The Blood Prince

Sovereign: Book Three

Josie Jaffrey

CONTENT WARNINGS & SERIES RECAPS

There is a full list of content warnings at the back of this book, and also available at Josie's website at the link on the left below.

Recaps of the Silverse books are available on Josie's website at the link on the right below.

CONTENT WARNINGS

www.josiejaffrey.com/content-warnings

SERIES RECAPS

www.josiejaffrey.com/series-recaps

By Josie Jaffrey

Stories from the Silverse: the World of the Silver

The Seekers Series
Killian's Dead (short story prequel, free to Josie's subscribers)
May Day
Judgement Day
Winta's Day
Valentine's Day
Dark Days
End of Days

The QuickSilver Trilogy
Kill Me Quick
A Quick Study
Quick and the Dead
QuickSilver Omnibus Edition

The Solis Invicti Series
A Bargain in Silver
The Price of Silver
Bound in Silver
The Silver Bullet

The Sovereign Trilogy
The Gilded King
The Silver Queen
The Blood Prince

Silverse Serialised Stories
Dead Box
Dead Road

Silverse Short Stories
Encounters: Silverse Short Stories

Other Fiction

The Deluge Series
The Wolf and the Water

Short Stories
Broken Wings (collection)
Ring The Bell

Prologue

The mountains of the Red were unusually crowded.

The two groups met in the pass at sunset, facing off in the corridor of stone like dancers lining up for a reel. One set wore shirts dyed red with blood. The opposite set wore no uniform, but seemed the more fearsome for it.

'We came,' one of the Red Shirts said, stepping forward. 'Now where's the boy?'

There was a laugh from the opposite line. 'Are you kidding me?' the laughing man said as he crossed the gulf between the groups. 'You think we're just going to give you that information?'

'What if I tell you we've already found it for ourselves?' the Red Shirt replied, smirking. 'Young, looks about twenty. Riding with the Invicti. Inherited that eye colour, didn't he?'

The laughing man didn't falter. 'You dinnae ken a thing. If you did, you'd have already snatched him. You think I'm an ejit, do you?'

'I think you're bluffing.'

The Scot shrugged. 'Then go it alone. When you realise your mistake, you'll come to us. I might not be feeling so cooperative, then.'

'You wouldn't be here at all if you thought you could take the Blue on your own.'

'And neither would you.'

The two men glared at each other. Stalemate.

They both knew the truth: there was too little uncontaminated blood left on the continent, and too many Silver. They could either find a way to make themselves immune to the cure, or they could attack the Blue. They'd prefer to do both, but they could do neither alone. They needed each other.

'Alright,' the Red Shirt conceded, 'but we're the ones who'll take the Blue.'

'My arse you are,' the Scot replied.

They glared at each other for another long minute.

'First to get the boy wins the Blue,' the Scot suggested. 'Bring him back here first, and you're in charge. But if we get him before you do…'

The Red Shirt narrowed his eyes for a second, almost suspecting a trick, but not enough to slow his avarice.

'Done,' he said, reaching out his hand.

The Scot shook it, and grinned.

The palace of the Blue was unusually quiet.

'Empress?' Claudia peeked her head around the edge of the gilded door.

This wasn't where she had expected to be summoned, but then there had been some reorganisation of the palace recently. The Empress spent most of the day in her rooms now, although no one knew how she passed the time.

She smiled at Claudia.

'I don't think the title's necessary anymore, do you?' she said, but a lifetime's habit was hard to break. Claudia simply nodded back.

The Empress was sitting cross-legged on a bed in the centre of the small room. Its height put her several heads taller than Claudia, despite her petite frame.

'Come in,' she said. 'Close the door and come here so I can look at you.'

Claudia entered the room cautiously.

The Empress regarded her for a few moments in which Claudia could feel her cheeks starting to pink under the scrutiny. With her translucent skin, the Empress wouldn't miss her anxiety.

'They were right about you,' she said eventually. 'You are quite lovely, in your pale way. Almost as though the blood would stain your skin. I can see the appeal, although it's not to my own tastes.'

'Empress?'

This conversation was taking an unexpected turn. Everything about this meeting was unexpected. She'd expected to be asked to feed the Empress, but apparently that wasn't on the agenda.

'Don't look so concerned,' the Empress said. 'I asked you here because I want to help you.'

'Help me?'

'Well, more accurately, I want to help your friend Julia. I've heard about my son's treatment of her. He's a bit out of control, you've probably noticed.'

Judging it unsafe to agree or disagree, Claudia said nothing.

'He gets that from me,' the Empress continued, her face cracking into a lopsided smile that bared a single canine. Then she seemed to remember herself. 'That's a bad thing, of course. I'm keeping an eye on him, but I'm worried about her. She seems to have got herself into a difficult position.'

That sounded painfully ominous.

'I thought we could chat,' the Empress added.

'Chat?' Claudia repeated.

'Daily, I thought.'

'Daily?'

The Empress narrowed her eyes.

'Are you able to speak in full sentences, or is it just one word at a time with you?'

Claudia's cheeks were burning now.

'I'm sorry,' she said. 'I was just–'

'Never mind.' The Empress waved her hand, as though she were dismissing the whole thing. 'It was a bad idea.'

'But–'

'I'm sure it'll be fine. Nothing to worry about. I don't leave the palace much myself these days, but doubtless all these stories I've been hearing about her and my son, and her involvement in some kind of rebellion, are all just fabrications. I'm sure she won't need my protection from the King and Queen, because what could she possibly have done wrong?' The Empress examined her nails. 'You can leave.'

Claudia felt the threat in the Empress's words. Was Julia going to be in trouble for going out into the Red? Had she become mixed up in something while she was out there? Even Lucas wouldn't be able to protect her from justice if she'd been involved with the rebels.

'No,' Claudia said. 'Wait, please.'

'I'm sure it's nothing,' the Empress insisted, looking out of the window.

'No, you're right, and I want to help. Please let me help.'

The Empress looked back at Claudia.

'If you're sure.'

'I'm sure. Just tell me what you want me to do.'

The Empress had another visitor after Claudia left. This one came in through the window, slipping from the roof to the ground then pushing back the shutters so he could climb into the lamplit room.

'Well?' he said.

Laila exhaled a laugh. 'Just as you said. So simple. So eager to please.'

'So well placed.'

'So you say,' she said, indicating her scepticism with a delicate eyebrow. 'Just remember: I get what I want first, then you can do what you like with her.'

'And if our goals align?'

'Then so be it, but don't make the mistake of underestimating me just because I'm temporarily human.'

He laughed. He shouldn't have. In the space of a second she had catapulted from the bed and pressed a bloodied finger against his cheek.

He tried to flinch away from the contamination, but she grasped his chin. He let her hold him there, not because he'd decided to let it happen but because she had power over him beyond the physical. She always had done, ever since he'd been a child.

'I saw something in you,' she whispered, tipping his face down to hers. 'I dragged you out of that place because we're the same, you and I. I suggest you don't forget who adopted you into this privilege.'

'I never have.'

'Good,' she said, pressing a kiss to his bloodstained skin, 'because I'm going to get my power back, and you don't want to be on the wrong side of me when I do.'

1

Julia had only been back in the Blue for a week, and already she was desperate to get back out again.

'I didn't think they'd go ahead with it this year,' Lucas said to her.

Julia snorted derisively and said, 'I was certain they would.'

They stood in the square, mingling with the crowd as they looked up at the temple. By rights, Lucas should have been seated with the rest of the Nobles in the rows of benches that flanked the steps. By rights, Julia should have sat there with him. But she hadn't wanted to mingle with them, and Lucas hadn't wanted to leave her side.

It felt better to be here in the square, shoulder to shoulder with the Servers, although the crowd was restless.

Last time they'd been gathered in the square for a ceremony of this kind, people had ended up dead. Blood had been painted on the temple in a four-word demand to the Empress, *Make no more Silver*.

Yet here they were at the Casting, waiting for the pick of the Candidates to be presented for ennoblement. Slim pickings this year, with only twelve Candidates having survived the Contamination.

'I suppose it's different now,' Lucas said, 'with the King and Queen back.'

Julia shrugged, but she suspected things would have been the same with or without the return of their sovereigns. Even if Laila had still been in charge, no Noble ruler would ever admit that they were intimidated by the demands of their people. They wouldn't be cowed into giving in to the will of the masses.

They were all the same, whatever pretty titles they held.

'*Intrate candidati*,' the priest called into square, finally managing to silence the audience on his third attempt.

He was joined on the temple steps by the twelve remaining Candidates, which set the crowd to whispering again. There were usually a hundred young men and women on display, but today these twelve were all the Blue could muster. With so much of the temple's bright stone exposed by the absentees, it was easy to tally the losses.

'*Instate sponsores*,' the old priest shouted, his voice cracking with its unwieldy volume.

The twelve sponsoring Nobles joined their Candidates. Julia was unsurprised to see that Rufus had managed to secure a spot in centre stage for himself and Marcella. Was that a good sign? Did it mean that he cared for her, perhaps enough to treat her more gently than he had treated Julia?

Julia was too far away to assess Marcella's condition, but her mind pencilled dark circles under Marcella's eyes, cuts on her wrists and bruises on her arms. Then she saw Marcella's chin dip to her chest as Rufus approached.

In Julia's mind, the goddess always had submission in her smile but defiance in her jaw. Marcella was never cowed, not really, she just pretended it.

Marcella never dropped her chin as she did now.

'He's broken her,' Julia whispered.

Lucas weaved his fingers into hers and squeezed.

'I shouldn't have left her behind,' she said.

'You had no choice.'

'There's always a choice.'

'But we would both be dead if you had chosen differently.'

She knew that it was true. Lucas had silvered for her, although he hid the silver in his eyes from everyone but her. He had told her what it meant for them to be bonded by that magic.

His life was now hers. If she'd tried to save Marcella from Rufus then she would probably have died, and Lucas would have died with her. Any chance of redemption for the Blue would have died with them.

Because Julia was going to change this city. She wasn't sure what she would change it into, and she wasn't sure how on earth she would make it change, but she was determined to do it, for Claudia's sake.

Julia had tried so hard to convince her friend that there were better things than the servitude she'd sought for herself. She'd spent the past week trying to change Claudia's mind, but she would not be changed.

The only way to free her was to change everything else.

'*Instate*,' came the command from the temple steps, but its tone was not the fragmented scrape of the priest's shout.

'Is that…'

'The King,' Julia said.

He didn't need to speak twice before the crowd quietened. They were mesmerised by him. He was half-hidden in the shadows of the temple's entablature, seated on a chair that looked a lot like the throne that had once graced the palace throne room. Even from this distance, his bright eyes felt as though they were looking into Julia's soul and finding it wanting.

The twelve sponsors stepped forwards.

'This is all?' the King asked.

The priest stepped back to where the King sat and spoke some quiet words, his hands flitting in shapes of penitent desperation.

But then Rufus stepped forward. Julia had managed to avoid him since the night they'd broken into the palace, the night when she had shot him through the eye. Seeing him now made her fingers itch for her crossbow, so she could do it all over again.

'It's not all,' Rufus called out across the square. 'There's another.'

He searched the crowd with his gaze.

'What's he doing?' Julia whispered.

'Get down,' said Lucas. 'He's looking for you.'

But it was too late. Rufus's eyes had already locked with hers.

'There she is,' he shouted merrily. 'Julia, come on up here. You too, Lucas.'

Rufus's usual entourage cheered from the benches on the steps, the gaggle of young Silver goading Lucas into a response.

'She's not a Candidate,' Lucas yelled back.

'Haven't you claimed her?' said Rufus. That was all that Julia heard, and all that the crowd would have heard, but even across the distance Julia could see that his lips were still moving as he stared intently at Lucas. He was talking directly to Lucas now, in a voice loud enough to carry only to Noble ears.

Lucas's jaw was tight with the clenching of his teeth.

'What's he saying?' she asked.

'Come on,' Lucas said, taking Julia's hand in his.

'Tell me we're not going up there.'

'Trust me, the alternative is worse.'

'Lucas…'

'I'm sorry, but this is the only way. He's not getting hold of you again, and if we have to play his game to keep you safe then so be it.'

'This is a mistake,' she said, but she let him tug her gently towards the temple steps.

It felt like a long walk. This wasn't the first time Rufus had dragged her up these steps while the rest of the Blue looked on and judged, but at least he wasn't actually by her side this time. This time, Lucas was there instead. He tightened his hand around her fingers and she knew he wouldn't let go.

Rufus smirked as they reached the top of the steps. His eyes met Julia's, then trailed over her cheek where the faint traces of his name were still stained into her skin. In a fraction of a second he was next to her, his fingers following the brushstrokes of the mark.

Lucas pulled Julia tight to his side, snatching her out of Rufus's reach, but not before her cheek had begun to burn under his touch.

'You remember what it was like, don't you?' he whispered to her, but in the next moment the priest was ushering Lucas and Julia through the gaggle of Candidates and sponsors, leading them straight into the dark seclusion of the colonnade surrounding the temple.

Not a second too soon.

The King was waiting for them there. Lucas went first, holding Julia's hand at his back so that she was hidden behind him.

The King raised an eyebrow at Lucas.

'The newest of my Invicti,' he said. 'This is a surprise.'

'For me as well, Your Majesty.'

'*Quem designas, Luca?*'

Lucas looked between the priest and the King, apparently unsure how to respond.

'You have no Latin?' said the King.

'I didn't have the education, Sire, and I never needed to know the rituals.'

'Until now.'

'Until now,' Lucas mumbled, throwing a petulant glare over his shoulder at Rufus, who seemed to be enjoying every second of his discomfort.

'No matter,' said the King. 'I simply asked whom you are nominating for the Casting.'

'Nominating? No one, Sire.'

'No one? And yet you stand here with this Candidate by your side, whom I am told you have claimed with your silver. Does that not make you her sponsor?'

'Honestly, Sire, I'd be happier if it didn't.'

'Then you spoke the truth when you claimed you were ignorant of the rituals.' The King lowered his voice and added, 'I also notice that you are hiding your eyes from me. I wonder why that might be so.'

'Everyone hides their silver here, Sire.'

'Not in front of their King.'

Lucas looked back at Julia, but she had no reassurance to offer him. He could hardly refuse the King's unspoken request to reveal the silver in his eyes, but if he saw that the silver had now extended into Lucas's irises, if the others saw...

Once that secret was out there would be no containing it.

But the King didn't push the issue.

'She bears your mark,' he said, 'and that is sufficient. Present your Candidate, Lucas.'

Lucas slid his hand around Julia's waist and brought her to his side.

A smile twitched at the corner of the King's mouth as his eyes landed on Julia's face.

'So it is you,' he said. 'The rebel friend of the biscuit thief. You have returned.'

'I'm sorry?' said Lucas, but the words hadn't been meant for him.

'That's right,' Julia said quietly.

'And I suppose that you have no desire to be a Noble.'

'Why would you think that?'

It had been some time since Julia had last considered the question. It was what she and Claudia had always wanted when they were younger, to be Noble. Julia had thought it was a fairytale fancy that she had outgrown, even if Claudia had not. From the way the King was talking, it seemed it might not be quite so unobtainable as she had assumed.

'In my experience,' he was saying, 'the true rebel would rather remain powerless than accept power that comes at the cost of ritual obedience. So the question becomes: what kind of rebel are you? Will it be your principles or your fear that dissuades you?'

'You're so sure I'd refuse?'

The half-smile was back, playing over the King's lips.

'Not fear, then,' he said. 'But I am correct that this is not what you would choose for yourself?'

'Yes,' said Julia, without thinking about the answer. It was a visceral response, that desire to remain of one of the people she called her own. She didn't want to be other, to be one of the creatures who were the instruments of their oppression. She didn't want to be another hand at the whip.

'It would succeed,' the King said softly to Lucas. 'If your feelings are as I suspect them to be, then it would succeed. I should approve your Candidate for ennoblement, but if she is not amenable then I doubt there will be any approvals this year. Are you sure, little rebel?'

'I'm sure,' Julia replied, trying not to take offence at the patronising diminutive.

'Then I offer you my sympathy, Lucas. You have a difficult road ahead of you, one that I have walked myself. You may wish to reflect on whether you are prepared to risk your life in order to give your Candidate the semblance of independence.'

As he dismissed them, the King's eyes lingered on Julia's. The sharp ice-blue cut into her, stripping away any illusions that she might have harboured about who had the power here.

She could say no to ennoblement if she wanted. Whether the Nobles would allow her to refuse forever was another matter entirely.

'He knows about the silvering,' Julia said as they strode away from the square.

'The King? Of course he knows,' said Lucas. 'He practically told us so, though not in so many words. He knew before he even asked about my eyes.'

'Not the King,' Julia said. 'Rufus.'

'You think *Rufus* knows?'

'Why else would he drag us up in front of the crowd like that?'

'Because he wanted to humiliate me. Because he loves making other people uncomfortable. Because he's a bastard. I can give you fifty reasons that have nothing to do with the bond.'

But Julia couldn't get the thought out of her head. Nothing Rufus did was without calculation, only right now she couldn't work out what he had to gain from this afternoon's performance.

'What does he want from us?' she said.

'Revenge.'

'But why would he want me to be a Noble? Surely that would just make his life harder.'

Lucas pulled her into the shadow of the palace, tucking them into an alley between its walls and the walls of the guardhouse.

'What?' Julia said after several moments had passed in silence.

'I'm thinking.'

'Well, think faster. I have to get back to the kitchen.'

Lucas had a room in the guardhouse now, cheek by jowl with the other members of the Solis Invicti. He wasn't in the dormitory with the new recruits, but he may as well have been. Visitors were discouraged and the living arrangements were apparently non-negotiable at the moment, so Lucas and Julia had watched their naive dream of cohabitation sail off into the distance just hours after Julia had agreed to stay in the Blue.

She was back in her old room in Livia's cellar, but now she was in it alone. It seemed empty without Claudia.

'He wants you out of control,' Lucas said eventually. 'That has to be it.'

'What?'

'You've never seen a new Noble, I suppose. Well, neither have I, but I've heard enough to know they're weak to start with, then they get hungry. Apparently it takes a while for them to calm down and start behaving like people again.'

Julia thought on it, tracing the zig-zagging path of the mortar in the wall with her fingertips as she tried to make the mental jigsaw fit.

'He's planning something,' she said, 'and he wants me out of the way.'

'Or he wants you, and he thinks it'll be easier to take you if you're weak.'

'It's a good thing I refused, then.'

A cloud passed over Lucas's expression. He had been holding onto Julia's hand as they spoke, but now he let her fingers slip between his own, breaking the contact as he looked away.

'What?' she asked.

'You said no.'

She should have known he'd want to talk about it. The problem was that she still didn't have the words to explain it.

'You don't want to be like me,' he said.

'No, I don't want to be like Rufus.'

Lucas shook his head gently. His dark hair tumbled into his eyes. Julia wanted to brush it away, but the moment felt too charged for contact.

'We don't live in decades,' he said. 'We live in centuries. But even if you live to be old in human terms, when you die I'll still be a child in the eyes of the Nobles. And when you die you'll take me with you.'

Oh.

Julia hadn't thought about that. She'd processed the reality of the bond enough to realise that she had to be careful with herself, because if she died in an accident, or at the hands of an angry Noble, that would mean Lucas's death too. But she hadn't thought about what it would mean if she were to die from natural causes, or of old age.

Lucas would still die. Simply by loving her, his life expectancy had been slashed to a tiny fraction of its potential.

'I'm sorry,' she said. 'I didn't think.'

Lucas kicked his heel against the wall behind him.

'I'm not complaining,' he said, 'not really. It's just something we need to accept. Something we need to think about. Maybe something that might change your mind.'

It felt as though it should be reason enough, but still her stomach roiled with revulsion at the thought of becoming ennobled herself. It was such an innocuous term for something so horrendous, being born of blood and born into blood.

A hundred lifetimes preserved in it, in a world comprised of copper stench and stain.

'You're asking me to reconsider?' she said, suddenly feeling sick to her stomach.

'I'm hoping that you might.'

But the thought alone made her mouth fill with a rush of saliva that presaged vomit. She could feel sweat prickling out across her skin. She wanted to run.

'No,' she said, swallowing back the nausea.

'Because of Rufus?'

'No. Look, I have to go. I'll see you later.'

She slipped away before he could call her back, running towards the safety of Livia's kitchen.

She didn't make it far before she was intercepted. Thankfully, the interceptor was a welcome one.

'Jules!' Claudia yelled as she threw herself into Julia's arms. 'It's been days. I half expected to find out that you'd left us again.'

Damn, Julia thought. That's exactly what she had been planning on doing. Claudia really was annoyingly astute sometimes.

'I wouldn't leave without saying goodbye.'

A familiar scent filled the air as a hand came to rest on the back of Julia's neck. She knew who it was from the way his touch burned.

'Really?' Rufus said. 'Then where was my goodbye, Julia?'

Claudia bowed her head and said, 'Master.'

Julia could have screamed with frustration. Why was Claudia still obedient to this monster, after everything he'd done? Probably because she was more sensible than Julia. She knew that compliance was the safest thing, that it might placate him, that it made Claudia invisible, but Julia just couldn't stop herself from playing into his hands. That was how she'd got herself into this mess in the first place.

Still, she wasn't about to start grovelling now.

'Lucas is just around the corner,' she said instead.

'I'm sure he is,' Rufus replied with a condescending smile. They both knew Lucas would already have been at her side if he'd been close enough to realise that Rufus was talking to her. 'You can leave us, Claudia. I'm sure my mother will have a use for you back at the palace.'

'Yes, Master,' Claudia replied, and then she left. She just bloody left, abandoning Julia in an increasingly dark corner of the square with a Noble she knew was dangerous.

Julia stared after her friend incredulously, shocked beyond words until she realised that Claudia was not taking a direct route back to the palace. She was heading straight for the guardhouse, where she knew she would find Lucas.

Julia should have had more faith.

Unfortunately, Rufus had noticed her change of course as well.

'Well, that's irritating,' he said, then his hand went to Julia's throat. She expected him to tighten his grip around her neck, but instead he let his fingers tease along the marks of Lucas's teeth, imprinted in her skin from that night in the Red when he had lost control.

'You were mine first,' Rufus said, moving his hand to the other side of Julia's neck, to where his own bite mark glowed pinkly against her skin. 'Do you think about how it felt?' he whispered, leaning close enough for his cloak to fall against her own. 'Do you remember the feeling of my teeth inside you?'

Julia snapped her hand up to push his own away from her neck, but he was a Noble. He was so strong that rather than moving his hand, she succeeded only in tipping herself sideways. He caught her, wrapping his free hand around her upper arm, then squeezing to the point of pain.

'It was different with him, I suppose. He would have marked you with his kiss first, to take away the pain.'

But he hadn't. When Lucas had bitten her, he had sprung from unconsciousness to action, his teeth latching into Julia's skin with no preamble.

'No?' Rufus said. 'Perhaps it was something different, then. But there's only one other thing I can think of that would have that effect… And surely Lucas can't have silvered for you. That would be inconceivable.'

Rufus's lips split into a smile that said, *Gotcha.*

He was reading her like a book.

She shook her arm, trying to get him to let her go, but he held her still. She'd known it would be useless. He was locked onto her now, and there would be no release. He'd locked onto her months ago, from the day they'd first met. They'd be dancing now until the bitter end.

'I may not have made my bite easy for you,' he said, 'but then you did shoot me in the eye.' He didn't seem angry about it. There was an edge of laughter in his voice, as though he were almost *pleased*. 'You always seemed like fun, but if I'd known you'd be like this…'

He stroked his hand up the side of her neck to her cheek. She glared back at him, denying an unwelcome instinct to lean into the touch that had become a caress. As his touch had softened, so had his eyes, turning his smile from a smirk into a devilish grin.

'Did he explain to you how it worked?' he said. 'Did he tell you how the mark works, how a kiss can take away the pain of almost anything?'

'No,' she said, 'and he'll be here any second.'

'Are you warning me, or yourself? I notice that you're not pulling away anymore, Julia.'

'There's no point, so I'm saving my strength.'

'Is that right? Or do you really just want to see how it would feel if I were to do it properly?'

His eyes lingered on her lips.

'I think you're in denial,' he said.

'Well, I think you're delusional.'

He leaned forward slowly while his grip on her arm softened into gentleness. Julia didn't even try to move, because what would be the point?

She'd anticipated a bite, but what she got wasn't that bad, yet it was so much worse. He kissed her. He pressed his lips to hers at the same time as his hand slid around her waist, pulling her close against him. She could feel the heat of him even through her cloak.

Then he was stepping back and setting her straight on her feet. He reached out to tuck a stray strand of hair behind her ear, and the gesture was so incongruous that she didn't even flinch.

'We'll have to continue this another time,' he said, with regret colouring his tone. 'Lucas is on his way. You'd better run.'

She looked at him in confusion for one last second, then for once she did as he said. She ran.

Livia was alone by the fire when Julia came in through the courtyard door, smoothing her clothes in an attempt to appear unruffled.

After all, everything was fine. She was fine. It was over. Rufus was gone, and she was home with Livia.

It wasn't unusual for the place to be empty these days, not now that so many had moved to the palace or been lost in the Contamination, but it still seemed quiet to Julia. There was the crackling of the fire in the hearth, and the bubbling roil of the kettle above it, but otherwise the house was silent as the grave.

That was a shame. In Rufus's wake, she yearned for noise and bustle.

'Well now,' Livia said as Julia joined her by the fire, 'that was something, wasn't it? You getting called up in front of the King like that. Next thing you'll be off plastering yourself in jewels and wearing clothes made new for you, instead of wearing hand-me-downs like the rest of us.'

'Unlikely,' Julia said, sinking down into her usual seat on the hearthstone. She rubbed her hands across her face, pushing away the sweat that had accumulated at her brows and around her eyes, not from the heat but from the panic. The day was chilly enough that she was grateful for her seat by the fire, but still she couldn't seem to stop sweating.

Livia looked at her cannily for a moment.

'What's up with you? I thought you'd be happy. Time was, being a Candidate was all you and Claudia spoke about.'

'Before we knew what it meant.'

'Ah. So that's the thing of it.'

Livia pushed herself to her feet and strode over to the cabinet in the corner, coming back with a small wooden box that Julia didn't recognise. Livia shook it gently, releasing a soft rattling and a spiced tannin scent.

'This'll see you right,' she said, making up a pot of tea for them to share. 'It's twice washed already, but it'll be good enough if we steep it a while. I could do with a cup too, the day I've had.'

'Oh?' Julia's eyes drifted up to the ceiling as she spoke, thinking about the two floors above them that were dedicated to nursing humans from the Red, floors to which Julia had never been invited. She'd only seen them by chance, during the Contamination. Without that glimpse, she would never have guessed that Livia was anything other than loyal to the Blue.

'That's right,' Livia confirmed, 'I had a patient. Gone back into the trees now, but he wasn't half difficult while he was here. The pig of it was that I didn't have Alba to help with him. Gods alone know where she's got to.'

'Alba? You mean Lucas's Baba?'

'That's what he calls her, is it?' An inscrutable expression passed over Livia's features. 'Yes, well, I suppose that makes sense, now that I come to think of it. I suppose he would.'

There was silence for a moment, and then, 'I don't suppose he said where she'd got to.'

'I don't suppose he did,' Julia replied, feeling obtuse. Why did Livia never tell her anything, even now? It irritated her, but nonetheless she was chastened by the look she received in response to her cheek.

Julia added, 'But then I didn't ask.'

'No, well, you wouldn't. I suppose he asked you about the ennobling though, didn't he? You didn't want to be one of them, then?'

So, they were back to that again. Julia supposed she would have to face the truth sooner or later.

'Do you remember that story you told us?' she said. 'You know, the one about the King waking up?'

'I remember.'

Julia sipped at her tea, relishing the warmth as it spread into her chest.

'I just thought he was going to change things,' she said. 'I thought the Queen was supposed to come back, wake up the King and bring us a cure for the contamination.'

'But you know what the contamination really is now. We both know what it really is.'

The Weeper vaccine. The Silver cure.

Julia had told Livia the truth the moment she'd returned from the Red.

'I know,' said Julia, 'but still, shouldn't *something* have changed? All the lives lost and battles fought and still things are happening exactly as they used to. The Candidates are still being cast, the Attendants are still bleeding, the Servers are still slaving, and above it all the Nobles are still taking exactly what they want from us. How is that fair?'

Livia settled back in her seat.

'Well, now, that depends on what you're asking. If you're asking how it's fair that they've used us for this long, then the answer is it's not. It's never been fair, and there's no wiping that blame away from them. But if you're asking how it's fair that they're still allowed to use us when you know very well what has the power to make them stop… Well, that's a different question, isn't it?'

Julia put her tea aside, no longer thirsty.

'What are you saying?' she said.

'You know what's in the blood of them outside the Blue. The way I see it, you've got a choice: either you accept things as they are, or you do something about it.'

Julia couldn't believe what she was hearing. Yes, she'd resolved to change the way that things were in the Blue, and yes, the thing that had motivated her was the knowledge that the contamination could be used as a weapon against the Nobles, but she hadn't quite put the two together into a course of action. The thought of actually using that weapon felt too extreme to contemplate.

But it was the logical end point, one Julia knew she'd have to accept.

Eventually.

'What about you?' said to Livia, deflecting.

'Me? I'm an old woman. I'll sit here and stitch up them as come to me, but I'm not going to war. You're going to have to find yourself some other allies, if this is what you want to do.'

Julia read the subtleties of Livia's expression.

'It's what you think I should do,' she said.

'I said nothing of the sort.'

'But you heavily implied.'

'Oh, I *implied*, did I?'

'Yes,' Julia said, levelling her gaze at the woman who was almost a mother to her. 'You did. Because this is what you think is right.'

'Well, *right* is all well and good, but *will* is a different kind of animal. Without that, nothing ever changes. So,' she said, leaning forward to take Julia's hands in hers, 'is this what you will?'

2

Cam found Emmy up in the north of the city, trailing her scent into the fields. She was standing with her foot on the bottom rung of a fence, staring out into the charred remains of the wheat stubble.

The Servers had burned it late this year. They'd had more pressing matters to attend to. The Weepers, the army, the battles, the bodies.

The pyres.

'Haven't had enough of the fire yet?' Cam called as he approached.

'Haven't had enough of the heat,' she replied, without turning around. 'The ground's still warm up here. Seems like it's gone cold everywhere else.'

'Daisies are still flowering, though,' he said, nodding at the flower she was twirling between her fingers.

She smiled ruefully. 'Sol's the only one who can find them. I don't even see them anymore.'

Cam leaned up against the fence and nudged her with his shoulder.

'He used to be that way once, too,' he said. 'You'll find your way back to yourself, Ems, just like he did.'

'Maybe. Maybe not.'

Emmy was right; it was warmer here, but the smoky scent of the air was cloying. It coated the back of Cam's throat, until all he wanted was to go back to the bunkhouse and have a drink. Vodka, for preference.

But Emmy seemed to want to talk.

'I used to think that turning Silver would turn me into a monster,' she said. 'Do you remember?'

'I remember.'

She'd agonised over that decision, until finally it had been taken out of her hands. It had been either turn Silver or die, and Sol hadn't been willing to allow the latter. He'd chosen for her in the end.

'And you thought I was an idiot for worrying about it,' she said to Cam.

'I never thought you were an idiot, Ems.'

In truth, he'd struggled to understand her reluctance at the time. Back then, it had seemed like the easiest decision in the world: turn Silver, live forever, protect Sol.

But now he could see the tyranny in their way of life, and nothing seemed that straightforward anymore.

Emmy shook her head. 'I don't know what I was thinking. As though the blood would contaminate my soul,' she laughed. 'Ironic, really, isn't it? And all it took in the end was one man. One worthless, human man to turn me into someone who's only useful for killing. It's probably a good thing that we've lost the baby, because god knows what kind of mother I would have made.'

She laughed again, but this time it sounded almost like a sob.

'Ems–'

'Don't, Cam. I know you're trying to help, but I'm not looking for sympathy, so please don't give me that look.'

'What look?'

'The one that says you think I'm better than I think I am. Because I'm not. Maybe I could have been once, but now…' She flicked the flower from between her fingers, sending it out into the field to land in the ashes. 'Now I'm exactly what he made me.'

'You don't have to be.'

She smiled unhappily.

'But that's the thing,' she said. 'I want to be. I *enjoy* it. This is who I am now. It's just that I hate seeing myself through your eyes these days.'

'I've changed too, Ems. We've all changed.'

She looked at him, assessing him thoughtfully.

'You don't smile as much anymore,' she said eventually. 'Except when you're with Felix.'

Cam smiled a little then. He could feel the heat creeping up his cheeks, but it was with happiness rather than shame.

'You blush more, too,' she said.

'He's a good guy.'

'You don't have to sell me on him. His blood's probably the only reason I'm here right now, so I'm already a Felix fan. But if you like him, then I'm happy for you guys.'

It felt awkward talking about the first flushes of his romance when Emmy was so unhappy herself. It had been a week now since they'd returned to the Blue, and still Emmy was spending most of her time alone. He couldn't work out whether she was having trouble adjusting to life outside a cell, or whether she was avoiding the King. Perhaps a bit of both.

'Have you spoken to Sol?' he asked.

She shook her head. 'It's hard. He wants to talk, I can tell. But he doesn't push it and, I don't know. Sometimes I'm glad he doesn't, and sometimes I just wish he would make me talk to him so I could hate him for it.'

'Do you want to talk to me?'

'What is there left to say? I had a little boy. He's gone. I don't know that we'll ever find him again.'

'Well, I'm not giving up,' he said.

She turned and leaned back against the fence, letting her weight sag against the bars. The afternoon sun was just starting to dip towards the trees in the west, and it caught the muted colours in her hair. It was drab, that heavy length of curls that charted her captivity. Broken and damaged, splitting at the ends.

'I've spoken to every woman in this place,' she said, 'and she's not here, the woman who took him from me. Either that or they're hiding her. I've thought about her every single waking second since I handed my baby over to her. I told myself I'd memorised her scent and every feature of her face, but in just a few brief seconds, how could I have done? How can I even know what I'm looking for? But without a trail to follow from her, I have no idea where to start looking for my son. It's hopeless.'

'It is not. I had no idea where to start looking for you, and I found you, didn't I? I mean, I know it took me a while,' Cam conceded, regretting the comparison, 'but it's not hopeless, is what I'm saying. Have you been able to remember anything that might help us work out how long ago it happened?'

She scrunched her eyes shut in frustration. Cam could see her jaw clenching.

'No,' she said. 'All I know is what that bastard told me, and we can hardly trust that, can we?'

Over the past week they'd had plenty of cause to regret the fact that Emmy had killed Charles, but she seemed to feel no remorse herself. Her fingers twitched whenever Cam mentioned his name, so he tried to keep their conversation abstract. Still, it would have helped to have a prisoner to question about these details, details that apparently only Charles had known.

Why had he taken Emmy? What had he been hoping to achieve? And, most importantly, when had her son been born? Without that information, they had no idea how old he would be now.

'I was under,' she said, going through the story for the fiftieth time. 'When they woke me up the first time, I must have already been out at least a month because we were in Charlestown. Then they moved me to the mountains. I didn't find out about the baby until I started to show, but it wasn't until nearly nine months after I woke up that I gave birth.'

Her voice cracked on the last words. There were details Cam hadn't asked, and that he would never ask, about that day. He would have changed the subject then rather than have her dwell on it, but she seemed determined to push on.

'So I was in stasis,' she continued. 'He must have had me drained when he took me, because my body was just frozen. The baby didn't start growing until I was awake again, and by then I think the world was already over. It was just rusted bedposts, buckets, gas lamps and coarse fabric. No plastic, no electricity, no plumbing, no toiletries, just lye and vinegar and everything smelling faintly of shit. Then the woman was somehow in my room, and there were footsteps thundering and she said, *Quickly*, and I couldn't move my legs but I was so desperate to get him out of there, to get him anywhere that wasn't that dank hole in the ground...'

She took a breath, deep and shaky.

'Then they put me under again, and then I was fighting and his throat was in my hand, and the baby was just *gone–*'

Cam wrapped her in his arms and pulled her close against his chest.

'It's okay.' He stroked her hair as her shoulders began to shake. 'We'll find him, Ems. Even if it takes a millennium, I promise you we'll find him.'

'What if he's not even Sol's?' she whispered into his shirt.

Cam didn't reply, he just squeezed her a little more tightly.

'You must have been wondering too,' she said, wiping her nose as she leaned back to look him in the eye. 'Everyone must have been wondering, right? I mean, I was gone for hundreds of years. What if it was… What if–'

'Of course he's Sol's,' Cam said, pulling her back into a hug. 'You silvered for each other. You're bonded. It's not like the Silver have kids all the time, Ems. It's not like someone who wasn't bonded to you could… You know. It just doesn't work like that.'

'We don't know what that bastard was doing while I was under.'

Cam couldn't think about that now, because he didn't want her to think about it either.

'We do know that no Silver couple has ever managed to have a child without a bond,' he said, although as he spoke he wondered whether that was true. Had Chloe and Darius had their little boy without a bond? Cam hadn't asked. Now, he wasn't sure that he wanted to know. To Emmy, he insisted, 'It just doesn't happen, so stop tying yourself in knots over this. Let's just worry about finding him, okay? Come on, everyone's waiting back at the palace.'

'I don't want to go there.'

'The bunkhouse then.' He pressed a kiss into her hair as he gently shepherded her away from the field. 'Let's get you cleaned up. You smell like a bonfire.'

'I *feel* like a bonfire. I just want to burn the whole world.'

'I know, Ems, but you're going to have to settle for a brisk walk and a hot bath.'

As they made their way south towards the square, Cam let his mind wander back to the questions he'd been avoiding. In truth, they had no way of telling whether or not the child was Sol's, not until they found him, at least. Because while it was true that the Silver didn't conceive outside the bond, they were also supposed to be turned human by the vaccine. Since Emmy didn't follow the rules in that respect, who was to say what could be possible?

So it came down to this: they didn't know where the child had come from, or what he would have become. That made it all the more urgent that Cam should find him before Emmy did, so he could do whatever needed to be done.

Because Emmy was right. Turning Silver hadn't made her into a monster, but it had sure as hell given her the power to turn into one now. He'd seen the glee in her eyes as she killed. It would happen again, and again, until there was nothing left of the friend he loved.

He had to stop her. He had to stop all of them, and he'd use whatever tools he needed to make that happen.

Cam had already made up his mind: the end of this year would mark the end of the Silver.

'We found two more today,' Naia was saying as Cam joined the Invicti on the bunkhouse sofas.

She and Konrad had been patrolling the edges of the Blue, looking for stragglers from the battle. They'd been doing it every day this week, and still they kept coming across more.

'Cured?' Tommy asked.

'No, still Silver, and they weren't trying to get out to the continent. They were coming back in from the Red. That's why there have been so many of the fuckers. They're trying to infiltrate us.'

'We don't know that,' said Konrad. 'We don't even know they were coming in rather than out.'

'Really? Because they had no blood or dirt on them, and I'll swear I'd never seen either of them before today.'

'What did you do with them?' Tommy asked.

'They're in the cells with the rest of them, down for now,' said Konrad.

The Invicti had moved the remainder of the Red Shirts and Lorelei's traitors into the guardhouse cellar. They'd had to build some new rooms down there to accommodate all the prisoners, but since they were keeping them drained for the moment they didn't need much space. They could have stacked them up like wine bottles if it hadn't seemed so crass.

The Invicti were waking the traitors one by one, then interrogating them to see whether they could bring them under the King's rule. So far they'd been entirely successful, but Cam didn't like to think about what might happen if they ever found one who wouldn't swear fealty.

These two new arrivals might be their first dissenters.

'Do you want us to keep them asleep?' Konrad asked Tommy.

'No. Let them wake up, then I'll go and talk to them. Maybe we can find out what they were hoping to achieve by sneaking into the city.'

'Probably just thirsty little bastards,' Naia said. 'They'll have been after the humans.'

Tommy nodded, but he didn't reply.

Cam knew Tommy wouldn't be satisfied with that explanation. They'd been discussing the problem only that morning, and they'd finally voiced the worry they both shared: Alistair.

With Alistair still out in the Red, there was no telling what to expect. There were still Silver left in Charlestown, and doubtless some Red Shirt survivors would have returned to Charles's fortress in the Ore Mountains. If Alistair were any kind of strategist, and all the Invicti knew that he was, then he would be trying to gather those forces together to turn them against the Blue.

Cam assumed that Alistair's aim would be to restore Laila to her former position, but that was a guess rather than a certainty. It would be a challenge now that she was human.

'We'll need all the guards we can spare to patrol the boundary fence,' Tommy said. 'Let's double the numbers, and then maybe we can work out where they're coming from and why. What about the cured traitors?' He said to Aaron.

As he was now human himself, Aaron had been judged the best person to handle the newly-cured.

'We've moved most of them out of the centre of the city. They're working in manufacturing, laundry, that sort of thing. Nothing that brings them into contact with the food, just in case.'

'Good,' said Tommy. 'The last thing we need is a load of disgruntled former Silver getting it into their heads to contaminate our food.'

'Well, you're just going to have to deal with that risk,' Aaron went on, 'because you need us. There are too many of you, and not enough uncontaminated humans left to serve you, so either you're going to have to get the pampered Noble bastards to pick up after themselves, or you're going to see a lot more of this.'

As he spoke, he pointed to his cheek. Like all of the contaminated humans from the Blue, he'd been stamped with a tattooed 'X' that designated his status. He wasn't wearing it well.

'You make up your own fucking minds,' he said, 'I've got shit to do.' He left through the back door, muttering grumpily as he went.

'Nice to see that this experience hasn't soured his mood,' said Adewale.

'Same old Aaron,' Zita said with a smile, but there was sadness in her eyes. If even she was moved to compassion by his circumstances, then they were all in trouble.

'I've been trying to work out if there's something we can do for him,' said Linh.

She was coping remarkably well with Gul's death, or at least she seemed to be. She'd thrown herself into her duties and that distraction appeared to be working, for the moment at least.

'Like what?' Bartek asked. 'A girl, maybe?'

'No! A way to turn him back. I'm looking at the Queen's blood.'

Cam opened his mouth to argue, but Linh wasn't finished.

'And before you get angry with me,' she went on, 'the Queen offered it to me. I didn't ask her for it. The King gave me some too, when he found out. I'm running some tests, but no luck so far.'

'And it's just Emmy and Sol who are immune to the cure?' Cam asked.

'Seems to be.'

'There must be something in that. Sol turned Emmy Silver, after all.'

'Or it could be the bond,' said Tommy. 'If that's the only way to pass on the immunity, then no wonder Charles didn't have any luck with his experiments.'

Linh sighed. 'There's probably not much hope. He was trying to accomplish this for decades, maybe even centuries. What are the chances we'll succeed when he failed?'

'Pretty abysmal,' Cam said. He schooled his expression into despondency, trying to match his mood to those around him, but the truth was that this felt like good news. Maybe the Silver could just fade away and take their violence with them.

'And Emmy doesn't know what tests they were running?' Tommy asked Linh.

'She says not.'

'I spoke to her again,' Cam said. 'About the baby.'

'Oh?' said Viv, sitting up as straight as her pregnant belly would allow. 'Where is she?'

'She's upstairs.'

Emmy had been sharing Cam's room since they'd got back. He'd been reluctant at first, thinking that it would make things a little awkward with Felix, but the woodsman hadn't wanted to come into the city anyway. He'd said he was happier out in the Red. Cam couldn't blame him for feeling that way, since he was yearning for the forests himself.

They both knew it wouldn't be long before Cam joined him in the trees again.

'I told her I'd go and look for the boy,' he said.

'Did she tell you something new?'

'No. Nothing new.'

Tommy raised an eyebrow. 'We still don't know how long ago this happened, then.'

'Nope.'

'You do realise that it could have been centuries ago? The kid could have grown up, maybe got cured out in the Red, then lived his human lifetime and died. You could be chasing a ghost.'

'I'm still going, Tommy. And don't try to tell me you need me here, because she needs me to be out there.'

'Okay,' Viv interrupted, sensitive to the changing tone of the conversation. 'Why don't the rest of us get started on the patrols?'

'Good idea,' Tommy said, his eyes never leaving Cam's.

It took Viv a while to manoeuvre her pregnant self out of the sofa, which had made a good attempt to swallow her, but when she was finally free she dropped a kiss onto the top of Tommy's head and ushered the other Invicti out into the yard.

'Dammit, Cam.' Tommy rubbed his forehead as though he were trying to smooth away the creases that had gathered there. 'You've barely been back in the city for a week, and now you want to go off searching the continent again? You have to know that you're not going to find this child.'

'You didn't give up this easily when we were looking for Emmy.'

'Because we had some reason to believe she was still alive, and at least we knew we'd recognise her when we saw her. What you're proposing now is entirely different. You're proposing to go back out into the Red and look for a boy of indeterminate age and indeterminate race, with absolutely nothing to go on except that he probably looks a bit like Emmy.'

'I'm not proposing anything. I'm telling you I'm doing it.'

'How?' Tommy got to his feet and started pacing. His face was now so red that Cam worried he was going to burst something. 'How the hell are you going to manage this one? For fuck's sake, you have *nothing*. Can't you see how hopeless this is? I feel like I spend my whole fucking life trying to talk you out of ridiculous decisions.'

'And if you'd succeeded last time, I would never have brought Emmy home. Come on, Tommy. Have a little faith.'

He looked at Cam for a long moment, then dropped back down on the sofa beside him with an exasperated sigh.

Cam had known he'd give in eventually. Tommy might have shouted the loudest, but he knew there was no point in arguing with Cam when he'd made up his mind about something.

'So, what's your plan?' Tommy asked. 'You're just going to scour the Red for orphan boys?'

'No, I'm going to try to find the woman. You know, the one who brought him here. That's the best place to start.'

'So you're going back to the mountains.'

'Yes.'

Tommy leaned back against the cushions and groaned.

'Oh, come on,' Cam said. 'It won't be that dangerous. We dealt with most of the Red Shirts, and it's not like I can't handle myself.'

'Against them? No problem. Against Alistair?' Tommy's brow knitted into creases again.

'Relax. I can take that old bastard. And anyway, I'm not going to Charlestown. I'm just going to sniff around up in the mountains and see if I can find someone who remembers seeing the woman pass through. That's all.'

'She might be dead too, you know. Odds are she never made it out of the mountains.'

'Maybe, but Charles told Emmy she'd escaped with the boy.'

'Right, because he never lied about anything.'

'Look, you're not going to talk me out of it,' Cam said, crossing his arms over his chest. 'It's just a quiet poke around. It's no big deal, and isn't it worth the effort so we know that at least we've tried? For Emmy.'

'Fine,' Tommy said, getting to his feet. 'Then I wish you luck on your hopeless mission. I just hope you know what you're doing.'

* * *

Cam had hung around in the lounge long after dusk, and long after the rest of the Invicti had eaten their dinner and gone out on patrol, or up to their rooms.

He'd wanted to leave the Blue immediately, but Tommy had persuaded him to stay a couple more nights before he set off. He couldn't really refuse, since he'd need time to get Emmy used to the idea of him leaving.

'He doesn't mean it, you know,' Viv said, joining him on the sofa. 'Tommy. He doesn't think it's hopeless, and he knows that if anyone can find the boy then it's you. He just doesn't want you to leave us again, that's all.'

Cam took the bottle of blood she offered him, clinking it convivially against her own.

'You know why I have to go, though,' he said.

'I'm not sure even you know that, Cam. I'm sure Felix is part of it, but there must have been something that kept you going out onto the continent for all those centuries, still looking for Emmy after all of us had given up hope.'

'I'm an optimist.'

'You *were* an optimist. These days I wonder whether you're just masochistic, spending all your time out in the Red with contaminated people, ignoring the risks. It's almost as though you want to be human.'

She raised an eyebrow at him, but the smiling tilt of her lips told him she was joking. She didn't realise how right she was.

He laughed, playing along. 'I don't know. I mean, have you ever wondered what it would be like if the contamination did spread?'

'You mean if we were all cured?'

'Yes. Sometimes,' Cam said carefully, 'I guess I wonder if it might be easier. I wonder if it might be better if we didn't live so long, if we weren't so strong. If we all lived on the same terms as the humans. Things might be more equal. Life might be fairer.'

'But there's always going to be inequality, Cam. Maybe not to the degree it exists now, but even if we were all human there'd be some of us who were more powerful than others, because of strength or intelligence or beauty.'

'And that makes what we do to the humans alright?'

'We do it to survive.'

'No,' Cam said, struggling to maintain a calm appearance. 'We do it because we have all the power, so we set the terms. We do it to make sure we keep our advantage.'

'Maybe. But I can't see the Nobles of this city lining up to surrender it all in the name of equality. People just aren't that selfless. Not us, and not the humans either. People can't just change their nature, not even for an idealist like you.'

This was a pointless discussion. Cam never should have brought it up – after all, he already knew Tommy's views on the subject – but part of him had hoped that Viv might feel differently.

She smiled and squeezed his leg.

'Is this because of Emmy?' she asked. 'I know it's been difficult for her. It can't have been easy for her to turn up here and see how little has changed since the Fall.'

'I don't think she cares,' Cam said, slumping back into the sofa. 'I don't think she's even noticed the Servers yet. She just worries about finding the baby.'

Viv nodded slowly, her gaze dropping for a moment before she looked back at Cam.

'Does she hate me?' she asked.

Shit. Not the question Cam had expected, and not one he welcomed.

He deliberately met Viv's eyes as he said, 'Of course not. Why would you think that?'

'You're a terrible liar, Cam.'

He dragged a hand down his face and groaned.

'Look,' he said, 'it's not that she hates you. You just remind her of what she's lost, you know? The baby, with your baby on the way. I think it's too much.'

'I guessed that when she stopped looking at me. I know we were never close like the two of you, but... I don't know. It was stupid of me to hope that our friendship would still be the same.'

'She's changed, Viv. You have to see that.'

'Well, it's been a long time.'

'No, that's not all it is. You didn't see her in the battle. She's *changed*. Sometimes I look at her and it's as though Emmy's just gone. She's either shaking in my arms or she's just something else, wearing Emmy's skin. I feel like a dick for even saying that out loud, but I'm worried about her. She's not the same person.'

Viv settled back into the armchair, wrestling the cushions into position. From the size of her, it was hard to believe that it would still be a month until she had her baby.

'Of course she's changed,' she said, 'and you have too.'

'Not like her.'

'But when you met her, she was just a girl. You were already hundreds of years old. She was just twenty-eight, and human. Of course she's changed. She's not just Emmy, anymore.'

'I liked *just Emmy*.'

'Me too,' Viv said as she took Cam's hand, 'but she's Solomon's bride. Despite everything that happened with Charles, I think this brutal version of her was the inevitable end. Things might not have played out as he planned, but Sol was always going to change her. In the end she's become exactly what our King always wanted her to be.'

'Which was?'

Viv shrugged and swigged at her bottle.

'His queen,' she said.

3

The King and Queen made their first official appearance the following day. The gong had been sounded – once, twice and a third time – and the inhabitants of the Blue stood in rapt attention to greet them.

It was the first time Julia had seen the sovereigns together without them both being covered head-to-toe in blood. The sight of their finery was almost anticlimactic. Almost.

'I've never seen a necklace like that,' Claudia said as they watched the procession that would bring the King and Queen to the edge of the palace steps. 'The way it wraps around her throat then drapes down her chest. What do you think it's made from? Copper? Fabric? And that headdress.'

'A bit much, don't you think?' Julia suggested.

'Not at all. It balances out the beading at the bottom of the dress. And *look* at that beading. I'd die for that beading.'

'Someone probably did.'

Claudia continued to enthuse while Julia tried to gauge the mood of the crowd. Claudia wasn't the only one speaking in tones of hushed excitement, and the grumbles were few and far between. Most of them seemed to be coming from the contaminated. They were off to one side, corralled by the guards into an area reserved for those marked with a cross on their cheeks. There had been more of them in the city recently, and far fewer bearing the designs that marked her cheek and Claudia's.

It seemed inevitable that one day there would only be crosses. They couldn't contain the contamination forever, not when everyone was living in such close quarters. If Julia were to hurry the process along a bit, would that really be such a crime?

She barely listened to the priest as he formally introduced their new monarchs, throwing around words like 'dynasty' and 'sacrament' as though the crowd were supposed to understand their meaning. To Julia, it was just noise carved into ritual, and it faded into the background.

If she could just get to one of the contaminated who lived in the city, just take a tiny bit of their blood, then her job would be done. She wouldn't need much to immunise herself, and then she could use her own blood to contaminate everyone else, one drop at a time.

She eyed the cross-marked group that had collected behind her in the square. It didn't take long for one of the guards to notice her attention. She was at least thirty feet away, but he still stepped deliberately between her and the contaminated crowd. With the Nobles guarding them, she'd never get close enough to get what she needed.

Perhaps it would be easier to take blood from someone in the Red. If she asked Galatea, the girl would give her a whole bottle. The journey would make that approach more time consuming, but easier in some respects.

'Well,' Claudia said.

The crowd around them was starting to move, and soon they were being pushed in the wrong direction by the force of the throng. Claudia snatched Julia's hand and tugged her off to one side, finding a quiet spot where they could speak before going their separate ways.

'It's like something out of one of Livia's stories, isn't it?' said Claudia. 'So romantic. But did you see her fingers flexing while the priest was talking about it?' She shuddered.

Julia looked over at the palace steps, now vacated, then back to Claudia.

'What are you talking about? What story?'

Claudia tilted her head. 'Weren't you listening at all?'

'Not really. Should I have been?'

'Yes! Because if you'd been paying attention, you'd know that there's a lost prince, and they're looking for him, just like a fairytale.' Claudia looked as though she were about to burst with sentimentality. 'Didn't you hear any of it?'

'So the King and Queen have a son?'

'That's what the priest said. Oh, I hope they find him. Wouldn't that be the perfect ending?'

Julia sighed. 'I love you, Claud, but you're a romantic fool.'

'And you have no joy in your soul,' she pouted. 'But look, I've been meaning to ask: are you and Lucas alright? People have been asking after you.'

That caught Julia's attention.

'Who?'

'Oh, you know. Just people,' Claudia said. 'After the Casting yesterday, people are interested. They want to know if you're spending a lot of time in the guardhouse.' She raised her eyebrows suggestively.

Julia was mildly scandalised.

'Well, you can tell them it's none of their damned business,' she said.

'Yes, but are you? Surely it's my business. Come on, Jules. I'm dying to hear about it. I've never been inside the guardhouse, and I want to hear about the Invicti. I want to hear about you and Lucas. You two are still a thing, aren't you?'

Julia leaned back against the nearest wall.

'I don't know, Claud. Yes, I suppose so. We don't see each other much, but yes. And I've never been inside the guardhouse.'

'But he's still feeding from you?'

'Not for a while now. The Invicti get bottled blood.'

'Oh. I see. Well, I've got to go. See you tomorrow, though?'

'Claud...' Julia called after her, but Claudia had already disappeared off in the direction of the palace, leaving Julia with the frustration of confidences unconfided.

She hadn't been intending to speak to Claudia about the immunisation issue, but it might have been nice to have at least a few minutes to speak to her about the Casting, or about what had happened with Rufus yesterday. Instead, she was left to puzzle it out for herself.

That would have been enough to worry about on its own, but now Julia suspected something might be wrong with Claudia. That abrupt exit was concerning. What was going on in the palace?

All the more reason to go forward with the plan that Livia had suggested.

But before she did anything else, there was someone she needed to see.

Julia had never knocked on the guardhouse door before. She'd let Lucas come to her over the past few days because she didn't want to intrude on his new life, and because returning to the guardhouse just reminded her of the day she'd fled the Blue.

The day she'd fled Rufus's teeth.

It was Cameron who answered her knock.

'Hey, Julia,' he said. He started to look over his shoulder, but then turned back to her abruptly, his eyes and nostrils widening.

'Hello,' she said. 'Is Lucas here?'

Cameron didn't say anything. He just stared at her.

'Is something wrong? Is Lucas alright?'

'No, he's fine, I just…' Cameron looked her up and down. 'Are you sure you want to see him right now?'

Julia tucked her hair behind her ears and smoothed down her dress, but everything was in its right place. The silver was in her ear, her dress was clean on this morning, and if there'd been something wrong with her face then Claudia would have told her so.

'Er, yes,' she said, 'I do. Is it a bad time?'

'Not for him. But, well, if you're sure. You'd better go round to the back door.'

Then he shut the door in her face.

Julia stepped back, startled. Had she done something wrong? Maybe only Nobles were allowed to use the front door. Perhaps she'd committed some breach of protocol by knocking on it. That was probably it. How thoughtless of her. She should have just gone to the back door in the first place.

She was still beating herself up about it when she turned into the rear courtyard and found Lucas waiting for her there.

'I'm sorry,' she said. 'I didn't realise I was supposed to use this door.'

'No, I'm sorry I…' he started saying, but then his face changed. 'What the hell, Julia?' There was a sudden bloom of red on his cheeks that had nothing to do with the heat of the sunny afternoon.

Now he *was angry with her too? What was going on here?*

'You're picking up some interesting language from your new friends,' she said, stopping a few paces away from him.

'And you're picking up some interesting scents.'

She charted the anger crossing his face, but she couldn't understand where it was coming from.

'Why the f–' He rubbed at his brow. 'Why the *fuck* is Rufus's scent mark on you?'

Oh.

Julia sniffed at her cloak.

'He stopped me in the square yesterday. Grabbed me. It must have rubbed off.'

She didn't see any need to tell him about the kiss. It had just been another part of Rufus grabbing her, she told herself, and it wasn't worth mentioning. It was just Rufus and his games.

She couldn't have been more wrong.

'Not his scent,' Lucas said, his jaw visibly clenching, 'his scent *mark*. Shall I tell you what the difference is?' He didn't wait for Julia to respond. 'Scent's just scent, but a scent mark is a mark of intent. There are scent marks of violence, which just let you know that something has been the subject of Silver anger, but that's not the one you've got all over you. The one you're wearing is a mark of possession, and there's only one way for a Noble to leave that behind. So when did you kiss Rufus?'

Damn.

She should have told him.

'When he grabbed me yesterday,' she said, speaking carefully because he seemed unbalanced. 'He kissed me, before he let me go.'

Lucas stepped towards her, closing the space until he could reach out and touch her. He didn't though, because his hands were clenched into fists at his sides.

'And you kissed him back,' he said with a softness that belied the menace behind the words.

'What? Of course not! I–'

'Don't.' Lucas held his hand up to stop her words. His expression was quickly tumbling from anger into despair. 'Just don't. Don't lie to me, please.'

'I'm not–'

'Gods, Julia! Just stop it! I know you're lying because the scent mark's reciprocal. It doesn't work if you fight it. I know you kissed him back because otherwise there'd be no scent mark on you.'

Julia's mind felt empty.

'That can't be right,' she said. 'It can't be.'

'It is.'

She stared at him helplessly. How was that possible?

'How long has this been going on?' he said in a tone so cold that it gutted her. 'Has it been just since we got back, or were you and Rufus always–'

'Stop,' she said, unable to hear him say the words. 'This is ridiculous. You know how he's treated me. You know what he did to me, to Claudia. How can you even think that there's anything between me and him? You know what he's like. You know that I'd never–'

'But here we are,' he said, spreading his hands. 'You've got his scent mark on you. You've got the scar of his bite on your neck. You've even got his name painted on your cheek.'

'And I didn't choose *any* of those things, Lucas. Not one of them. This is what I chose,' she said, tugging at the silver stud in her ear. 'Of all of these things that mark me, this is the only one I chose. Because I want you.'

'And when he kissed you, whether you accept it or not, you wanted him.'

Julia pushed her hair back from her face, fisting her fingers in it.

There was no point in arguing. He'd made up his mind. Nothing she could say could erase the reality of this scent mark she'd somehow acquired.

This twisted mark.

She couldn't understand how it had happened. The thought that she'd somehow allowed it, even enabled it, was more than she could take.

'I left the Blue to get away from him,' she said.

'But he keeps pulling you back,' Lucas said, 'and you keep letting him. You've always let him.'

'I didn't *let* him do anything.'

'Are you sure? Because the scent mark says otherwise, and it doesn't lie.'

'Lucas, please,' she said. Tears of frustration were already collecting in her eyes. 'Will you just listen to me? He cornered me and held me so I couldn't move. I can show you the bruise his fingers left on my arm.'

Lucas shrugged. 'It's just another one of his marks, isn't it?'

'Another one I didn't ask for! If he hadn't been holding me so tightly we wouldn't be having this discussion, because I would never have let him kiss me.'

But that wasn't exactly true.

Rufus had relaxed his grip, hadn't he? He hadn't been holding her at all when it had happened. He'd leaned in to kiss her, and she just hadn't moved. She'd let him slide his arm around her and pull her close against his body. There'd been no force in that gesture.

She wanted to deny her memory, but for the first time she began to wonder whether what Lucas had said about the scent mark might actually be true.

Maybe this time she had let Rufus leave his mark.

'Can we move past this?' she said, her voice cracking at the moment she realised his answer might be, *No.*

'I don't know,' he said.

She scrambled for something she could do change his answer. She needed him to believe her, because if he didn't then how could she move past this herself?

If only she could close the gap between them.

'Do you need blood?' she offered.

'I–' His expression soured. 'I just can't, Julia. Not with you smelling like him. I don't think I should see you until it wears off.'

'Oh. How long will that take?'

'It lasts about a day.'

'So I could see you this evening?'

But he was already backing away.

'Maybe tomorrow.' His eyes drifted off to the side. 'Sorry. I have to go. Patrol. You know.'

He went back inside without saying goodbye, leaving her alone in the yard with nothing but the weight of her thoughts to ground her.

The rest of the day was a boring procession of chores and self-recrimination. Strictly speaking, Julia didn't have to labour anymore. As a Candidate, she was afforded all the privilege of that rank and its life of leisure, but if she didn't spend her days scrubbing vegetables and mending clothes then what else was she going to do with her time?

'You've got a visitor,' Livia said that evening. 'I've left tea and biscuits in the kitchen.'

That level of hospitality could only mean one thing: a Noble. Lucas had obviously reconsidered, then. After the crippling shame of their meeting earlier that day, Julia wasn't sure that she wanted to see him, but then it was becoming increasingly apparent that she didn't know what she wanted.

'I'm going up now,' Livia went on, 'but you just shout if you need me.'

'Thank you,' Julia said, squeezing her hand briefly as they passed in the hallway. 'Goodnight.'

But it wasn't Lucas who was waiting for her in the kitchen.

'What are you doing here?' Julia whispered, suddenly feeling short of breath.

'I thought you might want to talk.'

'As if I'd ever willingly spend time with you.'

Julia turned on her heel and strode back the way she'd come, but Rufus was in front of her before she'd taken more than two steps.

'You seem a little less friendly than you did at our last meeting.'

Julia glared.

'Come and sit down,' he said.

'No.'

'I just want to talk.' He raised his hands in a gesture of surrender. 'I swear.'

'You've made promises to me before now that you've broken.'

'I made promises to my Attendant. Despite the fact that I can still read my name on your skin,' he said as his eyes settled on her cheek, 'you aren't that girl anymore. Are you? I think we're past deception.'

She still hesitated. She should have turned around and left, but she had to admit that she was curious, about his intentions as well as about her own distorted emotions. Anyway, he could have stopped her from leaving if she'd tried, although she wasn't entirely sure that he would have done. He could have forced her to sit down already, but he hadn't done that.

'Here, look: I'll pour the tea,' he said.

That decided her, because it was simply surreal. Her curiosity won out.

She took Livia's chair by the fire as he handed her a cup. He pulled up a stool from under one of the work benches.

'Biscuit?' he said, offering her the plate.

'We're not friends, Rufus.'

'Most humans would call me *Master*.'

Julia picked out a few stray tea leaves that were floating in her cup.

'I don't do that anymore,' she said. 'It implies that you're better than me, and I think we both know that's not true.'

He smiled sardonically. 'No, it implies that I'm more powerful than you, and we both know that is.'

'You still have vulnerabilities, and I know what they are. I watched the Queen kill Lorelei,' she said, hoping to strike a nerve. Lorelei and Rufus had been close, after all. 'She died almost as gracelessly as she lived.'

'Because you care so much about grace?' Rufus laughed. 'Oh, Julia, you vicious creature. The thing is, I'm almost glad she's dead. She was a petulant, dictatorial bitch. I'd had enough of her games.'

'So you're making people play yours, now?'

'Seems to me that right now you're making me play yours. So why don't we just be straight with each other instead? You can start, if you like.'

Julia watched the fire glowing in the hearth as she composed her thoughts.

'Fine,' she said after a few moments. 'You did it deliberately. You knew he'd be angry if you kissed me.'

Rufus laughed softly. 'Of course. But he's not angry because of anything I did, is he? Anyway, the scent mark's gone now. He'll get over it.'

She looked down into her tea. She wasn't so sure that he would.

'Why are you doing this?' she whispered.

'You're the one who did this, Julia. I'm sure Lucas told you as much.'

'But why me? You've been tormenting me since the day we met. Can't you just leave me alone?'

Rufus set down a half-eaten biscuit and leaned towards her, putting himself close enough to touch.

'At first, I just wanted to piss him off. He probably told you as much. We never got on, the two of us. We were both given up by our parents, and neither of us wanted people to think that we were like the other, because we didn't want to be lumped in together and branded. You know how it is.'

'I didn't know you were an orphan,' Julia said before she could stop herself.

'Well, the Empress adopted me, so I'm not.' He couldn't suppress a triumphant smirk when he added, 'Lucas is.'

Julia shook her head and said, 'You haven't changed.'

'I never pretended that I had. I'm just as depraved and sanguinary as I've ever been.'

'Then what are you doing here?'

'*You've* changed. You've outgrown him,' he said. 'You do know that, don't you? Poor little Lucas with his plants and his fairytales. You both went into the Red and came back just a little bit different, you more than him.' As he spoke, he leaned in and stroked the back of his fingers down Julia's cheek. 'He might have been the one who joined the Invicti, but you're the one who came back a warrior.'

'And you're still the same twisted monster you always were.'

'But you can understand me now, can't you? You feel the same rush and pull when you unleash your power. You know what it's like to take aim at someone's throat and fire. Or someone's eye,' he added with a smile. 'You felt the power in that, the sense of control, and you liked it.'

His fingers were playing with her hair now, twisting the loose strands into curls that wouldn't hold.

'I liked seeing it in you,' he whispered, 'but it's not enough. I want more. I want to see how sharp you become when your weapon isn't your crossbow, but your teeth. I want to see you like me. Silver.'

'That's not going to happen,' she said, leaning away from him. He let her hair slide through his fingers to unravel against her cheek. 'The Casting's over. It's too late.'

'It's never too late. Lucas can turn you whenever he likes. He silvered for you, didn't he?'

She said nothing. There was no point in denying what he already knew.

'Of course he has,' he said. 'That's the sting in it. That's what makes this so delicious.' He dragged Julia's seat towards his until her knees were nestled between his. 'He can feel you through the bond. Not much, just a little, they say. Enough to know what direction you're in, and sometimes, if your emotions are strong, enough to know what you're feeling.'

That was a terrifying thought. Could Lucas feel what she was feeling now? Would he know that she was with Rufus from the weight of the emotions thundering through her chest? Julia hoped not. The last thing she wanted was to hurt him again.

'What do you think you're feeling now?' Rufus murmured.

'Revulsion,' she lied. 'Nausea. Hatred.'

She sneered at him, but he just smiled back. It wasn't a pleasant smile, but neither was it unpleasant. It was calculating and hungry, and it was fixed on her. His blue eyes turned dark in the firelight.

'The bond doesn't care about your words, Julia, and neither does your heartbeat. I can hear it skipping.'

'Because you're too close to me. I don't like being crowded.'

'You keep lying to me. Are you lying to yourself as well?'

Julia tried to turn away but his hand was on her cheek, steering her gaze back to his.

'The only person lying to themselves is you,' she said. 'I don't know what you think I'm feeling–'

'Do *you* know? Because it's not revulsion, is it? I might be making you nervous, but it's not with fear. That's excitement racing your pulse.' He took her hand and traced the veins at her wrist with his thumb. 'I think you like courting danger. I think you miss the thrill of walking that line between safety and death. Is that why you let me in?'

'I didn't–'

'Lying won't assuage your guilt. Yesterday you kissed me back, and here you are now letting me hold your hand and pull you close to me. This is something you want, whether you admit it or not.'

She tried to push him away then, but he locked his grip around her wrist and held her in place.

'Let go,' she said.

'You don't want me to.' He was closer now, close enough for her to make out the reddish highlights in his dark hair. 'I won't wait on you, Julia. I'm not your pet Noble like Lucas is, but I'll give you a reason to give in to temptation if that's what you need. If you have to soothe your conscience, then I can make you believe you wouldn't have been able to refuse me.'

He leaned forwards, wrapping his arm around her waist to pull her against him.

'Rufus–'

'Try to get away. Go on.'

She wrenched and wrestled, but she couldn't move him an inch. He was as unyielding as stone.

'You can't fight it,' he said. 'Do you believe me?'

She met his eyes, then watched them slip down to her mouth. She didn't mean for her own gaze to do the same, but soon she was following the lines of his lips.

'It feels the same, doesn't it?' he breathed. 'When you sight down your crossbow, in that second before you loose the bolt. The anticipation of the kill. That moment when you feel the thrill of power. Can you feel it?'

The distance between them closed. Their lips touched a second after she realised he was no longer holding her captive, but by then it was too late. His hand was running up the back of her neck, weaving into her hair, and she was lost in the scent of lemons as they kissed.

'You see?' he whispered with his lips against hers. 'This is what you want.'

Julia put a hand on his chest and pushed him away. The force of it slid her chair back. She scrambled to her feet and backed over to the other side of the kitchen, wiping her mouth with the side of her fist.

'You have no idea what I want,' she said.

'Then why are you marked with my scent? Again?' he said, smiling as he stood from his seat by the fire. 'Face it, Julia: you're a predator, just like me, and what you really want is to come out and play. The sooner you admit it to yourself the happier you'll be.'

'I'm *nothing* like you.'

'You only think that because you've never had power. If I gave it to you, or if you took it from Lucas, what do you think you'd become? Do you really think you'd be like him, tending his pretty little garden, or would you rather be out playing with your prey?'

Julia walked around the kitchen, putting one of the work benches between her and Rufus. It wouldn't slow him down much, she knew, but it made her feel better to have it there.

'Lucas is ten times the man you'll ever be,' she said. 'He's kind, he's patient, he's loyal and he couldn't care less about fighting over power. He loves me.'

'Not enough to overlook this little indiscretion, though, I'll bet. What do you think he'll do when he finds out you kissed me again? After your little tiff this afternoon, I imagine he won't be best pleased.'

'You were watching me?' Julia's lungs emptied with the horror of it.

'I didn't need to. I could hear it from the house. And now that you're wearing my scent mark again, you might consider giving up on that fantasy. How many times do I have to tell you that you've outgrown him?'

Lucas wouldn't be able to move past it, she knew. Once, maybe, but after she'd let it happen a second time? Unlikely.

She had kissed Rufus back. She could still feel his lips on hers, and she could remember her own moving against them of their own volition. She could remember how his breath tasted of sweet lemons. How had she ever thought it was sour?

She knew that she'd hated him. She'd thought that she hated him still, but somehow her skin had stopped crawling under his touch. Somehow it had begun to thrill instead.

'I think you should leave,' she said.

'Why? Because you're afraid of what I'll do, or because you're afraid of what you'll do?'

'Just leave, Rufus.'

He shook his head with what looked like disbelief, smiling gently.

'You still need me to make this decision for you?' he said. 'Fine. I will. You like Marcella, don't you?'

'What?' Julia struggled to follow the change of subject.

'Marcella, my Candidate. You like her, don't you? You two seemed to get on well enough when we were all living together.'

'Yes,' she replied cautiously. 'I like Marcella.'

'And you wouldn't want anything bad to happen to her, since she's your friend.'

Dread settled in the base of Julia's stomach.

'Of course you wouldn't,' Rufus went on. 'So I'll make you a deal: if you come back to me, then I'll let Marcella go and never bother her again. You can come and go as you please, and you can even keep seeing your childish sponsor if you like, but your home will be with me.'

Julia's fingers curled under the edge of the workbench.

'You want me to go back to that house with you?' she said. 'You want me to live with you in the place where you almost killed me? Are you insane?'

He shrugged. 'I can get a new house if that's your only concern.'

'That is not my only concern.' She had to work to bite the words out, because suddenly her tongue felt numb. 'My main concerns are you, and my desire to stay alive.'

'I'm not going to hurt you, Julia. Well, not any more than you ask me to. You're a predator. Stop thinking like prey. Pay attention to what you actually want, instead of what you think you should want.'

'I don't want you!' Her yell was loud enough that she heard the floorboards creaking above them as Livia started towards the stairs. 'I'll never want you,' she said, more softly this time, 'and making me live with you isn't going to change that.'

'We'll see.' He smirked.

'Everything alright down there?' Livia called from the landing.

'Fine,' Julia called up. 'Sorry to disturb you. I'm turning in now.'

'See you in the morning, then.'

Rufus waited until they heard Livia's door shut above them, then he vaulted over the workbench and snatched a kiss from Julia's lips.

Lemon scent enveloped them again. Lemons everywhere, infuriating in the betrayal they announced.

'You'll always want me,' he said with a vicious grin, then he sauntered back towards the front door. Unlike Lucas, Rufus would never dream of using the kitchen entrance. 'I'll be back tomorrow for your answer. If you're worried about your pet gardener's finer feelings, then I'd stay out of his way in the meantime because darling, you reek of me.'

She picked up an apple to throw at his head, but he disappeared before she could hurl it. She'd had time to aim though, to feel that precipitous moment of balance, where the power of her intent settled in her chest.

Damn Rufus.

It had felt just like the prelude to a kiss.

4

'Viv's in trouble. The baby.'

Linh's voice roused Cam from sleep, even though it was just a whisper outside his door.

'What?' he whispered back. 'But it's not due for–'

'Like I said: she's in trouble. Come on. They need you.'

Shit.

Emmy was still asleep next to him, but he managed to slip out of the bed without waking her. She looked so tiny, all wrapped up in his blankets and still taking up only a third of the mattress. If it weren't for the dark hair spilling from the top of the bundle, then he might have believed she wasn't there at all.

'Where?' Cam asked as he pulled the door closed behind him.

'In the temple.'

'What? Why?'

'You'll see.'

Cam hurried after her. They only stopped to snatch a few bottles of blood from the cellar on their way out of the door. Viv would likely need them, and if she didn't then he was sure he could use the fortification himself. On a last-minute whim, he added a bottle of vodka to the bag as well.

When they arrived at the temple, he was glad he had.

'Holy shit,' he muttered under his breath.

Every piece of furniture in the place had been smashed to pieces. All the pews that they'd replaced after the Contamination now lay in splinters on the ground, except for the one piece that

Viv held in her fist. She was waving it at Tommy and Adewale, keeping them at bay while she backed towards the door.

'I'm not doing it,' she said. 'I don't care what the risks are. I'll walk out of this city right now if I have to, but you won't make me do this.'

'What's going on?' Cam whispered to Linh.

'The baby's not doing well. We want to take it out now, even this early, because I think we might have a better chance of saving it that way.'

'She doesn't agree?'

'I don't think she's really thought about it. She just reacted. She's scared, Cam.'

Cam took a step towards Viv, leaving Linh behind him in the doorway.

'Viv?' he said.

She whirled to face him, then turned back to Tommy and Adewale, stuck between the two groups. Her lips started to pull up over her teeth as she cradled her pregnant belly, making her look more feral than he'd ever seen her before. It was as though she didn't recognise them, not even Tommy.

'Viv,' Cam said, drawing her attention to him. 'I'm here to help. Why don't you tell me what's up?'

She said nothing. She was trying to back away from everyone now, taking her sideways towards the bare temple wall. There was nowhere for her to go, and Cam could see her desperation spiralling in the pinching of her lips.

She was a primed powder keg, and Tommy was the match.

'For god's sake,' he said, striding towards her, 'will you just listen to reason? We're trying to save the baby.'

Tommy was on his back in the space of a blink, and half a second later Adewale followed him to the ground. Viv had felled both of them and then retreated to the back of the temple, where the dais on which the King had slept rose into the alcove like an altar.

There was still no way out. She'd have to come through Cam. However erratic she might seem right now, she was putting the pieces together. There was only one way she was getting out of the temple. Cam and Linh would be the next ones down.

Viv tensed.

'Wait,' Cam said. 'Look, I'm not going to stop you. I just want to talk.'

He moved to the side of the door, holding out his empty hands in an attempt to appear unthreatening. When he was a few yards clear of the doorway he sat down amongst the rubble, pushing away enough broken wood to let him settle crosslegged on the stone.

'I'm not going to move,' he said. 'I'm going to sit right here, and Linh's going to come and sit with me. Aren't you, Linh?'

'Er, yes.'

Viv eyed them both warily as Linh joined Cam on the floor, but she didn't move. That felt like a small victory, since her exit was now clear. She could have left. She was choosing to stay, for now.

Cam could see the blood pooling under Adewale and Tommy's bodies. Even from this distance, it was obvious that she'd done enough damage to take them out of commission for a few hours at least. If Cam hadn't given her the option of running, he and Linh would be in the same position right now.

'Talk to me,' he said.

She took a step towards the door.

Shit.

'Viv, it's me,' he said as calmly as he could manage. 'Talk to me. Whatever it is, I'll understand.'

'You won't,' she said, shaking her head. 'You're the last person who'll understand.'

'I don't–'

'There's something wrong with him,' she said. 'The baby. I can feel it. He's... It's not right.'

'We know,' Linh said. 'That's why I'm advising that we deliver him by caesarian now.'

'No!' Viv yelled at her, so abruptly that Linh startled. 'You don't understand.'

There was a moment of heavy silence. Cam struggled to find something to say, anything that wouldn't make this situation worse, but during that delay all the fight had gone out of Viv. She crumpled to the ground, dropping her face into her hands as the tears began to fall.

'There's something wrong with me, too,' she whispered.

When she hadn't moved for a few seconds, Cam slowly got to his feet.

'Viv?' he said, approaching slowly. 'I'm coming to give you a hug. Is that alright?'

She didn't lift her face out of her hands, but she nodded once, sharply. He took that as a *Yes*.

She was shaking as Cam crouched down and pulled her into his arms. It occurred to him that she was probably suffering physically as well as emotionally, so he pulled a bottle of blood out of his bag and offered it to her.

'Would this help?' he asked.

She peeked between her fingers for a second, then slammed them closed over her eyes once more.

'That's the problem,' she mumbled into her hands. 'I don't want it. *He* doesn't want it.'

That didn't sound right. That didn't sound right at all. In fact, now that he came to think about it, *none* of this was right. Since when had Silver mothers struggled to give birth? Since when had Silver babies ever been in danger of dying in the womb? They were *Silver*. They were strong enough to survive explosions and decapitation, so childbirth wasn't much of a challenge.

Cam looked over at Linh, who was still sitting on the ground.

'What's going on?' he asked her, pulling Viv close against his chest so she wouldn't see the worry on his face.

'The baby's heart is racing,' Linh said. 'We need to get him out, now.'

She looked at Cam with an expression that was half fear and half despair, but he couldn't understand what she was trying to tell him. What was he missing?

'Have you listened to my heart?' Viv asked, finally moving her hands from her face to rest them against Cam's shirt.

He had. He'd heard the quickening beats, but he'd dismissed it as a normal part of the pregnancy. From the look on Linh's face, he guessed he'd been wrong.

'We're both changing,' Viv whispered. 'Aren't we?'

'Yes,' Linh said. 'I'm sorry. I need to get you to the surgery.'

'Changing?' said Cam, at the same moment the realisation hit him. 'No. That can't be right. Can it?'

'He's still small,' Linh said. She was by Viv's side now, trying to get her on her feet. 'What a mother's body can deal with is sometimes too much for a baby. It's not outside the realms of possibility.'

'But–'

'Just help me get her to the palace.'

He shut up and did as he was told.

The blood revolution had started, and Cam felt guilty as hell about it.

Of course it wasn't his fault, he knew that, but it could have been. It had been his end game, after all. Still, he couldn't say that he was unhappy about the way things had turned out.

Viv and Tommy, on the other hand, were inconsolable.

The baby wasn't a 'he' after all. It was a little girl, small but perfect, with ten fingers, ten toes, and two eyes of a blue so bright that they seemed to reflect the sky.

But blue was the only colour in them. There was no silver at all.

The baby was human. And after a few hours, Viv was too.

'How did this happen?' Tommy yelled, pacing the bunkhouse because he couldn't scream out his anger while he was with Viv at the palace. He didn't want her to know how upset he was.

And he was *very* upset.

From where Cam was sitting, it looked as though he was already in mourning for the two of them – his perfectly healthy wife and their perfectly healthy baby daughter – simply because they were no longer Silver.

'Linh said it was to do with the concentration of vaccine the baby received,' Cam said. 'Not enough to cure Viv, but enough to cure the baby, then it multiplied and the baby cured her.'

'Yes, I know that,' Tommy said irritably, 'but how did this *happen*? How did it all go so wrong?'

He dropped down onto the sofa next to Cam, letting the empty bottle of vodka roll from his fingers onto the floor. He'd necked the lot of it the moment he'd come back from the palace, much to Cam's regret. He could have used a drink right now.

'She's alive,' Cam said. 'The baby's alive. Is it really the end of the world?'

'Yes! Because in a hundred years they'll both be dead.'

'And so will you, with your bond to Viv. There are worse fates than a human lifetime. I know it might not be what you wanted, but…' Cam shrugged. It just didn't seem that bad to him. He was ready to stop fighting, and it was about time that Tommy did too.

Tommy dragged a hand down his face.

'It'll be a different life,' Cam said, 'but it could be a better one. You could take them both and go into the Red, find somewhere nice to settle. There's a whole world out there once you stop worrying about being contaminated by the cure.'

'But I'd still need uncontaminated blood.'

'Why?'

'I'm still Silver,' Tommy said, looking at Cam as though he'd lost his mind.

Tommy didn't understand.

He couldn't be drunk, not with his constitution, but he still didn't understand. Perhaps he was in shock, or perhaps the necessity of being Silver was so deeply ingrained that he hadn't even considered the alternative.

'You don't have to stay that way,' Cam said. 'You could turn yourself human.'

Tommy's face opened, then closed.

'No,' he said. 'I couldn't do that.'

'When your wife and daughter are both contaminated? Are you sure?'

'You and Felix manage,' Tommy said, clearly thinking that was the end of the conversation.

'Felix and I don't manage *anything*,' Cam replied. 'Every time we kiss, I know I might turn human. As for everything else... Well, we just don't. You can't live that way forever. You can't be scared of the people you love.'

'Oh, so you love the human now?'

'I wasn't talking about me,' Cam said, pushing himself out of the sofa and onto his feet. 'I was talking about you. *You* love a human. Two of them, actually. By the time I come back, you'll have changed your mind about staying Silver. Trust me.'

Tommy gaped up at him. 'You're not still going. Not after this.'

'*Especially* after this. Now stop being a dick and face up to reality. You need to go and be with your daughter, and I need to find Emmy her son.'

Cam grabbed his pack and left Tommy there, staring at the empty bottle like it held the answers he was looking for. Cam knew from bitter experience that it didn't.

One last mission, he told himself as he walked out into the courtyard behind the bunkhouse. *One last mission and I can give it all up. One last mission and I can be with him.*

'Are you going?' a voice called from above him.

Cam turned to see Darius leaning out of his bedroom window.

'Yes,' he said. 'We agreed it would be today.'

'I know. I just thought that with Viv–'

'No,' Cam interrupted, not wanting to be made to feel more guilty than he already did. 'I'm leaving now.'

'Alright. Can you give me five minutes?'

'Darius…'

'Please, man. Just five minutes.'

'Fine. I'll be in the square.'

Cam waited, and waited, but it was at least half an hour before Darius finally turned the corner around the side of the guardhouse. He had a pack slung over one shoulder, and a saddle balanced on the other.

'No,' Cam said. 'No way.'

'Oh, come on,' said Darius. 'The more the merrier, right?'

'No. The more the *less* merry.'

Cam had been banking on some time alone with Felix. It was torture to be close to him and unable to do much about it, but the good kind of torture. The kind of torture that Cam had been anticipating with a frisson of pleasure. But with Darius there, Cam would feel uncomfortable getting close at all.

'Come on, man,' Darius pressed. 'Just as far as the mountain lake. I've got to see Chloe and Alex.'

Cam opened his mouth to object again, but Darius cut him off.

'He's my little boy, Cam. Please.'

After the lecture he'd just given Tommy, how could he turn that down?

'Fine,' he said. 'But only as far as the mountain lake. Then Felix and I are going on alone.'

'No problem. I don't want to step on any toes. I'll be out of your hair in no time.'

Cam shouldered his bag, trying to ignore Darius's uncharacteristic enthusiasm.

'No more delays, alright?,' he said. 'I want to hit the shore by nightfall.'

'I'm right behind you, boss.'

Cam sighed. He could already tell that this was going to be a complete disaster.

* * *

They found the first body when they were about three-quarters of the way to the ferry crossing.

The trees were thick enough that it was difficult to pick out the path by sight, but that wasn't a problem for Cam. He'd come this way hundreds of times before, and he could navigate the route by smell alone.

At least, he usually could. Today the scent of decay hung heavily in his nostrils, all but eclipsing the salt tang of the lake shore that was their destination.

'Jesus,' Darius said, pulling his sleeve down over his hand then using it to cover his nostrils. 'Is this where we killed the Red Shirts?'

'No,' said Cam. 'We've already gone past that. It was the patch to the west that smelled like wet, burning leaves. This is something different.'

'Whatever it is, it stinks. How much further?' Darius hiked the saddle further up onto his shoulder, as though its weight were bothering him. It couldn't have been, because Darius was Silver and it would have weighed nothing to him, but he still wriggled under it like a bug under a stone.

'It's another couple of hours away.'

Darius groaned.

'I don't know why you even bothered to bring the saddle,' Cam said irritably. 'It's not as though you need it. The horses all have blankets.'

They'd left the team in a few acres of fenced grassland just west of the ferry crossing. Felix had been looking after them, so of course Naia had insisted on staying to help. Not that Cam had anything to worry about there. Felix wasn't the least bit interested in the Invicti's most flirtatious fighter.

At least, Cam didn't think he was.

'Come on,' he said to Darius.

But the other man had fallen behind. He was leaning against a tree trunk twenty yards back, hands braced on his knees, looking for all the world like he was struggling to catch his breath.

'What now?' said Cam.

When Darius looked up at him, Cam could see the sweat beading on his dark skin.

'Darius?' he said.

'Fuck, Cam.' Darius's words were snatched half gasps. 'I think I did something stupid.'

He held out his hand, palm up. Cam didn't need to move any closer to make out the red smear that stained it. *Blood.*

'There was a tree back there,' Darius went on. 'It was wet. I thought it was okay, but then…'

Cam followed the direction of Darius's gaze. He was looking into the undergrowth off to his right, at something that Cam couldn't see. He could guess what it was, though. In two strides he could pick out the fresher odour above the stagnancy of the others that surrounded them, and in four strides he had a clear line of sight to the body hidden in the holly.

'Shit,' Cam muttered. 'Why didn't you say something?'

'It was nothing,' Darius said. 'It was just blood. We've touched contaminated blood before and nothing's happened.'

But something had happened this time. Darius let the saddle slide from his shoulder, then followed it down into the leaf litter at his feet.

Cam caught him and took his hand carefully, looking for the broken skin that had allowed the blood to enter his system.

'Is this it?' Darius asked. 'Am I human now?'

Cam ignored his words and concentrated on the tiny lines that criss-crossed Darius's palm. He couldn't see a single break. The skin was smooth and clean, with just a small blotch of bloody discolouration at its centre. He turned his attention to Darius's arms next, then his face, before finally returning to his hands.

It was there, on the middle finger of his bloodied hand: a hangnail. A drop of blood had transferred from Darius's palm to the tip of his ring finger, and from there to the tiny cut the hangnail had caused.

'You're human,' Cam said, sitting back on his haunches. 'I can hear your heartbeat. Can you hear mine?'

Darius concentrated hard for a second, then dropped his head in resigned defeat.

'Fuck,' he said.

Cam didn't know what to say. Part of him wanted to celebrate, because this was what he had wanted. First Laila, then Aaron and Viv, now Darius. They were all regaining their humanity, drop by drop, and Cam hadn't needed to lift a finger to make it happen.

He would, though. He'd have to, because the rest of the Silver wouldn't be taken down so easily.

Darius wiped his forehead. 'Do humans always sweat like this?'

'When they're trying to carry ten stone's worth of equipment? Yeah, I think they do. You'd better give me your stuff.'

'We're carrying on?'

'Can you think of a better place for you to go right now? You can stay at the mountain lake. It makes sense.'

They already had one cured Silver in their community, after all.

'I'm not sure Chloe's going to agree,' said Darius. 'Last time I saw her she was… uncomplimentary.'

'Well, maybe this will change things.'

Darius rubbed at his eyes with his knuckles, as though he were trying to rub away tears.

Cam couldn't remember ever seeing him cry before. He was usually all bravado and suaveness, the kind of guy who thought people would judge him for showing any weakness, the same way that he would judge them. It was strangely mesmerising to see the real person spilling out between the cracks in his veneer.

Awkward, though. Really awkward.

'Hey,' Cam said, 'it'll be alright.'

'I was going to offer to stay with them,' Darius said, turning away to look back towards the city. 'I could have protected them. How am I supposed to do that now?'

'Well, maybe a protector isn't what she wants. Maybe it's not what she ever wanted. I don't know if you've noticed, but Chloe can kind of look after herself.'

'But what else have I got to offer her?'

Darius looked so genuinely perplexed that Cam wanted to shake him. Centuries with the Invicti had obviously rubbed off on him, and not in a good way. All he saw in the mirror was a blade.

'Why don't you just try being a father?' Cam suggested. 'Just be there for them. Do the day-to-day. Chop wood, hunt, cook. Hell, you could fish on the lake if that's what you want, but you could be part of that community if you tried.'

'Maybe.'

Cam waited for Darius to put himself back together, but after a minute had passed in silence it seemed as though that wasn't going to happen without a little nudging. The sun was already starting to pitch towards late afternoon, and Cam couldn't afford to hang around in the woods.

'Look,' he said, 'I know this is a lot, but we've got to keep moving. We're losing the light. Can you carry on?'

'Yeah, man,' Darius said, wiping at his face as he pushed up to his feet. 'Sorry. Yeah.' He took a deep breath. 'Let's get going.'

Five more miles brought fifty more bodies, some clustered in groups and others alone, their lips still painted with the blood that had conquered them. Someone out here was laying Weeper traps, and that made Cam cautious.

Then he felt a change in the air. He put an arm out in front of Darius, stopping them both in their tracks.

It was difficult to detect foreign presences in these woods, because everything here was so silent. There were no badgers, no foxes, no pine martens, no deer. Even the squirrels were few and far between, and the birds tended to keep to the edges of the island, where they were safe from the arrows of the Invicti. In these trees, it was always quiet. Nonetheless, the atmosphere had changed. Perhaps even the insects had fallen silent – Cam hadn't been paying enough attention to notice if they had been chirping before this moment – but something was setting his senses tingling with an overwhelming feeling of *wrong*.

He strained his hearing, sending his perception out in a spiralling pattern with him and Darius at its centre. He could tell from Darius's posture that he was trying to do the same, despite his compromised senses, but Cam found its source first.

He nodded towards the left. There was something there, about a hundred yards away from them: a mass of tiny noises. They suggested the friction of clothing against dry skin and the wet separation of lips.

How many? Darius mouthed at Cam.

He concentrated on the noises again. They spread for tens of feet in each direction, a horde of close-packed mouths gathered in the trees.

Lots, he replied.

Then came the first howl.

'Shit,' Cam muttered, securing his pack more tightly across his chest.

'They heard us?'

'No. Something else. Come on.'

'We're going towards it?' Darius said in disbelief as Cam started in that direction.

Cam didn't stop to explain. It wasn't as though Darius had anything to fear from them anymore, and Cam couldn't delay. He'd heard what had attracted their attention: the gentle sound of a knife snicking shapes into wood. It was both thrilling and terrifying; thrilling because it meant that Felix was close, and terrifying because it meant that the Weepers knew that, too.

There were so many of them.

Cam bolted into a run. He followed the rising sound of their hunger into an area of the forest where the trees had been thinned by fallen giants. The creatures howled as they arrowed towards a ragged tree stump. Its apex was crowned with a small bundle of wadded up fabric. Even from this distance, Cam could pick out the scents of nutmeg and cut branches that were stamped into its fibres like a nasal name tag. He could smell the blood, too, thick and fresh.

Unlike the Weepers, he could also see the trap.

The leader of the pack closed a fist around the material, then used both hands to shove it into its mouth.

Cam knew what was going to happen next, but he still had a breathless moment of doubt before the Weeper collapsed to the ground. The rest of the horde followed their leader shortly afterwards. A couple had latched their teeth into his flesh, dying human deaths as they were cured by the vaccine, then passing it on to those who bit them. The dominoes fell from that epicentre, and within seconds they had all simply dropped, hundreds of them, spreading backwards like a comet's tail from the tiny spot of contamination that was the blood on Felix's discarded shirt.

The forest was still once more.

'There are more every day,' Felix said, jumping down from the canopy of a nearby beech tree.

He looked just as he always did: red-tinged beard, piercing blue eyes and a body tautened and honed by hard living. Except now there were bite marks up and down the length of his arms. Some were red sand angry, others clearly days old and thick with scabs.

'What were you thinking?' Cam said, shoving the saddle at Darius before moving to the woodsman's side. He took Felix's hands in his and turned his arms this way and that, examining the wounds.

'I was thinking that I shouldn't let them get to the city.'

'And you decided it was better to take the Weepers down alone by letting them bite you than it was to come and tell us there was a problem?'

'I knew you'd be back.'

'Well,' Cam said, silently berating himself for not coming sooner. 'You could have taken better care of yourself while I was away. You're not supposed to let them bite you. There are other ways.' Cam nodded significantly towards the balled up shirt, still clamped between the fallen Weeper's teeth.

Felix shrugged. 'Not all of them are stupid enough to fall for a trap like this. The cuts'll heal.'

Cam had to concede that Felix had cleaned them well, and none of them looked infected. 'They'll scar,' he said.

'I'll add them to the collection,' Felix replied with a sardonic smile.

'Have you got the horses?' Darius said, looking around the clearing.

'Up by the crossing,' Felix replied, 'Naia's running them.' He looked at Darius carefully, then turned to Cam and raised his eyebrows.

'We ran across some of your earlier traps,' Cam said. 'There was an accident.'

'Yeah,' Darius said, 'I'm human now, so thanks for that.'

Felix was unmoved. 'It's not that bad.'

'Really?' Darius wiped his brow for the fifteenth time that minute. 'Because it seems a lot worse than I remember it being.'

'You get used to the sweat.'

'Maybe you did. Me? I need a dunk in the lake.'

'Come on, then,' said Cam. 'Let's go find Naia.'

She met them halfway, sauntering through the trees with three horses trailing from their halters behind her. It looked like she was taking three oversized dogs for a walk.

'I heard you bastards coming *miles* away,' she said. She grimaced at Darius. 'I wasn't expecting you, though. Fucking hell. What happened to you?' She waved a hand in front of her nose. 'Ugh, god, you stink of sweat. And mortality.'

Darius just narrowed his eyes at her.

'I need you to get back to the city,' Cam said to her, trying to derail the inevitable bickering that was brewing between her and Darius.

'What? You want me to leave you alone with the lumberjack? What a shocker.'

'So I don't count now that I'm human?' said Darius.

'Basically,' Naia replied. 'Honestly, if it wasn't for the stench, I wouldn't have noticed you were here.'

'Just take the blood,' Cam said to her, handing over the bottle from his pack. 'Go back and warn the others about the Weepers, then see if you can persuade Adewale to let you take another bottle to get you back here tonight.'

Naia looked sceptical, and rightly so. The cellar had emptied quickly over the past month, and with so few uncontaminated humans to replenish it their stocks were running low. Even the Invicti were on blood rations these days, and Cam had already been pushing his luck by snaffling a bottle on his way out.

'Be persuasive,' he went on. 'It'll work better if you don't deliberately provoke the person whose help you want.'

'I don't *provoke*,' she said. 'I just don't take any shit. There's a difference, you know.'

'Just tread lightly, okay? Things are a bit precarious right now.'

'Because I'm not the only one who's newly humanised,' Darius said.

'What?' For the first time, an expression of genuine concern crossed Naia's face. 'Who else?'

'Viv and the baby,' Cam said softly.

'The baby's here already? That was quick. And *human*? What, has Viv been doing the nasty with a *human*?'

'Jesus, Naia,' Darius muttered.

'I'm begging you,' Cam said to her, 'just try to be a bit more tactful with Tommy. It's something about the contamination being too strong for the baby to handle. If you imply anything else around him then with the mood he's in, you'll be down in the ice box with the traitors.'

'That'd be a relief for all of us,' said Darius.

Naia gave him a dirty look.

'Alright,' she said, shaking her head as though Cam were asking the impossible of her. 'I'll behave.'

'And hurry,' he said. 'We don't have time to hang around.'

With one final and pointed glance at Felix's backside, she handed Cam the halters and sped off towards the city, moving so fast that she might as well have blinked out of existence.

'Thank fuck for that,' Darius said.

Cam didn't vocalise his sympathy, but he felt it nonetheless. He and Felix shared a look that confirmed their mutual relief, and that was enough.

Darius rode Naia's horse to the shore, but Cam and Felix were on their own mounts: Hades and Sandor. It had become a running joke that the two horses were now as reluctant to be apart as were their owners, but Cam had stopped caring about the jibes. It was enough that Sandor was a calming influence on Hades. The beast had finally stopped trying to bite Cam's feet, although he still stepped on Cam's toes at every opportunity.

Darius didn't waste time when they got to the shore. He was stripped within a minute of reaching the pebble beach, leaving Cam and Felix with the horses. They were left to watch his naked arse running into the sunset-lit water with more haste than grace.

So much for the romantic reunion.

Then Felix reached out and laced his fingers with Cam's. It was enough contact to jumpstart his simmering frustration into outright longing.

'You came back,' Felix said, and Cam smiled.

'I'll always come back for you.'

5

Julia pressed her face into the mattress and screamed her frustration into the straw.

This wasn't supposed to be happening. What was wrong with her? Why was her body betraying her like this?

She couldn't seem to control the reaction she had to Rufus, but she wanted to control it. She wanted to push it away and never have it bother her again, because Rufus seemed to have no intention of ceasing to bother her.

No, would never be enough for him.

And he'd be back this evening.

She wanted to talk to someone about it, but there was no one she could discuss this with. She couldn't talk to Lucas, for obvious reasons, and the thought of telling Claudia that she had kissed Rufus not once, not twice, but *three* times, after everything he had done to them both...

How was she supposed to confide in someone else about this when she could barely admit it to herself?

She really had only one option. Perhaps it was good timing, all things considered. Perhaps she'd needed this impetus to get her to do what she knew she must.

While Livia was still asleep, she tiptoed up to the kitchen and gathered the essentials: food, water, medicine, needle and thread, just in case.

Her travelling clothes were clean and hanging from the back of her bedroom door. She shrugged out of her dress and pulled on the trousers and shirt, then set to the laborious task of tying up her boots. She'd want them now, with autumn bringing cooler weather. She'd be grateful for her short cloak too.

She grabbed her bag from the corner of the room, now stuffed with provisions, and that was the last of it. Her crossbow was already fastened to the loop at the back of her belt.

While dawn pinked the sky, she took one last look around the room and headed out towards the Red.

It was easier to leave this time.

This time, she wasn't running for her life. She might still be running from Rufus, but it wasn't Lucas that she was running towards. She was leaving him behind as well. This time, she was running with purpose. This time, she would bring contamination back with her into the Blue, and with it she would change the world.

It was full light before Julia reached the boundary fence. She didn't bother to search out a new path out of the city, she just stuck to the one she knew. That felt safer. She ducked and jinked as she wove her way amongst fallen trees and tumbledown houses, carefully working towards the gate where this had all begun.

It had been dark that night when she and Claudia had huddled in the roots of a fallen oak and watched as Marcus was ejected from the Blue. Back then, she hadn't understood any of this. Even if she had, it would have changed nothing. Lorelei would still have mounted her rebellion, the contamination would still have been dragged into the Blue, and they would still have been left at Rufus's mercy, because back then she'd known that she was just a Server.

Now she was something different. Yes, she was a Candidate, but that wasn't *all* that she was. She was new, and that new person had learned how to bring an end to the Silver.

She was the power of her knowledge, and soon she would be the power in her blood.

There was a heavy gust of wind that shook the trees on the other side of the boundary fence. Julia settled behind a pile of tumbled bricks, holding perfectly still. A few minutes later the wind blew again, in a strangely specific burst that moved only the trees that were nearest to the fence.

The Invicti were on patrol, moving at speed beyond the boundary.

Julia counted to three hundred, then the branches bowed once more. She counted again and there it was, regular as clockwork: leaves shaking from the boughs as the patrol passed by.

Perhaps it was someone she knew. Perhaps it was even Lucas, but that was all the more reason to avoid whomever was running the fence.

She used her three-hundred-second intervals carefully, creeping from tree stump to rubble pile until she was crouched by the gate. When the wood shook beside her, she waited twenty seconds before throwing the latch open and stepping out into the Red. She took a second to close the gate behind her and then she was running, diving headfirst into the forest.

When she was a hundred yards in, she knew she was free.

The woods embraced her. Julia had the benefit of hindsight now, so she knew where to aim her course. She didn't recognise any of the paths through the trees, but she knew that the ferry crossing was south of the city. She also knew that the forest was thick and wide, so she'd have to move quickly if she was going to reach the continent by nightfall. Frankly, she'd be lucky to reach even the shore by then, travelling on foot. Nevertheless, she put the sun on her left and tracked towards the ferry that waited to take her off the island.

It was unfamiliar territory. The only other time she'd passed this way, she'd been travelling at speed on Lucas's back. She didn't remember anything of that journey, so she didn't know the waypoints. She could only hope that she'd manage to make some decent progress before the sun rose too high for her to mark her course by it.

But the sun was only helpful for as long as she could actually see it. The trees were dense here and the space between was carpeted with ivy. It wound up the trunks and made the ground thick with vines that caught her feet. She could see the light, sort of, but as the day wore on it became harder and harder to determine the right direction. By the time the sun had passed overhead, she could no longer tell which way was south.

She was already on the verge of despair when she heard the first howl, cutting through the silent forest like the gong ringing out through the square.

Weepers.

The Weepers were on the continent, and if she couldn't navigate by the sun then she could navigate by the sound of the howls on the coast. Julia turned herself towards the noise, pulled the straps of her bag tight and started to run. She heard another cry a few minutes later and adjusted her course towards it. She must have been nearly at the shore now, because the howl sounded close. She was expecting to burst through the tree line at any moment. But then she heard the final howl, perilously close now, and realised her mistake.

The trees weren't thinning up ahead. She could see the canopy stretching into the distance, and yet the Weeper call had been close enough to raise the hairs along the back of her neck.

The Weepers were *here*. They were on the island.

And Julia's blood was uncontaminated.

Her feet stumbled over the ivy. She had to catch herself against a tree trunk to keep from pitching forwards, leaving a layer of skin on the bark. She forced her lips closed over her cry of pain and slipped into the shadow of the foliage just as a Weeper came into view.

She'd been running straight for it.

How could she have been so stupid?

But there'd be time for recriminations later. Right now, she needed to come up with a plan to get out of here before night fell. If she didn't get to the shore tonight, there was no way she was getting out of the forest alive.

Think. There must be something.

If the Weeper was alone, then she might be able to fight it off, but she'd never tried that before. She'd never had to, she'd just run. She couldn't run away from it this time, though. The moment it heard her footfalls, she'd be doomed. She couldn't climb away from it either, because the Weepers moved like squirrels in the treetops when they were chasing prey.

The only option was blood. It was always blood. It was the only way to defeat them, but she didn't have the right kind.

Damn Galatea and her worthless blood exchange.

So there was only one course of action left available to her: she huddled in the undergrowth and waited for the Weeper to pass her by.

* * *

Julia was shivering in a laurel bush when she heard the familiar thrumming blast of a Silver running by at speed. It passed close enough to send an unwelcome draught under her short cloak, but far enough away for the traveller to miss her hiding spot. She couldn't work out whether that was a good thing or not.

It felt as though she had been hiding for most of the day. In reality, it couldn't have been more than half an hour or so, but she was going to have to make a new plan soon. The light between the trees was beginning to darken, and still the Weeper hadn't moved more than thirty feet, side to side. She'd been watching him, tracking his course, but there was no pattern to it. He seemed to move blindly from tree to tree, but she couldn't tell whether he was sightless or not.

The worst thing was that, without contaminated blood, she had no idea how to take him down. Five times she'd raised her crossbow and sighted along it, but five times she'd dropped it, remembering the broken creatures that had chased her through the city on the night of the Contamination. Who was to say that a bolt to the head would be enough?

In the end, she had no other choice. Better to take a direct approach than to try creeping around it and find herself ambushed in the undergrowth.

She lifted the crossbow and found her target, widening her eyes against the fading light as her finger stroked the trigger. It released true. The arrow hit the Weeper in the cheek, the trajectory taking the point up into his brain and out of the back of his skull, so that only a couple of inches of the shaft protruded from his face.

He turned to Julia. For a second, she thought it had been enough. For a blissful moment, his spin seemed to result from the force of the bolt hitting him rather than from a deliberate movement.

But he didn't fall. Instead, he fixed his feet in Julia's direction and began to walk. Then jog. Then run.

She scrambled back through the leaf litter, dropping her crossbow somewhere in the ivy carpet.

He was coming so fast that she barely had a chance to get to her feet before he was on her. His bloodied hands grasped towards her throat. She shunted him back with an elbow to the stomach, but it didn't provide the distance she'd been hoping for. The Weeper's torso was so decomposed that it wasn't until her elbow met his spine that her strike found enough purchase to push him backwards. Until that point, all her momentum just went into sinking her arm into his flesh.

Still, it made enough space between them that Julia could get her foot against his hips. One sharp push and he was staggering backwards away from her.

Then the game changed. Perhaps he'd sensed his advantage trickling away now that Julia was fighting back, or maybe it was just the pack instinct kicking in, but it was bad news for Julia either way. He tipped back his head and howled.

That could only mean one thing: there would be more on their way.

Damn damn damn.

Julia pulled her knives from her belt. Wrapping her fingers around their hilts cemented her determination: she'd take this Weeper down or die trying. If more came, she'd take them out too, but first this one had to be dispatched. She could take him. She was strong. As long as she avoided getting his blood inside her, she'd make it out of this alive.

The Weeper was hesitating. He might have been waiting for the others to join him, or maybe Julia's kick had disorientated him. His bloodstained eyes didn't seem to be tracking her, just his face. It tipped from side to side in a grotesque dance, its rhythm regular and undulating like a simulated heartbeat.

Then he leapt. Julia launched herself forward in the same moment, her knives tucked in close to her body. As the distance closed, she raised them and slammed one into the Weeper's chest and the other into his throat.

The injuries didn't slow him down. His arms were already closing around Julia, fingernails scrabbling at her back and grasping at her hair. She could feel strands of it tearing free from the roots as she twisted in his grasp, but there was nothing she could do to loosen his grip. Only her hold on the knife in his throat was stopping his teeth from descending towards her face.

She had to get loose, or soon his bloodstained fingernails would find their way to her exposed skin. Then it would all be over.

She reared back and head butted him, smashing her forehead into his. There must already have been a crack in his skull, because the bone gave way under the blow and left a dent in his brow.

They both tumbled to the ground, and Julia rolled out of the creature's arms. She struggled to catch her breath, but the Weeper was moving again almost instantly, reaching out to wrap his hand around her wrist.

Julia's next gasp was more a sob than a breath. If even a caved-in skull wouldn't slow him down, then how was she supposed to win this fight?

But she wasn't completely defenceless. She'd managed to pull one of her knives out of his body as they'd hit the ground. The other was still stuck in the Weeper's throat. He made no attempt to remove it as he rose to his feet, dragging Julia's arm up with him.

Acting more on instinct than on conscious thought, Julia let her body go heavy as a corpse. The weight pulled the Weeper off balance and gave her enough reach to swing the knife down and slash the tendons at the back of his heels. He tumbled forwards, releasing her. She managed to scramble away just as the first of his friends came into view.

Now she was really stuffed.

There were at least four that she could see in the shadows of the trees, one clearly female but the others indistinct by reason of decomposition or the building darkness. She could barely make out their shapes in the dusk beneath the canopy, but she didn't need to count them to know that the fight was over. She had one knife, and they had a set of teeth each. They'd already zeroed in on her position. She had no time to go digging in her discarded pack for more weapons. They were already running out of the undergrowth towards her, their bodies shooting from the bushes like arrows.

She couldn't fight that many, but she couldn't outrun them either, so she raised her knife like a sword, dug her heels into the earth and prepared herself for the final clash.

But it never came. Instead, there was the thrumming again. It spun through the trees, cutting down the Weepers is a spray of gore. Julia only had fractions of a second to close her eyes before the noxious blood showered over her face.

By the time she'd wiped her eyelids clean on her sleeve, there was a woman standing in front of her. Julia recognised her from the journey back to the Blue with the Queen. She was one of the Invicti, distinguished by colourful tattoos that stretched from her neck to her fingertips, but Julia couldn't remember her name.

They'd never had a conversation, nor spent enough time together to get the measure of each other.

'Well?' she said to Julia. 'Aren't you going to thank me?'

Julia looked over the woman's shoulder to see the bodies of the Weepers laid out beneath the trees. They were no longer a threat. Like the one Julia had felled, they were incapacitated, but clearly still alive, still trying to move despite their broken bodies. Perhaps the only way to kill them was to use contaminated blood.

'Thank you,' Julia said. 'I wouldn't have been able to handle them all.'

'You wouldn't even have been able to handle one,' said the woman.

Julia cast her gaze pointedly towards the Weeper she had fought, who was hauling himself half-heartedly in their direction.

'Holy fuck,' the woman said. 'You did that? Wait a minute, you're the new kid's human, aren't you?'

'I was Lucas's Attendant,' Julia replied, putting the emphasis on the past tense.

The woman raised her eyebrows, but didn't ask. 'Well,' she said, 'he's going to flip his lid when he hears about this.'

'I'd rather he didn't hear about it at all,' Julia said, wiping her knife clean on her ruined cloak.

'You covered in Weeper blood? Of course I'm bloody telling him. He's going to have to watch you when you get back to the city, just in case.'

'I'm not going back to the city.' That was met with more eyebrow raising. 'And if I were going to turn into a Weeper then it would already have happened, wouldn't it?'

The woman took in the sight of Julia, blood-spattered with a red hand fisted around her remaining blade.

'You are one lucky fucker,' the woman said, 'I'll tell you that much. You'd better come with me. Don't go licking your lips or anything before I can get you somewhere you can wash that off.'

She strode towards the Weeper that Julia had felled and, putting one foot on its neck, pulled the knife out of its throat.

'This is yours, I suppose,' she said, handing it back to Julia.

'Thank you.'

As she took it and sheathed both knives, Julia felt a pinching in her palms that she'd not noticed in the frenzy of the fighting. She stared at the blood-stained skin, surprised to see that it was broken in places.

Then she remembered tripping on the ivy earlier. She'd fallen, hadn't she? She'd broken her fall on a tree with her palms, grazing them open. Apparently not open enough to admit the contamination of the Weeper blood, though. The grazes must have scabbed during her afternoon spent hiding in the undergrowth.

That was the only rational explanation.

'Well, come on,' the woman said irritably. 'We've got a couple of miles to go yet, and I'm not carrying you while you're covered in that shit. You'll have to walk yourself.'

Julia grabbed her pack as the woman disappeared between the trees. With night falling, she'd have to stay close to follow her.

'Naia!' a voice called as Julia's feet moved from leaves to pebbles.

That was the woman's name, then. It was familiar.

Julia could hear the slow waves of the salt lake now, the rush and pull punctuated by cries from the birds that picked the shoreline. The quality of noise was different here. In the trees everything had felt warm and close, but here the open space of the water seemed to swallow sound. In the darkness, it felt like eternity was stretching out in front of her.

Julia followed Naia's footsteps around a pile of fallen trees to where a small campfire was burning close to the edge of the forest.

'You made it,' Cam said. He was sitting by the fire with Felix and another of the Invicti, Darius, who was stirring a pot of something that smelled irresistible to Julia's empty stomach.

'Rescued a fair maiden on the way,' Naia replied as she waved Julia forward, her voice thick with sarcasm.

'Julia?' said Cam.

'You should've seen the number she did on one of the rot bags,' Naia went on. 'Carved through his Achilles tendons so he was wriggling along on his belly. Fucking hilarious.' Then she laughed, as though to prove the point.

Darius's face twisted in distaste. 'I'm so glad we're leaving you behind.'

Naia narrowed her eyes at him.

'Julia,' Cam said again, ignoring the others. 'What are you doing here? Are you alright?'

'I'm fine,' she said, 'thank you. I just need to wash off this blood.'

Cam turned to Naia. 'You want to take her down to the water?'

'What?' said Naia. 'Because I'm a girl? Fuck that. I've got rot bags to clear out, and I suppose you're going to want another horse for her.'

'Why do you always have to bitch about every little thing?' Darius said.

'Forget it!' said Cam, standing up from his place by the fire. 'I'll take her. Darius, go with Naia and bring back another horse.'

The other man started to protest, but Cam didn't even let him get a word out before ordering both him and Naia out of the camp. Julia couldn't say she was sorry to see them go.

'I'm sorry about those two,' Cam said when they'd gone. 'It throws off the dynamic having just two of them here. They fight like cats when the others aren't around. It doesn't help that Darius just got cured today, so he's feeling a little sensitive.'

'Because he's usually so easy going,' Felix said, and they both laughed.

Julia found herself smiling, despite the cold and the darkness and the infectious blood congealing on her skin.

'I'm lucky Naia came along when she did,' she said. 'I'm grateful, truly.'

Cam squeezed Felix's hand then moved towards the water.

'Come on,' he said to Julia. 'Leave your bag here and let's get you clean. We're going to have to burn your clothes, I'm afraid.'

'I have others,' said Julia, although she was already regretting the loss of her short cloak. It was the only outerwear she had, and without it she'd freeze at night. But it was too risky to keep it.

Cam held her back when they reached the tideline.

'They're in the water,' he said. 'That's how they made it onto the island. I'll go out first, then call you in when I've checked it's safe.'

'Weepers? In the lake?'

'They don't need to breathe,' he said, already stripping off his shirt. 'Apparently they've realised what that means. Wait here.'

He shed the rest of his clothing unceremoniously and waded out into the briny lake. Once he was waist deep he dove under the surface, sleek as an otter, and disappeared. The lake was a mirror reflecting the stars, rippling with the current, but unbroken. It stayed that way for a long time. As the minutes stretched Julia began to worry, until finally she started to wonder whether Cam would ever resurface. It shocked her when he finally did, breaking the surface in a shower of dark droplets.

'You're clear,' he shouted back to her. 'There are a few near the other shore, but I'll keep an eye on them.'

Julia stripped out of her own clothes hurriedly and self-consciously, but she couldn't wash in the same way. She could turn her back to Cam as she cleaned herself, but she needed to be thorough. She'd brought a rag and some ash soap from her pack for that purpose, in the hope that it would be enough.

'You're still carrying someone else's mark,' Cam said quietly as she scrubbed at her fingernails. 'Scent mark, I mean.'

'Oh,' Julia said, dipping her chin. 'You noticed that?'

'I know Lucas's scent. That's not it.'

Julia concentrated on a particularly stubborn stain on the back of her hand, scrubbing it almost raw before she realised it was a mole. The moonlight was not making this job any easier.

'That's why you've left the Blue,' Cam said.

'Yes. It was one reason.'

'And the other?'

To find some contaminated blood so I can turn every last Noble human.

Well, she could hardly tell him that.

'To find my parents,' is what she actually said.

'You think they're out here?'

'I heard about a lake up in the mountains where humans live, people who used to live in the Blue. I need to look there.'

Cam said nothing. His silence felt strange enough that Julia turned to look at him over her shoulder.

'That's where we're going,' he admitted eventually.

'Perfect,' she said, although it would probably make things more difficult. She'd only intended to go as far as Sabina and Galatea's community so she could get the contaminated blood she needed and bring it back to the Blue. The mountain lake had been a convenient lie, and the first thing that had sprung to mind in the moment. Now she'd have no choice but to go that far with them.

She finished washing the rest of her skin in silence. She'd left her hair until last because she knew it would take an age to tease the blood out of the strands. That's why she hadn't yet bothered to get it wet. That's why the sharp salt sting at the base of her skull came as a surprise.

She carefully felt around the area, rubbing it gently to loosen the blood. She'd lost some hair there, probably from where the Weeper had snatched at it during their fight. Then her fingertips found something hard and sharp, stuck in the skin. She pulled it out gently then held it up to the moonlight.

It was a claw-like shard, shoved into her scalp deeply enough to make it bleed.

The Weeper's fingernail.

Julia spent the rest of the night worrying that she was about to turn into a Weeper. She knew that what she had said to Naia was true – if she was going to turn then she would already have done so – but she still found it difficult to relax as the Invicti made preparations to cross over to the continent.

By the time they'd dried and dressed themselves, Felix had already made a bonfire from Julia's old clothes. She'd been left in a threadbare shirt and trousers. Her boots had survived largely unscathed, but they weren't enough to keep the rest of her warm.

'Here,' Felix said, handing her a blanket.

When belted around her waist, it made a serviceable coat. She smiled at the woodsman as she accepted it.

There was something about him that Julia found calming, and she needed that right now. For all their ice-blue colour, his eyes were warm. Especially when they turned on Cam. When those two looked at each other, Felix's eyes lit with the kind of mischief that made Julia long for Lucas, just so she'd have someone to hold her. She was going to miss him.

'Don't tell me you're crossing now,' Naia said when she and Darius returned. They didn't seem to be speaking to each other, but at least they'd stopped fighting. They'd also brought two more horses with them, making five in total: one each.

'We may as well,' said Cam as Naia and Darius joined them by the fire. 'It's more sheltered on that side. We'll only need three journeys across on the ferry.'

'Four,' Naia said. 'There are four of you, and four horses.'

Cam looked at Julia for a moment. 'No, three,' he said to Naia. 'You're taking Julia back to the Blue.'

No.

She couldn't go back without the blood. She couldn't go back to Rufus without a weapon that she could use against him.

But she had to give Cam a different reason.

'No,' she said, making her voice small, inviting Cam's pity. 'Please. I can't go back to the city. You know why I can't go back.'

She looked into his eyes, as though she were begging him not to make her share her secrets in front of the others. In truth, she'd rather not talk about the scent mark. She wouldn't mind Felix knowing, but the other two? Naia? She could already imagine the leering comments. Even the thought of them made Julia hot with shame, which in turn made her angry that she should be ashamed of something that was beyond her control.

She would wipe it away with blood.

'You're human,' Cam said to her, his tone soft. 'It's too dangerous. We can't risk it.'

'Why not?' she asked, her anger fuelling her courage. 'Darius is human.'

'He's contaminated.'

'Then contaminate me, too.'

'And lose another blood donor?' Naia said. 'Are you crazy?'

'That aside,' said Cam, 'I don't feel comfortable about contaminating you without talking to Lucas first.'

'I don't belong to him,' Julia said. Then she suffered the humiliation of watching all four of them tracing the faint lines of Rufus's name on her cheek. 'And I don't belong to *him* either,' she added, her fingers itching for her crossbow.

Julia stared at Cam, daring him to argue. He held her gaze steadily for so long that Julia thought she was going to break first, but then he looked over at Felix and, after a silent moment's communication, turned back to her.

'Fine,' he said. 'Come with us, but you stay uncontaminated, for the time being at least. We'll leave you at the mountain lake and collect you again on our way back. Alright?'

Julia could feel the tension in her body releasing. She would have slipped away and made the journey alone if she'd had to, but after her encounter in the forest she was happy enough to accept an escort.

'Thank you,' she said, with feeling. 'I do appreciate it.'

'I just hope you're ready to ride. We've got a long way to go.'

6

Julia was no better at riding a horse now than she had been when they'd returned to the Blue a fortnight ago. In fact, if anything, she was worse.

Cam had tried coaching her. He'd tried tying her horse's reins to Hades's saddle. Hell, he'd even tried tying Julia to her own horse, but she'd still managed to fall off at least once a day. In the end, he'd had to jury-rig an old-fashioned saddle, stirrups and all, from scraps of material they'd all scrounged from their packs. She was still the world's worst rider, but at least now she was more inclined to remain on the horse.

Cam had to give her credit, though, because she hadn't complained once. Even when they rode for sixteen hours a day, and even when she must have been chafed bloody with saddle sores.

She was nothing if not determined.

'Jesus,' Darius muttered as they crested the peak of the pass.

They could see Ana's little community spread out before them, though it wasn't so little now. There were a lot more buildings than there had been the last time they'd come this way. It looked as though Chloe had led a huge number of people back to this sanctuary.

'I didn't think I'd be nervous,' Darius went on. 'Why am I nervous?'

'It's your son,' said Cam. 'Of course you're nervous.'

Darius was sweating again, the beads shining like crystals on his forehead.

'Do you love her?' Cam asked him.

'What?'

'Do you love her? Do you love Chloe? I mean, you had a child together, so I assumed–'

'Yes,' Darius said, although he sounded uncertain. 'Yes, of course I love her.' He was more definite this time, but it still sounded as though he were trying to convince himself.

Cam smiled and clapped him on the back. 'Then you have nothing to worry about. Come on.'

Their reception in the settlement wasn't as grand as usual, but that was probably because the place was already bustling with activity. It seemed that new arrivals were no longer the novelty they had once been.

'Domnul Cameron,' Ana said as she met them at the edge of the lake. 'You certainly kept up your end of our bargain.'

'How many have come?' Cam asked.

'A hundred or so. I'm told that several were lost on the journey here.'

Cam nodded. 'Thank you for taking them in, Doamna Ana.'

'No, Domnul Cameron: thank you for sending them to us. We are stronger together. Are you staying this time?' She smiled, looking between Felix and Cam with a twinkle in her eye.

'Just for a few days, then we need to move on. We were hoping to leave our friends here though, for a while at least. This is Julia, and you'll remember Darius from our last visit.'

Julia said hello to the gerontocrat, but Darius's attention was elsewhere. He was looking over at the lake shore, where a small boy was paddling in the shallows. There was a woman close by, stooping to fish freshwater mussels from the mud and deposit them in a basket she held in the crook of her elbow. As Darius watched, she straightened and rested her hands on her hips. The little boy looked up at her and smiled.

'I can't do this,' Darius muttered. He started leading his horse away to the stables, but the movement must have caught the woman's eye. After exchanging a few words with another woman who was working nearby, she handed over her basket, left the little boy in the shallows and started striding through the silt to the shore.

'Darius?' she called.

He froze.

'I know that's you. You think you can just slink away without me noticing? You've got some nerve, coming here like this.'

Darius turned to face her.

The sight of him was enough to pull her up short. Cam could see the jerk as her feet stalled in the mud. Her eyes raced over Darius's exposed skin, taking in the myriad scratches and bug bites that littered his arms. It had been a hard ride, and a week of sleeping on the forest floor had taken its toll on his newly-human skin.

In contrast, Cam's skin was as smooth and clear as it always was.

'Show me your eyes,' Chloe said, walking closer.

'I can't hide them,' he said.

'Then you're human?'

'Yes.'

The hardness in Chloe's expression crumbled, giving way to a painful kind of hope that quivered her cheeks and made her eyes shine.

'So you're staying?' she said.

Darius shuffled his feet a little before he would meet her eye. 'I hope so.'

'Forever?'

'Will you have me?'

Chloe was already running. When she reached Darius, she jumped into his arms and wrapped her legs around his waist, smearing mud all over his clothes. He didn't seem to mind.

Their reunion was enthusiastic enough to make Cam clear his throat and look away.

'So prudish.' Felix smiled as he weaved his fingers between Cam's.

Ana was smiling too.

'It looks as though just the three of us will be staying in the visitor huts, Doamna Ana,' said Cam.

'*Your* huts, Domnul Cameron. Never anyone else's.'

'My huts, then.'

'I'll let you see to your own horses.' She was eyeing Hades with some trepidation. 'I remember this one. But perhaps afterwards you'd join us for some dinner in the hall?'

'We'd be glad to. We have some questions to ask, if you don't mind. We're trying to track down someone who might have come this way.'

'Oh? Well, find me after the meal, then we can talk alone.'

The food was delicious, but beyond that Ana had nothing to offer Cam. When her memory turned up nothing, she called some of the older members of the community to the fireside, but vague descriptions of a woman travelling with a baby were met only with furrowed brows and the shaking of heads.

They hadn't come this way, then, certainly not in Ana's lifetime.

There was no reason for Cam and Felix to stay. The only loose end to deal with now was Julia, but that could wait until the next day.

Julia opted to have the smaller of Cam's cabins to herself, leaving the newer hut for Cam and Felix. Cam didn't want her to feel deserted in a strange place, but she seemed to sense that his heart wasn't in his protestations. He wanted to be alone with Felix, and it was clear that Julia was happy enough on her own.

Which was just as well, because Cam wasn't going to be able to contain himself much longer. Felix had been teasing him throughout their meal, stroking his thumb along the inside of Cam's wrist, sitting so close on the bench that their thighs pressed against each other, then running his hand up Cam's leg until Cam was afraid he'd embarrass himself if he stood up from the table.

He threw the cabin door shut the moment they got inside, then threw Felix up against it.

'Are you trying to ruin me in front of these good people?' he said, pinning Felix against the door by his shoulders. Felix let him, his smile widening as his eyes darkened.

'They know who you are,' he said. 'They love you. *I* love you.'

'I think I love you too.'

'You *think*?'

Felix grabbed Cam by the waist and pulled him closer, close enough to kiss, but he didn't. Instead, he teased, brushing his lips over Cam's. When Cam tried to close the distance and catch Felix's mouth with his own, the woodsman pulled his head back out of reach.

'I think you need to be more certain than that,' he said, then he hooked a foot around Cam's leg and tumbled him forwards. It brought their lips crashing together in a kiss that was frantic with a mixture of relief and hunger that spun Cam's head. He let Felix turn them around until it was Cam's back against the door, but then Felix pulled away.

'Tell me,' he said.

Cam smiled, willing to play. 'That I want you?'

'I know you want me. Tell me the rest.'

Cam put his palm to Felix's cheek, letting the bristles of Felix's beard tickle his hand as he cupped his jaw.

'That I love your eyes, then,' Cam said, staring into their ice-blue depths. He fisted his other hand in Felix's shirt and pulled him closer, until there was no distance left between them. 'Or that I love your body. Is that what you want to hear?'

Felix leaned in to Cam, flattening him against the door, then kissed him again. This time his lips moved lazily, coaxing and persuading.

'Tell me,' Felix whispered, his blue eyes raising to meet Cam's, but there was something new in them now, a pinch of anxiety. Cam realised that Felix needed to hear the words.

'I love you,' Cam whispered.

Somewhere in the blood and struggle of the past months, Felix had become more than an addiction. It wasn't just that Cam wanted him, or that Felix intrigued him, or that he might have been the most attractive man Cam had ever met, although all of those things were true. Felix had become the constant. His touch had become the comfort Cam needed to steady him, just as it had become the catalyst that Cam needed to propel him from lamenting their existence into forming a plan to do something about it.

Felix was why he needed to find Emmy's son and put an end to the Silver. Without that, there would be no better world, and he needed to make a better world for Felix, not because he deserved it but because Cam wanted him to have it. He wanted to give Felix everything.

But for Felix to have that world, there could be no more Silver. They would all have to become like Felix: cured.

And that included Cam.

'Show me,' Felix said, and it took a few seconds for Cam to understand that Felix wanted to see his eyes. He wanted to see the silver leaking into Cam's irises, so he'd know that Cam truly was in love with him.

'You don't trust me?'

'I want to see it. Stop hiding your silver.'

'But that's not fair,' Cam said, stealing a quick kiss. 'What proof are you going to show me?'

'If your eyes are gold, then you'll have your proof.'

Cam grinned. 'But that's no fun. I'm sure you can find another way to convince me.'

Felix didn't hesitate. He pulled Cam against him and kissed him long and hard, showing Cam with actions what he could no longer show him in his own eyes. Cam reciprocated, and suddenly the air in the cabin seemed unbearably warm.

'Stop,' Felix said, breaking away. 'We have to stop.'

'I don't want to.'

'You know why this can't go any further.'

Cam sighed, stepping back as he ran a hand through his dark blond hair.

'I'm too old for this adolescent bullshit,' he said. 'I want you.'

'You have me. This is enough.' Felix smiled, but there was regret in it.

'No,' said Cam, 'it's not enough. It's not enough for me, at least. I don't want this to be the way things are between us. I don't want to be always holding back. I can't do that forever. I won't. It won't be like this forever, but... I'm sorry. I have to finish this first.'

'I just wish you'd tell me what "this" is. What are we doing here?'

Cam walked over to the fireplace and threw on a couple more logs, trying to find the words to explain why he had to change the world.

'Did anyone tell you about Emmy?'

'What about her?' Felix had walked over to join him now, settling onto the cushions that were laid out by the fire.

'What happened to her in the Revelation. No, I suppose they wouldn't have told you. She was human, you know.'

Cam dropped down onto the floor next to Felix, his long legs making him inelegant while Felix's dense musculature kept him compact and poised. He made Cam feel like a gangly spider.

'None of us knew what was happening in the beginning,' Cam went on. 'America went first. You know America? It was way on the other side of the ocean. Last time I went there it was just craters and ruins, but that was where it started. It was all Killian's fault, the bastard. By the time the Weepers reached us it was too late to stop them, so we just had to gather everyone in the cities and seal them off. Most of the humans died, but there were still hundreds of thousands left in London alone. There were that many people in the world, back then.'

'I'd heard about that,' Felix said, pouring them each a cup of wine from a bottle on the hearth. 'Wasn't sure I believed it.'

'It's true. Billions of people. That's millions of millions. Thousands of thousands of thousands of thousands.'

'Sounds crowded.'

'Not everywhere.' Cam sipped his wine. 'There were always places that were quiet. London wasn't one of them, but like I said, it emptied out after the Revelation. Well, we emptied it out. I thought we were just trying to keep people safe, but it almost didn't feel real. We had enough blood, and we'd planned for the worst, so nothing really changed except the Weepers at the gates. It was just, I don't know. Normal. Better, sometimes, because it felt like we were in charge. But it was never actually *us* in charge. It was Sol. When he lost Emmy, and we lost him, we lost everything else too.'

'Like?'

'The city, the noncontams. Shit, we didn't deserve them in the first place. Back then, I didn't see anything wrong with what we were doing. The humans got looked after, and we got the blood we needed. It worked. But seeing what that morphed into in the Blue… Now it feels like the slavery Emmy always said it was. She never wanted to be ruled by the Silver. She never wanted to *be* Silver either. She was always running off, driving Drew and Sol crazy because she just wouldn't do what she was told, but she was prepared to risk her life to be free.'

Cam smiled, remembering Emmy as she'd been back then: sarcastic, unpredictable and disobedient. There'd been a kind of power in that. She'd been stupid sometimes, but she'd been fun, too.

Now power was all she was. Pure, uncontrolled power.

'She thinks Charles is the one who broke her,' he went on, 'but I wonder if we hadn't already done that, by making her into what she is. And now she can't ever change back, because she's immune to the cure, and I feel like that's my fault. She was my friend, Felix.'

'She's not anymore?'

Cam pushed a hand back through his hair. 'Now I'm not sure what she is.'

Felix put his wine cup down and took Cam's hand. 'She'd be dead if she weren't Silver. The King would be dead too. There'd probably be no Silver left. Is that really what you want?'

Cam dropped his gaze, letting his eyes lose their focus as he searched for the words he wanted.

'I feel like I dreamt a perfect world and woke up without it,' he said. 'Except the problem isn't that I'm not in that world, it's that the world can't exist with me in it. I thought we'd all be gone eventually, with the cure, but that's never going to happen now, not now Emmy and Sol are immune. But maybe if just *most* of us are cured, that'll be enough.'

Felix sat up straighter as the implication of Cam's words became clear.

'You can't make that decision for other people,' he said.

'Like Richard didn't make it for you? Like you didn't decide for him?'

Cam could see Felix clenching his jaw. 'He deserved it.'

'I'm not saying he didn't. I'm saying that we live in a world of inequality and exploitation. I'm saying the only way to fix that is to turn all the Silver human, and they're not going to give up their advantage willingly. We're going to have to take it from them.'

'From you,' Felix said. 'You're one of them. Is this really what you want?'

'I want to be with you. Properly. '

'So you're taking them down with you? If you can't be Silver, then no one else can either? Is that it?'

'It doesn't matter whether I'm Silver or not. I'm going to die when you do, anyway. We're bonded now, or have you forgotten?'

That was what it meant for a Silver to love, after all: when you silvered, you died with your bonded partner.

'As soon as we've found Emmy's son,' Cam continued, 'I can give it up.'

'And what are you going to do when we find him? The King and Queen can't be cured, and their son will be the same.'

'Maybe. Maybe not. That's what we need to find out.'

Felix wasn't convinced. His lips were set in a line that expressed his concern without him needing to put it into words, but that wasn't what caught Cam's attention.

'You've got his eyes, you know,' Cam said.

'Hmm?'

'The King's. They're the same ice-blue as yours. I've wondered about that. It's not a common colour.'

Felix was still for a moment, obviously giving the idea some consideration, but then he shook his head. 'I'm too old.'

'We don't know how old their son is. Emmy doesn't know how long she was unconscious. He could have been born any time in the past five hundred years.'

'But we know he wasn't,' Felix insisted. 'We know he's about twenty.'

'What are you talking about? We don't know that.'

Felix leaned forwards, resting his elbows on his crossed knees.

'You've forgotten,' he said. 'That night with Peterke's people. I was in the trees. I heard them telling you that the Silver had come for their baby boys, about twenty years ago. They must have been looking for the Queen's son.'

Cam froze with his wine cup halfway to his lips. Could it really be that simple?

'I'd forgotten,' he said. 'With Peterke… I forgot about the boys. You're right. It makes sense. They took all those babies.' Cam dragged a hand down his face. 'Do you think they killed them?'

'They'd have no reason to keep them alive.'

But the pieces were starting to click into place in Cam's mind, and that didn't feel like the right answer.

'No,' he said. 'You were there in the mountains when we rescued Emmy. You remember all the soldiers with the Red Shirts, the young Silver who didn't know what the hell they were doing, who all looked–'

'–about twenty.'

Charles's army.

'He didn't kill those kids,' Cam said. 'We did.'

Both of them struggled to sleep after that. They hadn't contaminated all of the soldiers when they'd rescued Emmy, but the tens they had downed onto the blood-slicked floor would never have woken up. That was a lot for Cam to hold on his conscience now that he knew where the boys had come from.

Felix tossed and turned for a while, but since they were at the end of a week of hard riding, Cam knew it wouldn't be long before Felix dropped off in his arms.

He waited.

When Felix's breath became soft and regular, Cam slid one hand free and reached out for his belt. There was a knife hanging from it, which he slipped from its sheath and held up to his face, angling it to catch the wavering light from the fireplace.

Then he let the silver come, watching it trace a path along the blood vessels in his eyes, waiting for it to reach his dark irises.

He needed to see it for himself. He could analyse his feelings all he liked, but he wouldn't believe it himself until he saw the path of the silver snaking into the brown of his eyes.

He watched, and waited, and all too soon it stopped. The silver filaments didn't stray beyond his sclerae. No matter how long he stared at his reflection, his irises wouldn't silver.

He had lied to Felix.

Kisses wouldn't distract him forever. Sooner or later he'd ask to see the silver again, and then he'd find out for himself.

This wasn't love.

The next morning Chloe was waiting for them by the lake, with Darius and little Alex at her side.

The boy had changed since Cam had last seen him. His expression had always been pinched with anxiety that ill-suited his young features, but now it was as though his face had blossomed into joy. He was running in circles around his parents, dragging a stick behind him to make patterns in the soft ground.

'Happy families, is it?' Cam said, smiling to see them together.

'More or less,' said Chloe.

Darius just grinned, watching Alex run rings around him as though it were the most remarkable thing he'd ever seen.

This was the problem with the Invicti: you became so attached to your brothers and sisters in arms that you forgot there was another way to have a family. Tommy and Viv weren't the only ones who could be parents, but it had taken stepping out of their shadow for Darius to realise that.

Cam hoped they would all settle so well.

'You're staying?' Cam asked Darius.

'Yeah. I'll keep an eye on the girl until you come back this way, then you can take her back with you. That alright?'

'If that's what you want. Have you seen her?'

'Not yet.'

Dawn was only just peeking over the edge of the bowl that the mountains formed around the lake. It wasn't surprising that Julia was still in her bed, not after the ordeal she'd put her body through on the ride. She was made of tougher stuff than Cam had given her credit for, but she wasn't Silver, and she wasn't trained. She still had a breaking point.

'Who is the girl?' Chloe asked.

'She's human,' Cam said as they started to stroll along the shore, following Alex. 'She was born in the Blue, but she says she's out here looking for her parents.'

'You don't believe her?' asked Darius. 'You let her come out here and you don't even believe her story?'

'No, I believe it. I remember her parents leaving the Blue. I'm just not sure they're why she's out in the Red.'

'Oh?' said Chloe.

'She's quiet,' Felix said, and Cam nodded.

'I get the feeling that she's just waiting for us to leave. She watches. She plans everything she says carefully, and she wasn't like that with Lucas.'

'Her Noble,' Darius explained to Chloe. 'She left him behind in the Blue.'

That comment elicited raised eyebrows from Chloe.

'For good reason, I'm afraid,' said Cam. 'When we found her in the forest, she was carrying someone else's scent mark.'

'She was?' said Darius. 'Damn. That I did not know.'

'So you think she's running away?' Chloe asked.

'No,' Cam said. 'Lucas is a good kid, and anyway, she's too directed for that. I think she has an agenda. I just don't know what it is, but I don't have time to hang around here working it out either. Maybe you could try while we're gone.'

'You're not leaving already?'

'In a day or so. Just long enough to rest and resupply. We've got somewhere to be.'

Chloe nodded. 'Darius told me about Emmy's baby. I can't imagine what that must be like.' She looked down at Alex, touching her palm to his little head as he barrelled past, as though she needed to convince herself he was still there. 'They never tried to take him from me. I was in that cell for months, but they left him with me. I would have slit their throats if they'd tried.'

'Emmy did,' said Darius. 'She killed them all.'

There was a moment of silence, punctuated only by the wet slaps of Alex's footfalls in the mud, then Chloe said, 'Good.'

But Cam couldn't stop thinking about the truth: Yes, Emmy had killed Charles, but the other soldiers who'd died at her hands had been captives just like her. They'd been stolen from their parents and somehow turned Silver to create Charles's army. They'd been the same age as her son.

She might already have killed her own child.

'We're going back into the Ore Mountains,' Cam said, shoving the thought away. 'You were up there twenty years ago, weren't you?'

Chloe tipped her head. Cam had her attention.

'Do you remember a load of Silver coming out of Charles's compound, looking for baby boys?'

'Oh, shit.' She pressed her fingers to her lips. 'Yes. I remember that. When I was up in the Czech hills, before I had Alex. There were loads of people with little babies passing through, running from the mountains. You're telling me that's when Emmy had her baby?'

'Maybe. Were these people Silver?'

'One or two. Mostly humans.'

'Anything unusual about them?'

Chloe looked out over the lake as she fell into her memories. 'Yes,' she said. 'Shit, yes. A woman with a newborn baby. She was human, but she wasn't producing milk and the baby was Silver.'

'Maybe she'd just been cured,' Darius shrugged. 'Happens all the time.'

'I don't think so. She was feeding the baby her blood.' Chloe turned to face Cam. 'Are you telling me that was Emmy and Sol's little boy?'

'I don't know,' he said, but certainty was building in his gut. 'Do you remember anything else about the woman? What she looked like, her name, how old she was?'

'She looked like a human,' Chloe said, as though she were confused by the question. 'Muddy skin, muddy hair, muddy clothes. She was muddy all over. Her name though… I don't know. Some of them stayed up there in the mountains, the people who were helping her. Humans, mostly. They'd know. They're the ones you need to talk to.'

'Are there any of them left? I thought Richard rounded them all up when you moved over to Charlestown.'

'Then you thought wrong. Look,' she said, borrowing Alex's stick and using it to scratch into the silt of the lakeshore. 'Here are the Ore Mountains, coming down this way, and this is the mountain pass. Here's where Charles was holed up with the Red Shirts.' She marked it with a cross on her makeshift map, south of the pass that intersected the Ore Mountains. 'But have you tried looking here?' She added a question mark to the map, way north of the pass. If she was drawing to scale, then it was in an area that had been reclaimed by the ocean.

'You want us to look in the sea?' Cam said.

Chloe rolled her eyes. 'Find the island,' she said. 'Find the island, and you'll find the last free noncontams in the world.'

7

Julia woke with the taste of lemons on her lips. It must have been in their dinner last night, although she couldn't recall noticing the flavour in the food. She couldn't imagine where this community would get lemons either, given the climate up here.

Then she remembered who tasted of lemons, and doubled down on her denial.

She had *not* been dreaming of Rufus. Eurgh.

Time to get out of this hut and into the fresh mountain air, where she could wash the memory from her skin. Unfortunately, her thighs refused to cooperate. She had to roll off the straw mattress, which deposited her unceremoniously onto the floorboards, face first.

Great, she thought, *what now?*

She'd wanted to be on her way today, so she could find Galatea and her contaminated blood, but she had to face facts: she needed some time to recover first. Well, what she *really* needed was a bath. The fabric of her trousers had stuck to her saddle sores, and there was no way she was getting out of these clothes without soaking them off.

There was a knock at the door.

'Who is it?' she called, lifting her chin from the floor.

'It's Cam. Can I come in?'

Julia panicked. She tried to push herself to her feet, but that wasn't going to happen yet, so she settled for shuffling painfully into a seated position on the floor. It split the raw skin on her thighs and backside, but at least it was slightly more dignified than lying on the ground like a landed fish.

'Julia?'

'Alright,' she said, a little out of breath. 'Come in.'

'Are you okay?' Cam said as he pushed the door open.

'A bit uncomfortable.' She smiled through the tears of pain that had collected in her eyes. 'I'm having some trouble getting up this morning.'

'I can see. Do you need some help?'

No, she wanted to say, desperate not to show any weakness, but then she tried bending one of her knees and felt the fabric of her trousers pulling her sores apart. She sucked in a breath against the pain and said, 'Yes, please.'

'How bad is it?'

'Not bad,' she said, fighting the nausea.

Cam gave her a frank look.

'It feels bad,' she whispered.

'Okay. Hold on.' Cam hoisted her gently into his arms, holding her under her knees and around her waist. 'We'll get you cleaned up in the lake, then we'll take a look at you. Felix, can you grab some linens from the cabin?'

Julia hadn't noticed the woodsman until that moment, which said a lot about how much the pain was distracting her. He nodded from the doorway, rejoining them when Cam had already carried her halfway to the shore.

Thankfully, it was early enough that most of the community were still shut away in their huts. Julia could do without the spectators. There were just a few fisherman out on their skiffs in the centre of the lake, far enough away to afford them some privacy.

'Why didn't you tell me it had got this bad?' Cam said softly.

'I didn't want to slow you down.'

He raised an eyebrow in admonishment. 'Playing meek isn't going to work with me. It doesn't suit you, and you know it. You're not some wilting flower, but you've been trying damned hard to make yourself invisible over the past few days. Do you want to tell me why?'

Julia startled a little at that. She looked over at Felix, but he was giving her the same eyebrow she'd got from Cam.

Dammit. She'd thought she was being so subtle, but they'd noticed. They'd seen her trying to blend into the background, so no one would notice when she slipped away.

'I don't want to be any trouble,' she said. 'I don't want you to send me back.'

'But you *are* going back.'

'Not until you do. I'll have time to ask about my parents while you're gone.'

They'd reached the edge of the water now. Cam kicked off his boots and left them with Felix, striding out into the lake with Julia still cradled in his arms. He didn't speak again until they were out of earshot, the water up to his waist as he held Julia above it.

'The scent mark's worn off,' he said, 'but will that be the last time you wear it, or do I need to be worried for Lucas?'

Julia snorted. 'Lucas can look after himself.'

She hadn't meant that to be as scathing as the way it came out, but Lucas wasn't the one she was worried about right now. She was worried about the teethmarks in her neck, the lemon on her lips that morning, and how she was going to stop them both from happening again.

She was worried about getting that contaminated blood.

Cam was watching her.

'It's not that I don't care,' she said. 'It's just complicated.'

'Love always is.'

'I don't love him.' The words shouldn't have felt so bleak.

'Like I said: love's complicated.' Cam's lips twisted in a half smile that looked like sympathy. 'This is deep enough. Are you ready?'

Julia took a deep breath and nodded.

He lowered her slowly, the cold creeping into her flesh inch by inch. She almost wished he'd just dropped her straight in.

Between the water and her shivering, it wasn't long before the material had unstuck itself from her thighs.

'Will your clothes come off now?' Cam asked. 'I mean–'

But there wasn't any hint of a proposition in his words.

'They will,' Julia interrupted. 'Give me a second.'

It took a bit of wriggling, and Cam had to catch her more than once to stop her from falling over, but soon Julia was shivering naked in the water as she scrubbed at her hair and body, while Cam scrubbed at her clothes.

'I remember your parents,' he said.

Julia turned and stared at him, but his eyes were fixed on the blood- and dirt-stained rags in his hands.

'Well, I remember your mother, a little. Mostly I remember what happened after they left.'

'They were traitors,' Julia said, her tone deliberately level. She wanted to draw him out, but he wasn't playing along.

'So they say.'

'And what do *you* say?' Julia insisted.

'If your mother was a traitor for leaving the Blue,' he said, 'then doesn't that make you one as well?'

'You think I'm a traitor?'

Cam tossed her wet clothes around his neck and said, 'Do you believe in the Blue? Do you believe that it's fair for you and the rest of the humans to be treated the way you are by the Nobles?'

The seconds passed in silence as Julia watched Cam's face, and he watched hers. There were more people on the shore now, moving in Julia's peripheral vision over Cam's shoulders, but she held his gaze.

Then he said, 'You can't betray something you don't believe in.'

Julia blinked.

'Stay here and I'll fetch you a linen.'

The sores weren't as bad as Julia had feared. Her inner thighs were bruised and felt agonisingly awful, but there was no discolouration of the skin to betray her pain. The small areas that had been chapped raw were easily coated with salves and bandaged securely, so that when she pulled her clean clothes on she could almost ignore them.

Almost.

She could walk comfortably now that the wounds were clean and covered, despite the aching in her muscles. It would be another day or so before she was fit enough to start making her way back down the mountains, and there was no way she was doing it on horseback.

But she was starting to wonder whether she should go at all. Cam's words had her thinking, and not about her own loyalties. Now she was questioning his.

'Thank you,' she said to him as she emerged from her hut. 'I appreciate the help.'

Cam was leaning up against the side of his cabin while Felix crouched in the grass next to him, whittling away at a small chunk of wood. It looked bucolic, but the atmosphere was oddly tense. Julia saw the two of them exchanging a look as she emerged.

'What is it?' she said.

Felix stood as Cam took a step towards her.

'I spoke to Ana,' Cam said. 'About your parents. There's someone who can tell you about them, if you want to hear it.'

'My parents were here?'

Cam looked back at Felix again, and that's when the certainty settled like a lead weight in Julia's stomach.

'They're dead,' she said. 'Aren't they?'

'Yes.'

It should have hurt, that knowledge, but it felt like a relief. If they were dead, then there was no way they could have come back for Julia. Maybe they had always wanted her after all. Maybe they'd just died before they could retrieve her and save her from a life in the Blue.

Somehow that was better than finding out they were living out their days in this mountain paradise without her.

But hot on the heels of that relief came the guilt, for wishing her parents dead.

'I'm sorry,' Cam went on. 'If that's all you want to know, then that'll be the end of it. It's up to you. From what Ana said, I don't think it's a pleasant story, but if you need the whole truth then she's told me who can give it to you.'

Julia didn't speak. She just took a deep breath and nodded. Cam understood. He tipped his head towards the main settlement then led the way.

The route took them winding through some of the older houses whose wooden panels were weathered with age and rot. The journey was only a matter of a few minutes, but by the time Cam stopped in front of a shack that was bigger than the rest, Julia's palms were sweating and her clean hair was already sticking to the back of her neck.

'This is it,' he said. 'We'll wait out here, unless–'

'No, that's fine. Thank you.' Julia wanted to be the first to hear the truth, not just because she felt it belonged to her, but because if the story was awful then she might want to tell herself a different one. That would be harder to do if Cam and Felix knew the truth.

She stepped up to the door and knocked, wiping her palms on her trousers while she waited for someone to answer. It didn't take long.

'Yes?' The woman was about fifty, Julia guessed, but resplendent with grey-blond hair and sun-kissed cheeks. She looked like she belonged in the mountains, striding from peak to peak while the wind caressed her skin.

'Doamna Sofia?' Cam asked from over Julia's shoulder.

Julia's own throat was suddenly too dry to permit words. She could feel the muscles in her cheeks twitching with anxiety.

'Domnul Cameron.' Sofia smiled. 'I wasn't expecting a visit. I am honoured.'

'It's actually Julia here who'd like to speak with you, if you have a moment?'

Sofia looked Julia over from head to toe, her brow wrinkling with gentle concern. Julia wondered how much she already knew.

'Of course,' the woman said. 'Come in, my dear.'

She took Julia's hand and gently led her into the house. Sofia didn't flinch at the clamminess of her palm, which Julia considered a kindness, but it soon became clear that she was used to dealing with nervous women.

'There's no need to be worried.' She smiled as she ushered Julia into a chair by the fire and took the one opposite for herself. 'Whatever you need, no matter why you need it, I will do my best to help. So tell me: are you with child, or is it that you don't wish to become so?'

'Oh.' Julia could feel her cheeks flushing. 'No. It's nothing like that.'

She'd been too distracted to notice much of the room when she'd walked in, but she looked around now and realised why the place felt so homey. It had the warmth of Livia's hearth and the cleanliness of her surgery. There were herbs hanging from the ceiling joists in dried bundles above shelves of bottles labelled in a manner that Julia didn't recognise. On the far side of the room a few beds were pushed against the wall, unoccupied at present but made up with bright sheets as though they were being kept ready.

This was not only a place where Sofia lived, but also where she dispensed the medicines of her trade.

'You're a doctor?' Julia asked.

Sofia tilted her head from side to side, equivocating. 'A midwife, and a women's apothecary. Did you not know?'

Julia shook her head.

'Then what do you need of me?'

'Ana… Doamna Ana, she told us that you had some information about some people I've been looking for.' Julia swallowed, stumbling over her words. Why was this so hard? They were her *parents*, so why could she not admit that? In the end, she just said, 'I was hoping you could help me.'

Sofia sat back in her seat then gave Julia a look of stark assessment. Something in her had closed off, turning her welcoming attitude into one of suspicion.

'Their names?'

'A woman named Valeria,' Julia whispered. 'The man, I don't know. They left the Blue together.'

Sofia pressed her lips into a dissatisfied line. 'I can't help you.'

'But… Doamna Ana–'

'This is a place of safety for women. Do you understand? I don't betray their trust, even after they are gone. Not even for Ana.'

'Then it's true? They're both dead?'

'Domnişoară Julia, I cannot help you. Now, please.'

Sofia stood from her chair. She wasn't a tall woman, but her determination made her seem as though she were.

'Please,' Julia said, snatching her hand. 'Please. I… Valeria was my mother.'

Sofia froze. After a few seconds, she traced the lines of Julia's face, first with her eyes, then with her fingers. The gesture was filled with such sympathy that Julia was on the verge of deciding that she didn't want to know the truth.

'You're Valeria's girl?' she whispered, then shook her head. 'I wouldn't have known. You look like… You look too much like him.'

Sofia dropped back down into her chair, pulling her hair into a messy knot at the nape of her neck. Then she drew her knees up, tucking her feet beneath her so she was curled up in the chair like a child. It was as though she had deflated, transforming from striding matriarch to cowed damsel in the space of Julia's words.

'Is she dead?' Julia asked.

'Yes. I'm sorry.' The words were soft with pity, but Julia felt them as a pinch rather than a blow. She had already known her mother was gone.

'And my father too, I suppose.'

Sofia's pitying expression faltered, then darkened. '*Horatius.*' She hissed it like a curse.

'Was that his name?'

'They told you nothing of him, back in the Blue?'

Julia shrugged. 'I was a baby. Then a Server. Do you know what that means?'

'No power, so no knowledge. I know.' Sofia looked into the fire, then back at Julia. 'I was a Server myself, though much older than you when I left. I was working in the rice fields at the lake, so they probably thought I'd drowned. None of us could swim. It was a busy place, so easy to slip away. For Valeria, though, it was harder.' Sofia sighed. 'Are you sure that you want to know the rest?'

Julia wasn't sure at all. Her hands were already shaking in her lap, and her mouth was so dry that she had to clear her throat before she could answer.

'I think I need to,' she said. 'I think I have to.'

'Then we'll need some tea, and I'll start at the beginning. I hope your friends don't mind waiting.'

Julia sent Cam and Felix away. She reminded them that they'd be leaving for the north the next day, so their time would be better spent resupplying than it would waiting in the drizzle for her. Her real motivations weren't so honourable: she didn't want them to be so close. She was sure that Cam would be able to hear every word Sofia spoke if they waited outside.

These words were for her ears alone.

She promised to find them at dinner, which was enough to satisfy Cam, but not Felix, not quite. He trailed behind as the two of them walked away together, looking over his shoulder to watch Julia go back inside.

She couldn't parse the concern on his face.

'Are you ready?' Sofia had left a steaming cup of tea waiting for Julia on the arm of her chair. Its warmth was welcome.

'Yes,' Julia said, taking a deep breath. 'I'm ready.'

'Alright then. Your mother was an Attendant. No, wait. That's not the beginning.' Sofia pursed her lips, sucking at her cheeks as she thought. 'This is the beginning: The Empress had a son.'

Julia had been sipping at her tea while Sofia gathered her thoughts, but that made her look up sharply.

'You know him?' Sofia asked.

Julia raised a finger to her cheek, pointing at the faded name painted on her skin. The dye was nearly gone now, but if you knew what you were looking for you could trace the ghosts of the letters and the word they spelled. 'Rufus,' she said.

'Yes, Rufus.' Sofia leaned forwards in her chair to see for herself. 'What does the mark mean?'

'That I belong to him.' The words strangled Julia's tongue. 'I was his Attendant.'

'I see. And that's why you left the Blue?'

'No. Not this time.' Julia felt the shame burning in her chest, and she had to let it out. 'I left because we kissed.'

Sofia's expression turned wary. 'Do you love him?'

'What? No!' Julia put her cup down so violently that tea slopped over the edge and onto the arm of the chair. 'Dammit.' She wiped it up with her cloak. 'I didn't even want him to kiss me. It just happened. He's not... I mean, he's not a nice person. He's a monster. The things he's done.'

'But you kissed him.'

'He kissed me!'

Sofia raised an eyebrow at her.

'I'm sorry,' Julia said, trying to calm down. 'Can we get back to the story? I'd just as soon not talk about Rufus.'

Sofia's laugh was sharp and bitter.

'My girl,' she said, 'he's part of it. He was adopted by the Empress, you know. He's not her blood son. That's where it started, although I don't think she meant for it to happen as it did. You see, she had a favourite amongst her Servers, a man named Horatius.'

'My father.'

Sofia scoffed. 'I'd listen to the rest before you call him that. Horatius, he truly was a monster. I think the Empress liked that about him. She gave him free rein over her Attendants, or turned a blind eye at least. There were a lot of babies in the palace in those few years, my last ones in the Blue.'

'No,' Julia muttered, because she could see where this was going.

'I'm sorry.' Sofia looked down at her hands. 'But it's the truth. It's where you came from. Valeria wept for you to her last day, for leaving you behind, but you looked so much like him that she couldn't bear it. She hated him so much.'

Julia nodded. It felt true to her, that she had been conceived in hatred, because that's what the Blue was to her. The Nobles took what they wanted, and those to whom they bestowed their capricious favour had power behind them.

Like Horatius.

There was no love story to be found here. She'd been writing her parents' love affair her entire life. She'd imagined them sharing a glance one day over the well in the palace courtyard, her mother smiling reluctantly as her father told some awful joke. She'd imagined the trysts, the forbidden love, and their anguish at leaving her behind because it was the only way they could be together: by risking it all to run away into the Red, where they knew they might die. They couldn't risk taking Julia with her, not the little baby they loved so much, so they left her in Livia's care where they knew she'd be safe.

That was the story Julia had written for herself.

But it wasn't true. The truth was a darker kind of forbidden love. The kind of untrue love that's selfish enough to do what it wants.

She wondered if everyone in the Blue knew the truth, everyone but her. Was that why Livia would never speak about her parents, except in meaningless platitudes? Was that why the girls in the kitchen had always shunned her, because they knew how she'd come into the world?

Julia wanted to curl up into a ball and cover her ears against it, but that wasn't the end of the story.

'Your mother knew they wouldn't let her take you with her,' Sofia said, 'so she waited until you were born then ran as soon as she could. She didn't expect Horatius to come after her. None of us were expecting him, so we weren't on our guard. He got to her before we knew what was happening.' There were tears running down Sofia's cheeks now. She made no attempt to brush them away. 'She was my friend. She came here because I told her to follow me, but we never thought he'd follow her. He had the child, had *you*, and we thought that would be enough. To keep him away.'

'But it wasn't,' Julia said, feeling sick to her stomach. She knew how the story ended.

'I found them in the stables,' Sofia went on. 'She was on the floor, not moving, and his fists were covered in her blood. The men came out of the houses when I screamed, and they took care of him while we laid out her body.' Sofia's voice was quiet now, as though she were running out of words. 'She's buried under the hornbeam tree behind the hall, if you'd like to visit her grave.'

Julia shook her head, unsure what she should feel for the death of a woman who had mothered her unwillingly, then abandoned her to the care of a violent father and the Nobles of the Blue. She wanted to be angry, but she mostly just felt numb.

'You said it started with Rufus,' she said. She had to know the rest.

Sofia wiped her cheeks with her sleeve. 'They said he was born human, in the palace, an orphan, like you, but the Empress ennobled him when he was a child. People said it was because she loved Horatius, and it was the only way she could have a child with him.'

No. Julia shook her head, unable to pry the denial from her throat. *It couldn't be.*

'As I said,' Sofia went on, 'there were a lot of babies in those few years, before Horatius died. If the rumours are right, then Rufus must have been one of the first.'

'Doamna Sofia…' Julia begged.

Sofia shrugged awkwardly. 'I'm not certain he was Horatius's son. There were other men in the palace, of course, and plenty of babies without parents. But that was the story they told after Horatius's death. That's what they told us later, the women who made it here after your mother died.'

Julia rubbed at her temples, trying to soothe the headache that had suddenly sprung up behind her eyes. Her elbow caught her teacup and sent it smashing down onto the hearthstone, detonating in a shower of lukewarm liquid and pottery.

'I'm so sorry,' she said, bending down to gather the pieces, but Sofia stopped her with a hand on her shoulder.

'Leave it. It doesn't matter.'

'I should go,' Julia said, getting to her feet.

'I'm sorry I couldn't tell you a better story.'

Julia nodded, not wanting to admit that the thing that had bothered her most wasn't the story of her parents, but the story of Rufus's parentage. It was just another thing that made her shudder when she remembered the taste of lemons on her lips.

Sofia stood and put her hands on Julia's shoulders. 'You're not going to sleep tonight, are you?'

'Probably not.'

'Then here.' Sofia plucked a bottle from the nearest shelf and handed it to her. 'Drink it a short while before you go to bed. It'll help.'

'Thank you.'

Julia started for the door, but turned back as Sofia touched her arm.

'Try not to think too harshly of her,' she said. 'Everything bad that Valeria did was a result of something bad that had been done to her. It's like that, the Blue. You know that as well as anyone. The Nobles deal in pain, even when they're not the ones inflicting it. It wasn't your fault, Julia, but it wasn't hers, either. If you want someone to blame, blame them.'

'I do,' she whispered.

Her resolve hadn't needed steeling any further. She already had her plan. She was going to wait for Cam and Felix to leave, then she'd just slip away.

She was going back to the Blue, and she was going to put an end to the Nobles, once and for all.

By the time Julia returned to her cabin, worrying the bottle of sleeping potion in her hand, it was already dark. Cam was nowhere to be seen, but Felix was sitting under their cabin's overhang, carving intricate patterns into the structure's supporting beams. He stopped as she approached.

'Is Cameron here?' she asked.

'Gone to dinner in the hall.'

Felix turned back to his work, stabbing his knifepoint into the wood at an angle, then easing it along the surface by wiggling it from side to side, leaving channels scored in its wake. It was becoming a beautiful thing, and it was clear that Felix wanted to be left alone with it.

But Julia wasn't quite ready to be alone with herself.

'You don't like me,' she said, 'do you?'

Felix looked up at her for a moment, his expression giving nothing away. 'I don't trust you,' he said. 'It's different.'

She ducked out of the rain and sat on the barrel next to his, wrapping her blanket-cloak around herself tightly. Lightning was flashing on the distant peaks, but all she could hear was the thudding of water on the slates above them.

'Why not?' she asked.

'I don't know what you want, or why you're here.'

'Well, I got what I came here for. Sofia told me what happened to my parents, so I guess I can go back to the Blue now.'

Felix looked at her. 'That's not why you came.'

'It is,' Julia lied, trying to seed her words with conviction.

Felix shook his head and returned to his carving.

'Why are *you* here, then?' she said. 'Don't tell me it's because you care about some lost prince.'

'No. I'm here because I'm in love with Cameron.'

The words were spoken plainly, as a simple truth. It was one Julia had already worked out for herself, because it was apparent in everything the woodsman did, from the way that he guarded Cam's back to the way that the corner of his mouth twitched with the shadow of a smile every time he saw Cam's face.

It was doing that now, while Felix looked out along the path that led down to the lakeshore. Cam was on his way home.

'Lucas will always love you, whatever you do,' Felix said softly. 'And I will always be in love with Cam, even if he never loves me back.'

He spoke without emotion, but it was there, simmering underneath the surface.

'Hey!' Cam called to them, grinning wide. 'I brought you back some dinner. Bread, cheese, stew. Also some pie, which is *amazing*.'

He was holding a fabric-wrapped bundle in one hand, and two steaming bowls in the other. He handed one to each of Julia and Felix, then made his way towards the cabin door.

'Aren't you coming?' he asked when Julia didn't move from her perch on the barrel.

But she made her excuses, because she found she couldn't bear it.

She saw Cam's happy obliviousness, and the way that Felix was looking at him, and it was all too much. Felix's words had hollowed out their relationship until all she could see was the gap in its centre where Cam's love was missing.

The configuration was too familiar, and it was humbling to see it from the outside. It made her remember Lucas's expression when he'd scented Rufus's mark on her skin.

That was something she never wanted to remember, and not just because of what she had learned that afternoon.

Those kisses were the thing that made her a traitor. She might not have believed in the Blue, but her and Lucas? That was something she really could have believed in.

8

Cam awoke to find Felix still asleep in his arms, his suntanned skin sparkling with bleached hairs in the dying light of the fire. It made Cam long for the return of summer, for topless riding and river bathing. He kissed Felix's bare shoulder and slipped away gently, trying not to wake him. It was still mostly dark outside, and Felix could do with the extra rest. After all, he was only human.

Cam had a bounce in his step as he made his way to the lakeshore. It had finally stopped raining, they had a good lead on Emmy's boy, and Felix hadn't asked to see Cam's eyes again. With any luck, he'd just forget all about the silvering so they could make the most of their time alone together. That was certainly what Cam intended to do.

There was a shout from the direction of the pass. The distance was far enough that even Cam had to squint to make out the source, but after a few seconds it was irrefutable: there was a column of figures trailing over the edge of the crater's bowl, limping down towards the lake. By the time it approached the first of the buildings, Cam had already roused Ana.

'Friendly?' she asked him softly as they waited in front of the hall.

'Injured, and human. I would say they have no choice but to be friendly.'

That assessment seemed more accurate the closer the line came. There were no animals except a few scrawny dogs, and no carts, just a gaggle of fifty or so people carrying ragged packs slung over shoulders and chests.

They stopped several yards away and waited, looking behind them with anxious faces. After a few moments, a middle-aged man made his way to the front of the group. He was thinner than he had been when Cam had seen him last, his cheeks sunken and grey, but he was still familiar.

'Gergo, isn't it?' Cam asked in Hungarian. 'You've come a long way.'

The man blinked. 'I'm sorry. Have we met, sir?'

'Only briefly, a couple of months ago. In your camp, by the meadow.'

Gergo still looked at him blankly. Cam wondered how much of a toll this journey had taken on him. Moving on foot, they must have been travelling for weeks.

'I'm the one who found Peterke,' Cam reminded him.

Gergo's face fell. 'Of course. I'm sorry, sir, but I've forgotten your name. My wife... She was the one who remembered everything.'

'Cameron.' He didn't want to ask about Gergo's wife, but surveying the state of the caravan, he didn't have to. 'And this is Ana.' He gestured to her. 'She's the leader of this community. They speak Romanian here. Do you know the language?'

'Not much,' the man said, apologetically. 'My wife...'

Cam nodded, then turned to Ana and explained in Romanian.

'What is it that they need?' she asked.

Cam relayed the message to Gergo.

'Everything,' he replied. 'We have nothing left. We were hundreds, with the others who'd joined us. We rode while we could, then they attacked and we lost the carts. We carried on with the horses for as long as we could, then they took those from us as well. They tried to take our boys. Again, Cameron, they took our boys. And my wife...'

He dissolved into tears, sobbing into his hands while the others stood behind him and watched, looking between Cam and Ana as though they were waiting for a death sentence.

'They have nothing,' Cam said softly to her. 'They'd stay if you were willing to take them in.'

Ana looked them over. There were a few more men of Gergo's age, two young men, and the rest were women and girls. All of them were malnourished and many bore injuries serious enough that Cam wasn't sure they'd survive.

Ana kept her face carefully blank, but Cam could tell she wasn't impressed by what she saw. It didn't matter though, because she had pity enough to fill the lake and she'd never turn a supplicant away.

'Of course they can stay,' she said firmly. 'The rest of us can work a little harder until they're able to do their part.'

'Thank you, Doamna Ana. I'll do a share of that work myself, if it'll help.'

'We'll see about that. Let them settle in the hall for now, until we can make better arrangements.'

She didn't wait for Cam to translate before pulling open the doors and ushering the refugees inside, her expression filled with welcome and compassion.

'What is it that they're speaking?' she asked Cam as they filed gratefully past her.

'Hungarian. Do you have anyone here who can translate?'

'We have you,' she said, smiling hopefully.

He smiled back, suppressing a sigh. 'I guess we could stay another night.'

Cam had cause to regret that offer when he'd heard their story.

They'd dealt with the essentials first, making sure everyone was clean, fed and watered, then they'd set up makeshift beds for the newcomers along the length of the hall. Most of them were sleeping now while Ana's people tended to the wounds of the others.

'They walked through the night?' Ana asked, passing Cam as she came to throw a handful of bloody rags onto the fire.

'More than one,' he said.

She washed her hands in a bowl of hot water, wiping them dry on her apron. 'It will take them weeks to recover.'

'Will we lose any?'

'I hope not, after they've come this far.'

Cam scanned the rows of cots until he picked out Felix amongst them. His head was bent over a young girl's arm as he sewed up what looked like a bite mark. They must have run into some Weepers on the journey.

Felix was just tying off the last of the stitches when a man crouched down at his side, young and apparently uninjured, but with a look of urgency about him. He whispered frantically to Felix, but Cam couldn't make out his words.

Felix met his eyes across the room, then jerked his head towards the corner as he stood and led the young man in the same direction.

'Excuse me,' Cam said to Ana.

She nodded back at him, tired enough that her eyes were blinking closed. After Cam had dealt with this, he'd encourage her towards her own bed.

'This is Karl,' Felix said in German as Cam joined them. 'He recognised us and wanted to explain, didn't you, Karl?'

The boy nodded vehemently.

Cam didn't recognise him. He was perhaps eighteen, maybe twenty at a push, though his apparent youth could have been exaggerated by his pink cheeks and his golden curls. He looked like a cherub stretched out to adult proportions.

'Karl was in the mountains with Charles,' Felix said.

'Oh?'

'Apparently you knocked him out when we rescued Emmy.'

Cam looked more closely at the boy, but he could have been any one of the young men they'd felled that day. As far as Cam was concerned, he was a complete stranger, but his story was supported by the fact that he was looking at Cam in abject terror.

'Maybe we should sit down,' Cam said, indicating the benches that had been shoved up against the wall.

Cam and Felix sat on one, but Karl seemed wary of getting too close. He pulled out a stool and sat opposite them instead.

'Well?' Cam said. 'You're human, aren't you?'

Karl nodded. 'Again, for the second time. I was human before all of this, then I was turned back during the fighting in the Pit.'

'That's what Charles called the mountain compound,' Felix supplied, switching to Romanian.

'Not very imaginative.'

'Well, he hated the place. Said it was like living in a hole in the ground, hence…'

'The Pit.' Cam smiled. 'Good. He deserved to be miserable.'

Karl looked between the two of them during this exchange, but he didn't seem to follow their conversation.

'Tell me from the beginning,' Cam said to him in German.

Karl did, haltingly at first, then with more confidence as he saw that he had their attention, but the story was still garbled. It took some time for Cam and Felix to piece it all together.

It was clear that Karl had lived his entire life as a Silver in the Pit. All he knew was that he'd been raised to be a soldier, training to fight from childhood, but that still hadn't made him any good at it. Even Silver reflexes and strength couldn't help him when he was up against tougher kids with the same advantages, so that was how he'd ended up helping out in the laboratory. That's where he'd learned where he'd come from, and that all Charles's attempts to create immunity to the cure had come to nothing. He'd managed only to use Emmy's blood to make Silver like Karl: many times weaker, slower and softer than any Silver born or turned the conventional way.

Because Karl was one of the babies who'd been snatched from people like Gergo twenty years ago, when Charles had been searching for Emmy's boy. But instead of killing them, Charles had taken them away to the mountains and turned them Silver in his attempts to find something that would combat the cure.

His experiments had failed.

Then came the interesting part. After Emmy's rescue, the Red Shirts had chucked Karl's body out with the rest, apparently assuming that he was dead rather than cured and unconscious. When he'd come around, he'd seen the opportunity for a new life and had left the Pit behind him.

But then the Red Shirts had come looking for him. Or, rather, they'd come for every boy around his age, scouring the countryside and dragging those they found back to the mountains.

Which could mean only one thing: they were looking for Emmy's son again.

'He must still be alive,' Cam said to Felix in Romanian.

Cam could feel the relief flowing through him. He'd been haunted by the thought that Emmy might have killed her own son when they'd rescued her from the Pit. He could have been any one of the boys they'd encountered in those halls, just like Karl, but if what Karl had said was true then there was still hope.

'Why go after him now?' Felix asked.

'Perhaps they know we're looking for the boy too.'

'Or maybe Alistair knows something we don't.'

Cam had to admit that it was a real possibility. That being the case, there was no time to lose.

'You're both leaving tomorrow?' Julia asked.

Her tone was just a touch too eager for Cam's liking, but he nodded as he chewed on his dinner. They couldn't stay here any longer, no matter what Julia was planning. He just had to hope she wouldn't do anything stupid while they were gone.

The three of them had congregated in Cam and Felix's cabin to cook and eat together, since the hall had been given over to the newcomers. They'd spent the day down there, doing what they could to help, but now that Ana had located a couple of Hungarian speakers from amongst Chloe's cohort, there wasn't much reason for Cam to hang around. They already had more helpers than they needed.

'Do you think you'll find the missing prince?' said Julia.

'I think we have a chance of learning where to look. The problem is knowing how to recognise him when we see him. That's what I hope we're going to find out.'

'Then back to the Blue.'

'Yes.'

But Cam wasn't so sure. They had to find the boy first, and there was no telling how long that would take. In the meantime, Alistair could be gathering another army, but Cam couldn't stay away too long. Anything could be happening in the Blue. If Tommy hadn't pulled himself together yet, the Invicti could have imploded by now.

Felix gave Cam a look that said he shared that concern.

'What?' Julia asked, watching the two of them.

'I don't know what we're going to find when we get back to the Blue. Things… changed before we left.'

Julia tore a piece of bread from the loaf. 'Changed how?'

Cam looked to Felix, wondering how much he should share, but Felix just shrugged back at him. Apparently it was his call to make.

'You remember Viv?' Cam asked her.

'Of course.'

'Well, she had her baby.'

Julia stopped chewing, putting the bread down in her lap. 'Is everything alright?'

'Yes. Sort of. They're both human now.'

Cam watched the blood drain from her face. When she spoke next, her voice cracked a little. 'Was it deliberate?'

That thought hadn't occurred to Cam.

No, he told himself. It couldn't have been deliberate contamination, because the baby had turned human first and Viv had followed afterwards. It must have been as Linh had suggested: the tiny traces of the vaccine that Viv had picked up in the Red had concentrated in the baby's body, but had been too weak to turn Viv human. The baby was the one who had cured her.

But it was strange that Julia would assume that foul play was involved. He looked at her carefully, watching the way her eyes skipped over his. She seemed nervous, turning the bread in her hands while it showered crumbs over her trousers.

There was something she was holding back.

Had she overheard Cam and Felix talking in their cabin the other night? She didn't have Silver hearing, but maybe if she'd listened at the door...

She could have heard what he had planned. That would explain the look she was giving him now, a sideways glance that flicked between him and the door over his shoulder, as though she were looking for her way out.

'What do you know?' he asked.

'About what?'

She knew something – Cam could tell that from the way she was blinking at him innocently – but it might have nothing to do with him. He decided to tread carefully.

'About... people turning Nobles human deliberately.'

'I saw it in the Contamination.' Her words were careful and slow, but this wasn't news.

'Yes,' Cam said impatiently, 'with Laila. I know.'

'Lai... The *Empress* is human? Well, that explains a lot. It doesn't make sense, though.'

Now Cam was confused.

'If you weren't talking about her, then what *were* you talking about?'

Julia took a deep breath. 'Rufus,' she said. 'The Empress's son. You know he was working with Lorelei?'

Now that was news.

'I saw them talking together,' Julia went on. 'Then, on the night of the Contamination, I saw him with a case full of blood vials, contaminated I guess. There was a man with him, telling him to give them to any humans he cared about. To contaminate them, so the Weepers wouldn't get them.'

'And he ended up curing his own mother.' Cam tossed his empty bowl onto the ground next to him and rubbed at the back of his neck. 'Jesus. What a fucking mess. So what's Rufus's part in all of this? What does he want? Is he still working against her? Do we have to worry about him helping Alistair's army?'

'I don't know,' she said, but she still wouldn't meet his eye.

'Julia...'

'I don't know! I don't know what he's doing. If I knew then I'd tell you, and you can trust me on that.'

Felix leaned in and said, 'But he shouldn't, because you're not telling us everything.'

Julia looked at him, defiant, but Felix met her gaze and his was stronger. Eventually, her eyes dropped and her shoulders followed, until the fight had gone out of her entirely.

'I can't leave you here like this,' Cam said. 'I can't walk away without knowing what you'll do next. You must understand that.'

'His name is written on your skin,' said Felix.

'Because I was his Attendant. You know that.'

'Because he owns you.'

'No!' Julia yelled, her temper firing her from defeat to rage in split-seconds. 'He never owned me! He will never own me, no matter what he does. I will *never* be his.'

Felix leaned back on the cushions, raising an eyebrow at Cam as if to say, *You're welcome.* That had cracked her and, like the clouds clearing from the face of the sun, Cam could finally see the whole picture.

'Rufus,' he said. 'It was his scent mark on you that day at the bunkhouse, and then again when Naia found you on the island.'

Julia's next breath shuddered out from between her lips. 'I didn't want it. I hate him, Cameron. *Hate* him.'

He could see it in her face, burning in her eyes and simmering in the twitching of her lips. But there was guilt there too.

'And is that why you left the Blue?' he asked. 'To get away from him?'

'Yes. And no. I came to the Red... I came here to find a weapon.'

'But there's only one weapon that works against Nobles.'

Julia swallowed audibly then said, 'Contaminated blood. I know.'

The silence that descended then was almost complete. There was just the soft crackling of the fire and the sound of Felix's breath. Julia was holding hers.

'Contaminated blood,' Cam repeated.

A spark jumped out of the fire onto Julia's lap, but she didn't seem to notice it. She just stared at Cam while it burned itself out on her trousers.

'For Rufus?' Cam asked. 'Or for all of us? How far were you going to take this, Julia?'

'As far as I needed to.'

'To do what?'

Cam could see the pretence sliding away now. She'd given up hiding herself behind a meek veneer. Beneath the veil there was only a blaze of determination.

Well, Cam thought. *That's handy*. He could use that fire.

'Do you know what it's like for us in that city?' she said, rising to her knees. 'Do you know what they do to us, what *you* do to us? Our lives are nothing to you. You break us and drain us and rape us, and if we complain then you throw us in a cell and bleed us dry for the rest of our lives. You said it yourself: the Blue isn't fair. There's only one way to change that.'

Cam almost smiled, because it felt like validation. Instead, he said, 'I know,' but Julia hadn't finished yet.

'There are others who know what I do. What'll happen when word spreads, and all the humans decide to walk out into the Red? *Nothing*, that's what. They'll leave you all behind with no slaves and no blood, and there'll be nothing you can do about it. If I don't contaminate them, then someone else will spread the vaccine for me, because you can't contain that knowledge now. It's out, and the Blue is over. Finished. It doesn't matter if you stop me, because this isn't the end.'

Cam really did smile then. 'I'm not going to stop you.'

Julia looked ready to continue arguing, but she sank back onto her heels as she processed Cam's words. 'You're not?'

'No.'

She opened her mouth, then shut it again as a crease appeared between her eyebrows. 'But I'm going to cure the Empress's son,' she said. 'And after that I'm going to cure every Noble in the Blue.'

'Yes.'

'And you're going to let me?'

'I don't see any reason to stop you, especially since I was planning to cure the lot of them anyway.'

Julia looked at Cam for a moment, then turned to Felix.

'It's true,' he said. 'If you don't do it, he will.'

'But…' Julia plonked back onto the cushion behind her, tucking her hair back behind her ears. 'Well, that's… unexpected. You don't want to be a Noble anymore?'

'No,' said Cam. 'You're right: the Blue is already dying. I'm as eager as you are to speed up that process.'

'But they're your friends.'

Cam laughed. 'Are you trying to talk me out of this?'

'I wish you'd both talk each other out of it,' Felix murmured.

Cam turned to him. 'But you know how I feel.'

'And I don't want you to throw the rest of your life away. You don't have to do this just to be with me. There must be a way to make you immune, like the King and Queen. Maybe their son–'

'No.'

Felix pressed his lips together. He knew Cam wouldn't agree to run tests on his friends. Cam would doom them all to human lives if he could, but he wouldn't torture them like that, not even if they offered. It wasn't that he couldn't bear to hurt them; Emmy was more than familiar with pain. The hope would be the thing that broke them, because they'd fail, just like Charles had before them.

It would be better this way, when all of them were human.

'I don't want you to do it for me,' said Felix.

'And I told you: I made the decision before we even met. We find Emmy's boy, then I'm curing myself. It's the only way.'

'*Bitte nicht.*' Felix's ice-blue eyes were imploring him now. '*Ich liebe dich.*'

'*Ich muss,*' Cam said, reaching out towards him, but Felix just rubbed at his bearded cheek and looked away.

They'd argued this round and round, and it came down to one thing: Felix didn't want the weight of Cam's mortality on his conscience. Cam had tried to explain his bigger goal of natural justice, of freeing humanity, and Felix understood that, but it wasn't enough for him. He opposed the entire plan.

Cam wondered whether he'd guessed the truth: that Cam didn't love him. Without that piece of the puzzle, Cam's arguments for taking the cure lost their force. If he hadn't silvered for Felix (and he still hadn't – he'd checked again that morning) then he wouldn't die when Felix did. He could live for hundreds more years if he didn't take the cure. That was what Felix thought he'd be stealing from him.

But Cam didn't want those extra years. He was tired of living this stagnant life.

Felix stood and walked to the fire, showing Cam his back as he prodded at the logs. This was how the argument usually ended. Cam would slip his hand into Felix's later, and the man would let himself be kissed. Until then, this uneasy detente would continue.

'I've wanted this for a long time,' Cam said to Julia.

'I just… I don't understand,' she replied.

'Do you know what the world used to be like?' Cam leaned forwards, resting his elbows on his knees. 'Has anyone told you?'

She shrugged. 'Lucas told me fairytales. Kingdoms and palaces, rivers and castles. Wide open spaces with bridges and houses, where everything doesn't feel so… tight. Was it like that?'

'Sometimes. But towards the end, before the contamination even existed, it was different.'

Julia shook her head. 'I can't imagine a world without it.'

'We were still there, the Silver, who call themselves the Nobles now. The Weepers weren't, and the vaccine hadn't been developed. If you turned Silver then you stayed that way, because there was no cure to turn you back. But that's not the point: the point is that we were *there*, but no one saw us. We hid ourselves. That hierarchy in the Blue? It didn't exist. As far as humanity was concerned, the world was filled with human beings and nothing else.'

'But you still had to feed. How did you manage that without Attendants?'

'We stole what we needed, most of us from those who could spare it and wouldn't remember it the next day. Some of us were less careful, but there were consequences for them. We made sure of that. And because the humans didn't know we were there, the world was better. Not perfect, because they still enslaved, murdered and exploited each other. But better, I think, because at least most people were free. And they used their freedom to make things that changed the world.'

'Like?'

'Buildings, stories, art, transport. Electrical devices that would flood a dark room with the light of a hundred candles on command. Technology that recorded pictures and sound and turned them into plays that you could repeat over and over, each time perfect and exactly the same. Vehicles that flew to the moon, with people inside, and brought them back again. So many things that we lost in the Fall, because we caged people in the Blue and told them what they could and couldn't do.'

'I remember electricity,' Felix said from his place by the fire. 'We didn't have it for long, and only in a couple of rooms in the mountains, but we had it. They said it was powered by the sun, but then it stopped working and no one could fix it.'

'And the stories?' Julia asked.

'More than you could ever imagine,' said Cam. 'Millions of books, plays, sounds recordings, films... The world was filled with stories. Now it feels like there's only one story left, and we're getting to the end of it. I'm ready to start the next chapter. I want to see what happens when people have their freedom again. I want to see what they can build when they don't have to worry about the Silver or the Weepers, when all they have is a world full of space and each other.'

'But you won't see it,' said Felix. 'None of us will. We'll be dead long before the world is rebuilt.'

Cam shrugged. 'It's enough to see it start. That's what I think, anyway.'

They were quiet for a few minutes after that. Felix was still staring into the fire, and Julia was looking down into her hands, but Cam felt as though he were looking at the future. He could feel the excitement of it bubbling up in his chest and it filled him. He imagined the bones of broken buildings being raised from their graves and reinstated so that the shells humanity had left behind would ring with laughter again.

That was the hope this plan had brought him.

When he looked at burnt out masonry forced apart by trees and scored by violence, he no longer saw the blood that had been shed as the structures had fallen. Now he saw what they had been – a home, a shop, a school – and in their shadows he saw what they could become again.

The only thing missing was people.

'So,' Julia said. 'How do we do this?'

The plan sounded simple enough, but there were so many gaps in it that Cam's part could never be more than an outline. They didn't know what they'd find when they went looking for Alistair, or whether they'd find the prince, or if he'd be immune and, if so, how many other people he might have infected with his immunity, if such a thing were possible. Cam's greatest fear was that Emmy's boy might have been roaming around the Red making new Silver, because that would make Julia's part of the plan tantamount to mass suicide. The Blue would be left defenceless, Alistair's army would take over, and the blood slavery would continue.

But if they were very lucky, if everything went their way, then they might just pull this off.

The cabin was quiet after Julia left. Cam wondered whether he'd finally pushed Felix too far, and if this would be the thing that broke them. Telling himself that he just needed to give the woodsman some time, he left him by the fire and went for a walk along the lakeshore in the darkness.

It was a long walk, because for as long as he walked he could pretend that everything would be fine. When he returned, Felix would have his say and that might be the end of it all.

He hesitated at the door when he got back, for long enough that Felix noticed the silence and opened it to him.

They stared at each other. Cam had the horrible feeling that his world was about to fall apart.

Then, not for the first time, Felix offered Cam a bottle of his blood unbidden. It was still warm from his veins.

'For Julia,' he said, 'for your plan. I thought I'd save you having to ask.'

There was a smile playing at the corner of his mouth. It released the tightness in Cam's chest, because that was the moment he knew he'd be forgiven. Felix would fall asleep in his arms tonight, as he had every night since they'd left the Blue.

No matter whether Cam had silvered or not, he knew that was where Felix belonged.

9

Julia's part in the plan was by far the simpler of the two, but it didn't feel that way as she left the lake behind her and trudged down the mountain. From this vantage point, she could see the forests she'd have to wade through to get back to the Blue, laid out before her like a daunting sea of green. It was enough to make her grateful that Cam had insisted she take a horse with her, if only because it meant there was someone to carry her pack and the precious cargo that was nestled inside: a single bottle of contaminated blood.

Felix's blood.

She just wished that Cam's horse hadn't been the only one fit for the journey. Hades was immense, towering over Julia like a dark shadow, and Cam's warnings hadn't filled her with confidence.

Keep your feet clear of his. Watch out for his teeth, and if he tries to swing his head at you, make sure you duck.

She'd almost refused to take him, but Felix's arguments were too reasonable. She could carry more supplies with Hades than without, and she might be grateful for his legs in a few days' time once her sores had healed. Most importantly, if she was injured, or if she ran into any Weepers, then he could carry her out of trouble. He knew how to fly.

The horse turned his big head towards her and she jumped back, paying out the halter to put a couple of extra feet between them. He held her gaze, then tossed his glossy mane and bared his teeth, snorting as though he were laughing at her.

Which was just perfect. As if this journey wasn't already nerve-wracking enough; a sadistic horse was obviously the sidekick she needed.

Julia groaned aloud. After a few seconds, Hades made a similar noise. Apparently he was mocking her now, too.

But he behaved himself on the trek down to the forest. It took most of the day, during which a few apples and nosebags shoved in the horse's direction seemed to mollify him, and by the time they reached the densest cover it was almost dark.

That was when she needed Hades most: when the shadows started crowding in. She trusted his instincts more than she trusted her sight in the dusk. For as long as he kept walking calmly onwards, she knew there were no hidden dangers waiting in the trees.

But they couldn't walk all night.

Julia was starting to panic when she finally found a suitable tree: tall and strong, with thick branches that forked at angles that were convenient for her hammock. She managed to settle Hades without too much fuss, then climbed into the branches with some difficulty.

After the previous week's riding, her muscles were still sore and she wasn't as agile as she had been. It took her until full dark to get the hammock strung and tie herself into it, but when she had finished she was not met with the rush of relief she had expected.

There was now so much horror in Julia's head that she couldn't manage it anymore. She'd given each disturbing issue just enough attention to settle it, so it no longer brought tears to her eyes to think of it, then she'd arranged all her horrors neatly in the drawers of her mind, but they wouldn't stay closed. They kept popping open, spilling their contents into her thoughts at inconvenient moments.

Like now.

Her mother, who'd abandoned her, murdered by her father.

Lucas's betrayed expression when he'd scented Rufus on her skin.

Rufus, who'd bled her and kissed her, and whose father was...

She slammed the drawers closed, but she knew they wouldn't stay that way for long. There was the corner of something poking out from inside, and it would keep expanding until Julia couldn't ignore it.

So she tried to forge it into a weapon. She took her misery and shame and loathing and wrapped them into a blade that she could aim at the Nobles. She gave them direction and purpose.

It almost worked. The shame still bit at her cheeks, but it was quieter now, and it burned cooler. She could almost convince herself that wiping out the Nobles would wipe it away entirely, that she just had to bide her time.

Almost.

But maybe, for tonight at least, *almost* was enough.

By her fourth day in the woods, Julia's bread was rock-hard and the few apples she had left were starting to shrivel in her pack. Her remaining food choices were dried rice or dried lentils, and whilst those were doubtless nourishing, they weren't much help when she was so low on water that she barely had enough to drink, let alone waste boiling pulses.

It was time to go hunting.

She'd discovered over the past few days that Hades was incapable of stealth, so she left him tethered to a tree and crept through the undergrowth searching for her dinner. Four hours later, she'd managed to bring down a deer with a crossbow bolt to the head.

It was a lucky shot; she'd been aiming for its heart. Her hands were so shaky from the sleepless nights and hard travel that her usual marksmanship had entirely deserted her. At this rate, she'd be a wreck before she even reached the Blue.

She had to pull herself together.

Skinning the deer didn't help to steady her nerves. She'd managed squirrels on her own before, but she hadn't been prepared for the sheer scale of the task when a larger animal was involved. It made her feel vulnerable too, her back exposed as she crouched over the carcass, her cuts becoming messy as she tried to hurry through the process. Without Hades to act as her early warning signal, it was easy to imagine that every crack of twigs or crush of leaves was made by a Weeper coming towards her. Every noise stopped her and made her turn, rabbit-like, to track its direction, but every time there was nothing except mice and the breeze.

Until she heard the tinkle of metal on metal, like a rattling bridle, and whirled around to find herself face to knee with a familiar pair of trousers.

'Oh,' Julia said as her heart stuttered back towards its normal rhythm. 'It's you.'

Galatea laughed, making the knives at her belt chime against each other again. 'Don't sound too happy to see me, or I might think you've actually missed me.'

'Sorry.' Julia got to her feet, wiping her face with her sleeve. 'It is good to see you. Have you been tracking me?'

'A little. One of the girls saw you and your horse from the camp, when you went across the clearing yesterday afternoon. You shouldn't do that, you know.' Galatea leaned back against a nearby tree, crossing her arms. 'Anyone could be watching. Nobles, Were-People. You were lucky it was only us. Stick to the trees, skirt the clearings. And stop making so many fires.'

'I'm doing fine, and I'm not eating this raw.' Julia crouched down next to the deer carcass and started slicing off hanks of flesh. When she'd cut them to size, she skewered them onto sticks she'd carved to a point. 'It doesn't matter anyway. No one's looking for me, and the Weepers haven't found me.'

'Yet. But you're going back to the island, aren't you?'

Julia looked up from her work, resigned to the diversion. 'How did you guess?'

'You went straight past the track. You must remember the way to the camp, because we took that trail enough when we were hunting rabbits in the summer. You must have seen the marks, and I thought...' Galatea swiped her unruly hair away from her face. 'But you walked right past it, because you never really intended to come back to us, did you?'

Julia hadn't expected Galatea to care either way. She hadn't given it much thought at all. She'd only been at the camp for a few days, but she remembered now the way that Galatea had clamoured for her company during that time. The girl had been lonely, and she'd befriended Julia, who'd then abandoned her without a backward glance.

No wonder she looked so betrayed.

'I hoped that I'd come back,' Julia said, 'if I couldn't find my parents. In the end, that wasn't how things worked out.'

'So you found them, then?' Galatea said, looking down at her feet as she toed the leaf litter.

'In a way. They're dead.'

Her gaze moved back to Julia's. 'I'm sorry.'

'It's alright.'

'But then why don't you come back to the camp now? Sabina'll be pleased to see you. She'll probably mother you double to try to make up for it. You know you can't go back to the city.'

That was what Sabina and Galatea had told her when she'd seen them last: with the vaccine running in her veins she would never be able to go back to the Blue.

But she hadn't been contaminated with the vaccine after all. She wasn't immune to the Weepers, because the vaccine hadn't transferred from Galatea to Julia. She was still as welcome in the Blue as she had ever been. More so, probably, because of all the uncontaminated humans who had been lost over the past months.

Not lost, Julia reminded herself. *Killed.*

Killed by the Nobles she was intending to defang. That was her purpose.

'I've already been back,' she said, 'and I'm going back again.'

Galatea blinked. 'You what?'

'Let me ask you something,' Julia said as she wiped her bloody fingers on a handful of dry leaves. 'How do you know you made me immune?'

'What are you talking about? That exchange trick always works. I've seen Sabina do it a hundred times.'

But apparently it hadn't worked on Julia, because Lucas was still a Noble, despite having fed on her blood. Galatea had cut her skin, then cut Julia's and pressed the two together, but still the vaccine – the cure – hadn't transferred to Julia.

So what had gone wrong? Was the problem Julia? Or was it Galatea?

'And you're sure you're contaminated?' Julia asked.

'Of course I'm sure,' Galatea said, rolling up her sleeve to show Julia her arm. The Weeper teeth marks were white against the brown of her skin. 'Why? Are you worried about the Were-People? Did you want me to do it again, to make sure?'

'No,' Julia said, pulling her hand out of Galatea's reach. 'No, don't worry.' She tapped the bottle of blood in her pack. 'I have all the vaccine I need right here.'

Galatea's forehead wrinkled. She started forwards to grab the pack, but Julia threw it over her shoulder, taking it out of reach.

'What exactly are you up to?' Galatea asked.

'Revenge. Are you going to stop me?'

'Probably not, but can I warn you off? You're never getting onto that island, or if you are, then you're not getting off it again. The Were-People have all been going that way lately. All the howls are coming from across the water now. There are so many of them that even being immune might not be enough. I've seen them pile on top of people, crushing them before they even took a bite. You need to be careful.'

Julia collected her filled skewers. 'I'll take my chances. Now, wasn't there a stream somewhere around here?'

Galatea sang softly to herself as she led Julia and Hades to the stream, but her singing was more determined than the wandering melodies of that summer, as though she were trying to fill the space between them. Julia knew what Galatea wanted to say. She wanted Julia to come back to the camp, to build a life there with everyone else, but she didn't push again. In fact, she said nothing at all.

She didn't need to, because her silence was eloquent enough.

When Julia had washed up and refilled her canteens, she found that the silence had encircled her too. She didn't know what to say to break it, or if she even should. In the end, she fell back on the trappings of hospitality.

'Will you eat with me?' she asked. 'We could make a fire, sit for a while?'

But Galatea shook her head. 'I'll take the rest of the deer back to camp,' she said. 'They're expecting me, and since you're not using it...'

'Of course.'

'Alright. Thanks. Well, bye then.'

'Galatea, wait.' Julia said, following her into the trees. 'Don't be like this. I don't want us to part on bad terms.'

Galatea stopped and turned. 'We're not,' she said, 'but I'm not going to pretend that you're coming back either, not to the camp, not at all. If you go back to the island then you're going to die. That's your decision, but don't expect me to smile and wish you luck, because it won't do you any good. So, are you still going back?'

'Look, I know there are Were-People on the island. There were when I left the city. I found a way through then, and I'll do it again.'

'No, you won't. It's getting worse every day. I just hope that when you see it for yourself, you'll turn back around and come back to us, but I think you're too stubborn to admit that you might be wrong. So are you going to listen to me, or not?'

But she couldn't. She'd made a promise to Cam, and however many Weepers were around the Blue, she'd have to find a way to evade them. If she didn't, there would be no liberation for humanity. Without her, the plan would fail. Without her, the Blue would fall.

'Gala–'

Galatea closed her eyes for an endless second that felt like heartbreak.

'Bye, Julia,' she said, then she turned and walked away, leaving Julia to build her fire alone to the sound of the Weepers' distant serenade.

It turned out that Galatea was right: there were more and more Weepers the closer Julia got to the island.

It had been so long since she'd last encountered them that when she came across the first clutch, three of them huddled in the shady undergrowth, Julia froze. She'd become complacent over the past few days, complacent enough that the sight of them surprised her. It was only after Hades nudged her with his nose that she snapped out of her shock for long enough to scramble onto his back so he could carry her out of harm's way.

She was starting to think that the ornery beast had developed a soft spot for her.

The encounters became more frequent then, first a couple of times a day, then five, then twelve as she approached the island. In the end, she gave up walking entirely and put up with the pain in her thighs in favour of the safety Hades's saddle offered.

But it wasn't going to be enough. When she finally arrived at the ferry crossing on the shore of the salt lake, she could see the Weepers shambling just within the tree line on the other side of the water, waiting for darkness.

That was going to be a problem.

But it was more than just that. It was an indication that something had gone horribly wrong, because the Weepers were exactly where they didn't belong.

Shouldn't Naia be taking them down, as she'd said she would when Julia had left the Blue? Shouldn't the Invicti have been keeping them away from the city? Shouldn't they have been protecting their precious few remaining uncontaminated humans?

It didn't make any sense.

She watched for a few minutes, leaning forwards to stroke Hades's mane. He nickered softly, almost as though he were enjoying the attention. If he kept this up, she'd be forced to admit that there was some kind of tentative bond forming between the two of them. Imagine Cam's face when she told him. The thought made her smile for a moment, before she realised that she may never see him again. Unless their plan went perfectly, it was likely she wouldn't make it through this fight.

It was odd, but the thought of her own death didn't really bother her. She worried about how much it would hurt, but she wasn't afraid of being pulled into the darkness. The problem was that she wasn't the only one whose life was at stake. Lucas had silvered for her, so she was risking his life too with every reckless move she made.

The clouds rolled in over the lake and it started to rain.

That was when the Weepers moved. As soon as the sky darkened, even thought it wasn't yet midday, they came out from between the trees on the island and flooded the opposite shore, spilling down the beach and into the water.

There was no way she'd be able to cross here.

Instead, she rode north along the tideline, eyes darting between the water, the trees at her side and the opposite shore. It wasn't long before there was nothing moving in her field of vision, not a single Weeper ambling on the beach or bobbing in the water. That didn't mean they weren't there, though, hidden in the undergrowth or walking the bottom of the lake.

Julia rode a little further.

After a while she reached a stretch where the water seemed shallower. The rain had finally stopped, and without the disturbance of it splashing into the surface she would have sworn she could see the bottom of the lake. There was weed there, and the shadowy shapes of larger stones, but nothing that looked like it could be a Weeper. It was almost as though they knew to wait at the ferry crossing, because that was the most-travelled route to the Blue, but out here on the north-eastern stretch of the lake they were nowhere to be seen. Birds called gentle songs that communicated no alarm, squirrels raced up the tree trunks and the water lapped gently against the pebbles beneath Hades' hooves.

This was the best chance she was going to get.

As the sun cracked through the clouds, she pointed Hades at the opposite shore and urged him out into the water. He didn't need much encouragement. At a single squeeze of Julia's feet, he splashed quickly and noisily into the lake. She managed to pull her packs out of the way just in time, resting them on her shoulders as the water covered her thighs. Soon Hades was swimming beneath her, his feet kicking him along while she half-rode and half-floated above him.

It was raining again by the time his feet found the pebbles on the other side, the sky darkening into a dusk-like charcoal. It was the kind of weather that drew the Weepers out, even beyond the shade of the forest, and it made Julia antsy.

She was keen to press on, but Hades went down onto his knees as soon as they reached the cover of the trees.

That was not good. She must have pushed him too far. The run up the shore, then swimming with her on top of him…

She jumped off his back, panicking, but the moment she was clear he started rolling happily in the leaves, shedding the saddle rug as he kicked his legs in the air and wriggled from side to side.

'You're ridiculous,' she said. 'You do know we're in a rush?'

He nickered back at her, snorting and shaking his head as he rose to his feet again.

Julia collected the makeshift saddle from the mud, giving it a few cursory wipes. There was no time for a more thorough clean, not if she wanted to make it back to the city by nightfall.

'If you're quite ready?' she said to Hades. He nudged her shoulder with his head. She thought he was actually being affectionate until his nose disappeared into her pack and emerged a second later with her last, withered apple.

'You little thief,' she teased, pulling the leaves from his mane. 'Come on, then. Let's go home.'

But then there was a howl from the Weepers to the south, closer than Julia would have liked. She didn't stop to reattach the packs to Hades's saddle, she just hauled them over her shoulders and launched herself onto his back from a nearby tree stump. Without any guidance from her, he was already galloping towards the Blue.

The howls chased them as they fled. At first the calls came from behind them, from the direction of the shore, but as Hades's pace slowed over the next couple of hours they seemed to be catching up. By the time the evening started drawing in, the howls were at their sides, closing in and spurring Hades back into a gallop that Julia knew he couldn't sustain.

They weren't going to make it. They should already have been approaching the boundary fence – the strip of forest circling the Blue was thinner here than it was to the south – but Julia could see nothing but trees.

A Weeper lunged out of the shadows in front of them. Hades kicked it out of his way, trampling the body under his hooves, but it sent him into a panic that took them reeling off in another direction, turning a different way at every tree, until Julia was so disorientated that she couldn't tell where they'd come from.

'It's alright,' she said, leaning forward to stroke Hades's neck, but his eyes were rolling wildly now. He'd seen what was up ahead: tens of Weepers crowding the path.

The horse turned again and took them racing along another track, a narrower one, squeezing them close enough to the undergrowth that Julia mistook a Weeper's grasping hand for a branch, until it tightened around one of her packs and wrenched it from her shoulders. Not the pack holding Felix's blood, thankfully, although she nearly went with it to the ground. For once she managed to keep her seat as Hades plunged onwards.

But not for long. The next turn took them to the edge of a clearing, and the creatures were clustered on its opposite side, filling the spaces between the trees so densely that Julia could see nothing by skin and cloth.

Hades reared.

She scrambled for the reins, for Hades's neck, for the edge of the saddle, but nothing could stop Julia's slide from his back into the undergrowth. Her head hit the ground hard, jarring her teeth together, and for a single blissful moment everything felt quiet and floaty. Then the pain flooded in on a wave that pushed its way through her skull, and she could hear Hades squealing. Rolling onto her side, she saw him through the branches, stomping at the Weepers in a terrified frenzy, then he turned and pelted out of the other side of the clearing with the Weepers close behind him.

They were following him. Why, Julia wasn't sure. Perhaps they hadn't realised that she'd fallen from his back, or perhaps they thought Hades would lead them to more humans. Most likely, they weren't thinking at all, they were simply following his movement in the hope that it might mean food.

Whatever the reason, they were following the horse, and he was leading them away.

He was giving her a chance.

Julia did the only thing she could: she got to her feet, turned and ran.

Her feet flew over the ground, moving so fast that it felt more like a headlong stumble than a sprint. As she ran she touched the bottle through the canvas of her bag, just to check. It was still there, unbroken: her precious cargo. Trees strobed past on either side, thorns scratching her face and catching her clothes and her pack, but she didn't let it slow her down. Hades had given her a window, and she wasn't going to waste it.

She could only hope that she was heading for the boundary fence. She just prayed she would run out of forest before she ran out of strength.

But her panic couldn't fuel her forever. She could feel it sapping now, leaving her limbs weak and her head splitting with every thud of her feet into the ground. The Weepers wouldn't be far behind her. The calls were travelling away from her now, following poor Hades, but all it would take was one call for them to find her again.

They always found their prey eventually.

'Julia?'

She skidded to a stop, her feet slipping on the wet leaves as she squinted into the shadows. The figure there was familiar, and so welcome that it felt like a miracle.

'Lucas?'

Her course had been off, because he was standing to her left and the fence was behind him. She could see it through the tree trunks, rising lichen-green from the dirt. Lucas's own colour wasn't much better. There were dark smudges under his eyes, and his skin was a hue that didn't seem entirely healthy, even for a Noble.

Still, she didn't hesitate. She ran over to him, flinging her arms around his neck, holding on as he circled her waist with his hands and pulled her close.

'Thank you,' she said. 'Thank you so much. Your timing couldn't be more perfect.'

Julia's stomach reeled, and she opened her eyes to find that Lucas had carried them to the other side of the boundary fence. Her view of the Blue was obscured by a pile of fallen trees, but she knew the city was there. If she squinted, she could see the smoke rising from the fires burning in its hearths.

She was home. Despite everything she'd risked to get away from this place, not once, but twice, the safety of its walls now felt like a comfort rather than a restraint. That was a novelty.

'You're alright?' Lucas said, his eyes trailing over her body as he held her at arm's length.

'Me? I'm fine. Just taking a stroll through the forest, you know. Are you alright? You look like you're about to collapse.'

'You're alright.' His voice was quiet and strained, as though he were struggling to believe that it was true. 'You're here, and you're alright.'

A smile blossomed on his face. It made him seem bruised, emphasising the darkness that lurked in the hollows of his cheeks.

'When did you last eat?' she asked.

He framed her face with his hands, staring into her eyes so she would see each travelling thread of brightness in his own as he showed her his silver. The words he didn't say were written in the cracked sheen of his irises: *I love you.*

'I'm sorry,' was what he said.

'I'm sorry, too.'

And that was enough. He was sweet and warm and everything she'd missed in her weeks of cold and lonely nights. His fingertips were tracing her jawline, then sliding into her tangled mess of hair as they sought the sensitive skin at the base of her skull.

That was all the invitation she needed to kiss him.

The taste of him was rainfall in a drought, quenching and needful. It coursed through her, fresh and sugary and so strong that she could almost feel the mark it was leaving on her, the scent embedding in her skin.

Then his fingers were at her pulse, a silent request.

'Yes,' she breathed as his thumb brushed the skin of her neck.

He groaned a little as he broke their kiss. She'd almost expected to feel his teeth in her throat, but that wasn't Lucas's way. He wasn't savage. He was careful with her, slipping a knife from his pocket to nick her wrist before raising it to his lips.

He licked it first, a tiny caress of heat on her skin, then he closed his mouth over the wound and sucked. The pleasure it dragged through her veins was so strong that Julia had to lean against the fallen trees to stop herself from falling too.

This was what it meant to surrender to the bond. The scent mark, the blood on his lips, and the tether of desire stretching between them, pulling her into his arms. In that moment, she would have given up everything to keep him. But that was how the scent mark worked, wasn't it? It made her his.

As it had once made her Rufus's.

After a few seconds, she made herself push him away. He let her, discreetly wiping his mouth. It was an awkward gesture.

His eyes settled on her wrist, where a silver line now sealed the cut he'd left in her skin.

'Funny,' he said. 'I'd heard the stories about how silvered Nobles could cure their lovers' wounds. I didn't really believe it, though. Looks like it was true after all.'

Julia looked at the twinkling scab across her skin, then pulled her sleeve down to cover it. The bond wasn't something she wanted to talk about right now.

Silence settled between them.

'I couldn't find you,' he said eventually, 'and then they started taking people into the palace, and I thought I was going to find you out here, wandering around with all the others.'

'The other what?'

He shook his head impatiently, as though there were too many things to say and he didn't know where to start.

'It's all gone to shit,' he muttered.

Julia raised her eyebrows. 'As has your language.'

'Trust me, it's warranted.' He tugged her gently back towards him until she was wrapped in his arms with her cheek pressed against his chest. 'I missed you.'

'I missed you too.'

'Everything's gone wrong. Tommy's gone off the rails, the Invicti are scrambling – what remains of them, anyway. And then there's the Queen.'

'What about her?'

Held so close to him, Julia felt his sigh more than she heard it.

'People are missing,' he said. 'Humans.'

'Missing? How many?'

'I don't know. Lots.'

Julia pushed away enough that she could look up at him, but he was answering her next question before she'd even started to form the words.

'Not Claudia,' he said. 'Not Livia or Marcella either. All of them are fine. Well, as fine as they can be. But others have gone. And the Empress and the Queen are–'

Julia never found out what they were, because Lucas had frozen, his head tilted towards the city. A few seconds later Julia could hear them too: voices on the other side of the pile of trees, distant but coming closer.

'I can't speak now,' he whispered. 'They've got me on patrol so I can't leave the fence, but can I come and see you later? I'll tell you everything. Will you wait?'

'There are things I need to tell you too,' she whispered back.

So many things. Things she wasn't sure that Lucas would understand or support. Things she couldn't tell him, because he'd tell the rest of the Invicti. Things that she was scared to tell him, because they might shatter this fragile truce.

'So, I'll see you later?' he whispered again, his eyes darting between her and the fence.

'I'll be at Livia's.'

He kissed her lips one last time, quickly but gently. 'Wait here for a minute while I distract them, then you can slip past.'

'Wait,' she said, catching his hand. 'Cam's horse. Hades. He's somewhere out there.'

'I'll find him,' he promised, 'just get inside as quickly as you can. And be careful of Rufus.'

'Don't worry,' she said, forcing a cheerless smile. 'I'm not going anywhere near him.'

Julia was exhausted by the time she returned to her room, bypassing Livia's invitations to the kitchen hearth in favour of bed. However comfy the hammock was, she'd never stop missing the feel of a proper mattress beneath her, even if it was a poor one stuffed with straw.

There was a parcel waiting on the bed for her. It was a small bundle of material, wrapped with ribbon. There was no note, but then a note wouldn't have been of much use since Julia could barely read her own name. Livia hadn't mentioned anything about a gift, but its position on the bed was such that it might have been posted through the window bars.

Strange.

She took the time to unpack her bag, strip out of her travelling clothes and slip into her shift before settling down with the parcel in her lap. It unrolled softly and quickly, depositing its contents onto her bed. It was several moments before Julia could put what she was seeing into context, and several moments more before she could bring herself to believe it.

It was an earlobe, severed neatly and bearing a single stud that looked a lot like the one she wore in her own ear, except this one was copper rather than silver. Maybe that metal had been chosen because it complemented the hue of the skin in which it sat.

The dark, flinty tones belonged to only one woman of Julia's acquaintance: Marcella.

Marcella's ear.

10

Cam unwrapped the pack of bottles for the last time, his fingers shaking as he fumbled with the knots. It was cold this far north, and if Cam was feeling it then Felix must be freezing, but he didn't complain.

Cam had spent the day running at speed with Felix on his back, the wind whipping past them and snatching the warmth from their skin, but Felix had just clung to Cam more tightly, as though the proximity made the journey a pleasure rather than a chore. Still, whatever Felix pretended, they'd both be relieved when they reached the island Chloe had told them about.

If the bottles they had would take them that far. There were just three left, full of blood that had been donated by... Well, they didn't really know who had donated it, just as Ana had intended.

He and Felix had woken early that morning to a knocking on the door of their cabin, and Ana had been standing there with the crate, filled with bottles of blood that were so fresh Cam could see the heat rising from a few of them in the morning chill.

'A gift,' she'd said, 'to help you find the boy.'

'Doamna Ana, I can't accept this. It's not so simple as–'

'But you think I am simple, Domnul Cameron?' she'd said, in an indulgent tone. 'You think I have known you this many years without noticing your eating habits? Or did you think I was not blunt enough to seek answers from Doamna Chloe?'

Cam had smiled a little to imagine that conversation. He wished he had been there to watch those two locking horns.

'She told you about the contamination, then,' he said.

'She did. You will be satisfied with my word that this blood is not contaminated.' Then she'd passed the crate to him, placing her hand over his once he'd taken the weight. 'You can trust that we are as eager for you to find the boy as you are yourself. We have enough young men here of that age, and we'd sooner give our blood than risk them coming to harm. You've been our ally for centuries, Domnul Cameron. Today I ask you for more. Find these men and stop them, please, before it is too late.'

He'd taken the blood, and with that action he'd made a vow. There was no going back now. He'd cure the Silver who were living out here in the Red – Charlestown, the Red Shirts, and Alistair – and he'd save the sanctuary Ana's people had built by the lake in the mountains.

But first he had to find Emmy's son.

The blood had brought them this far, to the northern edge of the continent, and it wouldn't take them much further. They had to find the island before Alistair's people found them.

'Is that it there?' Felix said, pointing off into the gloom.

'I don't know. It could be, I suppose.'

The peak on which they crouched was overlooking the sea, but it was so high that mist had gathered between them and the water. They were squinting at shapes on the horizon that were practically invisible through the filtered murk, and it was impossible to tell which dark smudge might be an island rather than simply a shadow. Cam was starting to believe that their only option would be swimming out into the ocean, but this wasn't the salt lake that surrounded the Blue. This was the turbulent nexus of the North and Baltic seas, a freezing and endless flood that filled what had once been Northern Europe. The riptides were ruthless, and while they might not harm Cam, he wasn't about to let Felix follow him into the water. But he wasn't going to leave his man behind, either.

'Keep looking?' Felix suggested.

'For another couple of miles. She said north of the mountains, directly north, so if we don't find it along this stretch then we're not looking far enough out. If that's the case, then I guess we're going to have to build ourselves a boat.'

But a hundred yards further along the cliff, Cam spotted something. If the wind hadn't been so strong then he might have walked right on by, never noticing the rope attached to the overhang, but as he passed the jutting point of the land there was a snap. He stopped, turned, and tracked back until he zeroed in on its source: a line pulled tight from beach to peak, slapping against the cliff in the wind, zig-zagging down the rock face along a track of footholds that had been carved out of the stone.

'Holy shit,' he said. 'It's a path.'

'You think *that's* a path?' Felix asked, kneeling down next to him to peer over the edge.

'Come on, don't tell me you're sceptical.' Cam gave him a gentle nudge with his shoulder. 'You climb trees all the time without a blink. Don't tell me you're intimidated by this, when someone's helpfully pinned a guide rope right there for you.'

'Trees aren't three hundred feet tall. I don't trust other people's tools.'

'Did you want me to carry you?' Cam teased.

'Let's just get it over with.'

Cam went first, so he could catch Felix if he fell, but the woodsman was surefooted enough to make his own way down the cliff face. There was a tiny lip of beach at the base, just a few feet wide, but the stained undercut that loomed a few yards above their heads made it clear that there was often no beach here at all.

They were lucky to have turned up at low tide, and not just because it meant they didn't have to get their feet wet.

Now that they were below the mist, Cam could see the path stretching across the water. The island, if indeed it was the island, was still not much more than a distant smudge, but the lowering tide had revealed a raised bank that lurked just a few inches below the waves, leading them straight to it.

'It's a tidal path,' Cam said. 'Well, almost. I'm not sure the water's going to get any lower than this, so we'd better take our chances now. Are you up for some more speed?'

'Do you need more blood?'

'Yes, but one bottle should be enough.'

Cam downed it quickly, then crouched a little to let Felix jump onto his back. They were flying then, spray rushing up around them as Cam sped through the shallow water towards the island.

In comparison with the journey, the island itself was a bit of a disappointment. It was surprisingly large, but if they hadn't known to look here then they would have assumed it was nothing but an uninhabitable rock. Windswept and practically treeless, it rose out of the waves like a monolith. In fact, it was formed from a few separate peaks that clustered together like a clover leaf.

Cam and Felix found what they were looking for in the valley at the centre. In the sheltered lee of the crags, makeshift buildings leaned against the rock. In some places the stone had been hollowed out by nature and industry to create spaces that were just large enough to live in. It would support a small community, but this wasn't somewhere you'd choose to settle if you had any other choice.

Their reception was far from welcoming. Suspicious eyes peered out from the huts and caves that circled the space. Around the fires in the middle, hands busy gutting fish and weaving nets stilled as the two of them approached.

'Hello,' said Cam, waving his hand in a cheerful gesture. The reaction from his audience made him regret it immediately. 'We were told that you might have some information we need. We're looking for a woman who passed through the mountains with a baby about twenty years ago. Do you remember her?'

The expressions surrounding them changed from suspicion to open hostility.

'Lots of women with babies in the mountains,' said an older woman, bundled up against the cold but looking no less formidable for that. She was seemed to be the only person in the settlement whose hands weren't occupied with some form of work.

Around her, others muttered in disapproval.

Izcacus. The word hissed on the wind.

'This was a particular woman,' Cam persisted. 'She was human, but the baby wasn't. You'd remember her, because she was feeding him her blood, not her milk. We're just trying to reunite the baby with his mother. Please, if you know anything–'

'There's nothing for you here, Izcacus,' the old woman said.

That seemed to be the end of the matter.

Felix took Cam's hand and pulled him off to one side. 'Go for a walk,' he said. 'Let me try.'

Cam hated to leave it to Felix, but he was right: these people were never going to trust him. They looked at him and all they saw was an Izcacus, one of the creatures from whom they'd run here to escape. All they saw was a threat to their last sanctuary.

He gave Felix's hand a squeeze, threw his pack over his shoulder and strode back the way they had come.

It was up to Felix now.

Cam had expected Felix to soften them up a bit, but he hadn't expected *this*.

As he walked back into the settlement, a shout went up from the crowd that had gathered there. Cam couldn't imagine where they had all come from, because the twenty or so faces he'd seen earlier had now multiplied to more than a hundred, but the real miracle was that they were actually happy. Whatever Felix was doing, it was clearly working.

Cam peered over the shoulders of those at the back of the crowd just in time to see a group of objects flying up into the air, roundish and about the size of Cam's fist. The people watched them as they returned to earth, then erupted into laughter when they disappeared into the centre of the crowd.

What on earth?

This continued for a couple more minutes before the crowd finally separated to reveal Felix bowing graciously in its centre, one of the objects clasped in his hand while two soggy men got to their feet beside him. They were covered with bits of seaweed that stuck to their hair.

Cam raised an eyebrow at Felix. 'What was all that about?'

'It's a game we played when I was a child. You all stand in a group, frozen still, and you each throw a ball into the air, aiming for it to come down on one of your opponents' head.' He was smiling, an open grin that Cam rarely saw on his face. He'd clearly been enjoying himself. 'They play it with seaweed here, which makes the balls a bit harder to catch.'

'I can see that,' Cam said, peeling a slimy strip from Felix's shoulder. 'So, you've been making friends?'

'Enough that the vŭdce will speak to you. Come on.'

He took Cam's hand, weaving their fingers together, and led him towards one side of the settlement. The old woman was sitting there, watching them from across a small fire. It cast strange colours onto her face, the flames dancing blue and lavender as the salt burned out from the driftwood.

'You asked about the woman,' she said as they approached.

'Anything you know could be helpful,' said Cam. 'I know you have no reason to trust me, but we're on the same side. I think we can help each other.'

'So your friend said. Sit.'

Cam did as he was told.

'Your friend tells me that you knew Chloe.'

'I know her,' Cam said. 'We just left her, in fact. She's human now, living in a settlement in the mountains to the southeast of here, about three weeks' journey away. If you wanted to join them…' He left the question hanging, unsure whether she'd think him rude for suggesting they might want to abandon this rock for somewhere more hospitable.

She ignored the offer and said, 'I knew her well. She was a difficult woman: easy to love, hard to like.'

'Sometimes, but she's settled down now. She has a son.'

The vůdce pursed her lips and picked at her fingernails. 'Izcacus? Like you?'

'Not anymore.'

She nodded then, as though something had been decided. 'It would be better if that were the fate of you all.'

Cam looked at Felix. 'I told her,' he said, his expression grave but determined.

'Then you know I agree,' Cam said, turning back to the vůdce. 'You know that I need to find that baby, not just because he is my friend's son, but because he may have blood running in his veins that will make him impossible to cure. If he's spread that blood, if there are more like him out there, then I need to know that now. So, what can you tell us about the woman?'

The vůdce pulled a pipe from her blankets and filled it from a pouch at her feet, tamping the contents down with a large, flat thumb. 'We were still living in the mountains when she came through. She didn't try to deceive us. She admitted that the child wasn't hers. She said she'd rescued it, not caring that it was an Izcacus, because after all it was still a child.' She lit the pipe from a twig she pulled from the fire, sucking down a couple of deep breaths before she continued. 'We gave her a wet nurse, because she had no milk. That was a mistake. Or, rather, the wet nurse made a mistake. She tried to feed it from her breast and… Well. No one would offer their milk after that. They just wanted them gone.'

'So they left?'

'Eventually. We tried to take the child from her in the end. The old vůdce, she thought it would be one less of them. I can't say I disagreed. The woman left in the night, her hut empty and her pack gone the next morning. That was the last we saw of her.'

'You didn't see which way she went?'

'If anyone did, they didn't say anything to me about it.'

Cam sighed, defeated.

That was it then. They'd travelled halfway across the continent to find a clue that didn't exist. They were no closer to finding the boy now than they had been a week ago, and they were running out of time.

They'd just have to risk it. Cure their enemies, run back to the Blue and hope that all of them would turn as planned. It was too late to turn back now.

'Thank you,' Cam said, getting to his feet. 'I appreciate you talking to us.'

But the vůdce waved her pipe, urging him back down to the fireside. 'Not so fast, Izcacus. There was one more thing.'

He exchanged a glance with Felix, then sat down beside him once more, looking expectantly at the vůdce.

'You wanted to know how to recognise her, yes?' she said.

'I'm not sure a twenty-year-old description will be much use.'

'But she had a scar here.' The vůdce traced a line from her collarbone to the tip of her shoulder with the end of her pipe. 'And I remember her name: Barbara. The children called her Baba.'

They travelled as quickly as they could, but the journey to Charlestown was taking forever. Cam had expected they'd be on the move for a few days, but it took them the better part of that just to find their way back to the mountain pass. He could have used the last two bottles of blood, but they were keeping well in the cold, and he was going to need them later. Taking on both Charlestown and the Red Shirts without a reserve seemed like a suicide mission, so he held it back.

They could spare the time. They still had more than a week left before Julia would make her move.

'You're sure?' Cam asked Felix for the tenth time.

'Yes. I never knew a Barbara at Charlestown.'

'Maybe it was a false name. Maybe she never lived at Charlestown at all. Maybe she only ever lived at the Pit.'

Felix said nothing, he just plodded on through the mud. It was thick on the path as they wound their way up towards the peaks, caking their boots. They were aiming for the defile that would take them through the mountains and lead them down into Charlestown on the other side, but it was hard to navigate in the driving rain.

Autumn was short here. What had been greenery and grasslands just two months ago had already frozen over in the places where it wasn't churned to muddy slush, and snow had turned the summits white. The mountaintops formed a line along the old border, meaningless now except for the obstacle it presented. It was an obstacle they couldn't face tonight, not soaked to the bone with this icy rain. It would be dark soon, and it was already cold enough that Felix was rubbing at his fingers.

'We should stop,' Cam said. 'Set camp.'

'I can keep going.'

'I know,' Cam said, but he was pretty sure that Felix wouldn't last much longer. This wasn't like travelling on horseback; without Hades and Sandor they were relying on their own soggy feet to get them across the miles, and they had a few more days to go yet. 'If we stop now, we'll have a clear shot at the pass tomorrow. I'd rather do it in one stretch than get stuck in the middle with the lynxes, like last time.'

Felix didn't argue. They built a quick shelter, watertight enough beneath the trees, and lit a fire next to it using kindling from their packs. Felix didn't insist on gathering more wood, which had been his usual task these past few days. Instead, he practically tumbled down beside the flames the moment they caught, showing them his hands. They were an unpleasant shade of purple.

If he was going to get warm, that fire would have to be much, much bigger.

'I'll be back,' Cam promised, wrapping his cloak around the woodsman before stepping into the trees.

He worked as quickly as he could, but all the fallen branches were soaking wet and covered in mud. He found a serviceable stack in the end, delving in holes and corners, but it wouldn't make the kind of bonfire he'd been hoping for.

It's a start, he told himself. *Get it burning high, get him dry, and find more later.*

There was a cough as he approached the camp. It hastened his steps until he was chasing the noise through the trees, following it as it changed from a cough to a grunt to a moan.

There was a thud. Then nothing.

Cam dropped the branches and ran.

The first thing he saw when he reached the camp was the knife: the grip in Felix's hand and the blade plunging into his attacker's stomach. It wasn't enough, though. Felix had taken a blow to the face and his nose looked to be broken again, streaming blood down his chin. Worse, there was a rope pulled tight around his neck.

'No!' Cam yelled, loudly enough that the attacker turned to face him.

Tacitum.

His lips were sewn shut, but where the Tacitum they'd encountered before had been mutilated with string, this one had been silenced with a fine, golden chain. It didn't stop at his lips, either; it pierced through his cheeks, ending in golden studs that pulled dimples into his face where there should have been none.

Cam leapt towards them, meaning to pull the Tacitum away from Felix, but apparently all the woodsman had needed was an opportunity. While the Tacitum's attention was on Cam, Felix kicked the creature in the crotch hard enough to send it to the ground.

But his triumph was short-lived, because the end of the rope around Felix's neck was trapped in the Tacitum's hand. When he fell, he tugged Felix down to the ground with him, rolling them both into the fire.

The blaze might have been paltry, but it was still burning. When Felix landed on top of the Tacitum, trapping him against the white-hot coals, it would have hurt. The Tacitum stretched his sewn mouth with the echo of a scream.

'Move!' Cam yelled at Felix, helping him to scramble away as he wrenched the rope from the Tacitum's hand. 'Go!'

While Felix untied himself, Cam launched himself at the Tacitum. With Cam's centuries of experience, it should have been a matter of efficient seconds to dispatch the attacker, but his hands were shaking with fury and he couldn't focus his rage. Instead, the two of them wrestled in the remains of the fire, crushing the flames into the mud until Cam collected himself enough to extract the knife from the Tacitum's side and thrust it into his skull.

The lights went out in his eyes.

Cam rolled onto his back, soaked in blood, and let the mud seep into his shirt.

'You're alright?' he asked Felix.

'Fine,' he replied, but his voice was barely a whisper.

When Cam turned his head to look at Felix, he almost wished he hadn't already put the Tacitum down, because now he wanted to do it all over again.

The bottom half of Felix's face was smeared with blood. There was an angry red mark around his throat, and his clothes were pocked with burn holes from the fire. Beneath them, Cam could see darkened spots of skin showing through.

'Shit,' he said, getting to his feet. 'You're not fine.'

'Don't come too close.' Felix held up his bloody hands, warding Cam off. 'I'm covered in contamination.'

'I don't care. Where are you hurt?'

Felix ignored the question. Instead, he started to limp over to the Tacitum's body, wiping his bloody face on his sleeve as he did so. Cam realised what he was intending to do just a second before it was too late.

'Wait,' he said, tugging Felix away. 'We can't cure him.'

'You want to fight him again tomorrow?'

'No, but we need to know why he attacked us.'

Felix wrinkled his tired brow at Cam. 'We're not going to find that out from him.'

That was why the Tacitum had been created, after all: so that they couldn't give up the secrets of their masters if they were captured. With the Silver, though, there was always a way. Cam would find it, because he had to.

They were trying to take Felix from him. He hadn't missed the intention behind the rope around his lover's neck. If the Tacitum had intended to kill Felix then that's what he would have done, quickly, but instead he'd tried to lasso him and tie him up like a prize.

And this wasn't the first time they'd come for him, Cam realised. The Red Shirts had tried to take Felix once before, on the shore of the salt lake when the Invicti had been bringing Emmy back to the Blue. Five of them that time – *five* – separated off from the pack specifically to capture Felix.

That was more than an accident, and Cam couldn't afford to ignore it anymore. They were trying to take Felix away from him.

He wouldn't let that happen.

Cam gave the Tacitum lips and a tongue, carving the shape of them back into his flesh as he lay unconscious. It was gruesome work, but he could handle the blood on his hands. It seemed a small thing if it meant protecting Felix.

That was worth the battering of his conscience.

Felix washed himself in a stream while Cam worked. Cam joined him there when he had finished, rinsing the golden chain he'd retrieved from the Tacitum's lips. A strange keepsake perhaps, but a valuable one, for the gold if not for the craftsmanship. But it was beautiful, in a darkly fascinating way. At each end of the chain was a needle, sharply pointed but also edged like a razor and carved with symbols Cam didn't recognise. Those points were the metal that had pierced the Tacitum's cheeks, held in place by a ball of gold melted to their tips.

It was like a golden bridle.

Cam didn't want to keep it for long. It seemed heavy in his pocket, weighted with significance, but to him it held only horror. It was a special thing, but a cursed one, more an implement of torture than an ornament.

'Are you done?' Cam asked. 'Are you okay?'

'Yes and yes.' Felix's voice was still little more than a whisper, but then he'd always been soft-spoken. If Cam let his mind drift, he could almost believe the events of the evening hadn't happened at all.

But they had, and now they needed to make a plan.

'They'll send more,' Cam said. 'They could be watching us now. He was trying to take you.'

'I know.'

'I'll go scouting, to check it out, and to make sure our path is clear for tomorrow. We might need to pick a different route.'

'I'll come too.'

Cam looked at Felix's newly-set nose, his soaked clothes and blue-tinged fingers.

'I said I'll come too,' Felix repeated. It was clear that he wasn't prepared to stay behind. Perhaps that was for the best, because right now Cam didn't want to let him out of his sight.

They left the Tacitum tied to a tree. The rope wasn't to restrain him – he shouldn't wake for another twelve hours at least – it was to secure his body up in the branches, where the wildlife was less likely to nibble on him before they returned. The more damaged he was, the harder it would be to question him later.

'He's not worth the last of your uncontaminated blood,' said Felix.

'We won't need much to revive him, if we need to use any at all. We'll see how long it takes him to come around.'

Felix spat into the mud, his own blood dark in the moonlight. 'Do you know how they make them?'

'I've heard stories.'

'In the mountains, they make each other. It's a competition. They fight to take each other down, and the winner of each round cuts and sews the loser's mouth and tongue together, until there's just one champion left.'

'And who sews him up?'

'He does it himself, while he's still conscious. That's why he gets the gold chain.'

Like the chain sitting in Cam's pocket right now.

'Shit,' he said. 'I was afraid you were going to say that.'

'I know people think the Silver are monsters,' Felix said, 'but they've got nothing on the Tacitum.'

'Then we won't leave him alone for long. Come on.'

They moved at a quiet run, partly so they would get back to the camp faster and partly because Cam hoped the pace might keep Felix warm, but it also made it harder for Cam to pick out noises in the forest around them.

'What's that?' he said as they approached the pass.

They both stopped. Cam strained to the limits of his hearing as he scanned the surrounding trees for any sign of movement, but there was nothing, just the solid beating of Felix's heart. Still, he felt unaccountably jumpy.

There was a draught on the back of his neck, which wasn't surprising given that they were outside, but something about the direction of it was putting him on edge. He reached out to take Felix's hand, needing to hold on to him, just in case.

Their fingers touched, then a breeze sprung up around them, an unnatural rush of air, followed by silence.

Cam couldn't hear Felix's heartbeat anymore. He couldn't feel the warmth of his touch, or smell the nutmeg greenness of his skin.

He was alone in the trees with empty hands and the scent of Silver violence filling his nostrils.

Felix was gone, and the world was dark.

11

It was dark in the city, and quiet.

Julia had wanted to bring the blood with her, but it was too soon. Cam had been very clear about that. They'd agreed on a day, and she wasn't to make her move until then. So here she was, empty handed.

She hesitated on the doorstep, but Rufus must have heard her coming because she could already see his shadow approaching through the window. He'd know it was her, following his gruesome invitation to its conclusion.

She'd had no other choice.

'Welcome home.' He smirked when he opened the door, but then crinkled his nose in distaste. 'You stink of his mark.'

'And you sound just like him.'

The retort felt like another betrayal, because Lucas was nothing like Rufus. He wasn't the kind of man who'd cut off someone's ear just to get her attention. He was the kind of man who put her before his pride, who'd forgive without recriminating later.

But Julia feared that she was now passing beyond the reach of his forgiveness.

'You said you'd let Marcella go,' she reminded Rufus, her mouth drying at the sickening thought that she might be too late. What if he'd taken more than just her earlobe? What if he'd been torturing her all the time Julia had been off running around the Red with Cam and Felix?

Whatever had befallen the goddess would be her fault, because she hadn't taken Rufus at his word. She wouldn't make that mistake again.

'You promised,' she said. 'If I came back to you, you'd let her go. That's what you said. So where is she?'

He laughed. 'You think this is you coming back to me? You left. It's been *weeks*, Julia, then you turn up reeking of your sponsor, and you want me to trade you for her? No, I don't think so.'

He closed the door in her face.

Julia gaped at it. After all the fuss he'd made over her, after leaving her that foul package, he was sending her away. It made no sense. Why would he have behaved that way if he wasn't trying to force her here, to the surrender he wanted?

The worst thing was that part of her was offended by his rejection.

And then she remembered the game. What was it he'd said? *You're a predator, just like me.*

He was playing with her, seeing how far she was prepared to chase him. Maybe his pride was hurt, or maybe he just liked tormenting her, but either way he was going to make her fight for this. If she wanted to get Marcella free then she'd better be convincing.

Julia thumped on the door, listening as his leisurely footsteps came back towards her on its far side.

'Yes? Oh, Julia. It's you again. I thought I made myself clear: you *left*.'

'I left to find out what happened to my parents.'

He leaned against the doorjamb, hands in his pockets. 'Well, I could have told you that. Anyone in the Blue could've. They're dead. You didn't have to leave Marcella to my tender mercies to find that out.'

Julia tried not to let him see how much that guilt ate at her. That was probably why her next words came out a little less subtly than she'd intended.

'They told me Horatius was your father, too.'

Rufus blinked, then started laughing. 'You're not serious. You thought that piece of human excrement was my father?'

'It's not true then.'

'No.'

Julia felt herself deflating a little, with relief, but with some trepidation as well. It had been such a perfect reason to push him away.

'But even if it was true,' he went on, leaning in close, 'I wouldn't have let it stand in my way.'

Ugh.

'Well,' he said, 'I'm glad we could clear that up. Goodnight.'

This time, she jammed her foot between the door and the frame before he could close it again. Thank the Empress that her boots were sturdy.

He looked down at her foot, then back up at her face, expectantly.

'What's it going to take for you to let her go?' she said, forcing her fists to unclench.

'You really want me to tell you? It'll take all of the fun out of it.' He was teasing her now, the side of his mouth twitching with the promise of a sneer or a smile.

She took a deep breath, reminding herself why she was here: for Marcella.

'Alright,' she said, 'then let me tell you. First, you're going to invite me in.' She put a hand on his chest and pushed him back into the hall, slamming the door behind her. 'Then, you're going to get Marcella down here and tell her you don't need her anymore, because you've got me. I'm your Candidate now. After that, the rest of the night is up to you.'

'I don't think so.' He grabbed her wrist, his fingertips closing over the wound Lucas had left earlier that night. 'The thing is, I can scent him all over you, so strongly that I can almost see his tongue here.' He pressed the cut with his fingertip, sending a sharp rush of pain through her arm. 'And here.' He raised his other hand to her mouth, smearing her lips with his thumb. 'You're covered in him.'

'Then I'll wash.'

Rufus quirked an eyebrow at her. 'That won't wash away the mark. The way I see it, you have two options: either you come back when the mark has faded – and who knows what Marcella and I will get up to in the meantime – or you replace his mark with another one. It's up to you.'

Julia only hesitated for a second, just long enough to make herself ignore every instinct that was screaming at her to turn and run. That was enough time to let her other instincts come to the fore, the ones she wished she could deny.

She fisted her hand in his shirt and pulled him closer, wrapping her other hand around the back of his neck to drag his lips down to hers.

She might have pretended that he was Lucas, but Lucas didn't taste of lemon juice and spice. Lucas didn't kiss like he was waging a battle of wills with his lips. Lucas didn't tangle her hair in his fingers and press his hips into hers so forcefully that it was impossible to misunderstand his intentions.

Julia's own intentions were very different. She could feel the knife firmly tucked down the inside of her boot. She'd incapacitated Rufus once, and she'd do it again if she had to. If this didn't work, if he didn't give her what she wanted, then she'd take it from him by force.

But then the lemon scent of him enveloped her and she started to doubt herself.

'You still want this,' he murmured against her lips. 'You still want *me*. Did you think you were in control?'

She slammed him back against the wall. 'I am.'

'No, you're not.'

The next thing she knew it was her back against the wall, his body pinning her in place as he caught her hands in his.

'Don't you want this power?' he said. 'You could be so much more than this. You could be better, stronger. If you were like me, we could fight on equal terms, fuck on equal terms...'

She met his gaze. 'I don't need to be like you to take you down.'

'I'd like to see you try.'

The seconds stretched.

His eyes were dark and fixed on hers. There was a hairsbreadth of space between their lips, between their bodies, filled with the lemon scent of Rufus's mark. Then he softened his grip on her wrists, keeping eye contact as he gave up the strength of her restraints. Julia still hadn't decided what she was going to do with that freedom when the whisper came from above them.

'Julia?' It was almost too quiet for her to hear, but it was enough to make Rufus break away.

The goddess.

Julia looked up and over her shoulder to the staircase where Marcella stood. Alive and apparently well, despite her injuries. Her lower lip was swollen where it had been broken open, and there was a bandage where her right earlobe had been, but otherwise she looked unharmed. At least it looked as though she wasn't missing any other body parts.

'What the hell are you doing out of your room?' Rufus said.

'Apologies, Master,' Marcella replied. 'I didn't mean to disturb you.' But she gave Julia a look that said disturbing them was exactly what she had intended.

Rufus wasn't fooled. 'Never mind,' he said. 'Since you're here, you may as well help Julia wash that mutt's slobber off herself.' He turned back to Julia. 'Then in the morning, we'll talk.'

Julia started firing questions the moment Marcella had shut the bathroom door behind them.

'Are you alright? Did he hurt you? Is Claudia alright? Have you seen her? What's going on out there?'

'Julia, please.' Marcella leaned back against the door, closing her eyes for a moment. 'I'm well enough. I don't know about Claudia. I haven't left this house since the Casting.'

That had been weeks ago, long enough to feel like a lifetime to Julia, and Marcella had spent every moment stuck in this house with Rufus. Julia couldn't imagine it.

A Server joined them then, a rake-thin boy with sunken eyes but a cheerful smile. He was carrying two buckets of steaming water, and was followed by a couple of smaller boys carrying more. They filled the bath then left without saying a word, though Marcella nodded her thanks to them.

'They're not allowed to speak to me,' she explained. 'He tells them I'm too precious.'

'He's isolating you.'

'Of course. He thinks it makes me easier to control, more compliant, and if Rufus loves one thing it's being in control. He likes to make us dance, doesn't he?'

Julia took Marcella's hands in hers and looked her over, tracing the lines of violence on her skin. 'I'm so sorry I left.'

'But why would you come back? I thought you were Lucas's Candidate now. I thought you were safe.'

'None of us are safe, you know that. I came to get you out of here. He promised me an exchange. But it means...' Julia sighed, but there was no other way. She couldn't keep Marcella in the dark. 'I have a plan to get us out of this. Not just you, but all of us. I need your help.'

Julia whispered Cam's plan to Marcella while she bathed the scent of Lucas from her skin. Soon her brown limbs were pinked with the heat of the water, and she had run out of words.

'So, will you help?' she whispered.

Marcella smiled. 'Of course.'

'Then the first thing we need is the contaminated blood. It's stashed in my mattress back at Livia's. Can you bring it here once you're free?'

'Here?'

'We start with him.'

Marcella nodded, but Julia was worried as she helped her out of the bath and into a linen. For someone who'd seen Julia kissing Rufus less than an hour ago, she seemed remarkably willing to trust. It would have rattled Julia's faith had their situations been reversed.

Marcella slipped out of the room while Julia dried herself off, returning a few moments later with a stack of clean clothes.

'What you saw earlier...' Julia said. She caught Marcella's eye, then looked away, pretending to be absorbed in drying her hair.

'Do you think I'd judge you for it?' Marcella asked quietly, passing Julia a clean dress. 'Loathing is a force of attraction.'

'I am *not* attracted to Rufus.'

Marcella shrugged. 'He makes us dance. Your steps are different from mine, but you're still following his tune.'

'I'm doing what I have to do,' Julia said, tugging the dress on over her head. 'I'm making him believe what he needs to believe so he'll let you go. That's all.'

'You're still dancing,' Marcella said, but kindly. 'If you do it for long enough, eventually you'll forget you were only supposed to be pretending.'

'I won't forget what he is,' Julia insisted.

'I don't know. You might be surprised how much you cling to him when he's the only thing left in your world.'

Julia froze. 'Like he is in yours?'

Marcella was at the door now, her fingers already turning the handle. 'I'm sorry,' she said, 'but I've already made my bargain.'

When she opened the door, Rufus was standing on the other side. In his hand he held a familiar bottle. Felix's blood.

Julia tried to snatch it from him, but he pinned her to the wall by her throat and held her there as he popped the cork out of the bottle and poured its contents down the drain, chasing its residue down with a jug of water. The empty bottle he threw into the hearth, where it smashed in the fire.

And that was it. It was gone.

Julia had travelled for weeks, facing Weepers, suffering saddle sores and making deals with the Invicti, all to have her precious prize snatched away from her before she could use it.

'Give up,' Rufus whispered, leaning in close. 'You can fight me all you like, but I promise you one thing, Julia: you will never, ever beat me. And do you know why?'

She struggled against his hand, grunting as she tried to pry his fingers away from her throat.

'You don't want to,' he said. 'Deep down, what you really want is to let me win.'

Lucas came to the house the next day. Julia heard his voice in the hall below, then she heard his shouts echoing up the stairs.

Marcella had already left, but despite her betrayal it was difficult for Julia to blame her. Julia had almost got what she'd bargained for, after all. She'd replaced Marcella as Rufus's Candidate, just as she'd planned. She just hadn't expected to lose Felix's blood. When it had gone down the drain, her part in Cam's plan had gone with it.

Now she was stuck.

'Julia!' Lucas yelled from downstairs, but she didn't move from her seat on the edge of her bed. She worried what the consequences would be if she did.

This was her home now. This was the bargain she'd made. If she broke her promise to Rufus, then she didn't know what he'd do. One mention of Claudia's name had been enough to buy Julia's compliance.

Her bedroom door opened and Rufus lounged in the doorway, his arms crossed over his chest.

'Ready to break his little heart?' he asked.

She'd known this was coming, and she was dreading it. Still, Lucas couldn't help her now. She was going to have to find her own way out of this mess, and maybe it was better for her to scare him off.

Julia scowled at Rufus, but she got to her feet and joined him by the door.

'Oh, come on,' he said. 'It's not like you love him. I've seen his silver, with not the slightest trace of gold in it, so don't pretend this is going to come as a shock to him. Besides,' he said, leaning in to inhale the scent of her hair, 'we both know this is where you want to be. I'm just giving you a reason to give in.'

She jabbed him in the side with her elbow, but that just made him pull her closer, his arm snaking around her waist to rest possessively on her hip. He walked her down the stairs like that, holding her against his side, so that was what Lucas saw through the open front door.

'Julia?' he said, incredulously.

'Hello, Lucas.'

'What the hell are you doing here, and with *him*?' Then his face darkened as they approached the door. Julia recognised his expression: the same one that had haunted her, the look that told her he could smell Rufus's mark on her skin.

'I'm staying here,' she said, trying to keep her voice steady, 'with Rufus.'

'But... Why?'

'Do you really need to ask why she'd choose me over you?' Rufus sneered.

'Yes. Yes I do. Maybe if you weren't standing right next to her she might actually give me a straight answer.'

Rufus released her, holding his hands up in surrender. 'Fine,' he said. 'I'll leave you to talk.' But he snatched a quick kiss from Julia as he left.

When she opened her eyes again, Lucas was seething.

Dammit. She shouldn't have closed her eyes. Why had she closed her eyes?

'Why are you doing this?' Lucas said in quiet desperation. 'I don't understand. It's *Rufus*.'

'I know.'

'After everything he's done to you, how could you choose to be with him? How many of your scars are his?'

'About as many as are yours.'

Lucas's brows pinched together. 'That's not fair.'

'But it's true.' She shrugged, pretending nonchalance while her hands shook. 'Look, I don't want you to get hurt, Lucas. I'm sorry, but you really should leave. Please. There's more trouble on the way, and the Invicti will need you.'

'What are you talking about?'

But she couldn't tell Lucas about the plan, because if she did then he'd tell the rest of the Invicti, and they'd find some way to stop Cam. And he was her last hope.

'Did you find Hades?' she said instead.

'Covered in blood and dirt, but yes. He's in the stables and he's fine. Next time you can wash him yourself.'

'Thank you,' she said, trying to smile, but he was forcing so much distance between them now that it was hard to see her Lucas across it. He seemed to be diminishing, folding himself away into the shell of a man that she didn't recognise.

It's for the best, she told herself. It would have been better if she'd been strong enough to put that distance between them herself, but this was enough.

This would work.

'So that's it, then?' he said.

'I suppose so. You've moved on. You're with the Invicti now. It was time for me to move on, too.'

'I haven't *moved on*. You think just because… No,' he said, pointing his finger at her. 'No. I don't buy this, and you know why? If you're moving on, then why is my silver still in your ear? Every time you do this, Julia. Every time you push me away, but you keep the one thing that tells the world you're mine. Don't try to tell me that you want to be Rufus's Candidate when you're still wearing my mark.'

Her hand went to the earring of its own accord.

No.

She didn't want to give it up. It was his and it was hers, the sign that tied the two of them together. It was the solid thing she reached for when she doubted herself, to turn it between her fingers and know that it was real.

But she couldn't keep it, not now.

She unfastened the clasp and removed the stud, holding it out to him. 'There,' she said. 'Now Rufus's mark is the only one I'm wearing. Are you happy?'

'Am I *happy*?' He shook his head and looked away. When he took the earring from her hand, he didn't meet her eye. 'Goodbye, Julia.'

'Goodbye,' she said, then she closed the door so she wouldn't have to watch him walk away.

Rufus was waiting for her on the landing.

'I'll get you something prettier,' he promised.

But Julia knew there would never be anything prettier than Lucas's silver stud. It had been perfect, because it was one of a matching pair.

She spent the rest of the day in her room, looking out of the window as she tried to think of a quick and easy way to get more contaminated blood.

The problem was that there wasn't one. The quickest option was going into the Red to the north of the city, following the path to the fields where she'd seen Tatiana the first time she'd left the Blue. There were plenty of contaminated people there. But what would she do then? All of the humans working on that farm were heavily guarded by Nobles. She'd need a miracle to get what she wanted there.

The easiest option was a trip back into the Red to see Galatea, but there were two obstacles to that plan: firstly, she wasn't sure she'd make it through all those Weepers again, and secondly it would simply take too long. She needed blood, and she needed it within the next few days. If she didn't get it soon, then it would be too late for Cam.

There had to be another option. Perhaps there were still some contaminated humans in the boundaries of the Blue somewhere, but she'd been watching the streets all afternoon without seeing a single person with a cross painted on their cheek. Not that she'd seen many people at all. In fact, the Blue felt conspicuously empty and quiet.

She wished she'd had the chance to talk to Lucas about the people he'd said were missing. Something was going on in this city, something beyond the drama that was playing out between her and Rufus, and it worried her that she didn't know what it was. But she'd never given Lucas the chance to explain it. Still, there was no point in beating herself up about that. She'd done what she'd felt was necessary at the time, even if she regretted it now.

Which took her back to her biggest problem: before she could enact any plan at all, she'd need to evade Rufus.

He left her alone until supper time, then came knocking on her door.

'Yes?' she said.

He lingered on the threshold. 'Do you blame her for telling me?'

'Marcella?'

'Yes.'

Being in this room again had brought back the memories Julia had begun to suppress: the blade in her arm as the goddess bled her, the soft touch of Marcella's fingers as she bound her wounds, and the press of Marcella's tear-soaked cheek against Julia's hand as she'd lain in her bed on the brink of death.

Marcella had cared for her and loved her. How could Julia blame her for taking her chance to run? It was like blaming a starving dog for stealing a bone.

'I blame you,' she said.

'I suppose you should.' He came and sat beside her on the bed, but he didn't make any move to reach for her. 'Perhaps you should be disappointed that we're not siblings.'

'I'd rather not discuss it at all.'

'And you thought my father was Horatius, of all people. Laila hated him, you know, but then she hates most men. She hated my father too. It was my mother she loved.'

Julia didn't say anything. She didn't want to know about his history. She didn't want to bond. She didn't want to feel anything for him but hatred, for all he'd done to her and the people she loved.

'I did grow up in the palace, like you,' he went on, 'but you probably don't remember it. You were quite small. That was when we first met, when my mother still lived there with us. You know her. Quite well, actually.'

Julia couldn't help herself. 'Who?'

But she shouldn't have asked, because the moment he'd caught her interest he changed the subject.

'I don't understand why you want to cure us, when you could be one of us instead. Lucas could have given you that power. *I* could give you that power. Why would you want to wipe us out instead?'

'How can you even ask me that question?' she said, turning to face him. 'Power makes you evil.'

'Morality is a human construct, Julia.'

'No, morality is a construct you force onto us. If Nobles do wrong, then what punishment is there? None. And what rewards are there when you do good? None. But humans have to behave themselves, or they're punished by you.'

He put a finger under her chin and tipped her face towards his. 'Is that why you need me to give you permission to misbehave?'

'Do you really think that's what you're doing?' she said, pushing him away. 'You think that by keeping me prisoner here you're freeing me from something?'

'You're not a prisoner.'

'Excuse me?'

'You can walk out at any time, as long as you come back afterwards. This is your home, Julia. Your cage is in here.' He pressed a finger to her temple. 'Don't you want to come out and play?'

'Rufus,' she said, leaning towards him, 'I'm not playing with you. I promise you this: when I wipe out the Nobles – and trust me, I'm going to – I'm starting with you.'

She shouldn't have leaned in. That was where she'd gone wrong, because he took the gesture as an invitation rather than a threat. His lips were on hers before she knew what was happening, his hand on her thigh holding her to him.

But that wasn't the worst of it. Somehow her fingers were running up the front of his shirt and around the back of his head, pulling him closer to her. She stopped them in their tracks, jerking her hand away, but he caught her wrist and smoothed her fingers back along his neck.

'You can stop pretending you don't want this,' he said. 'There's no one here except us.'

'I don't want you,' she whispered, but the words came out breathy and wrong. So wrong. He was a monster, a sadist and likely a murderer too, so why was her body betraying her to him?

He chuckled, his teeth nipping at her lower lip. 'You can't lie to me.'

She pushed him away and walked to the window. Sitting on the bed with him suddenly seemed like a supremely bad idea.

The look he gave her was laced with frustration. 'How long are you going to keep denying this?'

'For the rest of my life, or until you're dead, which will hopefully be sooner.'

'Because you're going to kill me?' he laughed bitterly. 'You'd rather kill me than admit you want me, and you call me immoral.' He stood up and walked towards her. 'This is what freedom looks like, Julia. You take what you want because you want it, even if you shouldn't. You take your feelings and you act on them, without worrying whether or not it's right. That's what it's like to be a Noble. Don't you want to feel like that?'

Julia looked out of the window, focussing on the people passing by in the street below, not wanting to imagine herself as a Noble. She could almost feel the strength running through her muscles, the speed in her legs, and the power of her fists. How different her life would be if she could be that kind of weapon.

And she could. She'd lost the contaminated blood, and without it Cam's plan was doomed to failure. But that didn't need to be the end for her. Rather than defeating the Silver, she could decide to join them instead.

Rufus was behind her now, his hand on her shoulder, fingers tracing a slow line towards her neck.

'That voice in your head that's telling you to stop every time we kiss,' he whispered, 'that makes you push me away despite the fact that my mark is all over you, that makes you push me away despite your desire, wouldn't it be nice if once in a while it just *shut up*?'

She could feel his breath on the back of her neck. She wanted more of his warmth.

'You want me to turn off my conscience,' she said.

'I want to liberate you. You're still only human, but I could change that. Wouldn't you like to be free?' He pressed a kiss to her throat. 'All you have to do is say yes.'

12

'No!' Cam yelled.

His voice was sucked up into the darkness between the trees, sinking into the mud beneath his boots and fading into silence.

He ran the paths, leaping between the trees as he tried to track Felix's scent, but whoever had taken him had been moving at Silver speed, so the trail was thin. It wasn't long before the rain had washed it out of the air entirely.

'Shit.' His knees dropped into the earth and his head into his hands, the adrenaline flowing out of him as panic collapsed into despair.

Felix was gone.

Cam had lost him, and he had just two bottles of blood to get him back.

Charlestown or the Pit? There wasn't enough to get him to both.

But he knew how to choose.

When the Tacitum finally stirred, Cam had been waiting for so long that he was jittery with impatience. His fingers twitched on the blade he spun in his hand, twisting it recklessly along his knuckles. It was dawn now, but he'd found no rest during the night. He would find none until Felix was back in his arms.

He'd propped the Tacitum up against a tree and tied him in place, but the rope wouldn't hold him for long. Cam needed to get this over with quickly, before the creature recovered his strength.

'I know you're awake,' he said.

The Tacitum still had his eyes closed, but Cam could hear the increase in his heart rate as he rose into consciousness and realised he was in trouble. He couldn't know quite how much trouble, not yet, but that would become apparent when he opened his eyes and saw the look on Cam's face.

Cam wasn't prepared to wait for that moment.

'Do you want me to pry your eyes open?' he said, trailing the point of the blade along the Tacitum's cheek.

The Tacitum raised his eyelids sluggishly.

'Good. Now tell me where they took him.'

Turning his head, the Tacitum looked around the remains of the camp. The fire was still the mess it had been after their fight the previous night, because Cam had seen no point in rebuilding it; it wasn't as though he could stomach food, and he was too numb to feel the cold.

'There's no one here to help you,' Cam said.

The Tacitum grinned, splitting open his broken lips. 'But there's no one to help you, either.'

'You think I need help?'

Cam backhanded him across the face, slamming his head into the tree and cracking his eye socket. Cam felt the bone breaking beneath his hand, but the crunch and snap gave him nothing but satisfaction. They took him one step closer to his goal. He only cared about getting the Tacitum to tell him what he wanted to know. Everything else was irrelevant now.

That was why he felt so out of himself. It was as though his insides had been emptied out in that moment when Felix had been taken from him. All his gentleness had gone, siphoned off into determination.

But not determination for his original plan, because that was gone too. He no longer cared about the Blue, or curing the Silver, or the promises he'd made to Ana. He had a new plan now: he was going to find Felix, track down the people who'd snatched him, and make them pay.

Starting with the Tacitum.

'I am Tacitum,' the creature said, his words fumbled by his desecrated tongue. 'All you'll get from me is silence.'

'You seem pretty chatty to me. Not really what I expected from a champion. That's what this means, isn't it?' Cam pulled the gold chain from his pocket, letting the links tumble from his fingers so one of the needles trailed in the muddy leaves. The Tacitum's eyes followed it as it dragged in the dirt, his prize defiled. 'Some champion you are. I took you out in seconds. That's how the Invicti stack up against your *champion.*'

'Not all strength is physical,' the Tacitum lisped, but he was angry enough to spit the words through his bleeding mouth.

Cam laughed, at first just to rile the Tacitum, but then with triumph as he saw the effect it was having on his captive. He was straining against the rope, starting to pull it apart where it crossed over his chest.

'This is what I think of your championship,' Cam said, then he dropped the gold chain and crushed it into the mud under his heel.

The Tacitum roared. When he pulled free of the ropes, the force ripped the bark away from the tree, but Cam was ready for the attack. It was what he'd been waiting for. He'd swallowed two precious mouthfuls of blood in anticipation of this moment. The dose gave him enough speed to catch the Tacitum and slam him into the ground before he'd taken a step.

'Do you know what I think?' Cam said, holding the Tacitum down with a hand to his throat. With the other hand, he pulled the gold chain from the mud. 'I think you like to be in control. Am I right?'

The Tacitum struggled beneath him, but Cam kneed him in the stomach until he was calm, then held the bladed side of one muddy, golden needle over his eye.

'Felix – the man you tried to take from me – he told me you made yourself what you were, threading this through your lips, slicing your own flesh away so it healed together. Now, I can't imagine anything worse than that, but maybe you're different. Maybe your worst nightmare is the thought of someone doing that to you.'

The Tacitum squirmed, choking against Cam's hand. Cam pressed his knee into the Tacitum's stomach, pinning him down so hard that he started sinking into the soft ground.

'I wouldn't make it pretty,' Cam said, then he sliced the needle across the Tacitum's cheek. 'I could take your eye, then sew it up. I could take your teeth, one by one, then make you swallow them. There are so many things I could take from you, because I want to make you understand what it's like to lose a piece of yourself. So, where have they taken Felix? Charlestown? The mountains?'

Cam relaxed the pressure on the Tacitum's windpipe, but he just used the space to try to wriggle away. Cam slammed him back down and sliced his other cheek open. It was raining again now, and the water washed the blood into pink rivulets that disappeared into the mud.

'Every second you keep me waiting for an answer is a second I use to think of more things I want to take from you. Like your ears, or your fingernails, or your nose. Maybe all of them. So tell me: where have they taken him?'

The Tacitum glared at him, calling his bluff.

But Cam hadn't been bluffing. He didn't feel the horror of the gold chain anymore, because it was a weapon in his hand. All he felt was the ticking of the seconds as the Tacitum stalled, and Felix was taken farther and farther away from him. Weighed against the urgency chasing him on, the needle was light in his hand.

He could appreciate the elegance of its design as he thumbed the Tacitum's eye from its socket then used the razor-edged needle to cut it away. There were screams – of course there were screams – but Cam focussed on his task. It took a while to pry the golden ball from the end of the needle, revealing the sharp point, but then it was the work of seconds to sew the Tacitum's eyelid shut.

'Would you like to lose your other eye?' he said when he had finished.

But that had been enough for the Tacitum, who gave up his prize. It was almost a shame, because Cam had so much rage left to spend, but there would be others for him to use it on.

He found a leaf that was still stained with Felix's blood from the night before, nutmeg spiced, and forced it between the Tacitum's lips. Then he left him in the freezing mud with his mutilated lips and his chained eye, the cured and fallen champion.

It was more than he deserved.

Cam drank the last of his bottles and ran.

Charlestown.

It seemed fitting that it should be here, in the place where all this had begun. Cam remembered the last time he'd rescued Felix from this place, his first nose break and shattered tooth, and hoped he wouldn't be too late.

The journey had passed in a blur, literally, because Cam had pushed himself to a speed he hadn't even known he could obtain.

He'd flown up the mountains, into the ravine and through the pass, and now found himself in the trees on the other side, looking down at a broken version of old Dresden.

It had burned since he'd last been here, and recently. Smoke was still rising from its centre, black and noxious. Cam could only hope that Felix wasn't caught up in it, because the Tacitum hadn't known where exactly the Red Shirts would be keeping him. He'd known only that it would be here.

Cam had no plan. He'd run here thinking only of reaching Felix, of pulling him into his arms and burying his face in the woodsman's neck. He could almost smell his skin if he concentrated hard enough, like fresh-cut branches green with the spring.

Then he felt it. There was a tugging in his chest, so real that Cam looked down to see what was causing it. But there was nothing, just the sense of something drawing him on, an invisible tether pulling him towards the city.

He followed it.

Unlike the last time he'd entered the city, it was now full daylight, and also unlike that time, there was absolutely no one watching the perimeter. In fact, there barely was a perimeter anymore. The buildings had been pulled down in places, wrenched from their foundations into piles of smoking rubble that blocked the streets. On the outskirts of the city, that rubble had been piled into heaps that served as a mediocre barricade.

And there were bodies.

Cam picked his way through them, stepping over limbs and masonry on his way into the outer streets. He might have thought the casualties were human had it not been for the vials of blood smashed and broken around them, presumably once filled with contaminated blood. It was chemical warfare in its latest form, a trick that the Silver must have learned during their battles with the Invicti. Once someone had crossed that line, there had been no chance of return, but they'd gone beyond that here in Charlestown. These bodies weren't just cured, but dead as well.

That was more than Cam had planned for them, but he felt immune to the horror of it. It rolled off him, the stench and the heat and the cracking of skin, as though he'd carved it out of himself with every cut he'd made on the Tacitum's face.

For Felix.

He hurried on. His stride lengthened as he went, so he was sprinting by the time the dragging pull in his chest led him to a building in the west of the city. He hadn't seen a living soul since he'd crossed the barricade, but now he could hear the slow heartbeats of Silver in the upper storeys, and the fast rush of human ones in the basement. He decided to start there.

A quick recce identified a hatch set into the ground at the back of the building, wide and double-doored, as though it had been used to lower supplies into the basement from the street. It was locked up tight with bolts on the inside, but that didn't stop Cam; he just pulled the doors off their hinges and threw them aside.

There was no point in being quiet. The Red Shirts probably already knew he was here.

He dropped down into the darkness. Some light trickled in from a grate in the far wall, but it was barely enough for human eyes. Even with his enhanced sight, it took a moment for Cam to sift through the hundred-or-so faces that stared up at him from the shadows and determine that none of them was Felix.

Of course he wasn't here. The Red Shirts had a purpose for him, whereas these humans were just food.

'Run,' Cam said to them. They were already fighting to be first through the hatch when he reached the stairs.

A familiar figure met him at the top.

'You're the boyfriend, right?' It was the Red Shirt from the mountains, the one that Felix had met in the forest before they'd rescued Emmy. 'He said to expect you.'

'Get out of my way.'

The Red Shirt held up his hands in surrender, stepping back through the door to let Cam up.

Cam looked around for the trap. It couldn't be that easy. These Silver had travelled across the mountains, using up bottle after bottle of blood that they could ill afford from the looks of things, all just to snatch Felix away. There had to be a reason for that.

'Why did you take him?' Cam asked.

The Red Shirt shrugged. 'It was a mistake. Just a stupid mistake.'

'Then bring him down here, and we'll leave.'

'He's just upstairs. If you follow me I'll–'

'Bring him here.'

Something barrelled into Cam, and before he knew what was happening each of his limbs was pinned to the ground. He should have noticed them hiding in the corners of the basement, eight hearts beating slower than the rest, but he'd been trying to ignore the scuffle the humans were creating behind him and focus on the rest of the building. That had been his mistake.

'I knew you'd come for him,' the Red Shirt said, walking back down the stairs. 'I knew because that's what he told me. He told me all about your plan to turn us human, and he told me exactly how long we need to wait before every Silver in the Blue will be cured. After that, we can just walk in and take it. I suppose I should be thanking you, really.'

'What have you done to him?' Cam growled.

But the Red Shirt laughed and said, 'Nothing. Why would we hurt an ally?'

No.

Cam didn't believe it. He wouldn't believe that Felix had betrayed him.

'I'm not sure why you're surprised,' the Red Shirt said as Cam struggled against the Silver who were restraining him. 'He's always been with me. I'm his brother in arms, and I'm going to turn him Silver again, just like he always wanted. And you? You're the one who wants to wipe us out. You're the one who killed his lover.'

No, Cam thought, I'm *his lover,* but then he remembered the Weeper in the forest, back when he and Felix had been nothing more than a dream of a future that didn't seem possible. And if he believed the Red Shirt, it hadn't been.

None of it had been real.

'I didn't kill Otho,' Cam said. 'Richard did.'

The Red Shirt waved the comment away. 'Technicalities.'

'And Felix helped us rescue Emmy. He tricked you all, in the Pit. He stabbed one of you in the head. He hasn't betrayed me. He betrayed you.'

Because he loves me.

The Red Shirt tapped his chin. 'How do I explain this to you so you'll understand?' He crouched down beside Cam and gave him a frank look. 'He was playing you. He's always been playing you. He took one of us down – temporarily – in order to keep his cover, but he's always been my man.'

Cam couldn't believe it. The highlights reel ran through his head: the hot springs, the kiss by the salt lake, the cabin in the mountains and every touch, every smile they'd shared since then. How could that all have been a lie?

The Red Shirt laughed again. 'Did you really think he was on your side now, just because he made you think he wanted to fuck you? You should have left him to die. It's what he would have done to you.'

'Then get him down here. Let him tell me himself.'

The Red Shirt shrugged. 'It won't change anything.'

'Get him down here,' Cam said through gritted teeth. He wasn't in any position to be making demands, but apparently the idea amused the Red Shirt, because he went back up the stairs and called for someone to fetch Felix.

When his woodsman finally appeared, Cam felt as though his heart were breaking in two. Part of it surged with joy to see him alive, safe and with no new injuries, but the other part plummeted as he realised what that meant.

The Red Shirt had been telling the truth. Felix had betrayed him.

'Felix,' he said, but the name wasn't more than a whisper.

'You found him, then,' Felix said to the Red Shirt.

'He came, like you said he would.'

'Well, why are you telling me about it? Aren't we done here?' Felix didn't even look at Cam. His eyes passed over him, clinical and detached, noting his presence with no emotion. No emotion at all.

This couldn't be happening.

The Red Shirt was laughing again. Cam wanted to smash his teeth in with his fist.

'He didn't believe me when I told him,' the Red Shirt said. 'You should have seen his face.'

Felix's eyes met Cam's for a single, brief moment before breaking away.

'We don't have time for this,' Felix said. 'We've got to move if we want to get there before Alistair does. I told you: in two days' time, the Blue will be unprotected.'

Two days?

That wasn't right. Julia wouldn't be making her move for another week.

Felix caught Cam's eye again, and this time there was no mistaking it. He was trying to tell Cam something.

The Red Shirt was talking again, but Cam's attention was fixed on Felix's hand. There was a shine at the end of his sleeve, a glinting object poking out from behind his palm. As he spoke he pressed his finger against it.

There was a tiny thud as something liquid dropped into the dirt floor. If he concentrated very hard, Cam could scent the new blood in the air.

Felix's blood.

It gave him just enough warning. He stopped straining against his captors, letting his limbs go loose beneath their hands. They probably didn't even realise that they were reacting, but Cam could feel them easing off, applying just a fraction less pressure than they had been.

That was all he needed.

When Felix threw the bloodied knife towards him, Cam jerked his arm free and caught its hilt. One sweep sliced the blade across the arms of half of his captors, depositing the cure in their blood.

The effect was instantaneous. All of a sudden their grip was like wet paper wrapping around his limbs, and it was broken just as easily. He cut two more of the Silver before they realised what had happened to their friends, but the final two had been quicker on the uptake. They were already backing towards the stairs.

In the meantime, Felix had got himself into trouble. There was blood smeared on the Red Shirt's face, as though Felix had tried to force it into his mouth, but he'd clearly missed because the Red Shirt now had him pinned against the wall by his throat.

'You betrayed me?' the Red Shirt was yelling in his face. '*Me*? We're supposed to be brothers. We could have made you Silver again.'

Felix laughed, but it came out as a choking gurgle. 'You? Your soldiers were stupid enough to think *I* was the missing prince. You're incompetent. You'd never have made me Silver again, but we can make you human.'

Cam threw the knife.

It hit the Red Shirt in the shoulder. He dropped Felix and fell to his knees on the steps, reaching to pull the blade free, but it was too late. The cure had already done its work. Felix kicked him in the stomach, rolling him over the edge of the stairs and onto the basement floor six feet below.

The two remaining Silver had already disappeared into the building above them, leaving their newly-human comrades behind in the basement, clutching at their wounds in disbelief.

'You're alright?' Cam asked Felix.

'Fine,' he said. 'What now?'

'Now we need to finish what we've started.'

There were at least thirty Silver waiting for them at the top of the basement stairs, bristling with knives, bows and swords. They'd had time to prepare, but then so had Cam and Felix, and they only needed one weapon.

'Their hands!' someone yelled from the back of the crowd, but Cam had already spun through the centre of the room, wiping his bloody fingers across the mouths of everyone he passed.

Six cured. The cowards were already running for the exit.

Cam retrieved a crossbow that had been abandoned on the floor and threw it back towards Felix, who was waiting in the basement doorway. He caught it and swung it into position, letting the point run across his bloody skin as he did so. When the bolt met its target, that was another Red Shirt cured and out.

But the Red Shirts had seen him now, picking out the weak link. The other bows in the room focussed on Felix, then the air was thick with arrows.

Cam turned in time to see Felix duck back into the basement, avoiding all but one of the bolts. The one that found its mark cut through his forearm, sticking in the meat of the muscle, but he didn't let it slow him down. Instead, he pulled it out and flung it back at the crowd, taking another Silver crashing towards humanity.

'Bastards!' Cam yelled, throwing himself into the skirmish with renewed vigour.

It was only then that he realised he had one significant advantage over them: his speed. Despite the stakes, not one of the Red Shirts was moving at Silver speed. They must have been low on blood, because they were all as sluggish as Naia on a fifty-shot hangover. In the time it took Cam to flick blood into the faces of ten more of them, the knifemen had barely started moving towards Felix.

'Behind you!'

Cam turned to see a Red Shirt coming at him with a sword. A literal sword. It quickly became apparent that he didn't know how to use it, because it took Cam less than a second to deflect and disarm him, smearing blood in his eye in the process.

More than half of the Red Shirts were now cured and either down or gone. Cam could feel the uncertainty in the air. It was written in their hesitation, and in the way they shuffled their feet as they faced off against him. One more push, and they'd scatter.

Felix provided it. While they'd been concentrating on Cam and his Silver speed, Felix had procured another crossbow. He now hefted one in each hand, loaded with contaminated bolts, which he loosed before the Red Shirt's could react. The first took a chunk out of a Red Shirt's ear, the second another Red Shirt's finger, which left just nine Silver to oppose them.

The one closest to them had his hands up now, dropping his knife to the floor. A couple by the door were trying to make a break for it, but Cam was faster than them.

'No, you don't!' he yelled, corralling them back into the room.

They all raised their hands. Without uncontaminated blood, there was no way they could hope to take Cam on and win. Their surrender was encouraged by Felix, who already had one bow reloaded. He was weaving his aim between the remaining Red Shirts, keeping them on their toes.

'You're going to line up against the wall over there,' Cam said.

'But we surrendered,' one of them protested. 'You wouldn't kill us.'

'Up against the wall!' Felix yelled, picking up a sword from the ground.

Then he grinned at Cam. With his crossbow, his sword, and his broken nose, he looked like nothing so much as a disreputable pirate.

Suddenly Cam felt a pressing need to deal with the Red Shirts quickly so he could have some time alone with Felix. He had an overwhelming urge to reconcile. Maybe a few times, actually.

He didn't wait for the Red Shirts to reach the wall, he just sped along the line and smeared his bloody palm over their mouths.

'Now lick your lips,' he said.

They did so obediently, if hesitantly. One swing of the crossbow was enough to convince the few who'd been thinking too hard about whether or not to comply.

Once Cam was satisfied that their hearts were beating fast enough to be mortal, he sent them out into the burning remains of the city. The cured ones from the basement had already fled, probably in the same direction as the humans Cam had released when he'd busted in.

'Alone at last,' Felix said with a smile.

'You had me going for a minute there,' Cam admitted. 'I thought you'd switched sides on me again.'

Felix dropped the crossbow and came in close, close enough to push Cam's hair out of his eyes. 'You never have to doubt me.'

'You say that, but you obviously convinced them of the same.'

'Because they're idiots. They threw me out after I was cured, and thought they still had my loyalty.' Felix shook his head. 'So gullible.'

'And I'm not?'

'No.' Felix smiled. '*Du bist wundervoll, meine Liebe.*'

Cam took Felix's face in his hands, feeling the familiar tickle of his beard on his palms. Then he let the silver come, flooding his eyes while Felix watched. Cam could feel the moment when it crossed from the whites of his eyes to his irises, a beautiful sting that sang like the passage of tears.

He'd silvered for Felix. He'd known it in that moment when the tether had snapped into place between them, drawing him on towards this place.

But that wasn't all he knew. Yes, he'd silvered, but the metallic sheen ornamenting his eyes wasn't actually *silver*. It was gold, because the bond between the two of them was sealed, reciprocal and eternal.

This was forever.

'*Ich liebe dich,*' Cam whispered.

'Finally,' Felix laughed, leaning in to brush his lips across Cam's. '*Ich dich auch.* You believe me now, golden eyes?'

Cam kissed him, gently at first, but he couldn't hold himself back for long. He wanted to claim him, to mark him and be claimed in return. His kisses grew desperate, trying to say with their fervour what Cam didn't have the breath to put into words: that Felix was his love, his life, his home, and that he would never let him go again. He wanted to paint it across the sky, but the scent of his own mark on Felix's skin was enough.

It told the world that this man was his, in the same way that the gold in Cam's eyes told the world he belonged to Felix.

'*Für immer*,' Cam whispered against his lips, and Felix smiled.

'*Immer*.'

13

'Forever,' Julia repeated.

'If that's what you want,' Rufus said. 'But it's not just eternal life, it's a better life. Let me give it to you.'

The tray was still on the table in her room, holding the equipment the goddess had once used to take Julia's blood. It was all there: the blade, the cup, and the needle waiting to sew her up afterwards. Rufus walked over to it now, slicing his wrist open and letting his own blood drip down his fingers and into the cup. He offered it to her.

'You can have it all,' he said. 'You can be powerful. I can give that to you.'

She took the cup, but she didn't drink.

This wasn't right. Of course the thought of it was attractive, but this wasn't who she wanted to be. She didn't want power gifted to her, power bled from others who deserved it no less than she did. But most of all, she didn't want to be Rufus's creation.

Besides which, she had a promise to keep.

What was it that Marcella had said? *I've already made my bargain.* Well, Julia had made hers too, and her first bargain wasn't with Rufus, but with Cam. She was supposed to be unmaking the Silver, not letting herself be made into one of them.

She tried to pass the cup back to Rufus, but he wrapped her fingers around it.

'You could be exceptional,' he said. He raised his bloody hand to her face and traced the curves of his name on her cheek in red, then he leaned in close. Julia could already smell the acid sharpness of his scent.

'If you'd let me,' he whispered, 'I could be the making of you.'

But Julia leaned away.

This wasn't what she wanted. This wasn't what she wanted at all.

'I don't want you to make me,' she said. 'I'd rather make myself.'

She forced her hands apart and the cup dropped through them, spilling the blood in swirling coils on the ground. They both watched it spin to a stop, then Rufus snatched the front of her dress, pushing her towards the bed.

'And I told you I wouldn't wait on you forever.' He shoved her onto her back then pinned her down, one arm across her chest. 'If you need more of a reason, then I'll give it to you. I'll make it so you can't say no.'

He shoved his bleeding wrist against her mouth, smearing her lips open so his blood seeped in around her teeth.

'You'll change your mind,' he said, staring down at her as she gagged on the hot liquid. 'When you wake up, you'll be grateful. You'll see what it feels like to be a real predator, and you'll thank me. You'll never stop thanking me, Julia.'

The blood was drowning her. It was thick in her throat, burning in her sinuses as she choked against the assault. It bubbled messily from around his wrist, spraying his face red as she coughed out each breath.

'Don't fight it,' he said. 'Don't fight me.'

He took his wrist away, giving Julia one blessed second of relief before he was on her again, this time diving towards her neck. She had the barest moment to brace herself for the agony of it before his teeth sank into her skin.

And then… nothing. There was no pain, no terrible aching draw of blood through her veins, just a slight sting, as though a bug had bitten her.

Rufus grunted his confusion, then pulled his face away to stare at the nick he'd left on her throat. He tried again, biting at her neck so hard it pinched, but this time his teeth barely pierced the skin.

'What have you done to me?' he said.

Nothing.

She'd done nothing.

'Have you *cured* me?' he yelled, scrambling off her and over to the other side of the room. 'Is this some plan that you and Lucas cooked up together? I thought we had something, Julia. I thought this *meant* something.'

Julia rubbed at her neck, feeling the little divots Rufus's teeth had left in her skin, but there was so little blood. Just one tiny smear on her palm, one drop of contamination.

But it couldn't be the cure. She hadn't even cracked the lid on the bottle before Rufus had poured it all away. There was no more contamination in her blood now than there had been when Lucas had drunk from her last night.

'I didn't,' she said. 'I mean, you took the blood away, remember?'

But the suspicion that had been building at the back of her mind surfaced now, gathering momentum until it wouldn't be denied: her blood was contaminated after all.

She remembered Galatea telling Julia that her transfer had never failed, not until Julia tried it. And that wasn't all, was it?

There was the Weeper she'd fought in the forest, his blood in her scraped palms and his fingernail embedded in her skin. Then there was the deer she'd killed and eaten in the Red. It would surely have carried the cure in its blood, blood that should have turned Lucas human.

Which could only mean one thing: Lucas was immune to the cure.

'Why is everything so quiet?' Rufus said. 'What's wrong with me?'

Julia stared at him, watching him walk back towards her on unsteady legs, like a newborn foal. He knelt at her feet, taking her face in his hands.

'Julia,' he said. 'Please.'

He kissed her quickly, rushing up to meet her lips, but something was different this time. It took Julia a moment to realise that he tasted only of blood and wine. The lemon was gone, and there was no trace of the scent on the air.

'It's not working,' he said, pressing his nose into Julia's skin as he sniffed at her. 'Why is it not working?'

Julia put her hand on his chest and pushed him away, shoving him so hard that he sprawled onto the floor in front of her.

They stared at each other.

'I think you *are* human,' she whispered.

Which was not altogether a good thing. She'd unleashed the cure, but it wasn't time yet. Two weeks, they'd said. Two weeks for Cam and Felix to take out the army, but it had only been one. It was all happening too soon.

But Julia was prepared to make the most of it.

This is it, she thought. *This is how I cure them all.*

Rufus got to his feet and lunged at her, but he was so uncontrolled that it was the work of a moment to roll him onto his back and trap him beneath her.

'Welcome to the human race,' she said as she drew the knife from her boot.

It took a second for him to focus on it, to see it hovering over his heart, and his eyes went wide.

Then it came to her: this was what she wanted. She wanted to wield over him the power and control that he'd had over her. She wanted to feel the rush of strength that filled her now as she watched his understanding turn to fear.

Because she didn't want *him*, she'd never wanted him in any good way. What she wanted was to dominate him. To have him at her mercy, that was the purest kind of vindication. She wanted to hold his life in her hands and slowly, so slowly, close her fists.

That would feel like freedom.

But it was his kind of freedom, the kind that exploited and damaged because it knew there would be no consequences. So she made a choice: she wouldn't let it happen that way.

'I never wanted you to mark me,' she said. 'That was never what this was about. What I wanted was to mark *you*, the way you marked us.'

Julia could see the realisation in his eyes as she made her strike, but he was unused to his sluggish human reaction times. She'd already slashed the first cut into his skin by the time he clasped her wrist, and even then his grip was weak. She swapped hands to add the second mark, carving a bloody cross on his cheek.

Contaminated.

And then, at last, she felt satisfied.

'That'll leave a scar,' she pronounced.

She left him bleeding. When she stepped out into the day, all she took with her was the knife and a cloak. Everything else, she left behind.

* * *

'Lucas,' she called, running after him as he crossed the square. She'd waited in the alley by the temple, watching the guardhouse until he'd emerged at dusk. It had felt too reckless to go knocking on the Invicti's door.

He kept on walking.

'Lucas!'

'What is it, Julia?'

'I wanted to talk,' she said. 'To apologise.'

'I haven't got time for this now.' But then he noticed the blood on her neck, on her cheek, and he stopped walking. 'What have you done?' he asked, dragging her into a side street while he stared at the bloody knife shoved into her belt.

'Lucas, you're immune.'

'What? What are you talking about?'

'I'm contaminated. Maybe I've always been, since Galatea, or maybe it's just happened recently, but I'm contaminated. You drank from me, remember? By the boundary fence.'

Lucas closed his eyes for a second and took a breath, savouring the memory, or perhaps trying to forget it. 'I remember,' he said.

'And then today Rufus drank from me.' A flash of anger crossed Lucas's face, but she hurried on. 'He's human, Lucas. My blood cured him. Rufus is human.'

'Rufus is… So that's…' His eyes darted down to her blade. 'Please tell me you didn't.'

'Just a shallow wound.'

He looked at her, at her knife, and finally at the feeble bite mark Rufus had left in her neck. 'So that blood all over you, that's contaminated?'

'Ah, yes.' She hadn't thought about that. She'd just run from Rufus's house without a backward glance. She was so used to the gore of the Red that it hadn't occurred to her that walking around the Blue covered in contaminated blood probably wasn't a good idea. 'I'll clean it up,' she promised, 'as soon as I get back to Livia's. I'll burn the dress.'

But before she could protest, Lucas had leaned towards her, his lips closing over the wound at her neck. Then she felt the puncture, the skin yielding under his teeth in a way that it hadn't for Rufus. Only a little, though. This wasn't a feeding, this was a test.

He took one long, languorous pull from her veins, setting her knees wobbling. She may have moaned a little as well, but all too soon he was pulling away from her, leaving the silver mark of his healing on her neck.

'Watch my eyes,' he said, showing her his silver.

But nothing changed. His irises were still filled with the shining filaments that proclaimed his love for her, still silver, still waiting for Julia to turn them gold.

'Am I still Silver?' he asked.

'Yes,' she said. 'You're still Silver.' But what she was thinking was: *you still love me*. After everything she'd put him through, after rejecting him and coming to him now doused in the scent of Rufus's mark, he still loved her. How was that possible?

But he wasn't happy. He leaned back against the wall behind him, his head thudding into the stucco. 'This can't be happening.'

'Don't you realise what this means?' Julia said.

'This *cannot* be happening.'

'If you're immune, then maybe...'

'What?' Lucas said, his gaze snapping to hers.

She shrugged. 'Maybe you're the missing prince.'

He groaned and tipped his head back again.

'Why aren't you happy?'

'Because if I'm the prince, then all of this is my fault. I'm the reason everyone's going missing. If it's true then the Queen, the person responsible for making them disappear, is my *mother*, and in the meantime I can't find the one person who really deserves that title. I can't find Baba. I've looked all over, but no one knows where she's gone.'

Alba, missing. Why did that sound familiar?

Then it came to her.

'Livia mentioned she hadn't been able to find her,' Julia remembered, 'but that was weeks ago, before I left.'

Lucas turned to look at her. 'You're sure?'

'That's what she said.'

'Then I need to see Livia. Baba might still be safe.' He pushed away from the wall and started back towards the square. 'Goodbye, Julia.'

'Lucas–'

The gong rang out and Lucas froze. Seconds later, doors were already opening around the square, disgorging streams of people on their way to the palace.

'You've got to leave,' he said, turning back to her.

'What do you mean? That's the gong. We have to–'

'You have to leave.' There was panic in his voice now, pitching it high and strange. 'You're contaminated. You can't stay in the city. Do you know what they do to contaminated people they find in the city? You need to run, now.'

'Don't be ridiculous. You're not going to tell anyone, are you?'

'And you think that means people aren't going to know? Do you think Rufus isn't going to tell them? You have to go, Julia, and you have to do it now.'

But she couldn't. She had to wait another week. That's all it would take.

'No,' she said. 'I'm not running. Not anymore.'

Lucas stepped closer, his eyes pleading her to change her mind. 'Please don't make me turn you in.'

Julia couldn't believe what she was hearing. 'What are you talking about?'

'I'm one of the Invicti,' he said, speaking as though the word weighed a hundred tons. 'I'm sworn to the King. I've sworn to protect the Blue.'

And I've sworn to destroy it.

There was no way this could end well.

'So that's it?' she said, hand on her blade. 'You've become one of them, and nothing else matters? All the training, all this living under each other's feet. They've moulded you in their image. This person you've become, this isn't you.'

'And what have you become?' he said. '*Rufus*, Julia?'

'That was necessary to save Marcella. I'm sorry it hurt you, but it wasn't real. It didn't mean anything,' she said, although she wasn't entirely sure that was true. But she did know one true thing: 'It's over, anyway. You and the Invicti, when's that going to end?'

He looked confused at the suggestion. 'Never, I hope. You don't know what they've given me.'

'But I know what they've taken away. Have you forgotten what this city is? You used to want to change it.'

'I wanted to leave it.'

'And suddenly you don't?'

He pushed his hand back through his hair, tumbling the dark strands into a mess that she wanted to touch. It was a fleeting impulse, called to mind by the memory of her fingers on his skin, but it made her miss the intimacy they'd once shared.

There would be no going back now.

'I've found my place here,' he said.

'And you're telling me there's no place here for me. So yet again, we need to be apart.'

The gong sounded once more. Lucas looked towards the square and Julia knew she was losing him. This boy, this man who loved her, was slipping away as their paths diverged.

But she didn't want to let him go.

She grabbed his cloak and pulled him to her, backing against the wall so he framed her body with his arms.

'Julia, what are you–'

She went up on her tiptoes, offering him her lips, but he put his hands on her shoulders and pushed her back down.

'Don't,' he said, his nose wrinkling. 'Rufus's mark…'

'Then you mark me instead.' She pulled him closer. 'Please, Lucas. Please don't walk away from this.'

He hesitated, looking off towards the square, but Julia took his cheek in her hand, bringing his gaze back to hers.

'I'm sorry,' she said. 'I missed you.'

'But you wanted *him*,' Lucas sneered. 'I felt it through the bond, so don't try to tell me it's not true.'

She'd let that detail of the bond's function slip her mind. She'd done her best to forget it, because it was too awful to contemplate that Lucas might have felt her ambivalence.

'Maybe it was true,' she admitted.

'I felt it this morning,' he said, clenching his jaw. 'If you can't even admit your feelings to yourself then how can I believe you?'

'Then maybe it *is* true, but it's not what I'm choosing. When the choice is mine, truly mine, with no threats hanging over the heads of the people I love, I will *never* choose Rufus. I'll choose you, Lucas. It'll always be you.'

But he was shaking his head. 'I love you. You know I love you, and I can't stop feeling how I do about you, but I can't let you break me either.'

'Then let me prove it to you.' She grabbed at his shirt, holding him in place. 'You say you can feel what I feel through the bond, so listen to it now. What am I feeling, right now? If I'm pining for Rufus, the person I just cured and left behind me, then walk away and I'll never bother you again. But if the bond says I want you then please, Lucas, please give me another chance.'

He put his hand over hers as though he was about to push her away, but when he touched her he froze. He let his fingers linger on her skin, then slipped them along her arm, staring as he followed their movement with his eyes.

'I can feel you,' he whispered as he met her desperate gaze, his eyes wide as though he were seeing her for the first time. 'When I let myself. When I touch you.'

'I want you to touch me,' Julia said, pressing her palm against the side of his neck. 'Can you feel that?'

His eyes darkened and for a moment she worried that he'd read something in her that she hadn't intended. That worry increased as he broke eye contact and started scanning the street. A moment later he was hauling her into the building behind them and slamming the door at their backs.

'It's abandoned,' he said.

His words panicked her initially, but then one of his hands was on her waist, his other on her cheek, pulling her close. When their lips met, Julia felt like crying with relief. His mark was rolling over her already, the mint washing away the lemon as though it had all been a bad dream. He soothed her with it, offering himself to her like a gift rather than a challenge, because this wasn't the combative seduction Rufus had used on her. There was no game here, no fight to be won. It was so simple that she didn't even have to think about it, she just let him take her in his arms and kiss her.

By the time the gong rang for the third time, the two of them were watching the square from the rooftop. They lay on their bellies, tucked behind drifts of broken furniture and branches that had been stacked up for this winter's firewood.

Julia couldn't make out much of what was going on beneath them, but Lucas heard every word.

'They're checking everyone again,' he whispered.

'For what?'

'Contamination, they say.'

The Queen was standing on the palace steps beside the Empress, dressed in a shirt and trousers that clung tight to a figure so bare it was almost painful to watch. She looked like one of the humans Julia had sometimes seen released from the cells, so drained of blood that they were deflated, flesh flattened against bone. As the Queen walked towards the front of the platform, Julia could see the shake in her legs even from this distance.

'She's calling women out of the crowd to come to her,' said Lucas.

'Why?'

'Because that's what happens now. She gets them up on the steps, asks them questions and watches their reactions, listening to their heartbeats to see if they're lying.'

Julia watched as an older woman climbed the steps towards the Queen, half dragged by a member of the Invicti.

'This is what you do now?' Julia whispered.

Lucas didn't answer, he just kept his eyes fixed on the action in the square below. There were words exchanged, then the Queen leaned close to the woman, staring into her face. A few more mumbled words.

'Dammit,' Lucas murmured.

'What?'

But the woman was already being hurried down the steps and around the side of the palace. She barely struggled, but there were murmurs from the crowd as the guards led her away.

'What did she say?' Julia asked. 'Was she lying?'

Lucas grimaced. 'She wasn't very complimentary about the Queen.'

Before Lucas could expand on that, a boy was summoned up, perhaps fifteen or sixteen. The Queen accepted a cup from the Empress, then passed it to the boy. He hesitated, but eventually he drank its contents back.

'He's a Noble,' Lucas said through gritted teeth, 'one whose parentage isn't exactly clear.'

'A Noble? What's–'

'At least he was,' Lucas interrupted. 'He's not anymore.'

The boy was quickly led off in the same direction as the woman, too weak to fight the Invicti now, and then the Queen was summoning her next target.

'What will they do with them?' Julia asked. 'The woman and the boy?'

'The same thing they do with everyone these days: they'll put them outside. The boy will probably be okay – he's contaminated after all – but the woman…'

She'd turn into a Weeper. The first time she encountered one, she'd be turned into one of them. No wonder there were so many on the island these days.

'This is madness,' Julia said. 'Tell me you can see that. Please tell me you don't think this is right.'

'I know it's not, but I swore an oath.'

'So did I.' She whispered the words so softly that at first she thought Lucas hadn't heard, but then he turned to look at her.

'Who to?' he asked. Suspicion pinched his brows in a way that made her reluctant to tell him. He was one of them now, she reminded herself, and he was scrutinising her too closely.

'What if it was one of the Invicti?' she asked.

'Not possible.' He looked back down at the square.

'Because none of them have ever gone against the word of the King? What about Lorelei? What about Alistair?'

'Because the Invicti who survived the purge wouldn't betray him, that's why.'

Cam's words came back to her then.

'You can't betray something you don't believe in,' she said.

'But I believe in him.'

Julia looked over at the palace, where the King stood silently by as the Queen and the Empress herded more people up the steps. She couldn't understand why the King would allow this. Where was the man who'd helped her escape from the Blue? It was as though he'd been washed away in the blood of Lorelei's traitors, leaving only a ghost of himself behind.

'I don't know how you can believe in any of this,' she whispered. 'Look at him, Lucas. Do you want to fight for someone who would let this happen?'

Lucas shook his head. 'You don't understand.'

'Then explain it to me. What don't I understand?'

'I belong here,' he said, his voice growing louder. 'I belong with them. For the first time in my life, I belong somewhere. They accept me. They're my family, Julia.'

'Then why aren't you stepping up now? The Queen's searching for the prince, isn't she?' She turned onto her side so she could face him. 'That's what this is all about, isn't it? She's searching for *you*. She's questioning these women and testing the boys with contaminated blood because she's trying to find *you*, isn't she?'

'She's trying to find the prince,' Lucas said, with a sputtering spark of defiance.

'Lucas: you are the prince. You'd pass the test she just put that boy through, and you know it. We both do. You could stop all of this in a second. You could end this, so why are you still here? If this is where you belong, with the King and his Invicti, then why aren't you already running up those steps and taking your place at their side? They're your parents, her and the King, so why aren't you claiming them?'

He pushed himself to his feet and walked away, but not towards the stairs or towards the square. He wasn't leaving, he was just trying to evade the question.

'Fine, then I'll tell you why,' Julia went on. 'Because you know it's wrong. Because you don't want any part of this, do you?'

His back was turned to her, but she saw his shoulders sag. She stood and went to join him.

'I don't have a choice, do I?' he said. 'The only way to stop this is to hand myself over.'

'Not the only way. I'm going to change it,' she said softly, putting a hand on his shoulder to turn him towards her. 'The King waking up didn't change the Blue, and bringing the Queen back just made things worse, but we can cure this city.' She put her finger to the stains down her front then held it up, letting him see the blood.

'You're not serious.'

'Can you think of a better way? I don't want to give you up to them any more than you want to hand yourself over. This way, no one ever has to know. With my blood, we can cure the Nobles and make the humans immune to the Weepers. We can wipe the Weepers out, Lucas. We can actually make things better here, and I'm not the only one who thinks that.'

Lucas's eyes narrowed. 'Who?'

There was that scrutiny again, the suspicion that made Julia worry whose side he was on. She shook her head.

'Then don't tell me,' he said. 'Just tell me why.'

But she could find no words to explain the fundamental morality that drove her. He must have noticed her hesitation, because he put his arms around her and pressed a kiss to her lips.

'Convince me, Julia. Please.'

So she tried. 'You used to tell me fairytales, do you remember? They were about places where people lived together in a way that was fair. You told me stories about knights fighting dragons, clever children overpowering witches, and girls who killed their own monsters. Maybe you don't understand this because you're a Noble, but Lucas, *you're* our monsters.'

'The Queen, I know she's–'

'That's not what I'm saying.' Julia pressed her palms against his chest, trying to make him hear her meaning. 'It's the Nobles, all of you. You're what terrifies us. The worst of you, the ones like Rufus and the Queen, they know how to use us up. But even the best ones, the ones like you, still need our blood. You're still our monsters. You're what we have to kill.'

His arms loosened around her. 'You want to kill us now?'

'I won't need to if the Nobles are all turned human. Don't you see? This is the only way. With all of us human and contaminated, we have a chance to save this place. Without it, the Weepers will be a threat to the humans, contaminated humans will be a threat to the Nobles and the Nobles will keep the uncontaminated at their mercy. It's getting worse every day.'

He looked away for a few seconds, and when he looked back at her his expression was defeated. 'I know,' he said. 'This isn't a fight the Nobles can win, is it?'

'I don't think so. I think all we'd be doing is hurrying the inevitable. They're getting desperate, Lucas, and it's making them dangerous. You know what the King's allowing. You saw what happened today. How many more days like that can the Blue survive?'

He nodded, but he wasn't looking at her. His eyes drifted into the distance, unfocused and thoughtful.

'Look, maybe I could tell you a fairytale this time,' she said. 'And it wouldn't be a story about a lost prince who falls in love with a serving girl, because that's just where it started. Why don't we write the ending instead, about a girl who wants to save her people, and a knight who'll defy his King to do what's right. We could make that our fairytale. We could make it mean something, Lucas.' She took his face in her hands, looking into his eyes. 'I'd risk my life for this, but I'd be risking yours as well. So you need to tell me: what's our story?'

He pulled her close, holding her for a moment before he answered. 'It's about a girl warrior,' he whispered eventually. 'Determined enough to walk into the Red alone, strong enough to come back with allies and a plan, and the will to see it through. It's about the boy who loves her trying to earn the right to stand at her side.'

'Don't say that,' Julia whispered, the guilt of Rufus's kisses weighing on her conscience. 'I have plenty to make up to you.'

'Then we'll make an ending,' he said. 'I'm with you. I'm with you until the end of this, and after that we can start again. We don't have to have a *happily ever after*. We could have a *once upon a time* instead.'

'Alright,' she smiled. 'We'll cure them all, then start a new story.'

'And the ones like me and the Queen, who can't be cured?'

'Oh, don't worry about that,' said Julia. 'My ally has a plan, and he's on his way.'

14

'It was all just a distraction,' Felix said as they emerged from the wreckage of Charlestown. He and Cam had purged it over the past few hours, curing the Silver stragglers and contaminating all the humans. They'd also snatched the Red Shirts' remaining blood supply, which wasn't that impressive: twenty-odd bottles in total. It wouldn't last long.

'Alistair set it up as a contest,' Felix said. 'First one to find the prince gets to rule the Blue when the Red Shirts and Charlestown conquer it. But he never intended to play. He already knew who the prince was.'

'Alistair knows?'

'He does.'

'And?'

Cam turned to Felix, but the woodsman just shrugged.

'Shit,' Cam said. He stopped walking, stuck for what to do next. He was supposed to find the prince, cure all the Silver in the Red, then meet Julia back in the Blue. So far he'd achieved only one of those things, and that only partly.

'And the Red Shirts?' he asked, hoping they might know something.

'They're idiots,' Felix said, striding on towards the trees. 'It wasn't until they got me back here and Hans recognised me that they realised *I* wasn't the prince. By then, Alistair was already on his way to the Blue.'

Felix told Cam the rest of the story as they made their way across the rubble that surrounded Charlestown.

Hans had risen up to lead the Red Shirts after their defeat by the Invicti, but his authority was not well-established. That had presented an irresistible opportunity to Alistair, a way for him to get the extra fighters he needed without making a single concession to them. So that's exactly what he'd done. He'd used dissidents to divide the Red Shirts, sowing rebellion through the ranks. The soldiers had split and squabbled, by turns fearful in the face of their defeat and grasping at the opportunity for power the disarray presented. In the end, half the Red Shirts had been fed up enough to desert and join Alistair, leaving the rest to squabble on.

Those left behind had tracked the deserters to Charlestown, but by the time they'd arrived, Alistair and the others had already gone. Blame had been thrown, and the Tacitum were sent out on a last-ditch mission to find the prince.

But that hadn't been enough for the remaining Red Shirts. They'd been tired of being caught on the back foot, and had started to question whether Hans was the right man for them to follow. Then, inevitably, those who'd opposed him had presented an alternative leader. Felix hadn't recognised the name, and it hadn't mattered anyway, because the new hopeful had been slaughtered in the fighting that had broken out as his followers attempted to stage a coup. They'd used a lot of contaminated blood, and hundreds had been cured on both sides, from offensive and friendly fire alike. That was why Cam had arrived to find so few of them still alive, so little uncontaminated blood, and so many bodies strewn across the barricades.

In the meantime, Alistair and his new army had used the distraction to cover their tracks and disappear.

'They've gone to join the Empress, Cam,' Felix said. 'They're going to take over the Blue.'

'Shit. Alistair must already have Emmy's son.'

Felix raised an eyebrow. 'Or he's been in the city all along.'

'No,' Cam groaned, but it was a definite possibility. 'You think we're going to get back and find this Barbara woman in the Blue?'

Felix gave him an equivocal look.

What a kick in the teeth that would be, to have spent weeks out here looking for the boy only to find out that he'd been right under their noses the whole time. But whether he was with Alistair or already in the Blue, Cam and Felix's direction of travel was clear.

'Well, either way, we've got to head back there,' said Cam. 'With any luck, we'll be able to intercept Alistair before he reaches the city.'

'Then we're running?' Felix grinned.

'Don't tell me you missed me carrying you around.'

He reached out and took Cam's hand. 'I don't hate it.'

'Well, good, because yes, we're running. If we're going to have any chance of catching up with them, then there's no time to lose.'

They weren't going to make it to the Blue in a straight shot. Twenty bottles of blood was a lot, but not enough to get them all the way there, so they made a quick detour to the vůdce's island.

Unfortunately, they weren't the first ones to have that idea.

Cam could already smell the blood as they climbed down the cliff face, and by the time they were across the water the odour was thick in his nostrils. When they reached the shore, Felix jumped down from his back, trying to avoid the dark patches glistening on the rocks. There were a lot of them.

Their steps slowed as they walked along the tideline, not because they were marking the tracks across the ground, nor because they were trying to interpret the path of the violence that had been wrought on this place, but simply because they didn't want to reach the centre of the island.

It would be a known thing, then. When they saw it, *really* saw it, they wouldn't be able to deny what had happened here.

And yet somehow, when they finally rounded the corner into the camp, it wasn't as bad as Cam had imagined. That was the worst of it, because if they hadn't seen the blood on the path, if they couldn't smell the stench of decay, then they might almost have believed that everyone was taking an impromptu nap. People were clustered around the fires, knives in their hands as though they'd dropped into a slumber in the middle of their work. The bodies in the caves were the worst: mothers curled around their children, holding them tightly against the world. That hadn't saved them from the force that had broken this settlement apart. Nothing could have done that. The only thing that had kept them safe this long was the simple fact of their concealment.

Once they'd been found, that was the end.

'Did they follow us?' Cam asked Felix. 'Is this our fault?'

But Felix didn't answer him. He was already walking off towards the far edge of the camp, where a familiar figure was sitting crosslegged in front of a dying fire. Her chin had dropped down onto her chest, but her pipe was still clutched in one hand. In the other, she held a sheet of paper crumpled between her fingers.

'Can you scent them?' Felix called over his shoulder.

Cam closed his eyes, letting his senses search under the overwhelming glut of the blood. He knew what he'd find, and sure enough, there it was.

'Silver violence,' he said, 'a lot of it. And Alistair.'

'They're still stiff.' Felix said, teasing the paper out from between the dead vůdce's fingers. 'This happened maybe a day ago, I'd guess.'

Cam joined him by the fire, kneeling in the sandy dirt, and watched over Felix's shoulder as he smoothed the paper flat. It was coarse, grey and thick, but still finer than most paper they saw these days. The ink that marked it was higher quality too, unfaded and clear.

'Can you read it?' Felix asked, passing it back.

'Yes.' Cam's stomach dropped as he saw the shape of the words that curved across the page in neat little lines.

'What language is that?'

'English.'

Since the Fall, there was only one group of people that still used the language. It was archaic and ceremonial, having more in common with Latin than it did with the Romanian they spoke in the Blue, or the German, Spanish and Hungarian Cam spoke most commonly in the Red. But it was still sometimes used by those who had been living in England before the Weepers came, remembered only by those who had kept speaking it. To the Invicti it had become the language of their records, legible to the few who had lived through the world's demise.

This page had been ripped from the Invicti's records. Worse, Cam recognised the handwriting.

'It's from Viv's notebook,' he said.

Leaving it here was a message from Alistair to Cam, a proud middle finger that said: *this is your fault. I'm on my way, and you're lagging behind.*

'So they followed us here,' Felix said, 'and they wanted us to know it.'

Cam swallowed. 'It gets worse.'

Felix looked at him, waiting for him to elaborate.

'It's about me.' He smoothed the paper between his hands and worried at the corners as he traced the words across its centre. 'The words are about me. Things I said to Lorelei about the humans, things I said to Tommy. I think he knows what we're planning to do. And…'

Cam's eyes stuttered over the last line. This wasn't in Viv's handwriting, and it wasn't in ink either. It had been scraped onto the paper in charcoal, following on where Viv's final words had left off.

'And?' Felix prompted him.

Stay out of the way, or I'll cut the lumberjack down like a tree.

Cam couldn't say the words aloud.

'This bit here? It's a threat,' he said, then he looked up into Felix's beautiful blue eyes. 'Against you, if we interfere.'

Felix shrugged, but Cam wasn't taking it so lightly.

'I'm leaving you at the mountain lake with Ana,' he said. He balled the paper in his fist then threw it into the fire before rising to his feet.

'You're not.'

'I am.'

Felix followed him as he walked back towards the shore. 'Don't be childish, Cameron.'

'Look around you, Felix,' he said, his arms spread wide to encompass the blood-drained bodies that filled the settlement. 'All of these people are dead because of Alistair. I can't fight him if you're there. I just can't. I need to know that you're safe.'

'But you need me.' Felix took Cam's hands, wrapping them in his own. 'You need my blood so you can cure Alistair's army before it reaches the Blue. That's the plan, isn't it?'

'But that's not the only way I need you.' Cam broke one hand loose and cupped it around Felix's cheek, feeling the soft rasp of his beard against his palm. 'I can't lose you.'

'You're not going to.'

'But it doesn't have to be you. I can take the blood from Ana's settlement instead and leave you safe with them. After all, they gave us bottles of uncontaminated blood, so why not contaminated too? You don't have to be in harm's way.'

Felix smiled. 'You're just worried that–' he started saying, but then cut himself off. An unfamiliar look of panic crossed his face, then he said, 'How long have they been on our trail?'

Cam struggled to follow the non sequitur. 'What?'

'How long has Alistair been following us?'

'I don't know.' Cam picked back through his memories for any clue that he might have missed. 'There was nothing. It's not as though I haven't been paying attention, and how could they have tracked us? We were moving so fast, and when we came here the first time we came straight from… Oh god.' The bottom fell out of his stomach as he caught up with Felix's train of thought. 'Ana. Chloe. Alex. The lake. If Alistair followed us here, he must have picked up our trail before we got to the Carpathian mountains. He'll know we got uncontaminated blood from Ana's people.'

It swam before his eyes: his paradise, soaked in blood, just like this godforsaken rock.

'We have to get back there. Now.'

Cam felt like punching his frustration into the tree trunks, but that wouldn't help anyone, especially since they had no blood left to heal him up afterwards.

It hadn't even taken them as far as the mountain lake. The bottles he'd stolen from the Red Shirts had been old and degraded, as though the soldiers had been saving the last of their blood supply. They must have assumed their final battle would come to them in a guise different from the one they'd actually faced: a single, gangly, angry member of the Invicti.

They wouldn't care about it now that they were cured, but Cam regretted their lack of attention in keeping it fresh, almost as much as he regretted his own haste in contaminating the humans they'd found in Charlestown. If he'd been more circumspect, they wouldn't have had to spend the past three days walking.

'How long?' Felix asked as they trudged through the forest side by side.

'Another day, I'd guess. If we're lucky, we might make it by nightfall, but I doubt it.'

'But we'll keep going.'

It wasn't a question. They'd been running and walking for as many hours as Felix could manage, snatching only an hour or two of sleep here and there. Cam had carried Felix as much as he could, letting him rest in his arms, but it wasn't enough. Cam could see his feet dragging, making the woodsman clumsy in a way that he had never been before. His feet caught on tendrils of ivy, he walked into branches, and tree roots sent him staggering sideways until he resembled nothing so much as a Weeper.

He couldn't carry on like this.

'You need to sleep.'

'I'll manage.'

'Felix–'

'*Liebling*, I'm fine. Let's just get there first, and worry about sleep afterwards.'

They ran onwards, pushing their way through the undergrowth as they left the rolling foothills behind them. Soon they'd be climbing, and then the going would only get tougher.

'You never asked why,' Felix said.

Cam glanced over at him as they raced through the trees. 'Why what?'

'Why Alistair and the others wanted to find the missing prince.'

'I would've thought that was obvious. After all, he's Emmy and Sol's boy. Alistair's trying to take over the Blue, and if he has the prince then he can make them hand the city over to him in return for their son. It makes sense.'

Felix shook his head. 'But it's not the reason.'

'Then why does Alistair want him?'

'Same reason you do.'

'He wants to take him back to Emmy?'

'Nope,' Felix said, panting now as he ran. 'Alistair wants him because of his blood.'

'What?' Cam slowed to a walk, giving Felix time to recover his breath.

The woodsman bent over for a moment, resting his hands on his knees as he looked up at Cam.

'He found something out. Heard the others talking about it back in Charlestown. Thinks he can reverse the cure.'

'Can he?'

Felix shrugged.

'Shit.' Cam rubbed at the back of his neck. 'So he's trying to make a cure for the cure? Jesus, this is getting complicated. But Charles tried that with Emmy, and it didn't work. Why would

Alistair think it would work with her son? What's different about his blood?'

'Don't know,' Felix said, straightening up. 'Didn't hear enough to tell.'

'Did the Red Shirts think he'd be able to do it?'

'Yes, but that doesn't mean much. Gullible, remember?'

'Right, right.' Cam clasped his hands behind his neck. 'But if he did it, if Alistair managed to make something from the boy's blood that would turn cured Silver back to being Silver again, what then? We'd be screwed. There goes the plan, and there goes our advantage. He'd make the Empress Silver again, make everyone immune to the cure, and everything would just carry on the way it is. Nothing would change.' Cam pulled his hands over his head, dragging his hair forward into his face as he groaned.

'That's not true,' Felix said quietly.

Cam dropped his hands and looked at him.

'Something would change,' Felix went on. 'You could drink from any human you liked. Every Silver could, if you were all immune.'

'Shit,' Cam said again, kicking a nearby tree. 'You're right. And then none of you would be safe, because the Silver would just drink from whoever they liked. It'd be fucking carnage.'

'Like it was before the Fall?' Felix asked as they got moving again.

'No. No, before the Fall things were different. Well, before the Revelation. Humans didn't know we existed, and it made sense for us to keep ourselves hidden. There were so many of them and so few of us. But they know about us now. We can't go back to being their mythology, their monsters under the bed, at least not in our lifetimes.'

'Not in mine, anyway,' Felix said.

'Or mine. *Ich liebe dich*,' Cam reminded him. 'The bond is sealed. I die with you.'

Something flickered across Felix's face. 'And if we could use this cure for the cure?' he said. 'Turn me Silver again?'

'No,' Cam said softly. 'That's not what I would do.'

Felix's expression was impossible to read.

'Disappointed?' Cam asked.

But Felix just shook his head and ran on.

* * *

Eventually they started rising steadily, scaling the incline that would bring them to the basin of the mountain lake. The gradient wasn't helping Felix to stay steady. By the time the night closed in he was snatching his breaths, his hands shaking at his sides.

'Leave me,' he said. 'I'm slowing you down.'

'I'm not leaving you. I can carry you for the rest of the way.'

Felix shook his head, as he had so many times over the past few hours. 'Save… your strength. Might need it.'

'This is crazy. Let me help you, and we'll both get there quicker.'

It would mean Cam might not have anything left to give if there was a fight to be had at the lake, but at least they'd arrive sooner, and together.

But Felix just shook his head again. 'Go on ahead. I'll catch up.'

'I'm not leaving you.'

'Go!'

Felix's eyes were chips of ice, shining with determination, but still Cam hesitated. He was stuck between the urgency of getting to Ana's people and the sheer horror he felt at the idea of leaving Felix behind, particularly now that he was this worn out. There were wolves and bears in these woods, and if Alistair came for him now then he wouldn't stand a chance.

'Please, Cameron,' Felix said, catching Cam's hand to draw them both to a stop. 'Go. I'll follow.'

Cam searched Felix's tired eyes, but there was no room for argument in that look of his. He'd made his decision. Cam could only hope that everything at the lake was as it should be, so he could come right back here to fetch Felix to safety.

'Alright,' Cam breathed, tugging Felix closer until their foreheads rested against each other. Felix's was slick and cold. 'I'll see you in a couple of hours, alright? Promise?'

Felix pressed a kiss to Cam's lips. 'Promise.'

So Cam ran. He gave the distance all the speed he had, eating up the miles as fast as he could, but never fast enough to satisfy him. Still, it wasn't long before he was finally cresting the edge of the crater and looking down on the mountain lake.

It was still. There was no sound and, most worryingly, no light.

How late was it? Late enough for everyone to be in bed with their lanterns doused? Or just late enough that they should have been settling in front of their brightly-lit hearths?

It was impossible to tell, since Cam had lost track of time once night had fallen.

The moon reflected off the surface of the lake. It seemed about halfway up the sky, but it would track lower at this time of year, so Cam couldn't work out how close it was to its apex. For all he knew, it might already be midnight.

There was only one way to find out.

He tried to move silently down towards the huts clustered around the lake shore, but the shale slipped and slid under his feet so instead he arrived in a pattering shower of tiny stones. Holding his breath, he listened between heartbeats for the sound of movement.

No one was coming.

But that didn't mean the settlement was silent. He could hear the creak and slide of people shifting in their sleep, snoring gently into the night. That reassured him until the odour reached his nose: blood and broken bones, not coming from the area behind the hall that was designated for butchery, but from the far side of the cluster of huts.

That was where he found the graves, and that was where he found Ana.

'You came,' she whispered, her eyes fixed ahead. 'Too late, Domnul Cameron. Too late.'

'What happened?'

'They came for our blood, and they took until we had no more left to give.'

The old woman was wrapped in a blanket, her white hair unbound so the breeze plucked long strands of it free, swirling it out behind her. She looked as though she had come from her bed, bare feet shoved hastily into opincă – leather slippers that were too light for this weather. Her toes kissed the mounds of earth that hid their dead.

'When?'

'Two days ago.' She turned, facing Cam for the first time. The moonlight glittered off the sorrow that filled her eyes. 'I would think that nose of yours would tell you as much.'

'It doesn't tell me enough, Doamna Ana. Please tell me.'

She stared at him for a long moment, then let her eyes drop back down to the graves. 'Like you,' she said, 'they came in the night. They followed their noses to your cabin, and that's where we found them. Two of our men, good men, were the ones who found them. Our men assumed you had returned. They thought you'd crept to your bed so as not to disturb us, so they were taken by surprise. One was killed, the other forced to lead the invaders to my door.' She pulled the blanket more tightly around herself, shaking her hair loose from its constraints. 'They killed him at my feet.'

'Doamna Ana–'

But she carried on as though he hadn't spoken.

'They demanded that I reveal the uncontaminated amongst our number. By that point there were fewer – your friend Chloe had insisted that we contaminate everyone – but there were still nine who refused. The invaders gave me a choice.' She swiped at her nose, and the gesture drew attention to the shaking of her hands. 'I could either surrender the uncontaminated, or they would kill us all regardless. Everyone,' she said turning to him with pleading eyes. 'Everyone, against nine lives.'

He took her frozen hands in his, wrapping his warmth around them. 'There was no real choice,' he said. 'There was only one decision you could have made. I'm only sorry I wasn't here to prevent you from having to make it.'

She laughed softly, the bitter undertone of it cutting out across the lake at their backs as she reclaimed her hands and tucked them into her blanket.

'Choice,' she said. 'Decisions. Easy words for such a hard thing. They are my purpose, and they are mine to bear. Regardless of whether or not I had a real choice, as you say, I made it and I will live with it. My people don't have to, though. I'll let things settle, then step aside and take my decision with me. Let them blame me for it, because that blame is mine to carry.'

'No. I made a promise to you when I took the blood from you, and I broke that promise when I let the other Silver come to this place. Let the blame be mine, Doamna Ana, even if it means I can never return here.' As Cam spoke the words, his heart sank into his stomach. The thought of never coming back to this sanctuary, bloodied though it was; the thought of losing this place forever…

But Ana was already shaking her head.

'I don't blame you, Domnul Cameron. I am not a child, nor a fool. It was a vain hope that you might prevail over so many, but still I had hoped that you might. Hope.' She turned towards him, smiling as her tears began to fall. 'Such beggars it makes of us all, does it not? So much time spent scrabbling after things that might have been. We wish instead of doing, and mourn instead of moving on. The truth is that our losses were much smaller than they might have been, mostly because of Chloe's advice, and for that I am truly grateful. But still I cannot help but mourn that any losses occurred at all, and we both cannot help but feel the weight of those lives on our consciences. That seems to be the way of these things.'

They stood side by side for several minutes, watching the graves in silence.

Nine bodies' worth of blood, Cam thought. *Not enough to fuel an army for more than a few miles.*

It felt ghoulish to be so pragmatic, but urgency was pressing down on his shoulders. He needed to get back to Felix, and get on his way to the Blue.

'I'm sorry, Doamna Ana, but I have to leave you again. I need to go after them. Do you still have our horses? Sandor, and Darius's mare?'

But Ana didn't answer him. Instead, she said, 'They asked only for uncontaminated humans. They didn't ask after the bottles, so I didn't give them up. I knew you'd be back, as you always are.'

'Bottles?' Cam said.

'Our last. An emergency supply, if you like. Come with me.'

She led the way, shuffling quickly along the shore. Cam had expected that she might lead him to the hall, or perhaps to her own hut, but instead she kicked off her shoes and waded out into the shallows of the lake where a small boat was moored. She cast it free from the weight that anchored it, then hopped gracefully aboard as she slid the blades into their oarlocks.

Bewildered, it took Cam a moment to realise that he was supposed to be following her. He untied his own boots and rolled up his trousers, then splashed out to join her.

His mind couldn't help but flash back to the tidal path, the island, the bodies. Everything was locked together in blood and water, echoes and futures and this moment, right now, when the freezing water soaked his cuffs.

All he wanted was to get rid of the blood so he could make the water pure.

As it happened, that was exactly what Ana was intending him to do. Once Cam had scrambled into the boat, she sculled them out towards the centre of the lake with long, lazy strokes that belied their power. Even with Cam's enhanced vision, it took him a long time to work out their destination: a large wooden float that bobbed on the water's surface. When they reached it, Ana hauled on the line attached to it, tipping the boat to one side with her effort. Cam grabbed the object tied to its end as soon as it came into view beneath the dark glass of the lake.

It was a crate, filled with sixteen sealed bottles of uncontaminated blood.

'Doamna Ana, I don't know how to thank you.'

'Yes, Domnul Cameron, you do.' She reached over and squeezed his hand. 'So go and do what you must.'

There was a sound from beyond the lip of the lake basin, a howl racing up the side of the mountain from below.

'They come closer now,' Ana said as she picked up the oars again. 'More of them every day, calling at the moon like broken wolves.'

Weepers.

And Cam had left Felix alone in the woods.

'It won't be long before they come our way,' Ana went on, 'but we'll be ready for them. We know how to fight the dead.'

So did Cam, but he had to get to them first.

When they reached the shore, he took only a few moments to pack the blood into his bag and swig a bottle down, then he kissed Ana's hand and disappeared into the night.

The howls had intensified by the time Cam rose out of the lake's basin and plunged back down the wooded slopes. He was moving at Silver speed now, covering miles in seconds, but it still wasn't fast enough to reach the sickening howls before they peaked and, ominously, stopped.

There could only be two possible reasons for that: either the Weepers were dead, or they had their mouths full.

As it turned out, both were true.

The trees were thick here, so Cam heard the crowd before he saw them. He tumbled through the undergrowth just in time to watch the last of them falling. They had flooded towards Felix in a mass, maybe thirty of them, and the Weeper at the front had his teeth sunk into Felix's arm.

'Felix!' Cam yelled, but Felix was already detaching the Weeper's jaws from his flesh and kicking the body away from him. 'Are you alright?'

Felix smiled, holding up the shallow bite to show Cam. It was barely bleeding.

'How long did I live in these forests before you found me?' he said.

'Long enough,' Cam conceded.

'You worry about me too much.' Felix pulled a clean rag from his pack and used it to bind the wound closed, then he nodded up the mountains towards the lake. 'What's the news?'

'We're too late. Alistair's already been and gone. Eleven dead, nine of them uncontaminated.'

'I expected worse.'

'So did I. And there's some good news, as well: Ana set some more bottles aside for me, so I have enough uncontaminated blood to get back to the Blue.'

Felix looked up at Cam. 'You're not leaving me behind.'

Cam met his gaze. He didn't want to argue, because honestly he didn't want to let Felix out of his sight ever again.

'Alright,' he said, cracking open the first of the bottles. 'Then let's go and find Alistair.'

15

'Livia?' Julia called as they walked into the kitchen. 'Are you here? Is Alba here?'

There was no reply.

She went to the foot of the stairs, shouting up into Livia's quarters, but there was still no sound from the house. It felt empty and cold.

Too cold. Julia's insides churned as she realised what was missing, and rushed back into the kitchen to see that the hearth was full of burned-out ashes. Wherever Livia was, she must have been in trouble, because she never let the fire go out. *Never.*

'Wait,' Lucas said, catching her arm. His eyes slid along the corridor, towards the steps that led down to the cellar.

Julia froze. She listened for a few seconds and there it was: the undulating sound of a bottle rolling along stone.

'Oh, Empress,' Julia muttered, hurrying down the stairs.

'What?'

'The still. It's down here with her bucket brews, and the bottles of last year's stuff. She thinks she hides them, but she's not very good at it. If someone's got into them she'll be livid.'

But that wasn't what really worried her. She was remembering one evening a few years ago, when she and Claudia had come home late from the square to find Livia propped against the wall opposite their room with a bottle in one hand and a bundle of bloody rags in the other. They should have worked out about her private surgery back then, but after they'd cleaned her up and helped her to bed there'd been no more said about it. Julia and Claudia had preferred to forget the whole thing.

Livia was back in the same spot now, but this time her hands were empty. So was the bottle.

'My boy,' she whispered into her lap, then looked up at Julia with glazed eyes. 'You've killed my boy.'

Lucas and Julia exchanged a glance.

'Wasn't a good man,' Livia slurred. 'I know. You know he wasn't. She knew. Liked him that way, she did. But he... he... didn't *deserve...*'

Julia crouched down beside her. 'Livia–'

'And *you*,' she said, pointing a wavering finger up at Julia. 'Loved you, much as he could. Asked about you. *Cared*, in his way.'

'Livia,' she said, catching the old woman's hands in her own, 'I don't know what you're talking about.'

Livia crumpled, folding forwards to press her forehead against their joined hands. Julia pulled her closer, wrapping her in her arms.

'Grab the blanket from my bed,' Julia whispered to Lucas over Livia's head, nodding towards her bedroom door.

As soon as he was out of sight, Livia lifted her head again and said, 'Did you have to do it? Did he make you?'

'Do what?'

'My boy,' she sniffed. 'Why did you have to kill my Rufus?'

Oh no.

Rufus had practically told her, hadn't he? He'd said that Julia knew his mother.

Quite well, actually.

She should have put the pieces together sooner.

'He's not dead,' she said, rubbing Livia's back. 'When I left him earlier today, he was fine. He's just human, that's all.'

But that didn't seem to console her. 'She'll throw him out. S'where they all go, now. Chuck 'em out and watch 'em fall. Wait for 'em to die.'

She trailed off into incoherence as Lucas returned with the blanket. Julia wrapped it around Livia's shoulders, tucking it around a frame that seemed tiny without the force of her personality behind it. She was slumping sideways now, her face crushed against Julia's shoulder.

'I'll get her upstairs,' Lucas said, scooping Livia into his arms.

Julia just nodded and let him take her away, staring into the cracks in the stone floor as his footsteps climbed the stairs. When he came back a few minutes later, Julia hadn't moved.

'She's out cold,' he said. 'Look, about Rufus–'

'Can we not talk about it, please? I'm guessing you heard Livia, so you know what I know. Can that be enough?'

'Alright,' he said, looking down at his shoes for a moment. 'So what now?'

'Now we need to find the others. Is Claudia still at the palace?'

'She should be.'

'I'll need Marcella, too.' Julia was sure of that, despite Marcella's betrayal, or perhaps because of it. Marcella was an unknown risk that Julia couldn't afford right now. The goddess knew about the plan.

Which left Julia worrying about Rufus. Of course he would tell the Empress what Julia intended to do. Either they needed to act sooner than they'd intended, or they needed to get out of this house so they'd be harder to find. Probably both.

'I haven't seen Marcella,' Lucas said.

'So we start with Claudia.' Julia stood, gathering her energy for one more expedition into the dark city. The palace was as good a place to start as any.

But Lucas shifted his weight uncomfortably. He was reluctant.

'What's the matter?' she asked.

'I need to go on patrol,' he admitted. 'They're expecting me back at the guardhouse, then I'm supposed to go back to the fence. I'm with you, Julia, you know I am, but I can't just walk away from the Invicti. What would they say?'

'You go,' she said, stretching to her tiptoes to press a kiss to his cheek. 'I'll manage on my own.'

Lucas caught her around the waist and pulled her to him. 'I'll find you as soon as I'm done. Please try not to do anything too dangerous. And wait for me before you go to the palace.'

'But I have to find Claud.'

'Please.'

He kissed her, and somehow she found herself agreeing. She regretted it as soon as he'd left, but promises extracted with kisses didn't count, surely?

* * *

In the end, Julia was spared from having to break that promise because Claudia came to her.

Julia was in the kitchen, stoking up the fire so it would be warm in case Livia returned to consciousness before the next morning. It was unlikely, given that she'd managed to see away an entire bottle of her deadly home-brew, but Livia would need the warmth if she miraculously sobered up this evening. In any case, Julia reasoned it would be nice to be greeted by a fire when she came back from the palace through the cold night.

The courtyard door swung open, creaking on its hinges. At first Julia thought it was just the wind, but when she looked up, Claudia was standing in the doorway.

Julia smiled. 'I was just coming to look for you.'

'Then I've saved you a trip.' Claudia didn't smile back.

'Shall I put some tea on?'

'Real tea?' Claudia asked, closing the door behind her.

'Livia's asleep. She'll never know. Even if she did, I don't think she'd mind just this once.'

Claudia raised an eyebrow, but she didn't comment as she joined Julia by the fire. She kept her cloak on. Julia was still wearing hers too; it would take hours for the coals to warm the room.

'So–'

'You left,' Claudia interrupted, giving Julia a sidelong glance. 'Again.'

'Claud–'

'I was waiting for you, and you never showed. I looked everywhere, went knocking on doors, and no one knew where you'd gone. You should have told me. You could at least have asked someone else to tell me for you, if you couldn't be bothered to tell me yourself. You can't just disappear like that.'

'I'm sorry. There wasn't time.'

'Uh huh.'

'There wasn't.'

Claudia turned on her. 'And what else hasn't there been time for you to tell me? Something about Rufus, maybe, that you've neglected to share? Or maybe something about a plan to *kill everyone*?' She hissed the last words into a whisper.

Julia was taken aback. 'You think I want to kill people? I don't want to kill anyone. I just want to cure the Nobles.'

'It amounts to the same thing.'

'No, no it doesn't. I want to *stop* people from being killed, Claud, people like you and me. That's what this is about.'

Claudia folded her hands in her lap and pressed her lips together. This wasn't like her at all.

'Who told you?' Julia asked.

'Marcella came to the palace. She told me half of it. Rufus turning up this evening told me the rest.'

Rufus had made it to the palace, then. It wasn't surprising, but it was bad news nonetheless. Julia would have to move now.

'Have you told anyone else?' she asked.

'Is that all you care about?'

Julia reached out to take her hand, then thought better of it and turned the gesture into a move to hang the kettle over the fire instead.

'It matters,' she said. 'You must see that. If they know then they'll come for me.'

Claudia shook her head, her eyes finding Julia's. 'You know me better than that. I wouldn't do that. Marcella wouldn't, either. Rufus… I don't know. You tell me.'

Julia stood and walked to the corner cabinet on the other side of the kitchen, fetching out two cups and the teapot. The tea was there too, in Livia's wooden box. If ever there was a time to raid it, this was it. It might be Julia's only chance to get to Claudia.

'Did Marcella tell you what she did?' Julia asked as she returned to the hearth with the primed pot.

'Yes.'

'All of it?'

'Your plan? How she betrayed you to Rufus? The way you *kissed* him? Yes, I'd say she covered the important bits.'

So that's why Claudia was so angry.

'I was trying to save Marcella. But yes,' Julia hurried on as Claudia opened her mouth to argue, 'it was maybe more than that.'

Claudia's look was more jealousy than disgust. That worried Julia.

'How could you?' Claudia said, her tone dripping with betrayal.

'It wasn't what you think.'

'Then what was it?' Claudia scoffed.

The kettle was belching steam up the chimney, so Julia had a moment to gather her thoughts while she saw to it.

'It was almost like revenge,' she said eventually, filling the teapot, then sitting back in her chair as she let the leaves steep. 'Marcella said something to me. She said, *loathing is a force of attraction*. Maybe that's what it was. I don't know, but I took my chance to pay him back for both of us. You saw his face?'

'I didn't see much of anything.'

'I cut a cross into his cheek.'

The suggestion of a smile twitched at the edge of Claudia's mouth. 'You didn't.'

'I did.'

And there it was finally: Claudia's smile, flowing back onto her face with all the forgiveness it signalled. She might not understand what Julia had done, and it looked as though she was still confused about her own feelings for Rufus, but maybe they could move on from here.

'Imagine it.' Julia reached forward again, and this time she did take Claudia's hand in hers. 'I didn't know I was curing him, Claud. Not that I hadn't intended to in the end, but I had no idea I was contaminated at the time. And then… It was like nothing I've ever seen before. He was so *weak*. The way he fell.' She was talking quickly now as the excitement took her. 'The power of it. I can't describe that feeling. Now imagine what it would be like if we did it to all of them. If we cured them all, and took away their strength. Imagine what it would be like if suddenly we had as much power as they did.'

But Claudia didn't look convinced. 'We *can* have that power,' she said. 'You could have it any time you liked. That's what the Casting was for.'

'And how would that help you, if I were like them? How would it help anyone who wasn't chosen for the Casting? No. There's only one way to make this right.'

Julia leaned down to pour the tea, then held out a cup to Claudia. 'So, are you in?'

Claudia took the cup, but she didn't meet Julia's eye. There was no commitment there.

'I wish you'd told me sooner,' she said.

'I know, me too, but there really wasn't time. You've been at the palace. I didn't have any choice but to run when I did, because Rufus… Well, he made his intentions pretty clear. As soon as I got back I found out he'd taken Marcella, and there was nothing to do but go after her. You understand that, don't you?'

Claudia shrugged, but it was clear by now that she would be able to forgive, if not forget. She was just making Julia suffer a bit, but Julia guessed she probably deserved that. There was one surefire way to distract Claudia from a disagreement, though: gossip.

'Did you know Livia is Rufus's mother?' Julia asked.

Claudia looked up from her tea, her delicate mouth dropping open.

'No,' she said.

'Yes. Me and Lucas got back here this evening to find her rolling drunk in the hallway.'

'Like that time a few years ago?'

'Just like that, only with more of the drink.'

They were both silent for a moment as their memories took them back. The blood, the bottle, and Livia crying as though she were one of her girls, instead of the rock they all rested on. She'd always been the one who held them in line, and seeing her like that had felt so wrong that it had bewildered them both.

'Rufus's mother.' Claudia exhaled heavily. 'Well, they do say the Empress loved her. It explains a lot.'

'The necklace and the rooms? Yes, I suppose it finally does.' Julia remembered the other girls speculating about it, back when there had been others in this place. Now it was just her, Livia and this big, empty house. 'She's the one who told me to do this, you know.'

'You mean curing the Nobles?'

Julia nodded down at the teacup cradled between her hands, then reconsidered. 'Well, actually, no. She didn't tell me to do it. She suggested it in a way that made it seem like there was no other option.'

'Oh yes, that's Livia.' Claudia smiled.

'But now that it's come to it, and with Rufus being the first, I wonder whether she's changed her mind.'

'When have you ever known her to change her mind, Jules? She'd twist logic in circles if it meant she could say she'd never been wrong.'

Julia smiled then, too. It was true: Livia was nothing if not stubborn. She'd see past it in the morning. She'd have one mighty hangover, but she'd know that curing the Nobles was the right thing to do, even if it meant her son had to become human too.

'I just can't believe he came from her,' Claudia said. 'I wonder who his father is.'

'He didn't say.' As long as he wasn't related to Julia, she wasn't inclined to care.

She and Claudia sat together in companionable silence for a few minutes, letting the weight of their words settle over them. There was a distance between them that felt uncomfortable. Uncomfortable enough that Julia didn't know how to ask her next question.

'Claud,' she said eventually, 'I worry about you up at the palace. With everything going on with the Empress and the Queen, I want you to be safe.'

'I am,' Claudia said, but she looked away into the fire as she spoke.

'We both know that's not true. No one's safe in this city.'

'But there's no safer place for me to be. The Empress likes me. I do alright.'

'I can make you safer.' Julia took a breath, then let it out. 'I want to contaminate you.'

'What? No!' Claudia had been leaning forward in her seat, elbows propped on her knees, but now she pulled back, taking her teacup and her hands out of reach.

'You'll be safer that way,' Julia insisted. 'You've seen what they do now, throwing people out into the Red. If that happens to you and you're not contaminated, you won't stand a chance.'

'And if I contaminate myself then the first Noble who drinks from me will be cured, and then I'll be sent out into the Red for sure. They've got no reason to turn on me. Why would I give them one?'

'You think they need a reason?' Julia said. 'They're Nobles. You've seen what the Queen and the Empress have been doing. How can you stand behind that? They don't have any loyalty to you, Claud, and they don't deserve yours. Please, let me help.'

But Claudia took one last swig of tea, put the cup aside and got to her feet.

'I wish you wouldn't do this,' she said.

Julia sighed. 'And I wish I could make you see how wrong this city is. I wish you understood how much it needs to change.'

'Nothing's ever perfect.'

Julia laughed bitterly. 'The Blue is very far from perfect.'

But Claudia had never seen anything better. She hadn't seen the mountain lake, or the community Sabina had forged in the forest. To Claudia, the Blue was all there was, and living in the palace was more than she had ever hoped for herself.

'I wish I could show you what it's like out there,' Julia said.

'With the Weepers? I'd rather not, thank you.' Claudia was walking towards the door now, but Julia couldn't let her leave. She needed to keep her away from the palace and the Nobles' teeth, just until she'd finished her part in the plan.

'Don't go.' Julia said, standing from her chair. 'Please. Do me a favour and stay with Livia.'

Claudia stopped walking.

'Why? Where are you going?' she said.

'Somewhere it'll be harder for Rufus to find me. They'll manage without you at the palace for a night, won't they? I'd just feel better if someone were here for her when she wakes up. Please, Claud.'

'Fine.' She crossed her arms over her chest sulkily. 'I suppose I owe her that much.'

'Yes, you do. We both do.'

Claudia looked across the kitchen at Julia. She'd seemed defiant just a moment before, but now her lips were pressed together as though she were trying to hold back her tears.

'How did we get here, Jules?'

Julia wanted to comfort her, but there was nothing she could say. They were on opposite sides of this, each of them stuck in their own idea of what was best, and neither was going to be able to lever the other out of their rut.

'We grew up,' Julia said. 'We chose different paths, or they were chosen for us.'

'And now you're trying to choose for both of us.'

'No, I'm choosing for all of us. I know that's arrogant and high-handed, but it's what I think is right. I have to do it, and I'm asking you to let me.'

Claudia stepped away from the door, resting her palms on the counter that stood between the two of them, and it struck Julia for the first time how out of place she looked here now. She'd been just like Julia once, scrubbing vegetables by her side, but now

Claudia seemed to glow. Her clothes were clean, her nails well-manicured, and her hair had a lustre to it that hadn't been there before. While Julia's scars remained pink and raised on her neck, the bite mark on Claudia's pale skin was now little more than a ghost's kiss.

She was cared for in the palace, and it showed.

No wonder she didn't want to give it up.

'I won't tell them,' Claudia said, 'but I won't let you contaminate me, either.'

Julia let out a long breath.

'That's enough, for now,' she said. 'Thank you.' Impulsively, she moved around the counter and pulled Claudia into her arms, pressing a kiss against her cheek. 'Whatever happens next, I love you. I love you so much, Claud.'

'I love you too, you wilful idiot.' Claudia sniffed, wrapping her arms around Julia, and Julia felt the thunk of a tear dropping onto her hair. 'I just wish–'

'We both do. But this is the way it has to be.' Julia pulled away gently, smiling at her best friend in the world. She reached out to wipe the hair out of Claudia's tear-stained face.

'Look after Livia,' she said. 'I'll see you soon.'

'Take care, won't you?' Claudia said, wiping her eyes with the back of her hand.

'I will. And have another cup of tea,' Julia said with a smile. 'There's more in the pot, and it would be a shame to let it go to waste.'

Not that it mattered either way. The few drops of blood Julia had squeezed in with the tea leaves would already have put enough of the vaccine into Claudia's first cup to contaminate her.

The tea had served its purpose. Julia could only hope that Claudia would forgive her for it.

There was no more time to wait for Cameron's return. With Rufus cured and at the palace, and the Queen taking more and more people every day, Julia needed to act now.

She'd snatched the last few bottles of Livia's home-brew on her way out of the house. They were swaddled up with blankets in a bag she'd found in the cellar, but they still clinked gently as they rocked against her back. There was no one around to hear them as she moved out of the city, picking a path through silent streets.

The Blue was shrinking, and that was never more evident than after dark. What had once been a sprawling maze of busy streets and houses was now just a tiny cluster of light around the square, while the rest of the buildings remained unlit. Julia didn't have to walk long before she found an uninhabited house at the edge of the cluster, but still close enough to the others that smoke from its chimney wouldn't be a cause for suspicion.

Julia waited there, kindling a fire in the hearth. She unpacked the liquor next, lining it up in front of her as she sat crosslegged on the floor. The cut she'd made on her finger to contaminate the tea was still bleeding, but she used the blade of her knife to encourage the flow and to guide a couple of drops into each bottle, swirling it into the golden liquid. A few shakes later, and no one would be any the wiser.

She'd be able to make her deliveries when the morning came, and then there would be no turning back. For the moment though, she waited.

She wanted to sleep. After so long spent running from place to place, she wished she could curl up in front of the flames and let her eyes close, but it wasn't safe. Rufus would have told the Empress by now. Guards would be out looking for her soon, if they weren't already.

She had to wait.

She did so fearfully, wondering every second who would be the first to find her, and praying that it would be Lucas. Only he and a few of the Invicti would know her scent well enough to track her here, and she was relying on her assumption that those Invicti would protect her out of loyalty to Lucas, but she wasn't sure. She couldn't be sure.

So she waited.

The fire burned low. She threw a few more logs on, but that was the end of the stack. She'd have to start breaking down furniture if she wanted to be warm in the morning. Even now, with the roaring fire, the blankets from her pack and the rugs that carpeted the floor, she found herself shivering. The cold was inside her, in her bones, and it would be hard to shift.

When had she last eaten? She couldn't even remember.

The promise of something in her stomach was enough to shift her from the nest she'd made in front of the fire. A quick rummage in the larder turned up a few elderly potatoes. She buried them in the coals, slugging back a hit from one of the tainted bottles to ward off the chill in the meantime.

Then she waited.

She told herself she'd be better able to stay awake once she'd eaten, but by the time the potatoes were cooked through she was having to pinch the back of her neck to stop herself from falling asleep. Still, it was worth it. The soft, hot potato flesh was the best thing Julia had ever tasted. She used the blade of her knife to scrape out the innards, too impatient to wait for it to cool. When there was nothing but charred potato skin left, the roof of her mouth was burnt and blistered, but her belly was warm and full and that was all that mattered.

She could wait now, in this nest of warmth, until Lucas found her.

She could wait.

But the next thing Julia knew, she was swimming out of sleep as hands closed around her shoulders.

'I've got you.'

She tried to shake the fog from her head and the grip from around her body, but it held her strong. Her heart pounded so hard she felt as though it were trying to escape her chest, but then, slowly, she registered the voice, and its tone.

'Julia, it's me,' Lucas whispered. 'I've got you. Sleep,' he said, kissing her brow. 'I'm here. I've got you. Go back to sleep.'

With a sleepy sigh, she let him take her into his arms, warming her back as the fire warmed her front, lulling her back down into oblivion.

The next time Julia woke, it was to a sharp knocking at the door.

Lucas was already up, rebuilding the fire in the hearth. He looked at Julia and held a finger up to his lips, then made his way through the house to the front door.

Julia probably should have stayed where she was, but instead she bundled her blanket around her like a shawl and peered around the corner into the next room.

Lucas was already opening the door.

'Alistair?' he said.

Julia didn't recognise the man, but she did recognise the name. This couldn't be the same Alistair who'd run off to Charlestown though, could it? Not here in the Blue.

'Lucas, my lad. I followed your scent from the fence. Hope I'm not disturbing you. I wonder if we might have a wee chat.'

Lucas crossed his arms, barring the doorway with the breadth of his shoulders so that Julia could no longer see the stranger beyond.

'What are you doing here?'

The man laughed. 'Is it not obvious? I'm looking to make things right. Thought you might be willing to help.'

'After what you did?'

'What I did?' The man sounded almost offended. 'What did I do, really? I picked the wrong side, that's all, and then I fucked off out of your way and left you to it. I didn't cause any harm.'

'You betrayed us.'

'I can understand why the Invicti might see it that way, but you, lad–'

'I *am* one of the Invicti.'

Lucas took a step forwards and the man – Alistair – took a step backwards.

'Oh, aye,' he said. 'Yes, I see that. But come on, now. You must see things are changing round here. Laila's back in favour, I hear. Isn't that a good enough reason for a bit of reconciliation? Humour me. Come over to the palace and help me talk to the others. Go on,' he wheedled. 'For old times' sake. All those hours I spent training you to fight as one of us–'

'You're not one of us anymore.'

Lucas moved back inside the house, swinging the door closed, but Alistair held it open from the other side. There was just a crack next to the jamb to start with, but then he pushed, shoving Lucas back.

'You've forgotten me already? I'm offended.' Alistair walked past Lucas and strode into the room, taking in the mouldering air. 'Come on, lad. What are you doing out here, anyway?'

'Taking a break.' Lucas was still hanging onto the door, drawing Alistair's gaze back towards him and away from Julia. She took the cue and tucked out of view, flattening herself against the wall.

'Oh aye,' Alistair said. 'I know how it can get in the bunkhouse. All full of bodies and noise. Nice to have a wee bit of quiet. Shall we put on a brew, then?'

'I don't have anything here to offer you.' Lucas's tone was brusque.

'Aw lad, you don't know how to live. Well, aren't you going to invite me to warm myself by the fire, at least?' Julia heard his footsteps coming closer and screwed her eyes shut. It was a childish impulse, as though her being unable to see him would stop him from seeing her.

But Lucas called him back. 'I thought you wanted to go to the palace?'

'Keen now, are you?' Alistair laughed again, a confidential leer. 'I wonder why that would be?'

'Are you coming or not?'

Alistair's laughter followed them out into the street. Even after the door slammed behind them, Julia could hear it echoing beyond the walls.

He'd known she was here. He would have heard her heartbeat, her breath and the shuffling of her feet as she ducked out of sight. He had to have known.

Julia gathered up her things and prepared to move. If she didn't want Alistair on her trail, she had no choice but to find somewhere else to hide.

16

Cam tried to follow Alistair's trail, but he had passed this way too long ago. The scent was stronger in the settlement by the lake, where he and his followers had clearly spent some time as they wrought their damage, but it disappeared amongst the trees. Cam was left with little choice but to take a straight route back to the Blue, and hope that he and Felix might cross Alistair's path.

They didn't.

With every step closer to the city, Cam became more and more concerned about the decisions he'd made to get to this point.

This whole mission had been a fool's errand, driven more by his desire to be alone with Felix than by any hope of finding Emmy's son. Cam could see that now, so clearly. He'd cured the scant remains of the Red Shirts, yes, but the cost of that small victory had been high. He'd underestimated Alistair, and in doing so he'd caused the deaths of the vůdce's islanders, and eleven of Ana's people. There was no way he could convince himself that those losses had been worth his gain. It would have been better if he'd never left the Blue in the first place.

And now he'd provoked Alistair, so Felix was under threat as well. But he'd be safe in the city, Cam told himself. If he could just get Felix into the bunkhouse, then the Invicti would keep him safe while Cam cleared up the mess he'd made.

After a few hours' running, they finally reached the ferry crossing. Cam stopped to let Felix slide down from his back.

'How many left?' Cam asked him.

Felix shrugged the pack from his shoulder, rootling inside and making the remaining bottles clink against each other.

'Two,' he said.

'No point in saving it. It'll be dawn in a few hours' time, so we may as well run straight to the city. Are you ready?'

Felix looked as though he were dead on his feet, but he handed over the bottles. When Cam had drunk them down, Felix swung the pack over his shoulders and hopped onto Cam's back again.

'When we get to the Blue, you can sleep for days,' Cam promised. 'The bunkhouse is noisy, but it's warm and comfy. You can stay in my bed forever.' Assuming, of course, that Emmy had vacated it while he'd been away. Cam hoped he wouldn't get back to find her still hiding in his room.

'Sounds good,' Felix murmured. It sounded like he was already dozing off.

Then the Weepers started calling across the water.

'What the hell?'

Cam could see them peeling away from the tree line as they flooded the shore. He'd been expecting them, of course, because there had already been Weepers on the island when he'd left the Blue, but these numbers were inexplicable. There were hundreds. Each Weeper standing across the water was one fewer uncontaminated human. If they'd all originated from the city, then it was difficult to imagine how the Blue was still feeding its Silver.

All the more reason for Cam to cure them all.

But what had been happening in his absence? Where was Naia?

'We should wait,' Felix said, jumping back down to the ground. 'They're in the water, look. Wait till dawn.'

He was right. The Weepers could pull them from the ferry, and there would be no way to escape. Better to wait until the sunlight forced the creatures out of the water and under the cover of the trees, so they had a clear path across the lake. Once they were on the other side, Cam's Silver speed would let him avoid the Weepers as he ran back to the city.

'Alright,' he said. 'Then let's make the most of it.'

A few minutes' work was enough for Cam to build a basic platform in the trees. They curled up together there, huddling close against the cold of the night. Felix was asleep before Cam could even kiss him goodnight.

Cam watched him for a moment then rolled onto his back and stared up into the moonlit branches, thinking about everything they'd have to face tomorrow on their journey back to the Blue. He wondered why it was always so easy to leave, but so difficult to come back home.

When the sun lanced through the trees, it roused Cam first. It was already later than he'd hoped to rise, because with the trees this dense it took a while for light to penetrate the canopy. They'd already wasted a few hours of daylight.

Cam tried to shake Felix awake, but wasn't entirely successful. The woodman's eyes opened, and he nodded in response to his name, but he was plainly still exhausted.

'Come on,' Cam said, jumping down from the treehouse with Felix in his arms. 'Let's get you into a proper bed.'

The crossing was uneventful. The Weepers were out of the water now, as predicted. In their absence, there was something peaceful in the singing tang of the salty breeze. It brushed past them as Cam hauled the ferry across the water, rippling the surface of the lake while the passage of the vessel carved a furrow behind them. It seemed to be waking Felix up a bit, too.

'What next?' he asked.

'I don't know. We look for any sign of Alistair. We look for Barbara, too, if we can, but the most important thing is getting contaminated blood into Alistair and his army.'

Which was easier said than done.

After a minute, Felix asked, 'Have they beaten us here?'

Cam searched the air, but he could find no trace of Alistair's scent. If his army had used the ferry in the past couple of days then Cam would have been able to smell them on it, not to mention that their tracks would have been visible at the water's edge, but Alistair probably knew better than to take this route into the city. He would come from the east or the north or, if he was feeling really sneaky, he'd circle around to the west and try to creep in at the city's weakest boundary, even if it did mean travelling well out of his way.

It's what Cam would do if he were planning to infiltrate the Blue.

'I'll scout it out as soon as you're settled. If they're here, I'll find them.'

'Alone?'

He stopped hauling for a moment and gave Felix a candid look. 'You can't help with this one. You know that. You've more than done your part. Just let me finish this, and then it'll be over. After that, we can do whatever we want.'

Felix's eyebrow twitched. 'Whatever we want?'

'Yes.' Cam grinned. '*Whatever* we want.'

Felix smiled back at him. 'Well, alright then.'

That thought fuelled Cam as he hauled the ferry the remaining distance to the pebbled shore of the island. It was empty when they disembarked, but still the shadows moved in the dark spaces between the trees. He was going to have to jump over and around the Weepers, using the branches above to avoid grasping fingers.

'You'd better hold on tight,' Cam said. 'This is going to be a bumpy ride.'

'Or,' Felix suggested, 'we could just deal with them now.' He took his penknife from his pocket and used it to open the cut on his arm where the Weeper had bitten him, then passed the knife to Cam.

'When this is over,' Cam said, 'I'm never going to have to watch you cut yourself again.'

Then he sped into the trees. He only needed to go a few yards to reach the first of the Weepers. The blade slid in easily, then the creature was falling, dragged out of reach by clutching hands before it could even touch the ground. Cam stayed to watch the dominoes fall and by the time it was over, hundreds of Weepers laid out dead before him, Felix had joined him in the trees.

'I'm not sure that was better than just jumping over them,' Cam said.

Felix shrugged. 'It was always going to be their end. That's what you told me.'

There was no coming back once a human turned Weeper. Cam knew that, and it was what he'd told Felix after they'd watched Otho fall, but he hadn't needed to see more bodies today.

'You're right,' Cam said. 'I know we need to clear out the Weepers sooner or later. They won't last long after we do this thing anyway, but still.'

It was almost as though the past five hundred years had never happened. Every time the Weepers fell, he could almost feel Emmy at his side, just as she had been when they'd eradicated the

Weepers the first time around. Doing it again now was like being back at the Fall, at the point when the world had teetered and toppled, sliding them down into the darkness. This was their chance to climb back out of it, Cam knew that, but he also knew that there would be darker things to come before they could start to rise.

Cam carried Felix on his back and the knife in his hand as they sped through the trees towards the Blue. Whenever they encountered a Weeper – which was frequently – Cam would slice the knife across its skin as they passed, but he didn't slow to watch them go down. He knew what would happen, and that was enough.

The crowds thinned as they neared the boundary fence, which gave him some hope that the Invicti might have been at least trying to keep the Weepers under control, but the fence itself was unguarded. There were traces of Silver scent around the boundary, but no one stopped them at the gate, even when Cam slowed to a walk to let Felix down.

'How many were there?' Felix asked, looking at the bloody knife in Cam's hand.

'A lot. Too many.' He followed Felix's gaze down, resisting the urge to wipe the blood off on his clothing, then nodded towards the fence. 'Are you ready to see the Blue?'

'I'm not sure I want to.'

Cam sympathised. It was like the island all over again: the minute he opened the gate, they'd know how far things had degenerated. For now, he could stare at the greened wood and imagine that the Blue behind it would be the one he'd come home to centuries ago: sunlight catching on the shiny tiles, merry fires burning in every hearth, and children running in the streets of a city that hadn't yet ritualised oppression.

The damp had seeped into the wood, sticking the gate closed. Cam had to kick at it to get it to release. It swung open with a mournful rasp, revealing tumbledown ruins lit by a clouded autumn sky. It was not an inspiring sight.

'The Blue, huh?' Felix said.

'I know. It looks more like the Grey.'

Cam kicked the gate again to wedge it closed behind them, then led the way through felled trees and fallen masonry to the centre of the city.

When they finally reached the bunkhouse, it was clear even from the outside that the place was in disarray. There were empty bottles piled on the steps by the front door, and there was no smoke rising from inside. It was early in the day, but not early enough to explain why no one had seen to the fire.

Taken together with the unguarded boundary fence, it was enough to make Cam worry.

'Hey,' he called as he pushed through the door. 'Is anyone home?'

He was greeted with silence.

Cam and Felix exchanged a look.

'Hey!' Cam called again, louder this time. 'Where is everybody?'

This time there was a response: a thud upstairs, followed by the shuffling of feet. He heard someone else mutter, 'Shuddup,' but the sound was muffled by blankets.

He tried a third time: 'Get your arses down here, now!'

There was more movement, more shuffling, and eventually Konrad, Naia and Zita trooped into the lounge.

Naia rubbed at her eyes, yawning hugely. 'Great, you're home. Can I go back to bed now?'

'What's going on?' Cam said to them. 'Why is no one on patrol, and where are the others?'

'The others are on patrol,' said Konrad.

'All of them?'

'All three of them,' Naia replied, 'yeah.'

'Everyone except us and Lucas,' Konrad added.

'We didn't see anyone when we crossed the boundary,' said Cam.

'Bartek, Linh and Adewale are all out there,' said Konrad, 'but you probably wouldn't have seen them, because we're out of blood.'

'We're running the perimeter in shifts at boring speed,' Naia chimed in, 'which takes *hours* and is *exhausting*. Hence...' she raised her eyebrows and tipped her head towards the stairs.

'Fine,' Cam said. 'Go back to bed, but take Felix with you.'

Naia grinned wolfishly, looking suddenly much less tired.

'To *my* bed,' Cam clarified. 'Show Felix to my room, then you can leave him alone and go back to sleep in yours.'

Naia huffed out a dramatic breath, but she did as she was told.

'Come on then, Lumberjack,' she said.

Felix followed, but not before pulling Cam to one side and kissing him full on the lips. Cam blushed massively, much to everyone's amusement, but their smiles stopped short of laughter. No one seemed much in the mood for mirth today.

Once Cam was alone with Konrad and Zita, he ditched his pack by the door, kicked off his boots and threw himself down onto the sofa. His feet were burning from all the running he'd done over the past few days, and there was no point in worrying about his stinking socks – the lounge already reeked like something had died in it.

'Tell me what's going on,' he said to Zita and Konrad.

They took their seats on the sofa opposite him, eyeing each other cautiously.

'I'm not sure where to start,' Zita said eventually.

'Well, my first question is: where the hell is Tommy?'

'With Viv and the baby.'

'Where?'

'At the palace,' said Zita. 'It's where everyone is now, mostly. He hasn't been back here for a while, not since he came and collected all of Lorelei's traitors from the cells in the basement.'

That couldn't be good news. Tommy had been planning on interrogating the remaining Silver traitors, but here, with the Invicti. Why would he take them to the palace?

'Did he set them free?' Cam asked.

'We don't know. He sends messages, and we keep patrolling, but without more blood…' Zita shrugged.

'What about Emmy and Sol?'

'Also at the palace,' Zita said, but she and Konrad had exchanged a glance before she answered.

'What?'

'She's obsessed, Cam,' Zita said on a sigh. 'She got stuck in the idea that the woman who took the baby from her had to be in the city. First she started gathering all the human women to check for scent, then that escalated, and suddenly she was dragging them into the palace to interrogate them. People go missing, and then you see them by the fence days later, all of them turned Weeper and none of them looking like their last human hours were much fun.'

'She's gone power mad,' said Konrad.

'No,' Zita turned to him, 'she's just plain mad. The problem is,' she said, speaking to Cam again, 'the Empress is always right there, whispering in her ear.'

'Emmy's on Laila's side?' Cam said incredulously. After all the horror Laila had heaped on this place, and everything she'd done to try to stop Emmy from returning so that Sol wouldn't awaken, it seemed unfair that Emmy would make an ally of her. That sounded childish even in Cam's head, but he'd fought so hard to get Emmy back here. Lives had been lost, so many lives, in Laila's attempt to prevent that.

'But Laila tried to have me killed,' Cam said. 'She never wanted Emmy back. Doesn't Emmy know that?'

'I don't think she cares,' said Konrad.

Zita glared at him, then turned to Cam. 'You left,' she said softly. 'What did you expect? Tommy's basically out of action, the King's awake, the Queen's back, and she's not herself. You *knew* that when you left.'

'You're saying this is my fault?'

'No, I'm saying it's unfortunate, but this was predictable. You made your choice, and the Queen found another shoulder to lean on.'

'It sucks for us that she chose the Empress,' said Konrad.

'Former Empress,' Cam said.

'I wouldn't be so sure about that. Good luck getting through to her now.'

They'd been close, Emmy and Laila, back before the Fall. Strange friends, because Laila had always been ruthless while Emmy had tried to cling to her morals, but it seemed she'd abandoned them altogether now.

Maybe Cam could have stopped that if he hadn't left her behind to follow his own crusade, but he doubted it. From the moment Emmy had awakened she'd been drawn to the crush of bones and flesh. She'd practically spelled it out for him when he'd left the city: she was no longer the person he'd known. He'd softened over the years, but the abuses Charles had heaped upon Emmy had dulled her sensitivities and sharpened her into a weapon.

She was so far gone now that it might not be possible to blunt her edge.

'What are they planning?'

'We don't know,' said Zita. 'The Empress has been helping her look for the prince. Whatever else the Empress might have done, she's helping the Queen get what she wants. That's all the Queen seems to care about. She probably didn't even question the Empress's motives. We did, but so far we're none the wiser.'

'Shit.' Cam rubbed his eyes. 'Well, I've got more bad news. Alistair's on his way here with another bloody army, and he knows who Emmy's son is.'

'But you don't?' Konrad asked.

'No,' said Cam, frustrated. 'All I know is he's about twenty, and he's either here in the city or Alistair already has him.'

'Why would Alistair have him?' said Zita.

'Oh, right,' Cam sighed. 'I do know that: because Laila thinks she can use the prince's blood to turn her Silver again and make her immune to the cure.'

Zita and Konrad stared at him, then looked at each other before turning back to Cam. They didn't seem shocked or upset. More than anything, they seemed intrigued.

'Well, come on,' he said when they both stayed silent. 'We can't just sit here. We need to be ready when Alistair turns up, and we need some leadership.'

'So you're taking charge?' said Konrad, raising an eyebrow.

'On an extremely temporary basis. So Zita, you go to the palace, tell Tommy I'm home and see if you can get him to come back here. Konrad, you go knock on doors and get us some Attendants over here. We won't stand a chance against Alistair's army without a source of uncontaminated blood. In the meantime, I'll go out and scout the perimeter while I've still got enough blood in me to run at speed. Naia stays here to keep an eye on Felix. Alright?'

Konrad rubbed his face and yawned, but he said, 'Alright.'

Zita was already on her feet.

'When's the shift change?' Cam asked as they made for the door.

'About an hour. Mid morning.'

'Alright, we'll meet back here then. Now, let's get going.'

Cam felt strange running at Silver speed without carrying Felix. His movement was freer, but he also felt exposed without the warm weight of the woodsman on his back. It made him long for his bed in the bunkhouse, for the chance to share it with the man he loved.

That would be his reward, he told himself. In the meantime, he had a job to do.

He started by running north, up through the vineyards and charred fields. The ground wasn't warm now, as it had been when he'd stood here with Emmy a few weeks ago. Instead, the earth was cold enough to crunch under his feet, and the trees stood like the silhouettes of many-fingered hands on the horizon.

When Cam reached the boundary fence, he leapt over it then started to circle the perimeter clockwise, searching for any sign of Alistair's scent, or of the passage of many feet. Mostly he just found squirrels and the tracks of Weepers. In the northeastern corner of the Blue there was a gate that had clearly been used regularly. Cam wondered whether this was where the palace sent its victims to die.

He couldn't yet think of them as being sent by Emmy. The thought that she could be responsible for all these new Weepers made something twist in his chest.

Probably guilt.

Cam found nothing else unusual until he had almost come full circle. As he'd suspected, the western boundary had seen some action. There was no trace of Alistair's scent here, but Cam could pick out a whiff of something Silver on the breeze.

He followed it, plunging further into the forests to the west.

When he crept up on the camp, he was almost disappointed. Was Alistair really planning to take the Blue with this tiny band of Silver? There couldn't have been more than fifty of them in total, given the number of tents and provisions.

Cam crouched in the undergrowth as one of them – a woman with dark hair and strong shoulders – walked towards the tent nearest to him.

'Are you in there?'

'Yeah, give me a second,' a voice replied from inside.

A couple of minutes later a man came out and joined her. He wore one of the bloodstained shirts that were the Red Shirts' colours, but he'd covered it up with a loose jumper as though to distance himself from the association.

'News?' he said to the woman.

'Not yet, but it won't be long before we track the boy down. There are only so many places he can hide in the city.'

'Alright, then. Let's make sure we're ready when he's found.'

That was the information Cam had wanted: they hadn't found the prince yet, and he was still in the city. Armed with that knowledge, the Invicti stood a chance of getting in Alistair's way. They could find the boy themselves, then if they got enough blood they could come out here together and clean up this paltry little army.

He silently turned and started to make his way back to the city, finally feeling as though things were starting to look up.

Unseen by Cam, a dark-haired figure stood in the trees. He watched as Cam's back disappeared towards the Blue, then joined the others by the tent and smiled.

'Good work,' he said, clapping the man on the back. 'We'll make a spy out of you yet.'

'He wouldn't come,' Zita said when she joined the others in the lounge.

Cam had explained the situation to Adewale, Linh and Bartek when they'd come back from their shift on the boundary. They were now all sitting in the bunkhouse with Naia, waiting for Konrad to join them. Felix was still asleep upstairs.

'What do you mean, he wouldn't come?' Cam asked. 'How could he not come?'

Zita shrugged. 'Like I said, he wouldn't come.'

'You told him I was back?'

'Yes.'

'And you told him Alistair's heading here with an army, and that we've run out of blood?'

'Yes. I told him everything. He's still not coming. He wouldn't even let me in, so don't tell me I should have spoken to the King and Queen about it, because I tried that too. And the Secundus, well, he looked kind of sick. Something's not right there.'

'Shit.'

Cam really didn't need anything else to worry about right now. He was already on the cusp of despair when Konrad finally walked in with just a single clinking sack over his shoulder.

'Please tell me there's more than that,' Cam said.

Konrad scowled. 'I knocked on every damn door except the palace, and this is all I could get.'

'How many bottles?' Zita asked as he put the sack down next to the sofa.

'Twenty-one. Twenty-fucking-one.'

'For eight Invicti, running the boundary constantly, for a week.'

'Look,' Konrad said as he dropped into a chair opposite her, 'what was I supposed to do? Bleed them all dry? I did my best.'

'Then we don't use it to run the boundary. We keep it in reserve for the fight, and in the meantime we'll just have to make do without.' Cam looked around the room, counting heads. 'Where's Lucas?'

'With his girlfriend,' Naia leered.

'They patched things up?'

Naia leaned back in her chair and said, 'Seems like.'

That had to be good news. With Lucas's help, Julia would have a much better chance of spreading the vaccine amongst the humans of the Blue.

'Alright,' Cam said, slapping his hands on his knees and getting to his feet. 'This is the situation: we've got a small army camped at our door, the Secundus is out of action, and we need to find the prince before Alistair does. If we don't, he'll make his army immune to the cure and we'll lose the best weapon we have against them: contaminated blood.'

'So you know the prince is in the city?' asked Zita.

Cam told them what he had overhead in the woods.

'Alistair doesn't have him yet, but I'm guessing it won't be long before he tracks him down. I have one lead: the woman who took the boy from Emmy was called Barbara. Have any of you ever heard of a woman by that name?'

'Silver?' asked Adewale. 'I used to know a Barbara back in Scotland, but I think she got cured in the Fall.'

'No,' Cam said, 'not Silver. Human.'

'Called Barbara? In the Blue?' Konrad's expression was sceptical. 'Balbina or Blandina, maybe, but not Barbara. Who ever heard of a Roman called Barbara?'

Cam sighed. 'It was a long shot.'

If she'd even made it as far as the Blue then the woman had probably changed her name, or been given a new one. But if the name had been given to her, then maybe someone would know what it had been before it was changed. Cam wasn't going to find those answers here with the Invicti. If he wanted to know about a human woman who'd slipped into the city in secret, he needed to be talking to her peers.

'I have a question,' Bartek said, raising his hand. 'Why?'

Cam turned to him, puzzled. 'Why what?'

'Why are we fighting Alistair?'

Zita, Naia and Konrad looked outraged by the question, but the others just looked thoughtful.

'He has a point,' Adewale said. 'Our oath is to the King. The King is bound to the Queen, and the Queen is working with the Empress, for whom Alistair is working. There is only one side here, it seems.'

'One side and us,' said Zita.

'That Scottish bastard betrayed us, Adewale,' Naia said. 'I don't care how close you two were: he betrayed you. You can't pretend that never happened just because it upsets you. The Empress betrayed the Queen, too, and the King. I think our duty's pretty fucking clear.'

'I'm not denying what he did, but if the King and Queen have forgiven the Empress...' Adewale opened his hands, palms to the sky. 'We're soldiers, not leaders. We take our orders from the King.'

'And when the King gives no orders, and the Secundus won't lead us?' Zita asked. 'What are we supposed to do then? Because I'm telling you there's something going on in the palace, and it's nothing good.'

'Enough,' Cam said sharply. He needed the Invicti on his side to make this plan work, but he couldn't be honest with them, so he channelled Tommy's authority instead. 'The Secundus isn't here. We don't have a Tertius anymore, I know, but I'm stepping up. I think I've earned it. Does anyone want to argue with that?'

He looked from face to face, but none of them spoke up. He heard Naia mumbling under her breath, but she quietened down when he glared at her.

'Good,' he went on. 'Then I'm giving the orders around here until we work out what's going on. We're going to do what's right, and that means stopping Alistair and the Empress. Do you understand?'

They were all sitting a little straighter now, but it wasn't enough.

'I said: do you understand?'

Then they got the idea. All six shouted, 'Sir!'

'Good,' Cam said, 'then get on with it.'

Naia hung back while the others trooped upstairs, either heading to bed or to get ready for the next shift.

'How's the lumberjack doing?' she asked.

'Fine,' Cam said, narrowing his eyes at her. He'd checked on Felix earlier, and the woodsman had been sleeping like the dead. Cam hadn't had the heart to disturb him, so he'd just closed the door and let him slumber on.

'Is he done with you, yet?' Naia teased. 'Seriously, Cam, when's my turn?'

'You're ridiculous, and the answer is: never.'

She arched an eyebrow. 'Shouldn't you be asking him about that?'

'Trust me: he'd say the same.'

Naia opened her mouth to prod him further, but Cam had had enough. He let his silver come, flooding his eyes with the gold filaments that marked his bond to Felix. It was the romantic equivalent of baring his teeth at a rival, and it was the best way to get Naia off his back. And Felix's.

'Damn,' she sighed. 'You boys. What a waste.'

Cam rolled his eyes irritably, but at the same time he felt a surge of affection for Naia and the rest of the ragtag group that now comprised the Invicti. They were the closest he'd had to a family for so many years that, despite his reluctance, they'd wormed their way under his skin. His bonds to these broken remnants of their larger corps had been forged through every betrayal they'd suffered together, every loss, and now Cam was about to become a traitor himself.

The Invicti were not likely to forgive that.

Cam sent the next shift out to run the boundary at what Naia called 'boring speed', then started to plan his next move. He was sure there must be at least one human left in the city who had known this Barbara. Since they were working together, Julia was the obvious person to start with. He'd go and find her this afternoon.

As the front door closed behind the departing Invicti, Cam could almost pick up Alistair's scent on the breeze. He followed the memory of it out of the bunkhouse and down to the edge of the square, sniffing at the air, but he couldn't pick up any trace of it now.

He must have imagined it. That was enough to send him upstairs to join Felix for a couple of hours' sleep. If he was so exhausted that he was hallucinating smells, then he was no good to anyone right now.

Cam needed some rest. For the moment, Julia could wait.

17

The sun was high overhead and Lucas still hadn't returned. It had been hours now.

Julia had picked a new house, this one across from the first. When she climbed to the top floor, she had a clear view of the street below. She'd been watching all morning, growing steadily colder in the empty room, but there was no sign that Lucas was coming back. He wouldn't have stayed away by choice, not when he knew what she was planning to do, but he had his duties to attend to. Shirking them would just arouse suspicion.

It was past time for Julia to get on with her own work.

Cymbals chimed at noon, and they took her back to another world, one in which the Blue had been a sanctuary from the terrors that lay beyond the fence. They'd done this every year, at the end of the harvest: a celebration, *Ziua Recoltei*. The cymbals marked the beginning of the festival.

The cheerful sound felt incongruous given the desolation that surrounded her, but maybe that was the point. If managing to harvest the fields this year, of all years, didn't merit a celebration, then when would it?

Julia had a fleeting memory of the comfort her home used to hold. Perhaps she could understand why Claudia was so reluctant to shatter it, but that didn't make Julia any less willing to seize the opportunity the festival presented.

She checked the window again, but there was no movement outside. She was on the western edge of the city, and there was no reason for anyone to come out beyond the houses this way. It wasn't like the north with its fields, or the east with the lake, or the south, which was the quickest route to the boundary fence and the ferry. Here there were just the broken memories of what the Blue had once been.

She packed her blankets away, cushioning the bottles of tainted home-brew into her bag, and pulled her cloak up over her head as she stepped out into the street. It was cold enough that the hood wouldn't attract attention.

She strode towards the square, keeping her head down.

First call: the temple.

There ought to have been a crowd for Julia to blend in with, but there were only a few clusters of spectators gathered to watch the procession, if you could call it that. There were no dancers, no jugglers, no breathers of fire, just a line of bell-ridden men drawing a cart of produce from the north towards the temple steps.

That wasn't where Julia was heading. She gave the procession a wide berth.

Three bottles, three targets, and a morning of planning. She needed to maximise what little she had, so she'd listed out the places where a gift like hers was most likely to be shared around. Three buildings, and three chances to spread the vaccine.

The temple was the most obvious of the three. Livia's girls had enjoyed special dispensation to skip the daily ceremonies on the grounds that they were busy cooking for the Nobles. They weren't the only ones, either – other workers had similar dispensation, and the Servers in the palace were close enough to their gods that they didn't need to worship them in the temple – but the rest of the Servers would attend at least weekly. Now that there were so few left alive, daily attendance was encouraged in order to fill the space.

A bottle shared here could reach most of the Servers in a single sitting, and the best thing was that it would be utterly invisible. Not one of them would know they were contaminated until it was too late for their Nobles.

Julia walked down a side street and knocked at a building that backed onto the temple, one that had until recently been shared by the priest and priestess. The priest lived here alone now, since the priestess still hadn't been replaced. He opened the door on her third knock, looking as though he had just tumbled out of bed.

'Yes, hello?'

Julia had already pulled a bottle of contaminated home-brew from her bag, and the priest's eyes latched onto it.

'Oh, I recognise that bottle. Green wax. Her sign, you might say.'

Julia smiled. This was going to be easier than she'd anticipated.

'A gift from Livia for you,' she said.

The priest quirked an eyebrow at her and asked, 'The occasion?' But he had already taken the bottle from her, and was cradling it reverentially.

'*Ziua Recoltei.*'

He blinked. 'That's today?'

'And as a token of gratitude for the Casting,' Julia hurried on. 'For making me a Candidate.'

'Oh? Oh, yes. I do recall. Well, the best of luck to you and your sponsor, and do thank Livia for the, um.' He saluted her with the bottle as he hurried back inside, then slammed the door behind him. Clearly a man with important matters that needed his attention.

Julia had hoped that the bottle would make its way around his congregation, but it made no odds if the entire thing wound up in the priest's belly instead. He might pass around some other wine during that evening's *Ziua Recoltei* ceremony, but before he poured it out he would put a few drops of his own blood into the cup. That was how he shared his blessing with the crowd, but tonight he'd be sharing his contamination too. When the congregation went back home to feed their Nobles, they'd take out a good three-quarters of the Silver living in the Blue.

It was a good start.

But it was also the easy part. The Invicti would be more difficult. They didn't generally drink from humans, Cameron had told her. They drank most of their blood from bottles that they stored in the cellar under the guardhouse. Julia would never be able to get down there. The first time she'd infiltrated the guardhouse she'd done it with the assistance of the King, but she couldn't expect any help from him now. She was on her own.

She wanted to leave the bottle on their doorstep and run, but then she could only hope to cure one of the Invicti at most. Once the others saw what it did to the first of them, there's no way they'd take a swig themselves. She needed to engineer a situation in which they'd all drink at once, and be none the wiser until the contamination was already in their systems.

This would be so much easier if Cameron had made it back here, like they'd planned. Instead, she'd have to pretend the home-brew was a special *Ziua Recoltei* tradition of hers, and insist that all the Invicti should gather together and toast with it that evening.

That could work. *No*, she told herself, *it* would *work*.

She sighed and braced herself. Sneaking around the back would do her no favours, so she just knocked on the front door. When there was no answer, she took a deep breath and knocked again, more loudly this time.

Cam opened it eventually, his hair mussed and his eyes sleepy. Julia could have hugged him.

'You're back?' she said, stating the obvious, at the same time as he asked, 'What are you doing here?'

'Bringing this,' she whispered, hefting the bottle.

'You've started? I thought we agreed you'd wait two weeks.'

'Things changed.'

Julia's expression must have been grim because Cam's brow furrowed in response. He took a step forward, ushering her out into the square as he closed the door behind him.

'Come on,' he said. 'Let's find a crowd.'

They attached themselves to the back of a group of Servers and pretended to watch the *Ziua Recoltei*. The procession had reached the temple now, and the jingling men were unloading their offerings at the bottom of the steps. The produce would stay there in a grand arrangement until dark, at which point it would be free rein for the city's hungry humans. It would certainly go further this year with so few still alive.

'Now,' Cam said quietly, 'tell me.'

So she did. She told him about how her blood had cured Rufus, pre-empting their plan by days. Then she recounted the events of that morning: their visitor, the delivery of Julia's first alcoholic contaminant, and the plan that had brought her to the guardhouse door.

Cam was quiet as she spoke, but his mind was clearly whirring. His eyes followed her carefully, probing but never quite satisfied with what they saw.

'So?' she said when she had finished.

'Is there anything else I've missed?'

Julia ran back through her words in her mind, but that was it. 'That's everything,' she said.

Except the part about Lucas being immune to her contaminated blood. That was his secret, and Julia had sworn to guard it.

'Alright then,' Cam said. 'Give me the bottle of your moonshine. I'll take care of the Invicti once this is over, but if Alistair's in the city then we've got bigger problems to deal with first.' He rubbed at the back of his neck, watching the ceremony with glazed eyes. 'My part of the plan didn't exactly go smoothly. I just need a few more hours.'

'Then we're doing this?'

'I'm still in if you are.'

Julia smiled ruefully. 'Too late to turn back now.'

'Why, do you want to?'

'No,' she said. 'Never.'

'Good. Then let's get on with this.'

He held out his hand for the bottle. Julia passed it over, the whole thing tainted by two drops of contamination swirling within its boundaries. For a moment Julia felt as though she and Cam were those two drops of wrongness, swirling within the Blue.

That was the shape of their rebellion.

Last call.

If she was going to get caught anywhere, it would be here, but there was no way around it. There was only one path into the palace for a human, and it was through the front door.

Julia took a deep breath and stepped away from the crowd. Cam was already long gone, not back to the guardhouse but towards the west. He had his own tasks awaiting him, so Julia was on her own again.

Then a flash of blonde caught her eye. It was running her way.

'Claud?' she said. 'What's wrong?' At first, she suspected the worst – that Claudia had worked out that Julia had contaminated her – but there was no anger in Claudia's eyes. The other possibilities raced through Julia's mind. 'Is Livia alright?'

'She's fine,' Claudia said as she joined Julia at the back of the crowd. 'She's in a real stinker of a mood, but she's well.'

Julia looked back across the square towards Livia's house, Julia's home. On any other day, she would have rushed back to the kitchen to explain everything to the newly-sober Livia – about

Rufus and Cam and their plan – but there was no time left to lose. She had the last bottle of liquor in the bag slung over her shoulder, and she needed to deliver it before the first of the priest's congregation was contaminated.

After that, everything would get so much harder.

'The thing is,' said Claudia, 'I wanted to ask you a favour.'

'Oh?' Julia could think of only one thing that Claudia would want to ask her, and it was too late for her to grant it. The plan was already in motion.

'Don't look at me like that,' Claudia said. 'It's nothing bad, and you owe me one. Come with me.'

'I'm kind of in the middle of something.'

'It won't take a minute.'

Julia looked over her shoulder towards the palace. *Last call.*

'Jules.' Claudia put her hand on Julia's arm. 'Please. It's important.'

Julia sighed. She couldn't say no to Claudia. Even when they'd been kids, Claudia had always been getting them into trouble. It was Claudia who'd wanted to creep into places they shouldn't be, so she could watch little slices of the privilege that was denied her by her birth. She'd been the one who'd wanted to steal biscuits from the Nobles, and scraps of material that skimmed over her fingers like butterflies. But then Claudia had never actually stolen anything because she couldn't bring herself to break the rules, so Julia had done it for her. She'd always been Claudia's thief.

Now Claudia finally had the life to which she'd always aspired and Julia had turned her thievery against her friend, stealing her dreams from her by contaminating her blood without her knowledge. It was the only way to save her, but still the guilt was there.

Julia could spare her friend a few minutes of her time, even today.

'Alright,' she said. 'Where are we going?'

Claudia didn't reply, she just smiled and took Julia's hand, leading her towards the palace. Julia brightened up when she realised their destination. Maybe this wouldn't be an unwelcome distraction after all.

Claudia practically ran up the palace steps, dragging Julia behind her. When they reached the entrance the guard lifted an eyebrow at Julia, but nodded them through.

The doors closed heavily behind them. Without the sunlight, the cavernous hall was a patchwork of dark corners and lamplit alcoves that strobed past Julia's eyes as they crossed the floor. It should have been impossible for such a large space to feel claustrophobic, and yet...

She reached behind her to feel the shape of the bottle through her bag, comforting herself with its presence. She could do this.

'Why are we here?' she whispered, but Claudia didn't answer, she just pressed her finger to her lips and kept pulling Julia towards a doorway on the other side of the hall.

The back of Julia's neck was tingling now, but she let Claudia lead her through the door into a small room whose sole ornaments were a small table and two chairs.

'Sit here,' Claudia whispered, heading towards a door on the other side of the room. 'I'll be right back.'

'Claud–'

But she'd already gone, disappearing out of view as the door swung shut behind her. Julia should really have stayed there, but when Claudia still hadn't returned after what seemed like an age, she crept after her. There was a stone-paved corridor beyond, stretching off to right and left and dotted with doors on both sides. The biggest of them was almost directly opposite Julia as she exited: a huge, ornate affair of dark wood with precious metal inlaid to form patterns of shining curls. She definitely wasn't going to open that one, but she feared it might be where Claudia had gone – there were voices on the other side, though not quite loud enough for her to recognise.

Instead, Julia went right, moving deeper into the palace.

She bypassed the first two doors, feeling exposed this close to where Claudia had left her. The third stood open. Two women were talking inside in hushed voices. Julia pressed herself tight to the wall, watching as she waited for them to turn away so she could slip past.

One of them was crying.

'I never thought I'd be the last one,' she sobbed softly.

'You should count your blessings that she spared you,' the other replied.

'How can you say that?' The weeping woman rounded on her companion, and Julia seized her chance to creep by. She didn't hang around to hear any more.

She passed more closed doors that looked as though they might be sleeping quarters. Julia ignored them; they weren't what she was looking for. Eventually the corridor turned, taking her left, then left again, back towards the centre of the palace. That seemed more promising.

There was a crash as something fell in one of the rooms up ahead, then a door was kicked open so hard that the handle cracked the plaster of the wall behind it.

Julia slipped into the nearest room without stopping to check if it was clear, closing the door behind her. Since it was pitch dark inside, she guessed she was safe here.

'Get him!' a man yelled from the corridor outside.

There were more crashes, followed by the smashing of pottery and further shouting. It was a few minutes before everything quietened down again, by which time Julia had begun to feel uncomfortable. There was something strange about the room in which she'd concealed herself, a damp atmosphere with a smell like scrubbed pots and earth.

It reminded her of blood.

She waited no longer than necessary to move back into the corridor. She hadn't intended to look behind her, really she hadn't, but her head seemed to turn of its own accord to trace the edges of the dark stains that marked the stone slabs.

Something had died here.

She moved more quickly after that, racing along the corridors on light feet, until finally she reached the landmark for which she'd been searching: the courtyard garden. She remembered meeting Claudia there a few months ago, when she'd seen for the first time how happy her friend was here at the palace. Julia had almost understood the attraction back then: the comfort, the security, and the sweet biscuits were enough to make even Julia think twice about it.

But the palace she'd walked into today was not the same one that had been baked by this year's summer sun. This was a palace stained by blood and wrapped in a sense of unravelling panic. This was a palace that was sinking into dissolution.

Julia felt righteous in speeding its decline.

She followed the windows that edged the courtyard, since the glass doors that led out to it were locked tight. Eventually, she negotiated the right corridors and rooms to admit her into the kitchen on its northern side. That was where she had been heading.

She approached cautiously, but there was no need. The place was empty. That was unexpected and, although helpful, not necessarily welcome. Yes, it would allow Julia to plant her contaminant more easily, but it might also indicate that the kitchen wasn't much in use. If no one was cooking, then what was the point of planting her tainted bottle here?

Then she saw the pot on the hearth next to the fire. It was huge and filled with steaming, spiced wine. That was the tradition of the Nobles for *Ziua Recoltei*. The first of the year's grapes had just finished fermenting, so the new wine was mixed with apple brandy and honey, then warmed to make *vin fiert*. Heating it took away the sharpness of the fruit. At least, that was what Julia had been told. She'd never had it herself, never having been invited to celebrate the festival with the Nobles in the palace.

But all of the palace Servers would be invited this year. If she wanted to find a way to get everyone contaminated at once, then she couldn't have come up with a better delivery system.

Julia listened carefully for a moment, checking that she was truly alone, then made her way over to the hearth. The smell was tantalising. She dipped a finger into the pot to try it, but her face screwed up at the odd mixture of flavours. It was sharp and sweet and woody and the alcohol caught at the back of her throat. All in all, it didn't seem like she would be ruining it much by adding another ingredient.

Not the home-brew, though. Instead, she pulled her knife from her cloak and cut a new line deep into her arm. There were more than a few drops of blood, more than enough to contaminate the whole pot, which she stirred quickly before binding her arm with a rag and making her exit.

She was just heading back towards the front of the palace when Claudia found her.

'Where have you been?' she asked, looking frantic. 'I told you to wait.'

'You were ages. I got worried,' Julia improvised. She probably should have been worried, but she'd been so intent on her task that she hadn't thought about Claudia once.

'Well, come on.'

Claudia hurried her back down the passage to the ominous door.

'Claud…' Julia said, half a question and half a protest.

It was too late, though. Claudia had already thrown the door open and pulled Julia inside.

Julia's immediate instinct was to run. Claudia had brought her into the throne room. The Empress was there, sitting on a chair draped with fabrics so brightly coloured that they looked like flowers, and she was looking at Julia. There were a few guards lined up behind her, but none that Julia recognised. These were not the Invicti.

'This is her?' the Empress asked Claudia. 'She seems dirtier than she did the last time I saw her.'

Julia didn't understand. She looked over at Claudia, but her friend was smiling back at her as though this were the most natural meeting in the world. Just what favour *exactly* was Claudia expecting from Julia?

The Empress leaned forwards in her throne. 'Well, then. Thank you, Claudia. You may leave.'

Claudia looked uncertainly between Julia and the Empress for a moment, but it was clear that the words had been an order rather than a request. She backed out of the room and closed the door behind her.

'You look surprised to be here,' the Empress said once Claudia had left them.

'I am.'

'You shouldn't be. He loves you. Did you know that?'

Julia froze. Who was she talking about? She knew that Lucas loved her, but could it be possible that the Empress was talking about…? No, that was ridiculous.

'It was quite the revelation to me,' the Empress went on, hopping down from her throne. 'It always seems to be their downfall, though. All these men, who think they have control over themselves and everyone else, then they fall in love and surrender their strength to us like puppies. I wonder if you've really understood what that means, to have a person – one of us, a Noble – so wholly in your power.'

Lucas, then. She meant Lucas.

Julia didn't say anything, but she watched the guards. Two of them were moving along the sides of the room now, circling around to cut Julia off from the door.

The Empress moved towards her too, making her way down the steps that led up to the throne. She couldn't have been much taller than Julia, but somehow she seemed like a giant in this place.

'Almost perverted, that reversal,' the Empress went on, her voice light as though she were musing on something of interest, but with little actual importance. 'You're so utterly in our power, and that's the point, of course.'

As Julia had watched the Empress approach, the guards had closed in behind her. One of them grabbed Julia's hands, while the other dragged a sack over her head. She struggled against it, feeling little pieces of dirt raining down on her face from the lining, but struggling just made it harder to breathe.

'We like to keep you in the dark,' the Empress added, then Julia felt a blow to the side of her head.

She fell from her feet and into sleep.

When Julia sputtered awake her hands were free, but her head was still covered by the bag. She snatched at it, fear making her hands fumble so it took three tries to release herself. There was dirt all over her – the bag must have been used for storing muddy vegetables – but when she tried to shake her head, it throbbed.

'Took a fair old ding, did you?' a woman asked her.

Julia squinted at her surroundings and picked out a couple of figures in the gloom, one to her right and one to her left. The one on her right had his back to her, but the other was smiling at her from behind the metal bars that separated them.

'Alba?' Julia croaked.

'Yes, it's me.'

'We were looking for you,' Julia said as she felt at her scalp gingerly. Her fingertips came away clean, but there was a lump on the side of her skull.

'Well, you found me then, didn't you?'

'How long have you been here?'

'Not long. It took them a while to track me down, but they got me in the end.'

Julia could hear water dripping somewhere and everything smelled of dust and mould. They must have been in the cellars of the palace, because the floor was mostly dirt and the place looked ancient. There was only one oil lamp in the space, its flame flickering in the draught, and it was very draughty down here. By its light, Julia could see the bars that marked the edges of her confinement and separated her from the other prisoners. They ran from the floor to the ceiling, although the surface above her was more rock than plaster. The bars themselves attested to the age of this place, because the Blue just didn't make metal like that anymore.

Julia got to her feet carefully and rattled the bars, hoping their age might have weakened them, but they were stuck solid. There was no way she was getting free.

'We've tried that,' the other figure said, finally turning to face her.

Julia's stomach dropped into her feet.

Oh no.

'What are you doing here?' she asked.

'It's where they put me,' Rufus said, then he came and stood by the bars that separated their cells, leaning against them with his arms raised over his head. 'Apparently my dear mother didn't want to chuck me out into the Red, so until she decides what to do with me, here I am.'

'I'm not sorry for what I did,' Julia said, making her eyes trace the raw cuts that she'd sliced into his cheek. 'If you expect me to apologise, I won't. I didn't know I was contaminated, but even if I had, I still would have let it happen.'

'I know.' He looked at her from underneath his brows, but Julia couldn't read his expression. It might have been anger, but it could have been pain. 'You're a predator, Julia,' he said softly. 'I wouldn't have expected anything else from you.'

Then he turned and stalked back to the far corner of the cavern. Maybe he'd seen Claudia coming, because she was walking into the dungeon now, her bare feet just a whisper over the dirt as she approached the bars in front of Julia's cell.

Julia felt her fists clenching around the rough metal.

'Were you this angry with me?' she said. 'Is this some kind of sick revenge?' Then she dropped her voice to a whisper and tipped her head towards Rufus. 'All because of him?'

But Claudia seemed surprised to see Rufus, and even in the meagre light Julia could see the tears pooling in her eyes. 'I'm so sorry. Jules.' She sniffed, and then the words came out in a rush. 'I didn't know. The Empress asked me to keep an eye on you and Lucas. She said you were in some kind of trouble, but that if I talked to her about it then she'd keep you safe. I thought we were becoming friends. I suppose I was flattered.' Claudia looked down at her hands, blushing. 'Stupid, I know. Then she asked me to bring you here and, well…'

Julia sighed and thunked her head against the bars, making them ring softly. 'Oh, Claud.'

'Well it's not as though you told me anything,' Claudia sniffed. 'How was I supposed to know that Lucas was the prince? Isn't that the kind of thing you're supposed to tell your best friend?'

Rufus snorted and said, 'The prince. Perfect.'

'No one was talking to you,' Claudia snapped at him.

'And the fact that you're spying for the Empress,' Julia said, 'isn't that the kind of thing that you should have told me?'

They glared at each other through the bars.

But it was plain that Claudia's anger was already crumbling into misery. Julia hadn't been far behind. Claudia just looked so devastated that it was difficult to hold a grudge. She wasn't a manipulative person by nature, so it was hardly surprising that the Empress had managed to bend Claudia to her will. What was surprising was that Julia hadn't worked out what Claudia was up to. She'd let her guilt blind her.

'I was stupid,' Claudia said, wiping her face on her sleeve. 'I can see that.'

'It's alright.' And as far as Julia was concerned, that was true. She'd delivered the contaminant to two of her three targets, and Cam would take care of the third. She'd done her part. She'd walked into the palace knowing that she was gambling her and Lucas's lives for this plan, and whatever happened now, at least she'd succeeded. Even if she died here, she had done what she'd come to do.

There was some comfort in that. Not much, but some.

Claudia wrapped her hand around Julia's and pressed a kiss to her fingers.

'I'm going to get you out of here,' she said. But then she undermined her words by adding, 'Somehow.'

'Do you know what they're going to do?'

'No,' Claudia whispered.

'Then perhaps I can enlighten you,' said a voice from the darkness.

It took a few seconds for Julia's eyes to pick out his form in the corner of the room, then she wished she hadn't. When he stepped away from the wall the light from the lamp fell on his face.

The King was here, and he was not pleased.

18

Three things spun in Cam's head like a mantra: find the prince, cure the army, cure the Invicti. He still wasn't sure about the order of those first two – maybe cure the army, then find the prince? – but of one thing he was certain: curing the few remaining Invicti would be the last thing he would do, particularly since it seemed that he was down a soldier.

He'd been counting on Lucas's support. Maybe he shouldn't have been surprised. Alistair had trained the boy, after all, and so he'd spent more time with their newest recruit than anyone else had, it was just that Cam had never considered that Lucas might side with Alistair.

Cam's great army of Invicti was down from eight to seven.

When he left Julia in the square, he found himself heading west almost without thought. He'd intended to go back out to the camp to see if he could pick up any further intelligence, but then he crossed Lucas's trail, and he couldn't help himself.

He followed it.

He wasn't sure what he'd intended to do. Maybe he would have confronted the boy about Alistair, or maybe he just had to hear it from Lucas's lips before he'd believe it, but when the trail led him into a small courtyard and from there into an unfamiliar kitchen, Cam suddenly felt like a fool for letting his anger distract him.

There were more important things to worry about right now.

He was turning to leave when a voice called him back.

'Were you looking for something, Master?' the woman asked. 'Something I can help you with, perhaps?'

She was old for the Blue, and she looked about as downcast as Cam felt. Her eyes blinked vaguely from what seemed like a great distance, which was only lengthened by the shadows smudged beneath them. And yet she was familiar.

'Do I know you?' he asked.

The woman laughed. 'In my younger days, Master. You might remember me from them.'

'My name's Cameron.'

'Oh, I know that well enough, but I'll stick to calling you "Master" if that's alright with you. I'm Livia.'

Then he placed her. She'd been Laila's consort for a while, a long while in Laila's terms, and hadn't she carried Laila's boy?

Rufus, Cam thought. The boy Julia had just cured. No wonder the woman looked so exhausted.

'I'm sorry to intrude,' he said.

'Oh, you're not intruding,' she said, although the words sounded as though they cost her. 'Would you like a tea? The kettle's just boiled.'

'I can't stay.'

'Well, if you're sure.' She moved towards the threshold to see him out, pretending at politeness but giving the clear impression that she was ushering him from the house.

He let her, but as she was about to shut the door, a thought occurred to him and he turned back.

'There is one thing you might be able to help with,' he said.

She pulled the door open again, just enough to let her peer out at him suspiciously. 'What's that, Master?'

'I wonder if you ever knew a woman called Barbara. Probably came here about twenty years ago? She had a baby with her. And the children called her…' Cam searched his memory for the name the vůdce had used. Then it came to him: 'Baba.'

The woman's eyes widened. She hesitated for a moment before opening the door again with a sigh.

'You'd better come in,' she said.

Cam couldn't understand it. The soldiers he'd overheard at the camp had been very clear: the prince was still missing. But if Livia was to be believed, then Lucas was the missing prince, and if Julia was to be believed, then Alistair had already found him.

Several explanations presented themselves: either Livia was lying, Julia was lying, or the guards were lying.

Cam curled his fists as he raced back to the bunkhouse, tamping down the urge to start punching the walls.

Alistair had played him. The *bastard*.

It was beyond frustrating. All of this time, the boy they'd been looking for had not only been in the city, but he'd been one of the Invicti as well. Cam didn't want to believe it, but it made sense of everything.

He remembered the moment after Lucas had bitten Julia in the Red. He remembered the boy panicking for her, then panicking for himself as he told the Invicti that she was contaminated. But he hadn't been cured. Perhaps Cam should have suspected back then that the boy was immune, just like his parents.

Shit. Sol and Emmy were Lucas's parents.

That was going to take some getting used to.

And then there was the matter of Viv's notebook. Cam had never really understood why Alistair had stolen it, let alone why he'd gone so far as to parade it in front of Cam by leaving a page of it waiting for him in the vůdce's hand. But that notebook hadn't just contained Viv's notes, or the composition of the Red Shirts' army. It had contained Lucas's training notes as well. That was why Alistair had wanted it.

It all begged the inevitable conclusion that Lucas wasn't Alistair's accomplice after all. He was his prisoner.

Cam was already cursing himself for not putting the pieces together when he careened into the bunkhouse. Then froze.

It wasn't a place for the faint-hearted. The Invicti fought all the time, sometimes coming to blows over something as trivial as who'd eaten the last of that day's bread, but the scent of Silver violence never populated the bunkhouse because the Invicti's intent wasn't to harm their comrades. Not seriously, anyway. It was just rough-housing and drunken idiocy.

So when Cam barrelled through the door and was met with the stink of malice, he knew something was very wrong.

His mind jumped back to that page crumpled in the vůdce's hand, and the note Alistair had added to it.

Stay out of the way, or I'll cut the lumberjack down like a tree.

Cam had never moved so fast in his life. His feet flew up the stairs, carrying him so quickly that he was half running, half falling. But he could never have run quickly enough to save Felix.

He was long gone, the sheets in Cam's bedroom twisted and torn in the wake of his abduction. All that remained was a smear of blood and another page from Viv's notebook, placed dead centre in the middle of the ruined bedding.

I told you what would happen, it read. *This is on you.*

'Adewale!' Cam yelled, bashing on doors as he ran back along the corridor. 'Bartek, Linh, get up, now! We've got to go.'

Adewale was the first to emerge. He was still tying his trousers, but he didn't question Cam's orders. Linh and Bartek followed. The moment they were all gathered in the corridor, Cam held up the note for their inspection.

'Who was supposed to be guarding Felix?' Cam said, barely containing his rage.

The three of them looked at each other.

'Guarding him?' Adewale asked.

'Yes, guarding him!' Cam rubbed his face then pushed his fingers back through his hair. 'Oh, god. The others didn't tell you, did they?'

Three blank faces gave him his answer.

'Alright,' he said. 'Two bottles of blood each, then Bartek: go and fetch the others here from the boundary. Take bottles for them too. We're going after Felix, then we're going after the prince.'

'You know who it is?' Adewale asked as Bartek headed down the stairs and out of the building.

'Yes,' Cam groaned. 'It's bloody Lucas.'

'No.' There was a half smile on Adewale's face, as though he were waiting for the joke.

'Yes,' Cam insisted. 'Lucas is the prince. Now where would they have taken Felix?'

Linh said, 'The palace,' at the same time that Adewale said, 'The camp.'

'Shit, shit, shit.' Cam punched a hole in the wall.

He couldn't feel him. Cam should have been able to feel where Felix was through the bond, but there was nothing, so either Felix was too far away or something else was going on. Whatever the explanation, it was bad news.

'Breathe,' said Adewale. 'We'll check the camp first. It'll be easier to search. If he's not there, we'll go to the palace. Plan?'

Cam nodded as he extracted his fist from the woodwork.

'Thank you,' he said.

'Thank me later. Now let's go.'

By the time they'd got downstairs and drunk a couple of bottles of blood each, Bartek was back with the others in tow.

'What's the damn rush?' Naia asked.

'They've got Felix,' Cam replied.

'And Lucas is the prince,' Adewale added, 'and they've got him too.'

Zita turned and glared at Bartek and Adewale. 'So do you still think Alistair's on the same side as us?'

Bartek held his hands up in surrender, but that wasn't enough for Zita.

'*Why are we fighting him*, you said. *He's working with the Queen*, you said. Now look at this shit show.'

'Argue later,' Cam shouted over them. 'We need to go. Grab your weapons. The camp first, then the palace. Come on.'

As they ran out through the city Cam could feel his heart fluttering at the back of his throat, nervous and nauseating. What if he was too late? How long ago had Felix been taken? What if he wasn't at the camp or the palace? Cam knew he couldn't be dead, because if he was then the bond would have killed Cam too, but there were a lot of awful things Alistair could do to Felix without actually killing him.

Cam was starting to descend into panic when Adewale reached out and put a hand on his shoulder, squeezing lightly before breaking off to run a little way ahead.

Cam wasn't alone. They'd find Felix, find Lucas, and then Alistair would get his comeuppance. Focussing on any other outcome was pointless.

A few minutes after they crossed the boundary fence, Adewale stopped and held out his hand, indicating that the others should stop too. The trees had been at their most dense here, but now there were gaps where they'd been felled, presumably to feed the camp's fires. But that didn't make sense. The camp had been so small that they should have found enough windfall branches in the brush to sustain them.

The back of Cam's neck prickled with unease.

Adewale was walking amongst the stumps, counting the losses as he scanned the trees for movement. He tipped his head towards the west.

'The camp was this way?' Adewale asked.

'Just follow the scent trail,' Cam said.

They started into the trees on the other side of the clearing, following their noses. Alistair's scent was here now, faint but still recognisable under the blur of others that Cam didn't know. Too many others. It was a fog of unfamiliar smells, so thick that it almost masked Alistair's entirely.

Cam's unease increased.

'Wait,' he whispered to the others, but by that point it was too late.

They'd expected to ambush Alistair's men in their camp, but they hadn't considered that an ambush might have been laid for them already. Their enemies must have been sitting silently in the trees, training their heartbeats into low, slow rhythms, because not one of the Invicti realised they were there until they came swooping down from the canopy and into the clearing behind them.

There were so many of them, many more than the fifty Cam had estimated in that morning's recce, and they were all fuelled up on blood and moving at Silver speed. But the Invicti had their own supply, and that wasn't the only blood they'd brought with them.

'Darts!' Cam yelled to Naia and Linh. The two of them hung back from the fighting, letting the other Invicti shield them as they loaded darts into blow pipes and peppered the attackers with them. Each one had been dipped in contaminated blood that Naia had harvested. Cam hadn't asked where she'd got it from; he didn't want to know.

The first few waves of darts took out a good quarter of their ambushers, but that wasn't enough to stop the Invicti from being herded into the trees by their numbers. It wasn't long before they realised why their attackers had driven them in this direction.

Here was the camp, half a mile or so beyond the clearing, just seconds away at Silver speed. Cam gaped at it and swore. Nothing was as it had been that morning. Instead of a few tents scattered around meagre fires, there was a towering wooden wall decorated with spines that looked as though they'd been painted with blood.

Alistair and his men had been busy the past few hours.

'Again!' Naia shouted, shoving more tainted darts into her pipe and scattering them over the oncoming hoard. But it wasn't enough. Alistair's soldiers were on the top of the wall behind them, poised with their own tainted missiles.

Hundreds of them against seven Invicti.

And there was no way out now. The soldiers had circled around from the sides, backing the Invicti up against the wall so they had no choice but to fight the army head on or be crushed into the spines and cured.

Unless…

'Hold this,' Cam said, passing his pack to Linh. He had one advantage left: speed. Their enemies might have as much uncontaminated blood as the Invicti did, but Cam was faster than them. He knew that for a certainty.

He looked up at the wall, giving himself one last chance to reconsider, but this was the only way. He needed to get to Felix, and to do that the army needed to fall.

'Naia and Linh: darts!' he yelled. 'Everyone else: forward!'

Naia and Linh provided cover enough to let the others prepare their weapons. As their attackers fell back, the Invicti strode into the fray. Adewale was a spinning whirl of blades, while Zita leapt onto her first target like a frog, a tainted dagger clasped in each hand. Konrad was at the back of the group, shooting from his crossbow with a knife in his free hand, but most of the army had their attention focussed on Bartek. He always loomed over any battle because of his size, and this one was no exception. It helped that he'd chosen a club as his weapon, studded with blood-tipped nails. He never had been much for subtlety.

While they dealt with the army on the ground, Cam planned to deal with those at the top of the wall. He could see them readying little vials of blood, like the ones the Red Shirts had carried on their belts at Lorelei's direction. They didn't seem to have many of them, though, because they'd used none so far. That changed when they spotted Cam sizing up the footholds in the wood.

The first arrow stuck in the ground half an inch from his foot. After that, things moved quickly.

The spines would have been effective had Cam stayed in the centre of the wall, but instead he ran to one side, pushing through the army to reach its edge. From the side, the spines formed a ladder from the ground to the very top of the wall. The first one nearly snapped under his weight, but after that Cam moved like lightning, dancing upwards on swift feet. The arrows rained down, but he was quick enough to jink out of their way, swinging his body from side to side as he scaled closer to the top.

They were waiting for him. There was a group of ten or so clustered around the edge of the rim, as though they'd forgotten how the Silver could move. Maybe they'd never known. Maybe Alistair, who'd taught Lucas and the Invicti so much, had lacked the time to teach his own men. Either way, the jump surprised them when it came.

One leap snapped the spines beneath Cam's feet, but propelled him far enough that he landed in the centre of the wall's top, behind the majority of the defenders.

'Fuck!' someone shouted.

Arrows were flying thick and fast now, from in front of and behind Cam. He targeted the smaller group first, snatching an arrow out of the air and using its contaminated point to stab humanity into them. That left him with maybe fifteen more defenders to deal with, now ranged along the length of the wall. They were reaching for their vials and drawing their blades, as though they meant to coat them with blood, but Cam was quicker and he'd come prepared. His knives were already bloodied in the sheaths slung at his belt.

Then the scream rose up from the ground below, a scream of frustration and pain, and Cam's gaze snapped in that direction. He shouldn't have looked, but he recognised the voice. If he'd been paying attention to his own fight, as he should have been, then he would have seen that one of the defenders hadn't bothered to take the time to contaminate his blade. He would have seen that it was aimed straight at his stomach.

A fraction of a second's distraction was all the defender needed to run Cam through.

But it also brought him close to Cam. He had his knife in the man's side before he had time to gloat. The soldier dropped to his knees, and from there to the ground, but his comrades were crowding in close behind him so there was no reprieve. They were clearly keen to make the most of Cam's incapacity.

'Shit,' he muttered, his hand going to his stomach. He couldn't pull the blade out here. As soon as he did he'd lose a load of blood that he couldn't replenish, because the extra bottles were all in the bag he'd left with Linh down on the ground. But he couldn't take out all these defenders either, not with a sword through his stomach.

They saw their opportunity and closed in.

The first few obliged him by overestimating their advantage. They came in hastily, stepping within range of his contaminated blade before raising their own. Cam might have been injured, but he was still quicker than they were. They went down with little fuss.

The next wave was more cautious. They came in with arrows flying and bloody blades brandished. Cam wouldn't be able to avoid them forever.

But then he saw something out of the corner of his eye, a dark shape poking above the line of the wall behind the defenders. It disappeared for a second, but when it came back into view it did so in an explosion of tattooed skin and aggression. Naia burst over the spiked parapet, red spattered over her face and arms, and fell on the defenders with her blood-poisoned blades. It wasn't long before she'd fought her way through them.

The cured fled down the wall into the camp, leaving Naia and Cam alone on top of it.

'Thanks,' Cam said, his words tight with pain. 'Have you got the blood?'

Naia slung a bottle at him, which he caught awkwardly. He pulled the cork out with his teeth, and by the time he'd extracted the sword from his stomach and drunk the bottle down, Naia had helped herself to the weapons the fleeing soldiers had discarded. Here was the reason for the wall: a line of crossbow-like mechanisms fixed to its edge. They were each loaded with tens of bolts that were primed and tipped with contamination. This is what the defenders had been doing with their precious vials of blood.

Now Naia turned those weapons on the soldiers below them, firing again and again until there was only silence from the forest floor.

'That's it,' Naia said as they waited for Cam's wound to heal enough for him to move. It wouldn't take long. 'We've cured just about all of them.'

'And the rest?'

'Not just cured, but also dead. Most of them ran off, but some of them wouldn't back down, even after we'd cured them. Stupid fuckers.'

Cam got to his feet and stretched, testing the pain. The damn cut was still bleeding.

'Let me.' Naia wasn't known for her nursing skills, but in the circumstances Cam didn't have much choice but to agree.

'Is Bartek alright?' he asked. 'I heard him scream.'

'Bartek's fine,' Naia said, eyes fixed on Cam's stomach as she patched the wound with more aggression than was necessary. 'Linh isn't.'

That was something of an understatement. When they reached the ground, Cam was met with a sight that seemed gruesome even to him. Linh was suspended a foot or so off the ground, impaled on the spines and spikes of the wall that protruded from the front of her body. She'd been cured by their bloody tips, and now she was dead.

'They pushed us back,' Konrad said. 'I just got a scratch. Linh wasn't so lucky.'

'You're human?' Cam asked, but when he listened carefully he knew it was true. He could hear the thundering human heartbeat in Konrad's chest, and in the chests of all the cured soldiers who were retreating from them into the trees. There were just five Silver heartbeats in this forest now: Zita's, Naia's, Bartek's, Adewale's and his own.

'He's not here,' Adewale said, appearing from the far side of the wall. 'I searched the tents, but neither Alistair nor Felix are here. I'm sorry, Cam.'

Alistair had lured them here. He'd set this trap, taken Felix then waited for the Invicti to come and be ambushed, and for what? Like the game Alistair had played with the Red Shirts, it was a distraction to keep them out of the way.

'Just another fucking distraction,' Cam muttered.

Alistair still had Felix, and by falling into Alistair's trap Cam had lost two of his fighters, one of them to humanity and the other more definitively.

'At least she's not alone anymore,' Bartek said, wiping his eyes as he looked at the terrible display of Linh's body.

'Take her down,' Cam said softly. 'We'll bury her out in the yard with Gul.'

'There'll be time for funerals later,' said Adewale. 'We've got some business to settle at the palace first.' His tone wasn't unkind, but it held the same determination they all felt.

Naia clenched her fists. 'Damn right, we do.'

They left Linh's body in the bunkhouse cellar, in one of the recently vacated cells. She'd be safe there until they made it back from the palace.

They argued about how best to approach it. There were only three ways in: the courtyard garden and the front door were the two obvious routes, the two that everyone knew about. The less well-known entrance was through the tunnels under the temple. Cam wasn't even sure that Laila knew about that route – Tommy had found it when they'd first moved to the Blue and had it sealed up – and he was willing to bet that no one had ever told Alistair about it either.

That would be their best way in.

'How are we doing for blood?' Cam asked Naia.

'Four bottles.'

'Shit.'

Not even enough for one each. They'd already used two each today for speed and strength, then injuries had claimed a few more.

'You four take them,' he said. 'You'll need the strength. I'll manage.'

'You just have to hold out until we reach you,' said Adewale.

'I know. Now go. I'll follow, like we discussed.'

Adewale gave Cam a long look, then said, 'Alistair's mine.'

'Fuck's sake,' Naia muttered.

'He's *mine*,' Adewale said, turning on her.

'Fine, he's yours,' Zita said, pushing Naia towards the bunkhouse door, where Bartek was waiting. 'What do we care, as long as he dies?'

Adewale turned back to Cam, who nodded his agreement. 'Understood.'

They left.

Cam was alone then, sitting in the lounge as he waited out the minutes before he could make his move. Konrad was sleeping upstairs, perhaps because it was easier to sleep than it was to confront the reality that he was now human. Cam had thought about sending him out north to join Aaron, because if anyone could understand what it was like to be Invicti-turned-human it was their former cook, but it didn't seem to matter. If everything went as planned, everyone would be human by tomorrow.

He just hoped that he and Felix would live to see that new dawn.

He couldn't sit, not with that anxiety weighing on him, so he paced instead. It was strange to be in the bunkhouse, and in this room that was its heart, while it was so empty. He'd avoided this place for so long precisely because it had always been overflowing with people. Strange now that he suddenly hated its silence.

But it heralded something loud: the fracturing of the Blue's inertia. For centuries it had been on a slow but gradual slide towards its eventual breaking point. For centuries, nothing had changed while the Silver crippled the city with their unwillingness to change. Now, finally, it was shattering apart. Cam might not be around afterwards to pick up the pieces, but it would be worth it to know that he had broken its silence.

He looked out of the window and saw that the sun was well on its way below the horizon. The sky darkened incrementally over the next while, shading from yellow to orange to red, streaking rainbows up the winter sky. Soon the light was gone entirely, leaving nothing but indigo and the memory of sunshine in its wake.

Then, at last, it was time for Cam to go.

He expected the guard to be surprised to see him, but the woman opened the palace doors without comment. It was almost as though she'd been waiting for him.

A Server greeted him in the hall, a young man with dark skin and darker hair. He led Cam past Laila's audience chamber, past her rooms and to the door of the throne room, a space that he hadn't entered for decades. Apparently he'd be going in alone now, because the Server had already disappeared deeper into the palace on silent feet.

Cam didn't bother pretending stealth, he just slammed the door open and strode inside.

'Ah,' Laila said, 'I was wondering when you'd be joining us.'

She was perched on her throne with Alistair at her side. Guards lined the walls, some of them unpleasantly familiar. So this was where Lorelei's traitors had ended up. But there was no sign of

Tommy, and Emmy and Sol were nowhere to be seen. Weren't they supposed to be in charge now?

'I wasn't sure you'd be coming,' Alistair said. 'Cure them all, did you?'

'Except the ones we killed,' Cam replied. 'Where's Felix?'

'I've got him. He's alive.'

'I know,' Cam said, before he thought to stop himself.

Alistair's eyes twinkled at the slip. 'Oh, you do, do you?' he said. 'I thought you might have been labouring under that particular bond. But you can't feel where he is, can you?'

Cam gritted his teeth. The bastard had done something to Felix to affect the bond. 'Where is he?'

'Oh, you'll get him back,' Laila said, waving her hand dismissively. 'There's no need to be so dramatic. We're just keeping him until this ritual is over, and then you can do what you like.'

'Ritual?' Cam asked.

Then he noticed the trappings that had been assembled to his left, underneath the wide windows through which light streamed into the room. This must have been a church once, because there were votive scenes scattered across them in stained glass, but as each pane had broken over time their scenes had been replaced with darker ones. The lead didn't trace bible stories now, but stories from the Revelation and the Fall instead. Here were the bogeymen of the Blue immortalised.

On the floor beneath them, a wide copper bowl was suspended by an ornate tripod that seemed disturbingly sacrificial in nature. It didn't help that there was a blade already waiting in the bowl. The whole thing looked as though it belonged in the Delphic oracle.

'Did you notice it's a new moon tonight?' Laila asked. Cam hadn't, but now she mentioned it, he did recall that his walk to the palace had been lit by starlight and torchlight alone. 'Very auspicious, they say. I don't really care, but apparently it's necessary. We're not quite ready yet, though.'

'So you've got a choice,' Alistair said. 'Either you let the guards put you down, or I'll put your boyfriend down. Which is it to be?'

Cam didn't struggle as they closed in around him. He stopped himself from fighting back as hands grabbed his arms and pinned him against the wall. He still flinched when the blade slid into his heart, but he kept his eyes on Alistair to the very last second of consciousness, watching him even as he slid to the ground.

'Good boy,' Alistair sneered. 'If you're very lucky, we might even let you wake up.'

Cam's last thought as his sight faded into darkness was that four Invicti were no match for Alistair and his guards. But then it was too late, and he had already slipped away.

19

'Please don't be alarmed,' the King said to Julia. 'I have come to ask for your assistance.'

He was standing by the wall opposite her cell, leaning back against the stone with his hands in his pockets. The only way it would have been possible for him to look more at ease would be if he were horizontal.

Julia supposed that was what power did for you. The King was in complete command of the room, of the Blue, of the world, for all Julia knew. And yet, here he was asking her a favour.

Intriguing.

'I'm not sure what what you expect me to do for you from in here,' she said.

'It's something you would be doing for all of us, I promise you that.'

Alba and Rufus were silent in their cells, but Julia could feel the force of their scrutiny. Claudia had stayed where she was, holding Julia's hand through the bars.

'I'm not sure how aware you are of our history,' the King said. 'I gather there is some kind of fairytale, but I rather doubt its accuracy, so let me tell you this instead: some hundreds of years ago, I fell in love with Emilia, the woman you now know as the Queen. The world was somewhat different then, and Emilia was human. She was strong and determined, but so stubborn that she would never back down from a fight, nor ask for help when she needed it.'

He almost smiled as he spoke those last words. The shadow of an emotion flitted across his face before he locked it away behind his eyes.

'But she was kind, too,' he went on, looking off into space. 'Kinder than me. It became necessary to make her Silver. I believe you call it "ennoblement" now. That was supposed to be the end of our story, but then she was taken from me, and now that I have her back, she is changed. She is not now as she was before, as though the things that were done to her have burned away what remained of her humanity. I may not be known for that quality myself,' he said, meeting Julia's gaze, 'but I have enough remaining to see its lack in her. Cruelty is not my way, nor was it hers. I question whether it has lately become so.'

'She does it for her son,' Alba said from her cell. 'Anyone with half a brain could see that.'

The King looked at Julia, as though he were expecting an introduction, but Alba spoke again before Julia could oblige.

'I'm the one who carried him here,' she said. 'She begged me to take him, so I did. I carried him here, feeding him my blood. Your son, who your woman begged me to save for her. Your son, who I loved like he was mine. And you, standing there like your queen's the only thing in the world.' Alba looked the King up and down. It didn't seem as though she were impressed with what she saw.

Julia expected that to anger the King, but instead he turned to Alba and bowed respectfully.

'I owe you my thanks,' he said.

Alba humphed and crossed her arms. 'That you do, not that I begrudged the labour. As far as I'm concerned he's my boy, and I owed him nothing less than a mother should.'

'Then I owe you more than my thanks, for giving him what we could not. And of course you're right: Emilia still feels like the only light in the world to me. I never met my son, nor did I know he existed until a few weeks ago. He's a shadow to me, but for Emmy he is more than real, and her desperation for him makes her sharp.'

'Sharp enough to align herself with the Empress.'

'Apparently so. But I know what Laila means to do. I need your help to stop her.'

Julia rattled the bars. 'I'm still stuck in here. Are you going to break me out?'

'No,' the King smiled. 'That would be rather suspicious, don't you think? I thought perhaps the biscuit thief might be willing to assist.'

It took Claudia a moment to process the King's words, but when she'd unpicked them she turned to him with pink cheeks and a horrified expression.

'Me?'

'All I require is a contaminated human, and you would seem to fit the bill.'

Claudia smiled, relieved. 'But I'm not–' Then she put two and two together and rounded on Julia.

'What did you do?' she said, seething.

'Oh, didn't you know?' Rufus gloated from his cell. 'Apparently she's planning to contaminate everyone.'

'But not me!' Claudia thumped the bars, hard enough that flakes of rust drifted to the floor. 'We talked about this. You weren't going to contaminate me!'

'Then maybe we're even,' Julia whispered. She darted a pointed glance at the King, wishing Claudia would be quiet.

'So you had a plan of your own, little rebel?' the King said to Julia. 'Somehow I am not surprised. Well, allow me to assuage your fears by telling you mine.'

Cam woke with his face pressed into stone and the most crippling heartburn of his life. It came back to him after a few seconds: he was in the throne room, and one of Alistair's bastard guards had stabbed him in the heart. He wished he could remember which one, so he could repay the favour.

But for now, he was going nowhere. His wrists and ankles were tied, but more importantly he was lying in a pool of his own blood, and he had none with which to replenish it. He'd be useless until he could get more.

He lifted his head from the floor, blood dripping from his cheek, and tried to stop the room from spinning, with little success. Eventually, he managed to focus on the scene in front of him. Alistair had taken up position with his soldiers by the wall. Emmy was here now too, sitting in the throne with Laila at her side. Cam tried to catch his former friend's eye, but her attention was elsewhere.

There was a distinct air of anticipation.

Seconds later, a door opened at the back of the room and the King walked in, escorted by a couple of guards. It was clear that he was being forced rather than simply accompanied, but nonetheless he seemed perfectly at ease.

'Finally,' Laila said as he was led in.

'Apologies, Your Majesty,' said one of the guards. 'We had to search for him.'

Laila rolled her eyes and perched on the arm of the throne. 'Well, now that you're finally here, perhaps we can get on with this?'

'Perhaps if you were to tell me what *this* is?' Sol said, gesturing towards Cam.

Laila ignored the question and swept an arm towards the side of the room where the tripod stood ready for whatever ritual she was about to perform.

'Don't you remember how you made yourself, Solomon?' she said, walking down the steps towards him. 'You told me the story once. You told me so many fucking stories. On and on, every night while I was under the thrall of that bond. Like you are now, with her.' She gestured over her shoulder at Emmy. 'But I bet you never thought she'd turn into the bigger monster. You underestimated her, I think.'

'People frequently do.'

Sol was looking up at Emmy with love in his eyes, but her expression was pure determination.

'What is this, my love?' he said to her, rising up towards her. 'I thought we had decided against this, and yet here you are, bleeding out your friends to align yourself with enemies.'

Laila laughed at that and said, 'Is that what you think?'

But Sol's attention was fully on Emmy.

'I'm not an idiot, Sol,' she said, 'but Laila and I want the same thing, for now. I wanted our son found, and she needed him found. Once this ritual is over, we can take him away from here. We could go back home. Isn't that what you want too?'

Sol glanced back at Cam. 'And is that all you want? Will you kill your friends for it?'

'He'll be fine,' Emmy said, though she sounded as though she were trying to convince herself more than him.

'Do you know how many are already dead?' Sol persisted.

But apparently Emmy had had enough of listening to reason. She stood from the throne and leaned forwards until she was looming over Sol.

'He's your *son*,' she said, spitting the word. 'How can you not care?'

'He is my son,' he replied, reaching up to stroke her cheek, 'but you're my queen, and I'm losing you.'

The way that Emmy's face closed off was so definitive that Cam could see the barriers going up even through the fog of his weakness.

'I'm surprised you don't understand,' Emmy said to Sol. 'You know all about bargains, don't you? Well, this is the bargain I've made.' With that, she stepped away from his touch and returned to her seat, curling her fingers over the arms of the throne.

Sol looked at Emmy, then at Laila. After a moment, he put his hands in his pockets and said, 'I see.'

'You underestimate her yourself,' Laila said, returning to the side of the throne. 'Did you forget that she's steel beneath it all? I suppose that's what happens when people wear their power beneath the skin. It was never my style.'

'We all remember what your style was,' Emmy said impatiently. 'Can we get on with this?'

'Fine,' Laila pouted. 'Then let's go back to your origin story, shall we, Solomon? There's a reason Charles couldn't make Emmy's blood turn him Silver again, isn't there?'

Sol raised a lazy eyebrow, as though he were bored by Laila's words. 'You seem to remember it well enough,' he said.

'Then I'll tell you the reason.' Laila smiled wide enough to show her teeth. 'She wasn't born with the blood of the goddess in her. Like you, she was made with it, because that's what's in your veins. Do you know how many others there are left in the world like you and Emmy, that close to the blood origin? None. I know because I've looked. And as far as I know, there's only ever been one Silver who was born a pureblood, both parents so close to the source that he might as well have been born from the goddess herself.'

Emmy was looking nervous now, sitting forward in her seat as she anticipated the revelation, which is what made Cam realise: this *would be* a revelation for her. Laila hadn't told her who her son was, so neither Emmy nor Sol knew that it was Lucas.

This was the information for which Emmy had sold them out to Laila.

Information that Cam now had. If only she'd trusted him to find the boy, they could have stopped Laila together.

Cam groaned, and all three of them turned to look at him.

'Ems, what have you done?' he whispered, knowing it would still be loud enough for them to hear.

'You were never going to find him,' she said. 'It took you hundreds of years to find me. I wasn't prepared to wait that long.'

Cam felt like crying. 'But I did,' he said. 'I found him.'

Emmy's face froze, then broke into agony. 'You did?'

'I did. He's here. He's always been here. You've met him, both of you.' A tear streaked down Cam's cheek, then dropped from his chin into the pool of blood beneath him. It was too late, and none of it mattered.

Emmy gaped at him, her cheeks white and trembling. 'And?'

Perhaps feeling that she was losing the initiative, Laila waved at the guards. They opened the doors and dragged a kicking figure into the throne room, depositing him at the bottom of the steps. The hood of his cloak had been pulled down over his head, but now he shook it down onto his shoulders, revealing dark hair beneath. Cam didn't need the boy to turn around for him to know it was Lucas. He could recognise his scent. He could feel its constituent parts now: the fresh mint of Sol and the sweet richness of Emmy. How could he be anyone other than their son?

Stupid of him not to have worked it out before.

'This is your son,' Laila said to Emmy, 'and he's going to give me back my life.'

Down in the dungeon, Claudia was panicking.

'I can't do this,' she said. 'I'm a terrible liar. My hands shake and I get all flustered and start blushing. No one will ever believe me.'

Julia reached between the bars to take her hand. 'We need you, Claud. You heard the King.'

'I'll mess it up.'

'But you're the only one who can do it. The Empress is expecting you. You said so yourself.'

'Jules, I'm not like you. I'm not brave. I could never go out into the Red like you did, or stand up to the Nobles.'

Dammit. Julia could see Claudia's resolution ebbing away by the second. Now that the King was out of the room, her fear of the Empress was overwhelming her.

'You are so brave.' Julia took Claudia's face in her hands, training Claudia's eyes to hers. 'You're so much stronger than you think you are, Claud. Remember when we were small, and you pushed Tatiana onto her backside because she was making fun of my parents? Or during the Contamination, when you came out swinging that pole at the Weepers? Or just a few weeks ago, when we sat on that rooftop together and picked off Nobles with crossbows?'

Claudia covered Julia's hands with her own, wrapping her fingers around Julia's to lower them from her face.

'Because we were together, Jules,' she said. 'Because it was for you.'

'This is no different.'

But Claudia's lip was shaking. 'I wish you'd never contaminated me.'

'If I hadn't done it last night then I would have done it today. It's too late to change course. The contamination will already be spreading through the city by now, and I wouldn't have let you be one of the last uncontaminated humans left. The Nobles will bleed them dry if we let them. I wouldn't do that to you, just like I know you won't let the Empress win. For me, Claud. Please. For all of us.'

But Claudia didn't reply. She just dropped Julia's hands and wiped her eyes, stepping back from the bars.

'Claud…'

She turned away from the cells and walked back into the palace, giving no indication of which way she would jump.

'Well, you could have handled that better,' said Rufus.

'No one asked you.' Julia walked to the back of her cell and slid down to the floor.

'Livia spoke to you, then,' Alba said softly. 'I wasn't sure that she would.'

Julia turned to her. 'You knew?'

'We'd talked about it from time to time, but there are so many more outside the Blue that it seemed too dangerous.' There was reproach in her tone. She clearly thought Julia's actions would bring the Silver of the Red down on the Blue.

'We've dealt with them too,' Julia said, hoping it was true. She had to believe that Cam had fulfilled his part in their plan, because otherwise they were all doomed.

Cam had finally managed to get himself into a sitting position, but that had taken most of his strength. He was reduced to the status of spectator, watching Laila's machinations come to fruition, just as she'd intended.

Emmy stepped down from her throne and came to stand in front of Lucas. He was a few inches taller than her, though Cam supposed that many sons were taller than their mothers. How strange it was to think of them in those terms, these two people who seemed to be just a few years apart in age rather than entire centuries.

'I should have recognised you,' Emmy whispered, her fingers tracing Lucas's cheekbones. 'Your scent.'

He flinched away and, for just a fraction of a moment, her eyes darkened.

'Why didn't you?' he said.

'You saw how I was when the Invicti found me. Sol, your father… We were too far away. I was dropping back into the sleep. And then, when I awoke properly back here in the city, in the fighting, you weren't with the others.'

He'd been with Julia instead, shooting Red Shirts from the rooftops. How differently this might have ended if Lucas had been down in the melee with the rest of them.

'Lucas,' Emmy whispered. 'It's not the name I gave you.'

But Lucas betrayed no curiosity. Instead, his attention was on the trappings of the ritual that were set under the window.

'Why am I here?' he asked.

Laila saw the direction of his gaze and made her way towards the bowl, lifting the knife from its cradle. She waved a girl forwards from the back of the room, a girl who was vaguely familiar. Then Cam placed her: Julia's friend.

'I made a promise that I need to keep,' said Emmy, taking Lucas's hand in hers.

He shook her off, his face hard with suspicion. 'What kind of promise?'

'To turn Laila Silver again. She needs your blood.'

'All of it,' Laila said.

Lucas was already backing away, but Emmy followed him.

'I'll revive you afterwards,' she promised. 'It'll only be for a minute or two. I'll bring you back. I'd never let you come to harm. You have to trust me. I'm your mother, Lucas. I love you.'

But Lucas's eyes were wide with unease. 'You've been no kind of mother to me.'

Sol had been standing by quietly as this exchange took place, watching the boy's face as though he were trying to trace the lines of his own features in it. Now he stepped forwards and took Emmy's arm, holding her back when she would have chased Lucas further towards the door.

'There must be another way,' he said.

She turned to him with desperation in her eyes, but her words were pure resolve. 'This is the bargain I made.'

'You bargained our son's blood?'

'And how many people's blood have you bargained over the millennia? Yes, I bargained his blood, so we could find him, so we could be together. Are you going to tell me it wasn't worth the price? He's here, Sol,' she said, gesturing at Lucas with tears in her eyes. 'We've found our boy.'

But Lucas was looking rebellious, shifting his feet as though he were preparing to run. 'I'm not your anything,' he said, 'and I haven't made any bargains.'

'Then let's make one ourselves, shall we?' Laila said, gliding towards him. 'I think I can offer you something that'll change your mind.'

Lucas scowled and opened his mouth to reply, but before he could do so a crowd of guards entered from the back of the room. They were dragging an old woman with them. After a few seconds, Julia was hauled in behind her.

Laila smiled at Lucas. 'Would you care to reconsider?'

Julia was thrown to the floor. She skidded along the polished stone, coming to a stop at Lucas's feet.

'Julia,' he whispered sadly as he helped her up. 'I thought you were safe.'

'What is this?' said the King, looking between Laila and Julia.

'This is blackmail,' said Laila. 'Surely you recognise it. You always were a master of manipulation, Solomon. I might not be as strong as you anymore, but with one arrow at that girl's head, none of that matters.'

But there were far more arrows than that aimed at her. Julia could see them circling the room, every other guard armed with a bow that was pointed straight for her. Lucas pulled her closer, wrapping her in his arms.

'Maybe your bloodline silvers more than most,' Laila went on. 'I don't know, but either way I know this: your boy's in love. You know well enough what that means.'

Julia felt Lucas's arms stiffen around her as the Queen's face fell. The King had already known about their bond, but he looked no less grim. If Julia was killed, it would take Lucas with her to the grave.

'Please, Lucas,' the Queen said. 'Just do what she asks.'

But Lucas didn't look at her. His eyes were on Julia.

'Is it done?' he asked her, his voice soft. Julia heard the question beneath it: *If we died right now, would the plan still work?*

He was asking for permission.

Julia gave him her assent with a sad smile. 'There's nothing left for me to do.'

If she'd been sure that she could rely on Claudia, then she would have denied him. In the absence of that faith, this was the best way to ensure that the Silver of the Blue would be cured, and that they'd stay that way. They couldn't let the Empress finish the ritual, and at least they'd go together.

He stroked his fingers down her cheek, then reached up to his ear to take out the earring he'd once given her. He fixed it back in her own lobe now, settling the silver stud in place as though it had never been gone.

'How will you do it?' she whispered.

'Like this.'

When his lips met hers, they were bittersweet. This would be their last kiss, their last embrace, the last time that the air around them would swirl with the honeyed mint fragrance of his mark. It was the best of goodbyes, and yet the worst.

'Your decision, Princeling?' the Empress asked.

His reply was to drop his kiss to Julia's neck, fixing his teeth in her skin. Julia was vaguely aware of a ruckus behind her, but all she could feel was the bliss of Lucas's bite. She pulled him closer, pressing his head against her neck as she felt the delicious pull of the blood through her body to his lips. If she had to die, then she couldn't think of a better way to go. The caress of his hands on her back, the scent of him filling up her nose and mouth, and the crush of their bodies close, so close, chased the drag through her veins into ecstasy.

The room had just begun to spin when she felt herself wrenched from his grasp, his bite mark already healed by their bond at the moment his lips left her skin.

'No!'

At first Julia thought the scream had come from her lips, but then she saw the Queen holding Lucas back. Her fragile arms were corded with strength, but her expression was pure desperation.

'I'll hold him,' she said to the Empress. 'Let's just get it done, and then everything will be fine.' She cooed at Lucas. 'It'll be fine.'

'Let me go!' He writhed in her grip, trying to slip free, but with no success. She was stronger than she looked.

'You can't force him. You know the blood has to be given, not taken,' the Empress said to the Queen, her exasperation clear from her tone. 'Plan B, then. Bring her here.' This last command was directed at the guards, who were now dragging Alba forwards.

'I can walk on my own, thank you very much,' the old woman said, muscling out of their grip. The guards didn't seem to care as long as she kept moving in the right direction.

The Empress turned to Lucas. 'It's easy for you to be the martyr, isn't it? Dying with your lover would be so terribly romantic. But it's different when you have to watch someone you love dying. Would you like me to show you?'

She brandished her blade at Alba.

'You think I'm not willing to die, too?' Alba said with some asperity. 'I'm old. What do I care for death? It'd be worth it to see you toppled off your perch.'

Laila backhanded Alba across the face. Alba would have slapped her right back, but the guards caught her arms and held her in place.

The Empress held the knife to Alba's neck and looked at Lucas. 'Well?'

Julia could see him hesitating. He looked from her to Alba as though he were juggling their lives in his head.

'It's alright, my boy,' Alba said, smiling.

But that wasn't the decision he made. Instead, he turned to Julia and said, 'I'm sorry,' then stopped struggling against his mother's grip.

Julia couldn't blame him for it. If it had been her choice and Claudia's throat, her answer would have been the same.

'Good,' the Empress said, seeing his surrender. 'Then maybe we can get on with this while we still have the moon.' She waved at the guards, who took Alba back to the other side of the room. Julia was dragged off in the opposite direction and deposited unceremoniously on the floor.

The sticky floor.

Then she noticed Cam for the first time. He looked about as pale and bloodless as she felt.

'Hi,' he said weakly. 'Everything going well, then?'

'Oh, sure,' Julia said, forcing a smile. 'Perfectly according to plan.'

'Well, I've got everything under control here, as you can see. But you didn't happen to bump into Felix, did you?' His eyes were so hopeful that Julia almost couldn't bear to disappoint him.

'No,' she said after a moment's pause. 'I'm sorry.'

Cam nodded to himself. 'Sounds about right.'

Over on the other side of the room, the Queen kissed Lucas on the cheek and released him. 'It's for the best,' she said.

Lucas wiped the kiss away and took a step back, but the guards were already there, shepherding him towards the tripod where the Empress waited.

'You'll see,' the Queen muttered as she returned to the throne. 'It'll all be fine. You'll see.'

Then the Empress called for Claudia, as the King had said she would, and passed her the blade.

'You know what to do,' the Empress said.

Claudia looked down at the knife in her hand, then her eyes met Julia's across the room. Ever so slightly, Claudia nodded.

Julia's heart gave a little jump. Was she going to do as the King had asked?

The Empress returned to the throne then, joining the King and Queen.

'I don't buy all this magical nonsense,' the Empress said. 'Why should it make any difference if the ritual's performed at new moon or not, by a human or a Silver, virgin or otherwise? Ridiculous.'

'And yet you follow it,' said the King.

'Because I'm not so arrogant as to assume I'm right.' She turned to the guards. 'Bring my son.'

They left the room, reappearing a minute or so later with Rufus in tow, but they weren't the only newcomers. Guards rushed into the room, bundling in after the others until the space behind the throne seemed uncomfortably full. They all had scarves pulled up over their faces, covering their mouths.

'What's going on?' the Empress demanded.

'We're under attack!' said one of the guards. 'They're spraying contaminated blood.'

That explained the masks, then.

'Your Majesty,' a second guard interrupted, speaking more calmly, 'the Invicti are in the building.'

The Empress cut her eyes towards Cam. 'Oh, really?' she said.

'I've sent the last few down to the cellars to bring the blood up. Don't worry, Your Majesty. We'll be ready for them when they come.'

20

Cam smiled. He'd recognised the voice even through the muffling of the mask, then he caught the flash of bright eyes and dark skin above it, and there was no doubt.

That was no guard.

'Cover the doors until we can finish this,' Laila instructed Alistair, then she turned to the window. 'Claudia, start the ritual.'

Cam heard the girl swallow. She clasped the blade in her hand and beckoned Lucas towards the bowl that waited on top of the tripod.

'I'm sorry,' she whispered, but Lucas just shrugged. He'd resigned himself to this.

'What the hell is going on?' Rufus asked, joining the royals by the throne.

'I'm restoring us both to our former glory,' said Laila. 'You do want to be Silver again, I take it?'

Rufus didn't reply, which Laila seemed to take as agreement, but Cam saw Rufus's gaze seeking Julia out. To him, the boy's loyalty looked shaky at best.

But that wouldn't stop the ritual.

Claudia had taken Lucas's hand in hers. Now she stretched his wrist over the bowl.

'Ready?' she said to him.

'Just get it over with.'

She took him at his word, slicing the blade across his skin. The bowl must have been designed to amplify the sound, because the noise of his blood hitting the copper was like a waterfall thudding into the sea. It seemed to pour, filling the bowl until it overflowed and cascaded down the sides onto the floor. Claudia dropped Lucas's wrist and backed away from it, trying not to let it reach her bare feet, but the Empress wasn't done with her yet.

'The other one too,' she said, nodding Claudia back towards the bowl.

Claudia hesitated until the guards pointed their arrows at Julia, then she stepped gingerly into the puddle of red and reached out for Lucas's other wrist. He offered it willingly enough, though he was no longer entirely steady on his feet.

Claudia cut again. This time there was nothing but overflow, extending the pool far enough that it was lapping at the steps of the throne.

Rufus's lip was curling.

'Distasteful, I know,' Laila said to him, 'but these rituals always are.'

'Is that enough, now?' Emmy asked. She was poised on the edge of the throne, anxiously twisting her hands around each other.

'Not yet.'

Sol said nothing. He just watched, his gaze intent on Claudia as she held Lucas's wrist above the bowl. There were tears in her eyes, but still she held him there.

Julia got to her knees as Lucas fell to his, but Cam grabbed her cloak and held her back.

'Wait,' he whispered.

'They're killing him,' she sobbed.

'This won't kill him. He's stronger than that. You'll see.'

But he didn't look strong right now. He slipped in his own blood, sliding down onto the floor. His gaze found Julia's one last time before his eyelids drifted closed.

Then, finally, Laila said, 'That'll do.'

Julia felt as though she were about to crack apart. Every drop of blood that poured from Lucas's veins may as well have been coming from hers, because it weakened her just the same. She wanted to go to him, to gather him in her arms and pull him out of harm's way, but she could barely crawl. He'd taken more blood from her than she'd realised.

Her gaze was so fixed on him that she barely registered the crashes coming from outside the throne room.

A pair of guards barrelled through the door carrying a crate between them.

'They're coming!' one of them shouted.

'One bottle each,' said the other.

'Wait for my mark!' Alistair yelled at them all. 'No need to go wasting it, is there, now?'

The crate made its way around the room quickly, hands grasping for the bottles of salvation that the pair were handing out. When they reached Cam and Julia, one of the two – a giant of a man – bent down as though to check Cam's restraints, but Julia saw him sliding a bottle into Cam's hands as he whispered silently in his ear.

He saw her looking. His mouth was hidden behind his scarf mask, but from the twinkle in his eyes, he might have been smiling.

Meanwhile, the ritual was proceeding uninterrupted.

'Time to uphold your part of the bargain,' the Empress said, ushering the Queen towards the tripod.

The Queen went straight to Lucas's side, holding his face in her hands, but the Empress hauled her up to her feet again.

'There'll be time for that later,' she said. 'Claudia, the blade.'

Claudia handed it over, then stepped back out of the blood. Her tears were falling freely now as she looked over at Julia, mouthing, *I'm sorry.*

But Julia wasn't sure why she was apologising. Was it because of Lucas, or because the King's plan hadn't worked, or because Claudia hadn't tried to implement it?

The Empress used the blade to stir the bloody contents of the bowl, then handed it to the Queen.

'You're sure about this, Solomon?' the Empress asked. 'Because she's going first. If we've missed something out of the ritual, she'll be the one to suffer for it, not me.'

'I'm certain,' he said, and he looked it. Even Julia didn't notice the tightness around his lips, and she was searching for it.

The Empress turned back to the Queen, but as she did so, her eyes caught on Claudia. Claudia's wrist, to be precise. Julia followed her gaze and saw the cut there, a deep slice that was seeping blood down her hand.

Claudia's eyes went wide as she saw the Empress's attention. She tried to cover the cut with her hand, but it was too late to pretend that it wasn't there. Even now, the blood was dripping through her fingers to the floor.

'What have you done?' the Empress said, her voice a low whisper as she strode towards Claudia, who was either too scared or too stubborn to run. When the Empress's fist connected with her cheek, she went down hard, sliding in Lucas's blood. 'You've ruined it all!'

Cam wasn't sure what trick Claudia had pulled, but he was going to make the most of the distraction. The bottle Bartek had given him was still nestled safely in his hands, the only uncontaminated bottle in the whole room. If he picked the right moment, he could heal himself in time for the fight he knew was coming.

Laila was hurrying back towards the tripod, snatching the knife from Emmy's hand as she passed. 'Guard!' she called, pointing to one of them at random. It didn't look to be one of the Invicti, but Cam couldn't be sure.

'Empress?' the guard said, stepping forward.

No, Cam thought, *definitely not one of the Invicti.*

'Give me your hand,' Laila said.

He hesitated a moment, which was apparently too long, because Laila simply reached out and stabbed him in the arm. He grunted at the initial impact, then smiled as though he were trying to be a good soldier. But when the wound kept bleeding several seconds after Laila had withdrawn the blade, his expression changed from tolerant to anxious.

'It hurts,' he said, covering the cut with his hand. He blinked a few times. 'Have I gone deaf?'

'Shit!' Laila yelled, throwing the knife to the floor. It skittered over the stone and came to rest at the feet of another soldier, who retrieved it from the floor with a tattooed hand. 'Bloody fucking bastarding shit! It's contaminated,' Laila said to Emmy. 'The whole fucking lot of it is contaminated. And you,' she turned on Claudia, 'are going to regret the day you ever fucked with me.'

'Contaminated?' Emmy said. She looked at Sol, noting his equanimity, then her face twisted in horrified realisation. 'You did this.'

'I love you,' he said. 'You wanted our son back so much that you were willing to bargain his blood. Do you doubt that I'd bargain your eternal life to save your humanity?'

Then the shouting started outside. At first it was just a few raised voices, but then something exploded, so violently that Cam could feel the floor shaking.

But it didn't distract Emmy. 'You're trying to cure me?' she said to Sol. 'Me?'

Another guard slipped in through the door, covered in dust and blood. 'They're coming,' he gasped. 'I'm the last one. The others are gone.'

'Do not open that door again!' Alistair yelled.

Sol was walking down the steps towards Emmy now. 'There's nothing I wouldn't do to bring you back to me,' he said, then he dipped his finger into the blood-filled bowl and brought it to his lips.

Emmy lunged forwards to stop him, but it was too late. Sol might be immune to normal contamination, but this was more than that. Cam didn't know it yet, but this was the same magic that had made the Silver in the first place, the ritual by which Sol had attained eternal life, now reversed by Claudia's contaminated blood.

It was humbling to watch. This was the god king Cam had followed his entire life. He was the torch that had given Cam a reason to keep fighting, who'd set the example that he'd followed as he climbed his way up through the ranks of the Invicti. But now the fire was dimming. The glimmer was ebbing out of his hair, his skin, his eyes, until he was nothing more than a man.

'What have you done?' Emmy screamed, grabbing his hand and pulling him towards her. 'Sol,' she whispered. 'What have you done?'

'I've reclaimed my humanity,' he said. 'You could do the same.'

'Don't you dare,' Laila said. 'We made a bargain, Emilia.'

The far wall of the throne room shuddered, the door cracking as something slammed into it from the other side.

'Bottles ready!' Alistair yelled. 'On my mark.'

Another impact, this one hard enough to shake pieces of plaster down from the ceiling.

'Mark!' he yelled, and the guards obliged, each of them drinking down their portions of blood, even Alistair. Only three figures failed to comply: the giant standing next to Cam, the girl with the tattooed hands, and the dark-skinned man who'd now circled the room until he was standing directly behind Alistair.

The third crash brought the door in, but by that point there was a lot going on.

Cam took the opportunity to pop open the bottle of blood with his bound hands. Julia helped him raise it to his lips, and within seconds he was healed up and ripping out of his restraints. As soon as he was free, he carried Julia to Lucas's side.

'Stay here,' he said.

Moving at lightning speed, he snatched a few bottles of blood from the guards as they dropped them to the floor in horror. They'd revive Lucas just as well as if they were uncontaminated. His immunity would protect him.

The same couldn't be said for the guards. They were shouting now, looking at each other in accusation, trying to pick out the traitors' faces in a sea of their masked companions. When the first person shouted, 'Over there!' it made the rest turn just in time to see Adewale plunging a knife into Alistair's heart.

The Scot's eyes widened in surprise for half a beat, then he fell like a stone.

Meanwhile, Naia and Bartek had made it over to the door, which they were now opening to admit Tommy and Zita.

The cavalry was here, and Cam couldn't wait to join them.

In the blood pool under the windows, Julia had Lucas propped up on her knees.

'Is he alright?' Claudia asked, crawling over towards them.

'You little idiot,' the Empress raged, bearing down on Claudia. 'After everything I did for you.'

To Julia's surprise, it was Rufus who caught his mother's hand before she could swing her knife down on Claudia.

'It's over,' he said. 'Your guards are all cured. Your general is dead. How likely do you think your people are to obey you when you don't have the strength of your army behind you?'

The Empress's lip curled with affront. 'You'd stand between me and these humans?'

'We're all human now. Maybe it's time for new alliances.'

He took the knife from her hand with more ease than Julia would have thought possible. With one last, disgusted look at her son, the Empress turned and ran from the throne room, slipping out through the side door. No one tried to stop her. They all had bigger problems.

While the Invicti put down those guards who refused to surrender, Julia grabbed for the bottles Cam had left her and tipped one of them to Lucas's lips. The blood flowed into his mouth, but then overflowed, pouring down his cheek and into Julia's lap.

'He's not swallowing,' she said, looking to Claudia in panic.

Had something gone wrong? Had the tainted blood on the floor somehow cured Lucas, just as it had cured the King?

'Of course he isn't swallowing,' Rufus said. 'It's old, contaminated blood. His body doesn't recognise it.'

'Look,' said Claudia, 'if you haven't got anything helpful to say, then maybe you should just bugger off.'

He sighed, then knelt down beside Julia and took a knife from his pocket. 'I hope you know that this goes against all of my principles,' he said as he sliced his own wrist open. 'I never thought I'd be the one to save Lucas, of all people.'

The moment he pressed his bleeding skin against Lucas's mouth, Julia could see Lucas's throat start to work, swallowing the blood down.

'It's working.' Julia smiled her relief, then said, 'Thank you,' to Rufus. When she looked up she found he was already looking back at her, his gaze roaming around her eyes until it settled inevitably on her lips.

'Think nothing of it,' he whispered.

That was the first thing Lucas saw when he opened his eyes and found Rufus's wrist in his mouth. He spluttered against it then pushed it away, sending Rufus skidding a few feet back across the floor.

'Don't feel obliged to thank me,' Rufus said to Lucas sarcastically, holding his wrist close to his body as he got to his feet. 'I only saved you.'

They glared at each other until Claudia interrupted by shoving a bottle of blood into each of Lucas's hands. 'Drink up,' she said. 'You're going to need your strength. We've got work to do tonight.'

Meanwhile, the Invicti were rounding up the guards, but there was one last problem left: Emmy.

The ritual blood clearly had no effect on Lucas – he was sitting in a puddle of it and still seemed entirely Silver – but it had cured

Sol. Logic suggested that it could do the same to Emmy, and if either of them had needed to be cured, it was her.

But she wasn't listening to Sol.

'You want me to give up immortality?' she yelled at him.

'My love,' he said, 'I've already done that for both of us, or did you forget our bond? When I die at the end of my human life, that will be the end of both of us.'

'Then why?' she laughed, edging towards mania. 'Why does it even matter if I stay Silver?'

Cam stepped towards her. 'Do you remember when you were human?' he asked softly.

'That was a long time ago.' Her voice sounded small and distant.

'Not so long for you as it was for us,' Cam persisted. 'Do you remember what you thought of us? *Monsters*, you called us. You didn't want to be like that. You didn't want to lose your humanity, to reach the stage where you'd look at a human and see a resource rather than a person. The woman who thought that is still in you, Ems, but what you're doing right now? That's not her.'

'That version of me's a long way gone,' she said, looking at him with oubliette eyes. 'I thought you'd understand that. We can't go back to being who we were.'

'So it's not worth trying to be better versions of who we are? You don't really believe that. You could fool anyone else, but not me, Ems.'

'What do you expect me to do?' The words were half a challenge, but Cam could feel the edge of desperation in them. Part of her wanted to be told what was right and wrong, as though she'd forgotten how to tell them apart on her own.

'I'm not asking you to do anything I'm not intending to do myself,' he said. 'This power's going to break you if you don't give it up. You're disappearing into it. So take the blood. Everyone in this city will be turning human within the next few hours. Join us.'

Sol offered her the bowl. It was brimful with the blood of her own son, whom she'd insisted should be bled out for the sake of a stupid bargain Laila had tricked her into. She remembered the Silver she'd cured, one after another, and sent out into the Red. Their faces blurred with those of the women they'd slaughtered while searching for Alba. So much blood. Blood pooling under

Cam as he'd lain on the floor while she'd looked on impassively, blood under the tripod and soaking between her toes, blood on her hands.

So much blood. What was a little more?

She dipped her finger into the bowl, then looked up at Cam.

'You won't regret it,' he promised.

So she rolled her fingertip across her tongue, putting an end to the gods of the Silver.

Cam pulled Emmy into his arms, kissing her hair as he squeezed her tight.

'You won't regret it,' he said again.

As they parted, her eyes drifted sideways to where Lucas sat on the floor, downing bottle after bottle of blood.

'And him?' she asked, her voice so quiet it was barely a breath.

Cam smiled. 'I think we just made him our new king.'

The Invicti had found Felix locked in one of the palace's strongrooms with Viv and the baby. All three of them had been held captive to ensure the compliance of the people who loved them. Felix had been unconscious, knocked out by Alistair's drugs, which was why Cam hadn't been able to track him. When Cam finally extricated himself from the mess upstairs and made his way down into the bowels of the palace, he found the woodsman sitting on the floor cooing over the baby.

'Don't tell me you're getting broody now,' Cam said, leaning against the door jamb. 'That's the one thing I can't do for you.'

Felix smiled, beaming so widely that Cam found himself reflecting the expression.

'What?' Felix said. 'We can't adopt?'

Viv went to the door and hugged Cam, wrapping him tightly in her arms. 'Is it over?' she asked. 'Is Tommy okay?'

'Yes and yes. He's up in the throne room if you want to go find him.'

She took the baby from Felix and left them there, racing off to find her love. Cam's was already here, just a few feet away from him, smiling up at him as though he were plotting the downfall of Cam's virtue.

'So what now?' Felix asked, getting to his feet.

'I don't know. I was thinking maybe a long engagement. I'd want the ceremony at the temple, so we'd need time to rebuild it properly first. Then maybe a honeymoon in the Transylvanian mountains. I hear they're beautiful this time of year.'

Felix smiled and kissed him, and Cam kissed him back soft and long, pouring all his empty worries into this moment of resolution. They were together, they were safe, and their enemies were vanquished.

'You're in a good mood,' Felix said.

'I'm counting my blessings.' Cam took the woodsman's cheek in his hand, running his fingers into the soft pile of his beard. 'But we lost Linh.'

'I'm sorry.'

'We were lucky not to lose more. Konrad's cured, Emmy and Sol too.'

Felix drew in a long breath, surprised. 'I didn't see that coming. And the others said Lucas is the prince.'

'That's right. Sol and Emmy's son, the only Silver left who's immune to the cure. He might not be the strongest of us yet, but pretty soon he'll be the only one. I think that makes him the most powerful.'

'So what are you going to do about him?'

'You know,' Cam said with a smile, 'I'm not going to do anything at all.'

Felix raised an eyebrow. 'Nothing?'

'Nope. Nothing. You and I have a life to live together, and I've wasted enough of it already. Lucas is a good kid. I think he'll do alright.'

Felix smiled back. 'I think so too.'

Lucas tracked Marcella into the kitchen, where she was hiding with the rest of the palace Servers. Julia was gratified to see that the spiked *vin fiert* she'd left on the hearth had almost entirely disappeared.

'Is it over?' Marcella said. She stood amongst a gaggle of frightened girls and boys, none of them much older than she was.

'It's over,' Lucas said.

Claudia went to join the Servers, pulling those she knew into her arms and asking after those who were absent. Julia understood now what Claudia had been trying to protect from Julia's rebellion, but she was no less glad that she and Cam had been successful.

Things would be better. Julia would make sure they were, but first she had to make sure every human in the Blue was contaminated.

Marcella's skills were invaluable in that regard, as were her connections. No one would have paid attention to Julia if she'd tried to tell them how they were liberating the Blue with contamination, but Marcella was a perfect figurehead. She was well-known, so she could access people Julia would never have reached alone, and she had an easy charm that Julia had no hope of ever achieving. People just liked her. They didn't much like Julia, but that didn't matter.

It came down to this: Julia had done her part, and now it was Marcella's turn.

Marcella drew a little of Julia's blood, as she had so many times before, but it was different now. This blood didn't go into Rufus's cup, but into bottle after bottle of the wine that Claudia and her Attendant friends were liberating from the palace cellars. When Marcella had taken a cup's worth from Julia, Claudia offered her arm too.

'Are you sure?' Julia asked her.

'A bit late to ask my permission, don't you think?' She laughed, but there was no bitterness in its tone. This was Claudia's way of inching towards forgiving her.

When every bottle was contaminated, they made their way towards the square, Lucas blazing the trail. That was where the celebration would be. Marcella had issued the invitations, carried to every house in the Blue on the tongues of the palace Servers, and by the time their little band reached the square it was already filling up.

Everyone would come.

They'd make a proper *Ziua Recoltei* now, with fire and dancing, but their harvest wasn't reaped from wheat or vines or trees. They weren't collecting grain or grapes or the apples that lay rotting in the earth of the Blue's orchards. No, they were harvesting the Nobles with blood, and gathering a new crop of humanity.

This was the end of the Silver, the Red and the Blue, but it would also be the beginning of something new.

* * *

Cam explained himself badly. It was difficult to distill his ideology into simple words when to him it felt so complex, but in the end he just said: 'It's what's best for everyone.' That seemed to sum it up.

Tommy rubbed his forehead. 'Everyone, Cam?'

'In the long run, yes. Better that we go all together now than have these few starving themselves to the last moment. There's no more uncontaminated blood, Tommy. That's it. There's no other choice.'

The Secundus exhaled heavily then nodded.

Cam handed him the bottle. 'Alright?' he said.

'Alright.'

Then they went out to join the others in the courtyard. The grave hadn't been difficult to dig. After all, it wasn't that long ago that they'd moved this earth to make space for Gul. Doing it a second time had been easier.

'Well,' Tommy said once they'd all gathered together. He looked around at them, so few left now. Konrad and Aaron had come for the funeral, as had Viv with her and Tommy's little girl, and Felix was standing at Cam's side as always, but there were just six Silver left: Tommy, Cam, Adewale, Naia, Zita and Bartek.

Tommy said some nice things. It was good and proper, but it was all just words. That wasn't how the Invicti mourned their lost brothers and sisters.

When Tommy had finished his eulogy, Cam passed around the cups. Tommy filled them, then lifted his own into the air.

'To Linh and Gul,' Tommy said.

'To Linh and Gul!' the Invicti echoed back at him.

'To the last of the Silver,' Bartek added, and the others repeated the toast. Then, as one, they lifted the cups to their mouths and drank the tainted liquid down.

Except Cam. He watched each of them swallow, then he waited to be sure. Once he was satisfied with their bewildered, blinking faces, he turned to Felix and smiled, letting his silver pour into his eyes. Well, not his silver anymore; his gold.

Then he tipped his own cup back and waited for the weakness to overwhelm him.

It was pretty instantaneous.

The other Invicti didn't take it well.

Cam was hardly expecting them to celebrate, but some of them were downright violent. When they discovered that Tommy had okayed it, they turned their anger on him instead. Well, Zita and Naia did. Bartek was surprisingly sanguine about the whole thing once he'd had time to think it through, and Adewale took it like a punishment he deserved. Alistair was a burden that no one could persuade him to lift from his shoulders.

'Of course *you* wanted this,' Naia was screaming at Tommy and Cam. 'You're both boning contaminated humans!'

'You will be from now on too,' Zita quipped.

Felix just raised an eyebrow at Cam. A very eloquent eyebrow. *Not yet*, it said, *but soon*. Looking at him now, Cam could hardly believe he'd managed to wait this long.

'Look,' he said to Naia, 'hate me for this if you want. It was my plan, and my choice, because it was the only way. There's no more uncontaminated blood. Would you rather have shrivelled up and desiccated than live a human life?'

'Those tattoos won't be pretty when you're all wrinkly,' Konrad piped up.

'At least they're pretty now,' Naia snapped at him, 'which is more than I can say for your face.'

'If I were you,' Zita said, 'I'd be more worried about your nymphomania. If you're not careful, you'll be the next one having babies.'

They all laughed at that, except Naia who was pink-cheeked and furious.

'You bastard, Cam,' she said. 'What have you done to me? Am I not allowed to enjoy anything anymore?'

'It's not all bad,' Cam said, throwing her the remainder of the bottle of home-brew. 'It'll be much easier to get drunk.'

She popped the cork out and took a slug. 'Cheers, then.'

Then it was time for him and Felix to go. They'd told the others they were going to clear out the last few Weepers, but that wasn't really necessary. They would die out on their own over time, because there was only contaminated meat left in the Red.

What Cam and Felix actually wanted was a little time alone. They might come back to the Blue one day, and they'd always be close enough to visit, but for now Cam needed some distance. He suspected they all would, for a while at least.

'We'll see you next month?' Cam said. They gathered their packs and made their way around the circle saying their goodbyes.

'We'd better,' said Viv, giving Cam a hug.

Naia's farewell was less exuberant, but she gave him a grudging handshake. They were a good twenty yards away before she delivered her parting shot.

'And you can take that fucking horse with you!'

Cam and Felix were not the only couple leaving the Blue. The former gods of the Silver were out in the wilderness too, bundled up in the ruins of an old building. It only had three walls, so the fire was more a necessity than a luxury.

'Sol,' Emmy said, clinging onto his hand. 'Why does it hurt so much?'

'It will pass, I promise.'

'Ah.' She clutched at her neck. 'My throat's so dry. Why does it burn? What's going on?'

'Shh,' he whispered, pressing a kiss to her brow. 'Here.'

She looked down into the cup he offered her. 'But this is–'

Blood.

'I may not have been entirely honest with our new friends. The truth is: there is nothing that can undo what we are, you and I. We are Silver, and we shall always be Silver.' He stroked her hair back from her face as he spoke. 'It was a temporary effect, nothing more.'

'Then what was the point?'

'To make them less afraid. To give our son space to breathe. To give you time to heal. I collected a bottle of the ritual blood for when you need it, but right now we need you Silver so we can travel. This is normal blood, so drink,' Sol said.

She did, surprised at how much her body craved it. After one bottle was empty he passed her another, and another, until she almost felt like her old self again.

'Do you remember life before the Revelation?' he asked when she had finished.

She'd thought of little else in every waking moment since Charles had taken her. She'd watched the passage of time in the rusting bed posts, the dampening walls and the simplified produce, and all she'd wished was to return to a time that was now lost forever.

'Do you miss that life too?' she asked.

'In a sense. You remember what it was to live as a human with no knowledge of our kind, with no fear of vampires lurking in dark corners. You must see that this is a freedom we can offer them, the freedom of ignorance. You and I can go back into the dark. I seem to recall that you enjoy being in the shadows with me.'

He trailed the back of his fingers down her cheek, down the side of her neck, coming to rest in teasing strokes around her collarbone, but it didn't soothe her. Instead, she fixated on what they'd lost.

'But we'll live apart from Lucas,' she said.

'For the moment. Perhaps not forever.'

'The things I did–'

'Are done. He may understand one day. He might forgive. For now, is it not enough to know that he is happy? You and I can still have our eternity, if you're willing to take it.'

Epilogue

When springtime reached the rooftops of the Blue, it found Lucas and Julia already planting out their garden for the year. There were vegetables and herbs and every variety of fruit that they could grow in the climate.

'So,' Julia smiled, 'how does it feel to be the last Silver on Earth?'

'A little lonely.' Lucas grinned, pulling Julia closer.

Julia smiled back at him. 'I don't believe that for a second.'

'Hey, Jules!' Claudia called up from the house below. 'Rufus and Livia are coming for dinner.'

Lucas groaned. 'Again?'

'Yes, again,' Claudia shouted. 'Alba wants to know if you've got any mint up there.'

'Not yet,' Julia called back down. She wasn't sure whether Claudia was trying to romance their former enemy or just make friends, but either way it was awkward as hell. Still, they all enjoyed seeing Livia, and at least Rufus's continued presence made Julia sure she wasn't dreaming. In real life, not everything could be perfect.

She sat back on her haunches to survey her work. Not bad for a day's planting. 'We'll have to make room for some mint somewhere,' she said to Lucas. 'We'll never hear the end of it if we don't.'

'That can be arranged.'

He had a smear of dirt on his forehead and his hair was being blown here and there by the wind. Julia didn't think she'd ever seen a more attractive man in her life. She wiped her muddy hands on her trousers and put her arms around his neck, pulling him closer for a kiss.

He smiled against her lips.

'We don't have to stay here forever,' he murmured. 'I know you wanted to leave the city.'

She laughed. 'But you're the King now.'

'Of what? This place is just a pretty pile of rubble, and plenty of people are leaving, starting fresh. We could do that too.'

'But plenty of them are staying.'

Julia remembered the overgrown rooftop paradise of Lucas's old garden, overflowing with produce, buzzing with bees, strewn with chips of terracotta and mortar cracked apart by persistent foliage. It had been beautiful and yet dilapidated, like the tree-contorted buildings she'd found in the Red.

Perhaps the Blue would be that way soon. That would be alright with her.

'We could stay,' she whispered. 'For now, at least.'

He kissed her again, and it suddenly didn't seem to matter where they were. She was with him, with Claudia, Alba and Livia. Wherever they ended up, she'd feel like she was home.

In the mountaintops of the Red, Felix and Cam were expanding their two small cabins to form one large one. They'd need the extra space now that their family was expanding too.

Mihaela had found them on their way home. A little girl of six with huge eyes and dark hair, she'd come careening out of the undergrowth chased by Weepers, practically flinging herself under Hades's hooves. Felix had scooped her out of harm's way while Cam had experienced his first Weeper bite. Strange how much it seemed to hurt when you knew it was going to take more than a few minutes and some fresh blood to heal.

Mihaela was playing with Alex now while Darius and a few of the other men were helping with the construction. Chloe and Ana were off meeting with the council, receiving visitors from the Blue and from Sabina's sanctuary, as well as numerous other settlements that had popped up over the past few months. The continent was fairly bustling these days, and Cam had worried for a while that the lakeshore community might disintegrate as people spread, but so far that wasn't happening. The new matriarchy certainly seemed to resonate with Chloe, and she was keeping her people close. Cam didn't think it would be long before she was running this place, now the biggest settlement in the world.

It was amazing how much things could change in just a few short months.

'Nearly done,' Felix said, wiping the sweat from his brow. 'Mihaela wants to stay at Alex's tonight. That okay with you?'

Cam shrugged. 'If it's okay with Chloe and Darius.' Then he noticed the grin playing at the corner of Felix's mouth. 'Did you maybe suggest to our daughter that she wanted to spend the night away?'

'I may have brokered a deal with Chloe,' Felix said, moving closer.

'What kind of a deal?'

'Well, we get both the kids tomorrow night,' Felix leaned in, whispering into Cam's ear, 'and tonight we get to try out our new bedroom.'

'That's a hell of a deal.' Cam was grinning now too, suddenly eager to pay their helpers off in home-brew and get them out of the house as soon as possible.

'I can be extremely persuasive,' Felix said, then he kissed Cam in a way that promised more to come.

If you enjoyed the *Sovereign* series, why not read *Encounters: Silverse Short Stories*? It contains sixteen short stories set in the world of *Sovereign*, including two from Laila's perspective set before and after the *Sovereign* series, and one from Solomon's perspective explaining how he came to be the Gilded King in the first place.

***

Join my Readers' Club and receive a FREE short story

www.josiejaffrey.com/subscribe

***

Please leave a review!

If you enjoyed *The Blood Prince*, I'd be so grateful if you would please review it. Book reviews can make a huge difference to the success of a novel, particularly those of self-published authors like me. If you have time to leave a review, even if it's just a sentence or two, then I'd really appreciate it.

***

Explore the rest of the Silverse…

This book is just one small part of the Silverse, a whole world of vampires that's waiting for you to explore. There are more novels, short stories, serialised story episodes, and even audio drama podcasts. They're all interrelated, although each series stands alone.

Find out more on my website at www.josiejaffrey.com

Acknowledgements

I really don't know where to start with my thanks for this book. As the culmination of not just one series, but all of my Silverse novels, *The Blood Prince* was probably the toughest thing I've ever had to write. So while I'd like to give huge thanks to all the usual suspects for their contributions and support, my thanks really should be doubled, trebled and quadrupled because of the immense amount of emotional labour involved in the past few months to get me to the end of this journey.

So, to Vicky and Zoe: huge thanks for your beta reading, and for all the books and gin.

To Ali at Wallingford Bookshop: thanks for the books and coffee, for plugging my work to publishers, for recommending *Supernatural* to me, and for yelling at me when I felt like giving up entirely.

To family on both sides of the pond: thank you so much for your support, and for not asking how my book sales are going.

To Martin: the cover is amazing, as are the covers for the entire *Sovereign* series. Thank you for all of your hard work.

To everyone who has read and reviewed my books: Thank you so much. Your reviews are everything to me. In those moments where everything felt desperately difficult, seeing how much you have enjoyed this series was the motivation I needed to keep going. I hope this last instalment has lived up to your expectations.

And lastly and mostly: thank you to Max for picking me up every time I was down, and for being the most supportive partner I could ever imagine. The cats and I would be lost without you.

CONTENT WARNINGS

General warnings:

Post-apocalyptic setting; humanity has been mostly wiped out by a virus that turns them into zombie-like creatures. Small communities of humans are isolated from the abandoned outside world, which is considered contaminated.

General warning for violence.

General warning for blood/gore, including blood drinking, description of injuries, zombie-like creatures, dead bodies.

One of the main settings is a city controlled by vampires where humans are considered servants/slaves. Issues of power disparity/class divide/consent under slavery discussed briefly.

No racism, no homophobia (main character relationships are F/M and M/M), no ableism, no animal cruelty, no misogyny.

No sex; some kissing (teen appropriate).

Some swearing (up to and including 'fuck' but not frequent).

Specific warnings:

Blood drinking as sexual/pleasurable behaviour.

A main character tortures minor character for information.

A main character finds out she was conceived by rape.

A main character is temporarily, and side character permanently, under the control of a sadist; he injures them, keeps them locked in his house, and emotionally manipulates them. Main character subjected to emotional abuse disguised as romance.

A side character is a mother who had her baby stolen at birth.

A side character has a difficult childbirth; not graphic, mother and baby fine afterwards.

Minor characters whose mouths have been sewn up.